I0712266

ZERO SUM CONCLUSION

0 ⟺ : 3

TITLES BY THOMAS LOPINSKI

Zero Sum Conclusion
2024

The Art of Raising Hell
2015

Document 512
2012

SPECIAL THANKS

SPECIAL THANKS to my family, Author Marketing Experts, Steve Bender, Gayle Hoskins Bibb, Tom Fullerton, Hank and Betty, Ink Tracks Editing, John Lopinski, Tracy Lundin, Flo Selfman at WordsalaMode.com, Glenda McMurray, Matt Sigmon, Jose Ramirez at Pedernales Publishing, LLC, Don Terbush, P. Jestin Trahan, Sue Woods and Carl Wurtz for all of their input. Last but not least, a very special thanks to John Christian Gleichman: my best friend, my confidant, my de facto story editor, my drinking buddy, and the one person who never shies away from letting me know what stinks and what should stick.

ZERO SUM CONCLUSION

by

THOMAS LOPINSKI

ZERO SUM CONCLUSION

Published by Bunsen Creek Pub
First Edition 2024

Copyright © 2024 by Thomas Lopinski

All rights reserved. No part of this book may be reproduced or utilized in any form or by any means, electronic or mechanical, including photocopying, recording or by any information storage and retrieval system, without permission in writing from the publisher. Inquiries should be addressed to the author.

This is a work of fiction. Names, characters, places and incidents are either products of the author's imagination or are used fictitiously. Any resemblance to actual events, locales or persons, living or dead, is entirely coincidental.

ISBN: 979-8-9892536-8-5 Paperback Edition
         979-8-9892536-9-2 Digital Edition

Library of Congress Control Number: 2023918468

Author services by Pedernales Publishing, LLC
www.pedernalespublishing.com

10 9 8 7 6 5 4 3 2 1

Printed in the United States of America

CONTENTS

PART III — ONE YEAR LATER

*It's 84 years after 1984 and everything in the world
has changed, but nothing is really different.*

PART I

EDGAR

CHAPTER ONE

BURBANK, CA

Two Months Earlier, 2068

EDGAR GORMAN LOOKED UP at the clock on the wall and sighed. It was after midnight. Once again, he'd lost track of time. Not only had he lost track of time but he'd become lost in the moment, lost in another world, and, subsequently, lost in a space. A space between reality and fantasy where he was able to unwind and tune out all the troubles in his world. A moment when he could just be himself, in a place where there were no shadows, no haunting voices, and no dreams left unfulfilled.

He dipped his brushes in a large cup of water and debated whether to properly clean them or take care of it in the morning. With a subtle yawn, he rubbed his eyes and turned away. The freshly painted canvas in front of him stared back the reflection of a puzzling portrait. It was a portrait of a man whose unremarkable past was quickly being replaced with an elusive future. Scattered in between the wrinkles and scars on his face lived unkept promises and unknown desires. One thing for certain was that everything would soon change for Edgar Gorman.

Although his path in life had been set in stone by decisions made decades earlier, it was not burdened by alternative theories on what might have been. There were no alternative theories in the year 2068. They'd all been replaced with predictable facts. Facts about which path in life you'd choose, where you'd live that life, and how long you'd live.

It was a byproduct of the Second Civil War that changed everything in America, and for good reason. The only other alternatives at the time were sheer chaos and mayhem. When people took to the streets in hand-to-hand combat, neighbor against neighbor, fighting for what they believed in and each believing their views were worth dying for, you had utter chaos.

Nevertheless, our country endured.

Thirteen days later, cooler heads prevailed and the Second Civil War was over. A constitutional convention convened nationwide where many underlying issues and ignored problems were finally addressed. Everything from conspiracy theories, to string theory, to online privacy, to what it meant to be a patriot were discussed and dissected. Every option on how to heal the country was laid out on the table, then analyzed and summarized. In the end, it became obvious what had to be done and a new nation arose from the ashes. The destruction of America as predicted by many, mostly outside our borders, had been thwarted.

Edgar dipped a rag into a cup of silvery solution on the table and wiped the palette dry. His painting was finished. Another masterpiece of acrylic shapes and designs waiting to be displayed … but where? A subject for discussion for another place and time. He just grinned and sighed.

His wife sauntered in and nonchalantly bowed her head with approval before saying, "Your best work yet."

"You think so? I wasn't sure about the colors, never am."

Evelyn placed her delicate hand on his shoulder and caressed it gently. Her auburn hair dangled playfully as she flipped it back and replied, "Where have I heard that before? The colors are just fine. They're your colors."

In most settings, that statement could've been misconstrued in many different ways. It seemed esoteric in nature, possibly condescending, but in this setting, it was meant as a joke. Her tone of voice was gentle. Yet, to those who'd viewed any of his mother's paintings and witnessed the explosions of colors swirling within them juxtaposed against Edgar's, they made perfect sense.

"I guess you're right," he surmised. "Definitely my colors."

She kissed him on the cheek, ran her hand through his hair, and said, with a hint of sarcasm as she walked away, "I'm always right."

That she was. She was exceptional in that way. In reality, she knew more about him than he knew about himself. Every whispering sigh, every ache of regret, and every squint of happiness in some way or another had been observed and absorbed by her. She didn't like hearing her husband doubt himself but knew once he'd vocalized his concerns, he'd return to the loving man that he was.

She gazed up at a wooden plaque hanging above the doorway that read:

Yesterday's the past, tomorrow's the future, but today is a gift.

It reminded her each time to be thankful for what she had and not to veer off course. It was much easier these days for her to slip into that dark place. Although her journey in life had been filled with many wonderful memories, the last couple of years had been tough, especially the last few months. They'd even made her doubt her own existence and question the meaning of it all. She glanced at the sign again and smiled.

Edgar knew how to smile away concerns and glaze over responses when it came to making her happy. Even though she was more than willing to hear his complaints and listen to his aspirations, he knew that too much of a good thing could turn into something bad quickly. It was better to smile and move on.

After all, such were the ways of a Back-Ender. To assume there could be any other outcome was fruitless. Such normal thoughts were nonexistent these days, all replaced with assumptions. If it was a good thought, then it was assumed. If it was a bad thought, then it was discarded like soap bubbles. Those thoughts were never meant to be ingested but only seen as flickers of light, glimmers of sadness, and not meant for consumption.

Your demeanor was paramount in the year 2068. Our leaders had figured out that if they could control a person's character with rewards and penalties, they could keep the peace. They even kept score. Without it, the Second Civil War would've never ended.

Certain feelings were no longer left to the imagination. People realized that they didn't need to exist. Society had found a way to endure without constant fear, without the need of emotional provocation or the burdens of overwhelming stress. All that had been mitigated. All that had been negotiated out of the discussion with the advent of Demeanor Scores.

Everyone had one and everyone abided by them. It followed you around like a ray of sunshine, or a dark cloud, depending on the kind of day you were having. There were demeanor points given for complimenting others, smiling, and acts of kindness. Points were taken away for swearing, cutting in lines, and raising your voice. For those who accumulated enough points, rewards were bestowed on them in the form of trips abroad or more privileges.

Punishment, on the other hand, was dealt with swiftly and nonnegotiably. Those whose Demeanor Score dipped below a certain point were sent off to camps for rehabilitation and sometimes training. These measures may have seemed harsh, but when the leaders met at the Constitutional Convention of 2033, they knew nothing less would suffice. The harsh realities of uncivil discourse in America had led to bloodshed with a rebellion of twisted ideologies fighting against hard-wired idiosyncrasies. All wires had crossed and all relationships were in jeopardy. In the end, neither side wanted to give in to the other nor listen to their point of view. A cleansing of the mind was needed. A whitewashing of beliefs and principles became necessary for the country to prevail.

Edgar stared at the painting and then at the clock. They tugged and pulled at each other like taffy. *Shall I place it on a shelf or underneath*? He pondered the thought. It was the same question he'd asked himself every time a painting was completed.

His wife knew what he was thinking and lifted the canvas off the easel to admire. "Let's put it in the living room tomorrow. I think it'll complement the others nicely."

"You're too kind," replied Edgar.

"You're too modest. You really do have a knack for this stuff." She hesitated to say more and instead declared, "Let's go to bed."

He turned away and replied, "Of course."

The next morning, Evelyn awoke with a headache. She'd had them before but this one was unrelenting and insisted on being recognized. She called her doctor's office and explained the situation. "Unfortunately, Mrs. Gorman, your ACP readings have shown that nothing can be done in the long term. I can prescribe you an opioid or mild sedative to ease the pain if you wish," replied the nurse on call.

"Can't I get in to see the doctor, maybe run a few more tests?" she begged.

"We've already run the tests, more than once. Your Advance Care Predictors have concluded with a 98% accuracy rate that the headaches will worsen and eventually become fatal. I'm sorry. Please fill out a prescription request online if desired and I'll have it filled before the week's end." Evelyn slammed her palm on top of the CompWatch and ended the call. She removed her eyeglasses and wiped her tear ducts dry.

"What'd they say?" asked Edgar.

"Same thing as before. It's useless."

"Damn doctors."

"Damn insurance. If only I'd taken the Premium Care Option that you have."

"Yeah, but how would you have known, and look how much it would've cost. Your SSI would've been eaten up before you know it. Everybody goes with the normal option these days."

"I know." She grabbed a tissue off the table, placed it around her nose and puffed. Then she tapped on her CompWatch a few times and said, "I'm down to twenty-five thousand in my account. Looks like I'll have to find a real job soon before I go below the threshold."

Their eyes locked as they both nervously chuckled and contemplated what that meant. Edgar suppressed any ominous thoughts and raised a slight grin off his upper lip. "Don't worry, I'll be able to retire in a couple of years and we'll be fine. We just have to make it until then."

He was a Back-Ender with health insurance benefits that would last him a lifetime. A small price to pay for working thirty years in an approved occupation before taking his SSI. At least, on paper. His salary was set by the state, sufficient to cover the costs of owning a home, putting food on the table, and enjoying some of the finer things in life. Not too many, but just enough to squeak out a decent middle-class livelihood.

Evelyn, on the other hand, was a Front-Loader. When the Solid Start Initiative became law after the Constitutional Convention of 2033, she jumped at the opportunity to begin life with a million dollars. Who wouldn't, especially, since the financial markets had agreed to revert the value of all currencies back to mid-twentieth century levels? A million dollars was a lot of money and most people took it without blinking.

The architects of that Constitutional Convention had devised a system, quite cleverly, to deal with an insolvent Social Security and Medicare program, which had threatened to bankrupt the whole country. It was a stroke of genius. With one swipe of the digital pen, they were able to wipe out both poverty and the federal deficit. Every US citizen had a choice: either you became a Front-Loader and received a million dollars upon your eighteenth birthday, or you became a Back-Ender and retired after thirty years of service with two million dollars and a lifetime of health benefits.

Evelyn forced a smile wide enough to expose a set of enchanting dimples and said, "You're right, we'll get by. I haven't even come close to being shipped off to Dunes."

"I won't let that happen," sternly replied Edgar. "Not with you or me or even that silly sister of mine."

Evelyn laughed, "I think she's better off than both of us now. I mean, early on, yeah, it looked like she wasn't going to make it, but she finally turned things around. She took that million and made something of herself, doing what she wanted. That's how life's supposed to be."

She caught herself before her next sentence, realizing where the conversation was going, and just grinned. Edgar lowered his head and peeked at the canvas on the easel. He chipped away at the dried beige and green paint swatches on his hand with his fingernails and tried to rub off the reality of his situation. He and his sister had chosen completely different paths in life and there was nothing he could do about it. He also knew that his wife didn't mean any harm by her comment, but her words were as truthful as the night is black.

On the other hand, he'd survived twenty-eight long years of satisfying work at the Bureau without getting himself shot or killed. The goal line was five yards away and he could almost taste retirement at this point. To think otherwise was counter-productive and that was the last thing he needed affecting his Demeanor Score.

The Solid Start Initiative, or SSI, had breathed new life into millions of Americans after its creation. It had allowed many people to pursue their dreams, their passions, without the hindrance of trying to figure out how to put food on the table or keep a roof over their heads.

SSI also allowed those who weren't so creative or adventurous to pursue a more conservative path in life. By working in an approved field instead of taking the money, a person could build a future, enjoy decent benefits, and feel confident that they'd be taken care of after retiring. The program had soothed the nation's soul.

Evelyn reached out and with her hand gently caressed his shoulder. "I'm sorry."

Don't be," replied Edgar. "You're just stating the obvious. No use crying over spilled milk, now, is there."

"Spilled milk? You are dating yourself there. Who drinks milk these days?"

He chuckled, "You're right. Most young kids don't even know what it is, do they?"

"I guess not," she replied. "Still, I shouldn't have gone there."

He inhaled deeply and said, "It doesn't bother me anymore. Don't worry, we're almost there, and don't you worry about the doctor. Those ACP results are bullshit. Look how wrong they were with me. I never developed diabetes nor did I die of a heart attack. It's just a way for insurance companies to justify their premiums."

Evelyn slid the table away and hopped onto his lap. She coiled her long slender arms around his neck and gently pressed a cheek against his forehead. "That's right. You'll live to be a hundred, just like your mom."

Edgar kissed her on the cheek and squeezed tightly. "I need to get ready for work. We'll figure this out. After all, we have the best of both worlds, right? Both our front and back ends are covered."

Evelyn melded her body into the sofa and crossed her legs. Edgar knew that pose. It was her deep thinking pose, her "nothing good can come from this train of thought" pose. Before she had the chance to sink any further, he said, "We've had a pretty good go of it, haven't we? A trip to Europe before they closed the borders, a new climate-safe home, no more cyber-attacks, no more pissed-off neighbors. Not bad considering the alternative."

She allowed the words to soothe her soul and leaned back into the headrest. "You're right. We enjoyed every penny of my million dollars and have your two million to look forward to. If it just hadn't been for the... well, you know."

He leaned over and placed his forehead against hers with each hand on both sides of her head. "If I had to do it over again, I wouldn't have changed a thing. How were we to know what those ACP tests would reveal and what it would cost us? People avoid them like the plague now, if they can."

"You see, right there. That's why I love you." She grinned and lowered her head. "You always know the right thing to say. Let me make breakfast."

As Evelyn rose from the couch and turned to move into the kitchen, she paused and staggered. While regaining her step, she pressed the palm of her hand against her temple and pushed hard. Edgar froze. His mouth was wide open but unable to speak. A sudden gasp was all he could muster. As he rose from his chair, she collapsed to the floor.

Two hours later, she was dead.

CHAPTER TWO

CEDARS SINAI PLAZA, LOS ANGELES, CA

Present Day, 2068

EDGAR EXITED THE ELEVATOR and squeezed a button on each side of his CompWatch. An image of a business card opened on his contact lens displaying a name and room number. After releasing the image, he walked down the hallway to a water fountain and bent over to take a drink. Brown droplets sputtered onto the stainless steel basin. "Fucking dark ages," he grumbled.

Inside the doctor's office, he stopped at the counter and announced, "Edgar Gorman."

The desk clerk looked up but didn't make eye contact. She found the name on a schedule, handed him a digital notepad through the slot and said, "Please fill out the highlighted areas and return it to me."

Edgar recognized the form immediately and replied, "I just filled this same thing out yesterday at the clinic."

Through a glass window thick enough to repel a staccato burst of artillery, she replied in a muffled tone, "I'm sorry, but it's required, you know. Article 3, Section 4 of the Revised Constitution. You can have a seat in the waiting room. When you're finished, bring it back up to the counter."

"What?" Edgar pointed to his ear.

The clerk pushed a button activating a microphone and

repeated her explanation. A moan slipped off Edgar's lips as he shuffled into the empty adjoining room. Ergonomically designed chairs lined both light blue walls, with a table positioned in the corner. Propped up next to the lamp was a large electronic tablet flashing a gallery of views from dozens of magazines. Each photo randomly bounced from side to side like two poles of a magnet, as a "Click Here" box relentlessly followed along.

On the far wall was a digitized poster with the words "Your Demeanor Score" written across the top. He approached it and leaned in for a closer look. It read:

> "In order to form a more perfect union, it is our patriotic duty to become better citizens. Your Demeanor Score is a measure of your personal growth as a human being and the contributions you make to society. Demeanor Score levels above 1,000 can earn you certain benefits not available to other citizens. Scores below 250 may activate a Zero Sum Conclusion. Learn more by visiting our website at www. demeanorscore.gov."

Edgar perused the list of examples on the chart that outlined how to increase your score. "I can do that," he confirmed as he continued reading, "I can do that, I can't do that, I thought that was illegal." The receptionist peered over the counter when she heard the last few words and looked up at a camera in the corner of the room. Edgar just smiled, scratched his head, and took a seat.

When he completed the form and returned the pad, the clerk said, "Thank you. The doctor should arrive shortly." Edgar glared over at the clock on the wall and grimaced. Then he peered over at the poster next to the camera in the corner of the room. With a feigned grin, he sat back down and closed his eyes.

A nurse ambled into the reception area as the desk clerk turned around and giggled. "Looks like someone had a long night."

"Did I ever," yawned the nurse while wiping away wine splotches from her lips. "That Dylan MacMillan sure knows how to throw a party." Her shoulders shivered as she mused, "And he's so cute."

"What time did you make it home?"

"Who says I did?" she replied with a wink and strolled away.

At the end of the hall, a side door opened and Dr. Bevan quietly scurried down to his office. As he passed the nurse, he whispered, "What do we have this morning?"

"Only the one patient that was sent over last night. This one's marked urgent. The FBI agent needs to be evaluated and re-certified before he can continue field operations. He took the fitness test yesterday."

"Can't this wait? I speak at a conference in two hours."

"Apparently not. The physician sent over notes and marked them 'STAT.' MAGMA needs this completed today."

The nurse showed the doctor the request and he commented, "Why they wait until the last minute is beyond me. Well, send him in then."

She gently caressed a frown and replied, "Oh, by the way, our system's down again. I'll have to dictate everything."

"Again," winced the doctor. He handed his digital notepad to her and said, "Here, update my notes and bring them to me when they're ready."

A few minutes later, the doctor returned to the nurse's station and asked, "How much longer?"

"Sorry, I had to request printouts from the clinic. System's down, remember? They just arrived."

"Well, make it quick." He peeked at his watch and grumbled, "I'm running out of time."

The nurse nodded and rubbed the back of her neck as the doctor stomped away. While burping up remnants of last night's Champagne, she massaged her weary eyelids, stretched, and declared, "Okay, you can do this." She pressed the "Dictate" button and recited:

Name: Edgar Gorman
Height: 6' 3"
Weight: 210 lbs...

She continued transcribing Edgar's medical history into the pad for another five minutes, only stopping long enough to proofread for any errors. "No, I didn't say 'then,' I said, 'than.'" She shook her head and continued reading. "Oh my God, how could you come up with 'plowing' instead of 'following'?"

A message dinged on her computer screen from the doctor. It read: "How much longer?"

The nurse glanced up and typed, "I'm on the final page." Then she began dictating the doctor's summary from yesterday's visit:

"In conclusion, the patient is in physical good health overall. In 2061, he was treated for *diabetes* but is now in remission. *Be aware* that signs of mental *stress* and *psychosomatic* behavior were observed during the exam. The patient has requested medication to remedy insomnia."

Doctor Bevan now hovered over the nurse's desk like an ominous fog as she finished the last words. Before she had time to react, he snatched the notepad out of her hands and said, "Good enough. Get the patient in the room and let's get on with it."

The nurse nodded and scurried into the waiting room. "Mr. Gorman, please follow me." She escorted the patient to the doctor's office, pointed to the sofa, and shut the door behind him. The dimly lit room reeked of solitude and tranquility, with its beige cotton couch surrounded by overgrown potted plants and the sound of a trickling waterfall seeping in from the walls. Along the baseboard on the wall away from the window was a 3D hologram of a riverbed meandering over rocks and limbs with a twinkle of green, blue, and white flowing within.

Edgar circled the couch a few times before sitting down. He knew why he was there but that did nothing to calm his nerves. Physical examinations were black and white. You knew right there and then whether your blood pressure was elevated or heart rate rapid. Psych examinations, on the other hand, more resembled a Tarot card reading. He unconsciously rubbed his ring finger and sat down.

"The bathroom is next to the kitchen here if you need it," the doctor shouted from the adjacent room. No doubt a subject that came up often with patients, due to the hologram. "A cup of coffee?"

"That would be nice."

Dr. Bevan poured and asked, "Cream, sugar?"

"No thanks."

The doctor entered the main room and handed Edgar the cup. His patient took a sip and didn't comment on the hint of hazelnut. Everyone noticed the flavoring, at least those not preoccupied with other thoughts. The doctor noted it on his notepad. He glanced at his chart and asked, "Edgar Gorman, correct?"

"Yes."

"Thank you. As you know, MAGMA requires a complete evaluation of FBI agents every four years."

"MAGMA? When did they take over?

"I'm not quite sure when or why. I suggest you ask your congressman."

"I don't even know who that is."

"I don't either, I'm afraid." He ran his finger down the chart. "I see that you passed the physical portion of your evaluation yesterday. Congratulations."

"Thank you."

The doctor sat down and continued reading his medical history while chewing on the side of his mouth. Each breath whistled through his nose as if it were his last. Every few sentences, his double chin jiggled in syncopation with his earlobes. *Nothing out of the ordinary with his blood results or vital signs*, he internalized. *I wish I had those cholesterol numbers.*

Then he took another sip and read the final paragraph outlining the prior doctor's conclusion. Before he could finish, coffee dribbled off his lips as he fought back the urge to spit it out. His face went flush while unchecked emotions surfaced out of nowhere. While pretending to still be reading, his eyes registered his patient's every movement: *Tight shirt stretched open in between buttons, no doubt a sign of weight gain; five o'clock shadow, probably hasn't showered in days; an unexpected swipe at the tissue box, overt aggressive behavior.*

Edgar felt the doctor's eyes upon him and cleared his throat while navigating a more comfortable spot on the couch. This snapped Dr. Bevan out of his trance. He smiled and said, "Please forgive me. I'm almost finished reading your history."

Edgar nodded politely.

He reciprocated and read the summary again:

"In conclusion, the patient is in good physical health overall. In 2061, he was treated by *Diane Beatty,* who is now *missing. Beware* that signs of mental *duress* and *psychopathic behavior* were observed during the exam. The patient has requested medication to remedy insomnia."

He ran his fingers through his newly crusted mustache as traces of dried coffee granules fell onto his lap. With a nonchalant touch of a few fingers, he quickly searched "Diane Beatty" online. One entry for a doctor stood out. It read:

"A leader in the field of mental health, Dr. Diane Beatty disappeared outside her home on October 1st in 2067. The case is still

under investigation since a body has not been found, but no suspects have been officially charged."

Doctor Bevan sipped his coffee while trying to decide how to proceed. Edgar had settled into the couch and turned his gaze to the windowpane. *Was he just bored or daydreaming,* Bevan wondered, *or showing more symptoms?* He added a note to his record: *Patient is showing signs of possible Depersonalization Disorder. Will explore further for any emotional detachment or loss of touch with reality.*

He reread a portion of the previous doctor's summary: "*Beware that he is now showing signs of mental duress and psychopathic behavior.*" He wondered what the physician meant by "psychopathic." Not a lightly used term in any setting, but even more unusual coming from someone outside the mental health field. He thought about excusing himself from the room and placing a direct call to the physician, but time was running out. He still needed to prepare for his conference.

Instead, he set down his cup and decided to continue as if nothing was wrong. "So, Mr. Gorman, I'm sorry about your loss."

"Thank you. The last few months have been rough."

"It says in your file that your wife died from a brain aneurysm."

"Yes."

"Did it come on suddenly?"

"No, she knew it was a possibility."

"I see." Dr. Bevan scratched his neck and asked, "Yet it went untreated?"

"The doctors said it was inoperable. At least, the doctors she was allowed to see."

"That must've been difficult for both of you."

Edgar tilted his head and studied the doctor's eyes, searching for any signs of empathy. There were glimmers but his animated jowls and bloated cheeks overshadowed any real depictions of sincerity. Then he gazed toward the window on the other side of the room. "Of course, it's been difficult. It's been downright unbearable. I haven't had a good night's sleep in months — thus, part of the reason why I'm here."

"Of course."

Dr. Bevan nodded his head and continued studying the notes. As he read the file, Edgar noticed a flash of light shooting across the window. It rekindled images of Evelyn in the hospital on that decisive day they learned of her diagnosis. His mind wandered as he recalled the memories.

꘡꘡꘡

The hustle and bustle of gurneys and orderlies crammed the hallway. Instead of escorting Edgar and Evelyn into his office for a heart-to-heart chat, the doctor on call stood in the corridor with one foot angling toward the operating room. The flashing red light above his head repeatedly distracted his train of thought while he delivered the devastating news on Evelyn's condition.

Evelyn's shoulders collapsed upon learning it was a brain tumor. Edgar quickly grabbed his wife's arms and escorted her over to a chair. He gently stroked her hair while the vibration of her pounding chest bellowed through the backrest. "Don't worry, we'll figure this out. It's not as bad as it seems."

She laid her head next to his and replied, "It is, I can feel it." Then she melted into his arms and said, "I don't want to lose you. I'm not ready to die."

The on-call doctor stood in front of them but remained silent. Edgar nervously looked up waiting for him to throw a lifeline but none came. The man's hollowed out expression sank any hope of an encouraging response. "I'm sorry, Mrs.

Gorman. There's nothing we can do here. Consult with your insurance and primary care physician as soon as possible."

The red lights continued blinking above. Each time they glowed, the doctor unconsciously tightened his cheeks. Finally, with the soft clap of his hands, he added, "I'm sorry, but I'm needed in the Emergency Room. Good luck to both of you." Then he scurried down the hall and disappeared.

❧❧❧

Dr. Bevan finished reading and noticed that his patient was daydreaming. He cleared his throat. This caused Edgar to snap out of his reverie. He lowered his head and relaxed back into the sofa. "Sorry, Doc. I just needed a moment there."

"No need to apologize," the doctor replied, "your feelings are normal. What you've experienced over the past few months are a natural response to tragic events. A person is expected to experience several stages of grief and emotions. It takes time."

"Which ones would you say I'm showing now — denial, anger, regret, hostility? — because I'm feeling them all."

The words rested between them like a rug ready to be pulled out from underneath at any moment. The silence lingered a bit too long, causing the doctor to glance at his patient's damning summary while clearing his throat again. Then he rose to his feet and sauntered over to the window. He pulled up the blinds, letting in as much sunlight as possible, hoping it would warm up the conversation, and replied, "Pain comes to us from many different sources. Are you looking for something to just calm your nerves or is there a physical pain of some kind too?"

"Listen, Doc, I'm sorry, but I've been at my wits' end these past few months and just need something to calm the nerves so I can sleep. The sooner I get back to work, the sooner I can take my mind off everything else."

Dr. Bevan returned to his chair and replied, "I see. Let's continue the evaluation first and then decide on the correct treatment from there."

"Do we have to? Can't you just prescribe me something and be done with it?"

"I would if I could, but the doctor who conducted your physical left a few notes in his overall conclusion that — how should I say — require further exploration on my part. Otherwise, I could lose my license."

The comment made Edgar pause. He wasn't sure why, but it seemed out of place, definitely unanticipated. "Care to elaborate?"

The doctor glanced at his CompWatch and suggested, "Let's just continue for now since I'm pressed for time and you want to get out of here as soon as possible. Why don't we just go over a few more questions and conclude today's session. How's that sound?"

Edgar replied, "Wonderful."

"As you mentioned, the circumstances surrounding your wife's death and your subsequent grief, I take it, were unsatisfactory? Or, how should I say this, maybe unexpected?"

"Not so much unexpected as uncontrollable, I guess."

"In what way?"

"In every way, doc. They said her condition was incurable but, in reality, it couldn't be cured under her health plan. If she'd had my health plan, she'd probably still be alive today."

"She was a Front-Loader, I presume," replied Dr. Bevan.

Edgar nodded. "And to top it off, they took her remaining twenty-five grand and applied it toward unpaid medical care that she never even received. By the time I realized they were deducting it right out of our checking account without sending bills, it was too late. They said they couldn't go back and credit us."

The doctor didn't need to ask for more details. He was already acutely aware of hidden fees popping up like crabgrass on medical statements. He decided to move on. "Before the diagnosis, how was your relationship with your wife?"

"What do you mean?"

"Did you get along well? Were there any problems with other family members, neighbors, colleagues? I see her final Demeanor Score was only 380, down from 850 two years ago." He scrolled the page and added, "And yours is now at 425. That's quite a substantial drop in just a few months."

Edgar gazed over at the window before answering, "What can I say? The more people I meet these days, the more I like my dog, and he's been dead for years now. In my line of work, you meet a lot of shady characters — you know what I mean, not the cream of the crop. After time, it just wears you down."

The doctor nodded. "Why don't you just get another dog?"

"I don't think I can take another heartbreak."

"Understandable." Dr. Bevan added another entry to his notepad: *Patient is unable to maintain relationships.* Then he closed the cover and said, "Law enforcement is a stressful occupation, thus, why we have these evaluations periodically. It's all part of the guidelines set up under the Revised Constitution as I'm sure you're aware. It is my job to identify any candidates that might possess character flaws which could lead to possible confrontations in the field, causing harm to the public."

"Yeah, I remember what happened in the twenties and thirties," said Edgar. "FBI was a four-letter word back then."

"Exactly." The doctor wriggled in his chair and added, "It's nothing personal, all part of the evaluation process. You just, unfortunately, came up for review shortly after a very tragic event in your life. The mental duress can be overwhelming for anyone in that situation."

"Doc, you make it sound like I'm some kind of crazy person. I'm fine. My wife and I got along fine. Everything's fine." Edgar waited for an acquiescent response but none came. A soundless static occupied the space between them as the doctor remained still. As the seconds ticked away, Edgar finally lowered his guard and confessed, "We just had a couple of tough years following her diagnosis, you know. Who wouldn't? She was everything to me, my best friend. My only friend, for that matter."

"I see. Have you recently had any problems thinking clearly or urges to do harm to yourself or..."

"Now you're really making me out to be some kind of wacko. I just need something to calm my nerves so I can sleep at night. If I can do that, everything else will go back to normal."

"Okay, Mr. Gorman. Let's move on. Please tell me about your sessions with Dr. Diane Beatty."

"Diane who?"

It says in your medical summary that you were seeing a Dr. Beatty in 2061."

Edgar's brow tightened as he lifted his head off the sofa. He recalled the events of 2061 in his mind and only one came up with any significance. "2061, that was the year my blood levels were elevated and they thought I had diabetes. Luckily, the number went down when I cut back on drinking but I don't know of any doctor named Beatty."

The doctor reviewed the patient's summary while observing his mannerisms. Delusional thoughts and abnormal thinking were blatant signs of mental illness, but were usually accompanied with other symptoms like restlessness, a repetition of words and, most importantly, memory loss. He straightened up in his chair and asked, "Are you saying that you don't remember seeing a Dr. Diane Beatty?"

Edgar crossed his legs and with an irritated tone replied, "I don't know a Dr. Beatty, never have, probably never will. I've never visited her, never heard the name before, and don't really understand why this is an issue."

A drumbeat of fingertips glided over Dr. Bevan's notepad as

he wrote, *Patient is showing hostile tendencies and repetitive cognitive impairment.* Edgar was sitting up rigidly now and searching through his pockets as if trying to pull a rabbit out of a hat.

"Can I get you something?" asked the doctor.

He shook his head. "It's been three years now without a cigarette. Sometimes I just fall back into the old routine and have to catch myself." Edgar found a toothpick in his jacket, pulled it out, and placed it between his teeth. "This'll do."

The doctor nodded and typed: *Past history of addiction.* Before lifting his fingers, he erased the note and replaced it with: *Past and present problem with addiction.*

"I can give you something to calm your nerves and help you sleep at night." He stood up and asked, "More coffee?"

"No, thank you."

As Edgar watched him leave the room, he realized that something was amiss with the session. Why would a Dr. Beatty be listed on his chart? Why was the doctor taking so many notes? On the wall in the corner was a painting. It was a print exquisitely framed behind a glass mirrorpane of Edvard Munch's creation "The Scream." It was one of his favorites. He marveled over the many shades of orange and blue fighting for recognition in between the outlines of blackness. The sexless, twisted creature screamed and swam through streams of tormenting brush strokes, lost and alone, even in the presence of others.

In a way, Edgar felt the same. Between the dismal routine of a job he didn't want, a wife he'd lost, and a life with little meaning, he felt trapped. It was the reason he took long hot baths. There, he could think in peace, there he could reflect, and there he could scream underwater.

Dr. Bevan studied the video feed coming from behind the two-way glass mirror of the painting. Edgar's greenish-blue eyes glistened off the golden rays coming from the window as the doctor poured himself another cup of coffee and returned to the room.

While peeking at his watch, Dr. Bevan said, "Well, I think we're done here for today. I'll file my report and we'll continue from there."

"Continue from there?" Edgar questioned. "I thought this was a one-time thing, you know, to get recertified."

"It is, but considering your present state of mind and the circumstances surrounding your wife's death, I think it would be advisable to continue these sessions. That's totally up to you, of course."

"State of mind?" questioned Edgar.

Dr. Bevan entered a few words on his pad and Edgar's CompWatch dinged. "I've sent you a prescription for Clozapine. That should help calm your nerves."

"Clozapine — isn't that for, you know..."

"Don't believe everything you read. They have many different versions of the drug these days that can treat everything from schizophrenia to diarrhea. This dosage is 50% methylenedioxy-methamphetamine."

"What's that?"

"Ecstasy. If you wish, schedule an appointment with the front desk for next week. In the meantime, I'll go ahead and file the report and we'll leave the door open to whatever you choose to do." He glanced at his watch again and added, "Thank you for your time. You're free to go."

As Edgar shut the door behind him, the doctor switched applications on his notepad and logged on. A few seconds later, the pad rang and answered, "Homeland Security."

"Hello, this is Doctor Arnold Bevan opening case number 982209390. Level 3."

The voice in the pad replied, "Information has been received and confirmed. A case is now opened and standard protocol implemented. One hundred points have been added to your Demeanor Score."

The doctor scratched the back of his head and in a solemn tone asked, "Will this mean I can now go visit my wife in Canada?"

"It appears that your score has reached that level."

"Thank you."

THE PHISH POND

"IT STARTED WITH RIPPING OFF TAGS *from pillows. Then the subject moved on to jaywalking for no apparent reason." Somewhere in an unknown corridor of Southern California, a short man dressed in a white lab coat and white tennis shoes paced the floor in a windowless room. He turned to his colleague and exclaimed, "In broad daylight!" He raised an inquisitive eyebrow before concluding, "And, finally, Edgar Gorman progressed into outright psychosis? Something's wrong with this report."*

His colleague studied the electronic notepad in his hand and replied, "It just doesn't make any sense, does it? Why would we not have predicted this sooner? This should've been flagged months ago."

"Maybe he's working with them." The short man glared up at a glowing neon hologram positioned in the upper corner of the wall next to a set of monitors. The word "GRID" blinked with a repetitive snarl in bright red letters.

"Should we call it in?" asked his colleague.

"Not yet. His Futures Exchange is still positive and generating value."

CHAPTER THREE

FORGOTTEN MEMORIES

EDGAR TROTTED DOWN the flight of stairs and left the building out the side door. Instead of heading over to his car parked on the other side of the plaza, he shuffled across the street and turned right. A ping rang out as his face flashed across a nearby window. It read, "Edgar Gorman, your health profile and ACP readings have been updated. Your Demeanor Score is now 400, down 25 points."

He froze and stared at the glass, "How can that be? I thought it was all tied to how nice you were."

A slight drizzle drifted down through the gray skies above. It was the middle of summer and fifty-eight degrees. He checked the weather forecast. "Four More Weeks of Cold" was the headline. His head wavered between trying to make sense of it all and trying not to care as he continued walking. A few blocks later, he opened the gate and entered the Cedars Sinai Retirement Center.

"Good morning, Mr. Gorman," greeted a robotic voice from the front desk clerk. "We weren't expecting you today."

Edgar grinned and nodded as the smell of disinfectant and chlorine lingered in the air. "Yeah, sorry. I was in the neighborhood. How's Mother?"

The robotic desk clerk maneuvered around behind the counter searching for the proper forms while answering, "Oh, you know. Some days Mrs. Gorman is better than others. Unfortunately, it won't be long before she quits recognizing you completely. I can tell. Half the time she doesn't know who *I* am and I see her every day." The desk clerk stood rigid and blinked. Then on cue: four, three, two, one, it sniffled and sighed, "I'm gonna miss her. She is a wonderful lady." It reached for an electronic notepad and laid it on the counter. "Here you go, please log in."

As Edgar checked the appropriate boxes on the form, he asked, "Is she up?"

"Yes, she's been up for hours, as usual."

"Oh, good. I'm just gonna check on her for a minute." He left down the hallway as the desk clerk bent its elbow and waved with the grace of a knight in armor.

The door was open to his mother's room, as it was with all the rooms nearby. It was much quieter too compared to other floors. No machines beeped through the day nor did the nurses run down the hall shouting orders. Instead, a staff of robotic caregivers roamed the hallways, wirelessly chatting among themselves while one sole nurse with a heartbeat monitored them.

Leslie Gorman rested on her side, facing away from the door and looking out the window. Even though she could barely see the tops of a few high-rise buildings and palm trees across the street from her bed, it was still a fairly nice view of the outside world compared to most. The walls were sparsely covered with featureless pictures of flowers and fauna. On the nightstand was a photo of Leslie with her two children and a separate glass-framed photo depicting her wedding day with her now-deceased husband.

"Good morning." Edgar crept in and waited for a response.

His mother rolled over on her back and said, "Can I help you?"

"It's me, Mother, Eddie."

"Oh, of course, I wasn't expecting you today. Is it Saturday already?"

"No, it's not. I was just in the area and thought I'd stop by."

Leslie smiled and replied, "Well then, it's my lucky day. Come in, come in. Sit down." She sat up on the side of the bed and slowly rose to her feet.

"How've you been, Mom?"

"Oh, the same. Some days are better than others."

"I guess I could say the same," replied Edgar. Leslie lumbered over to the armoire, opened it, and pulled out a light blue dress. "What are you doing?"

"Getting ready." His mother removed her pajamas and draped them over a chair.

"Mom, cover up!"

"Oh, you've seen me naked a hundred times, Eddie."

"Yeah, but not that way." He pointed, turned away, and grimaced. "Anyway, getting ready for what?"

"Honey, they don't let me stay here for free. My money ran out a long time ago. I didn't plan on living this long, you know."

"I didn't realize that. Why didn't you say something?"

"Say what? You're in law enforcement, dear, and a Rear-Ender. Your money won't come until after you retire."

"Back-Ender, Mom, but I could be helping out."

Leslie put her fingers to Edgar's lips to quiet him. "Rear-Ender, Back-Ender, it all means the same. I'm doing fine as it is." Edgar rolled his eyes and sighed. It wouldn't be a visit with his mother without a little stinging sarcasm.

Leslie paused to study her son. Edgar could tell she didn't like what she saw. "How come you never smile anymore? You used to smile all the time as a child."

"Well, life does that to you, Mom, you know — plus gravity."

"At least you haven't lost that sense of humor." His mother sat down at the vanity, grabbed a brush, and stroked her hair. "I'm doing fine," she confirmed while continuing eye contact in the mirror. "Thank God I was grandfathered into that silly program and not like those other unfortunate souls."

"No doubt. You'd been long gone by now."

A grin unfolded as Leslie added, "It's not hard work, son. I just keep an eye on the robots, make a few beds, and they leave me alone the rest of the day." Then she buttoned up her blue dress and added, "I've had a good life — traveled the world a few times, explored jungles, stood up for what I believed was right, and even fought off some bad guys." She leaned her head to the side and reflected, "I've made some good memories, and spent every damn dime of that million dollars the government was stupid enough to give me. What more could I ask for?"

"It wasn't all good," replied Edgar.

"Yeah, I know, but better than most. A minute of feeling sorry for yourself is a minute of happiness you missed out on, dear." His mother walked over to the window and stared out into the morning sky. "I know I was a sucker for bad boys when it came to picking men. Ever since your father died, well, you know, it was just hard to fill those shoes."

"Yeah, you sure did know how to pick 'em."

"You remind me so much of your father. The same delivery, the same determination, the same eyes." She mulled over the thought and added, "At least I outlived them all."

"Well, women are supposed to live longer than men, you know, because they have more to say."

His mother let out a hearty laugh. It was a wonderful laugh — short and sweet in timbre, but solid and pleasant to the ear, the kind that made you want to laugh in return just to hear her laugh again. She turned around, adjusted her collar and said, "You sure do know how to bring a smile to my face, honey."

"You too, Mom."

Leslie turned toward the television and commanded, "Elixir, turn on Channel 12." The volume was down but the screen showed a news anchor on the left side of a split screen with the President of the United States on the other.

"I can't believe you still use voice commands. You do know that they can hear every word you say."

"Not with the volume down." Leslie continued getting dressed and Edgar shook his head. There was no use arguing with an old woman who had dementia over surveillance technology.

"Oh, I love hearing this man talk. You know he was a child star before he went into politics. Elixir, turn up the volume."

"Mother, everyone knows that."

"Yes, but did you know that he singlehandedly saved the Networks from total disaster?"

"You mean 'Network.' There's only one."

"Not at the time, dear. There were many back then."

"But he was only seven years old. How can that even be possible?"

Leslie stared at the screen and replied, "I don't remember, but it happened." She pointed and added, "There it is, scrolling across the bottom of the screen. And that chin, those eyes, it's all right there." A smile blanketed her face as she continued. "I loved his shows."

"I don't remember you ever watching any TV growing up."

"Now that you mentioned it, me either." Leslie shook her head for a moment before nodding, "Well, I do now. I mean, look around. What else is there to do? Besides, we need him now more than ever. Just look at how he's turned this country around and kept the peace."

Edgar placed his hands on the chair next to the vanity and scooted it in as his mother sat down again. "Kept the peace?"

"Yes, maybe you don't remember," replied Leslie as she applied foundation to her face. "Years ago, we were under attack daily by those fascist-sympathizing cyber-bullies. And the violence and unrest, oh my, it was everywhere, all day long." She pointed at the monitor and declared, "He and his party stopped it all, that man right there. I tell you, he's a savior, the chosen one."

Edgar's head slowly swayed as he searched for a tender response. "He has done a lot of good, I'll give you that, but don't believe everything you hear when it comes to violence and poverty. Believe me, I see it every day. We just don't see it on our news feeds since MAGMA took over."

"MAGMA? What's that?" she asked.

"The private conglomerate that took over operations years ago."

Puzzled eyebrows raised and lowered on her forehead. The lines on her face revealed a lifetime of expressions but this look only showed emptiness; a hollowed-out crevice where the memories once were.

Edgar chose his words carefully. This wasn't the mother he remembered as a child. That woman would take off for weeks on excursions into the wild with men she barely knew. That woman taught him how to load a pistol before he learned how to tie his shoes. That woman was now gone, a victim of a slow creeping disease that turned cognitive thoughts into grains of sand. Those memories had been replaced with television commercials and mindless chatter from her news feed.

"MAGMA is the conglomerate made up of Mega, Appo, Gooble, Macrohard, and Alpha that took over control of most government agencies years ago. They now run SSI, Homeland Security, the Department of the Interior, you name it. Everything except the military. From what I'm told, they'll soon be running the FBI and CIA too."

Leslie grinned sheepishly and replied, "I knew that." An advertisement came on the screen. She stiffened her shoulders and groaned, "I can't believe that Taylor Swift lady is still doing reverse mortgage commercials. When is she ever going to retire?"

"Didn't she die a few years ago? I'm sure she did." Edgar leaned in for a closer look. "See, in the bottom corner of the ad. There's that symbol signifying it's a deep fake."

Leslie opened a bottle on the table and shook it with a finger over the lid. "I guess anyone can live forever now. Why, is beyond me." Then she dabbed a few spots on her forehead and around her eyes. Edgar brushed back her mother's bangs, allowing the silence to soothe them both. These were the moments he wanted to remember. Before he could think another thought, his mother asked, "How's your sister?"

"Lotty's doing fine."

"I know, but we both know what she's capable of, or, should I say, not capable of. Is she all right? Is she going to survive?"

Edgar stiffened his shoulders and replied, "Mother, she's doing ten times better than I am. You do remember that she took the million dollars and left when she turned eighteen?"

"Yes, yes, I remember some kind of scuffle with that guy I was dating. What was his name? Oh yeah, Bill. Wild Bill the Bull-Shitter."

"Bill the Bastard is more like it."

Leslie snickered and nodded her head. "I guess so. He could be an asshole, for sure."

This was another subject he didn't want to revisit. He glanced at the clock and hugged his mom. "I should go."

Leslie firmly grabbed hold of her son's sleeve and pulled him in closer. "I know I've been a terrible mother."

"No, don't even go there. That's not..."

Leslie shook her head and interrupted, "It doesn't matter anymore. Hear me out, please." Edgar nodded. "I know my boyfriends were hard on you, but it wasn't all bad."

"They were hard on all of us," he replied.

"Yeah, maybe at times, but they knew where to draw the line with me. With you and your sister, not so much, and I shouldn't have tolerated it." Leslie's eyelids gently quivered, "It's just that after your father died, I kind of lost my will to live, for a long time. He was one of a kind. And the way he died, well, you know."

"You never did tell us how he died. Why?"

His mother wiped away any remaining blotches on her cheeks before replying, "It was a long time ago. It all happened so fast. I don't remember." She stared into the mirror and continued, "He just did. It doesn't matter now. You turned out all right in the end and that's what matters."

Edgar leaned in and gingerly agreed, "I guess."

As she pushed back her hair and wrapped it with a tie, a light brush of sincerity gleamed over her face. "I know I haven't left you anything as far as money goes."

"That doesn't matter, Mom."

"There is the house, though, and at least that's something."

"That's a lot these days."

"Still, there's something I need you to do for me."

"Sure, what is it?"

Leslie tried to gather her scattered thoughts together and put them into words. "It has to do with the pottery I've made, my paintings, that kind of stuff. They're all a part of me and who I am. The only things I'll be remembered for after I die. I know it sounds corny and all, but please keep them after I'm gone."

"Mom, we'll always remember you."

"I'm sure you will for a while, but then I'll just become, what's that silly song from the twentieth century, 'Dust in the Wind.'"

"Of course, we won't forget you. I'll make sure of it." Edgar peered into his mother's eyes searching for clues about what was going on inside her mind. "Why are you being so serious all of a sudden?"

Leslie stood up, closed her eyes, and placed her hands on both sides of her son's face. It was as if she was trying to telepathically channel vanishing thoughts using Edgar's brain waves. She sniffled before adding, "I wish I could explain it, but I can't right now. It'll come to me again, I'm sure, and I'll write it down this time."

"I love you, Mom. Don't forget that."

"I won't." Her eyes fluttered just enough to keep the tears from forming. Then she grinned and said, "Anyway, let's change the subject. How's that lovely wife of yours? You never bring her with you anymore."

Edgar lowered his head and lamented, "Evelyn died a few months ago."

"Oh, yes, of course. I'm sorry, dear. So sad what they did. I liked her a lot."

"Me too."

While stroking his arm, she batted away the tears again and asked, "So, how are you holding up?"

Edgar wiped his own eyes and replied, "Some days are better than others, you know. I'm still getting over the initial shock, but..." His words faded as his thoughts began to wander.

Leslie pulled her son in for a hug and said, "I know it's tough. It took me forever to get over your father but the key is finding a cause worth living for, or dying for. Either way, just find a cause. That's how I got over losing your father. Maybe it'll help you forget about your loss."

"Not a bad idea. I'll think about that one."

Leslie nodded and tossed her head back with a confident flair. "Hey, who turned down the volume on the TV? I was listening to our President." She fumbled through the settings while Edgar shook his head. There it was again. He knew it was only a matter of time before his mother slipped away forever.

"Okay, Mom. I have to get to work."

Edgar patted her on the back and kissed her forehead. On the way out of the building, he double-tapped the lens on his CompWatch and brought up a photo. It was a picture of his mom shortly after giving birth. The hologram flickered and wavered in the sunlight so he ducked under a tree to study it in the shade. "Elixir, search in my 'Event Library' and play the Gorman family videos from late 2032."

In a confident but soothing mechanical voice, Elixir responded, "I found Gorman Family Video, Burbank, 2032: #1 created at 07:30 a.m., Saturday, December 4, 2032; and #2 created at 12:00 p.m., December 4, 2032. Should I keep searching?"

"No, that's it. Play #1."

The screen on the lenses faded to black for a moment. Then the words "Retrieval Mode" flashed as images gradually took form. Edgar flipped through the "Settings" and muted the "Music Option," while selecting the "All Camera Angles" box. Another alert box popped up reading, "You have two new camera feeds that have been shared. Do you want to include them in your stream?" Edgar clicked on one of the streams to read the source title: "Burbank Water and Power Department, created at 07:15 a.m., Saturday, December 4, 2032." He clicked "Accept."

Gradually, the fragmented pictures turned into actual video footage as the events from years ago came into view:

❧❧❧

GORMAN FAMILY VIDEO #1, 12-4-2032, 07:30 A.M.

From the camera angle on a telephone pole down the street, a man quietly crept behind the bushes lining the front yard. His semi-automatic .22 rifle was tucked against his armpit with a finger gently caressing the trigger. One eye bulged out of its socket over the gunsight with laser focus. The other was tightly shut and twitching. He scanned the sidewalk, stopping long enough at each car, when it happened.

A gray tabby cat jumped out of a truck bed and scurried for cover under an oak tree in the next yard. One shot, two shots, three shots rang out, the last one grazing the door of a classic VW Microbus across the street. The car alarm sound woke the neighborhood so forcefully that the leaves on nearby trees shuddered. The neighbor raced out the front door with one arm in his robe while repeatedly clicking a key fob. The noise finally stopped. The man in the bushes lifted his rifle to his shoulder and aimed.

"Bill, what the hell are you doing?" The feed switched to a camera near the front porch recording Leslie's cry as she yawned and rubbed her eyelids.

"Get back in the house. He's one of them."

"One of them? What are you talking about? He's our neighbor. We've known him for years."

"Oh, but have you? Who's to say he's actually the person you think he is."

Leslie had both hands on her hips and replied, "I've lived here for years now and I know my neighbors."

"Yeah, but he's still one of them. There's a civil war going on right now, in case, you hadn't heard."

"Put down that damn gun!"

Leslie's words were loud enough to attract the neighbor's attention. He squinted in their direction and waved as he bent down to pick up a paper flyer that was floating across his driveway. Another shot rang out from the bushes. It missed its target but shattered a corner panel of his living room window. Fragments of glass scattered across the newly speckled concrete. The neighbor, still bowing and clutching the flyer, glanced at the damage and then at Bill. In one swooping motion, he lifted the robe over his head and ducked back into the house.

Bill aimed and pulled the trigger but it didn't fire. He squeezed again, but nothing. He yanked on the bolt action and tried to load the chamber manually. Instead, the gun slipped out of his hands and landed on the ground, dislodging it on impact. A bullet spun through the bushes across the front porch and pierced his car tire. As air hissed out of the plies of rubber, Bill yanked the rifle off the ground and grunted.

Leslie stood motionless during the whole episode. Her hands had unconsciously moved down to her sides while her mouth opened wide exhaling years of built up frustration with her boyfriend. She didn't say a word. The corneas of her eyes swam in anger as they darted from one image to the next. She relaxed her shoulders and ambled over to the side of the house. There she turned on the water faucet to the sprinklers.

Bill jumped up to his knees and cursed, "What the hell?" Spray coming from sprinkler heads behind and in front of him now showered his body. He tried to cover his face. He tried to cover the sprinkler. As the moisture frustrated and soaked his ego, he cried, "Turn it off, dammit," but no one was listening. Leslie was already in the house and slamming the door shut behind her. He looked down at his muddy kneecaps and began crawling alongside the house. At the corner, he turned and faded away into the backyard.

From his bedroom window on the second floor, a young Edgar Gorman watched the morning exchange. The new camera feed from a streetlamp captured the view in front of both houses. His head shifted from the bushes to the car tire to the window across the street. A curtain in the neighbor's bedroom window opened. A girl, two years younger than he was, and sporting a head of wavy hair draping down past her shoulders, discreetly waved. Edgar returned the gesture while trying to conceal a blushing smile.

Then he rushed out of the room and down the stairs. The security camera in the hallway captured video of him at the bottom colliding with Bill.

"Bill, how could you!" asked Edgar.

While drying his head with a kitchen towel, he replied,

"How could I what? Were you watching? That's dangerous, you know."

"Looking out my window? Why'd you try to shoot our neighbor?"

Bill marched into the living room, grabbed the remote, and turned on the TV."

A newscaster spoke as a banner flashed across the bottom of the screen reading "THE COUNTRY IS AT CIVIL WAR — Four dead in Mississippi. twenty wounded. THE PRESIDENT HAS BEEN ASSASSINATED."

"That's why. It's the big one," he said. "Everyone saw it coming but no one did anything to stop it."

The newscaster stood in front of a burning church in Jackson, Mississippi, as firemen set up hoses. With a deep low voice, he began his commentary:

"Three hours ago, the states of Mississippi, Alabama, and Louisiana announced that they were seceding from the Union for the second time in the history of our country. Texas and Florida are expected to soon follow. Violence has broken out in cities and towns across these states as neighbors are taking up arms against each other, fighting with whatever weapons they have in guerrilla-type warfare. In some instances, going door to door. There are several reports of people being hunted down in their own back yards using weaponized drones. The National Guard has been deployed to restore peace as officials work on a solution."

The newscaster paused to listen through his earpiece. "We have breaking news. There are similar reports of outbreaks of violence happening in other states across the country. We don't know if there've been any casualties yet, but authorities are advising people to stay indoors until further notice. We understand that the newly sworn in President is scheduled to speak at any moment from the White House."

A burly man dressed in sleeveless, worn-out army

fatigues and wearing a baseball cap entered the picture and shoved the newscaster to the ground. As he grabbed the microphone and stared into the camera, the screen went dark.

"Jesus, the whole world is falling apart," sighed Leslie.

"I think it's only here in the States." Edgar looked down at the news feed coming from his phone. "It says that all flights to Europe have been grounded until further notice."

"Why Europe?" asked Bill.

"Who knows, maybe they don't want us there."

Leslie ran her hand through her hair and said, "What a mess." Before he could reply, she smacked Bill on the arm and asked, "What in the world has gotten into you? Why would you shoot at my neighbor? They haven't done anything?"

"It's only a matter of time. Check out the new bumper stickers they put on their car."

"Bumper stickers?"

Bill walked over to the window and pulled back the curtain while keeping his distance. "Look." Leslie peered out cautiously before moving away. "Yeah, they have a couple of bumper stickers on their car. So what?"

"So what? Did you get a good look at them? One is a peace symbol and the other looks like the face of some old communist leader, probably Fidel Castro or that Che Guvarro guy. Fucking extremists, I tell you."

"How does putting a peace symbol on your car make you an extremist? And it's Guevara, not Guvarro."

"Who would put a peace symbol on their car unless they were some kind of Commie fanatic?"

"Well, maybe someone who was a pacifist. It means nothing."

"Even worse. That means they'll just roll over for anybody."

"That's not true. They're good people. Why, we were just over there a couple of months ago at a barbecue."

"Well, that was then. We're at war now. Everything's changed. It's us against them."

Edgar leaned in closer with his face against the glass. "That's not a peace symbol. It's a Pisces sign, and that looks like a bear, not a person, on the other sticker."

"Let me see." Bill squinted and replied, "It's hard to tell from here. I still think it's a peace symbol."

Leslie peered over his shoulder again and then backed away. "William P. Vandercamp, what's gotten into you?" She gazed over at her son for an uneasy check on reality. He'd seen this look before with other boyfriends in the past. It was a face swelling with exasperation but drenched in heartbreak.

"Well, I wasn't going to hurt anyone with that pea shooter. Just put the fear of God back in them." Bill hung his head and added, "I was aiming for a shoulder or leg, not for the heart, you know."

Leslie sighed, "When you're sitting in jail for attempted murder, please remember the stupid stuff you said — like that."

The phone rang. She checked the number, then stared at her boyfriend while shaking her head. "Boy, have you done it now." She answered, "Hi Laurie... Yep, yep... I know... I'm so sorry... We'll pay for the window. What can we do to make this up to you? Yep, yep... I will, you can bet. By the way, what month were you born?... I thought so. Bye."

Leslie ended the call, looked at Bill, and said, "She was born in March. First, you kicked Lotty out of the house just for following her dreams, now this. I need you out of the house and gone by noon."

☙☙☙

The hologram screen darkened after the video ended. A virtual alert box flashed over Edgar's CompWatch, scrolling the following message: "WARNING – This device will reboot in 30 seconds. WARNING – This device will reboot in 30 seconds."

He selected "Close" and exited the hologram screen. "Fucking reboots," he muttered.

He tried to reflect on the video footage. The two new feeds captured much more of the episode than what he'd been able to access years ago. He didn't know whether to laugh or cry. At the time, no one was laughing, as the whole country was dealing with a cultural mental breakdown laced with misguided anger. The political landscape had finally come unhinged and boiled over to the point of violence. Yet, thirteen days later, the Second Civil War was over. Hundreds of people had died at the hands of their neighbors or local militia. It was hard to tell the two apart. Both sides finally came together and agreed that senseless killings were not going to solve the country's problems. Drastic solutions were needed.

When compared to the conversation he'd had with his mother about the world as she knew it only minutes ago, it made his head spin. Was everyone better off now than they were back then or had everyone's perception of the world just changed? How did technology advance by leaps and bounds while social issues seemed to be stuck in a nineteenth-century time warp?

His phone screen turned black for a moment as a little dial churned in the middle. A few seconds later, a combination of pleasantly short harmonies dinged, soon followed by the message "Reboot Complete."

CHAPTER FOUR

LOOKING OVER YOUR SHOULDER

EDGAR LEFT THE RETIREMENT CENTER and walked toward the parking garage to get his car. As he rounded the corner, he decided to duck into a coffee shop and order a drink. *What was that flavor in the doctor's coffee,* he thought? As he stood in line, a ceramic cup hit the concrete floor, shattering everyone's moment of privacy. Instinctively, he reached under his jacket for his weapon. The barista apologized to everyone while picking up fragments from the floor. Edgar removed his hand from the holster, trying not to draw attention, and lowered the flap.

He looked around the room to see if anyone had noticed, but everyone was back to going about their own business. Lovers chatted and cuddled in the corner, students pecked away on touch screens and focused on their studies, while employees cleaned tables and bussed dishes.

Everything seemed to be back to normal with one exception: a man who'd just come in and grabbed a seat at a table near the doorway. He looked familiar, yet Edgar couldn't quite place him. From the Hawaiian shirt down to the brand new baseball cap, his outfit screamed, *I'm totally out of place.* Their eyes crossed paths for just an instant before the man turned his gaze to a TV screen on the wall.

The whole coffee shop was now glued to the dialogue box scrolling on the bottom of the TV as the newscaster described the scene at Capitol Hill:

"Congress has finally agreed to place a constitutional amendment on the ballot one year from now. By then, the five-year trial period allowing MAGMA to subcontract all day-to-day operations of certain government agencies to the private company, Forest Dunes Corporation, will have concluded. These agencies include Homeland Security, which has jurisdiction over other branches such as FEMA, the Secret Service, and U.S. Immigrations and Customs, plus the Department of Labor and the Department of the Interior. The FBI will also be rebranding and transitioning its workforce over to Forest Dunes during this final year of the contract. The Department of Defense, CIA, and all branches of the military will remain under government control for now.

"After the trial period has ended, a referendum will be circulated nationwide asking voters to amend the Constitution permanently. If three-fourths of all voters agree, as directed by Article Five of the Revised Constitution, H.R. bill number 96754 will become law and the Thirty-Seventh Amendment.

"In other news, the high today of sixty-eight degrees was two degrees lower than last year, thus increasing the latest cooling trend to a record thirteen weeks, surpassing last year's heat wave of twelve weeks. Scientists still can't explain the long periods of inconsistent weather, but the National Oceanic and Atmospheric Administration says that we have seen this pattern before in the past and are confident that normal weather patterns will return shortly.

"Latest figures from the United Nations show that the world's population has declined another two percent this year..."

Edgar watched the man stare at the screen. Something didn't feel right. He turned back around and asked the clerk, "Where's your restroom?"

"In the back," motioned a young boy behind the counter as he rang up the next customer.

Edgar moved down the hall to the rear of the building and exited out the back door. *Better safe than sorry,* he surmised. Then he backtracked his steps around the block and took the long way to his car. As he turned the corner heading to the parking garage, a dizzying array of morning rush hour pedestrians sucked him in before he had the chance to respond. Bodies shuffled on and off the sidewalks and into buildings as he danced between, them making his way to the other side.

He descended the stairs to the second level and glanced back up. A silhouette slid into the garage from the outside ramp. It was the man from the coffee shop. This was no coincidence. He unsnapped the strap on his holster and flipped back his jacket while racing down the steps to the next level.

Suddenly, a buzzing sound came from his CompWatch. An image of his boss, Isabel "Izzy" Moreno, materialized on the crystal. It wasn't a live feed, but the stock photo from her badge. That meant she didn't want to be seen and was either undercover or in the middle of a major situation. He tapped on the earpiece connected to his contacts and answered, "What's up, chief?"

"Don't get me started, *compadre*."

He chuckled and grinned. This was Izzy's signature saying, her mantra on life, if ever she had one. "I won't, but I'm kind of rushed for time here."

"Where are you?"

"I'm in a parking garage being followed."

"Being followed. Are you sure?"

"Yes."

"By whom?"

Edgar jogged back up the stairs to the next landing and peeked over the railing. "Some guy wearing a stupid Hawaiian shirt with a ball cap. He also has on a pair of white sunglasses."

"Sunglasses? Show me a video feed."

Edgar activated a camera lens and directed it toward the landing, while zooming in with his earpiece.

"Ay yai yai," hummed Izzy.

"Don't ay yai yai me. What?"

"The white glasses. Have you ever heard of Dill Electronics?"

"Of course, I think."

"A few years ago, the company invented this gadget called a Digital Data Organizer. It was on the market for about a week before the government swooped in and seized the whole stockpile, classified all their records, and removed the trademark from the Library of Congress."

"Holy shit. I've heard about DDO glasses. I thought they were outlawed."

"Not outlawed, but restricted."

"Restricted, to whom?"

"Uh, law enforcement."

"Well, why then don't we have them?"

"Edgar, we couldn't even afford the I.T. support, let alone, be high enough on the list of officers who would get a pair. I hear they're still in development and a year or two from being ready for use. Something to do with medical side effects that really screw with your mind if you wear them too long."

"Then who would use them, CIA?"

"That's my guess, but they usually give us the heads up in these circumstances."

Edgar ducked back down and headed to the lower level of the structure. "Circumstances, what do you mean 'circumstances'?"

Izzy's response was jumbled and inaudible.

"Shit, Izzy, you're fading in and out. I didn't hear what you said. What do I do? This guy's got the whole Internet hooked up to his brain. There's no way I can lose him. Can you come get me?"

There was a long silence between them before his boss cleared her throat and said, "I can't."

Edgar peeked up over at the stairwell before asking, "What are you not telling me?"

Izzy sighed and replied, "Your clearance level has been

downgraded for some reason. I don't know how or why but I'll get to the bottom of this. Until then, I can't do anything."

Edgar winced and squeezed his fist, "That goddamn shrink."

"Shrink?"

"Yeah, I just left his office a few hours ago. You know, part of the re-certification bullshit we go through now."

Izzy chuckled, "What did you say to him?"

"Nothing, I swear. He was, you know, kind of weird."

"Well, that explains things. Give me a couple of hours to figure this out. I'll text you when it's safe to come in."

"Maybe I shouldn't come in at all? I mean, it'd be like walking into the lion's den."

Izzy took a more somber tone and said, "Normally, I'd agree with you but, well, we have this boy in custody. It's a 26A, the same scenario as that case a month ago in the state of Jefferson, Old Oregon to be exact."

"Same charges?"

"Yeah, and the same M.O. I'd like to interrogate him before the Dunes agents come and take him away."

"When are they scheduled to show up?"

"In about four hours."

"I wanna be there when you talk to him."

"I thought so. That last case hit a nerve with all of us. I'll contact you when I figure this out."

The sound of rusted steel rubbing against concrete echoed off the walls of the stairwell. He knew what that meant. The man was coming down. "Okay, gotta go."

After disconnecting the call, a door squeaked from above. With lightning speed, Edgar raced toward his car and ducked behind a pillar. Even from the underground level, he knew the DDO glasses picked up every movement. All it took was a security camera link or a cell phone signal. He had to think of something soon or the slightest movement would give away his position.

The sound of footsteps grew louder. They weren't just any footsteps, though — no, these were puzzling. Rubber squished against rubber like a play toy in the jaws of a big canine. The two feet squeaked along, inching closer with every stride.

Edgar's eyebrows tightened into a crown of confusion as he whispered, "This can't be CIA." He scrolled through his CompWatch and brought up a Spotify playlist. "Let's see how dumb this guy is," he muttered as he scanned his music settings for a "Shared List." Sure enough, another name popped up. Then he linked their accounts and turned the volume up all the way.

The man approached with his pistol drawn, choosing each step with hesitation. A blur of red light flashed onto his lenses. There was movement coming from a pillar next to a black sedan. Then it vanished. He pushed a button on the side of the glasses and whispered, "Backup requested on the lower level of the Cedars Sinai Medical Center garage on Beverly." His hands shook as he focused his gaze on the column, adjusted the vision on his glasses and crept in ever so lightly.

When he was within a dozen feet, a high-pitched, distorted electric guitar blasted into his earpiece, unannounced and unrelenting. Heavy Metal music roared out, causing him to momentarily lose his balance. He moaned and ripped the glasses off his head.

Edgar swung around and tackled him before he knew what hit him. He jumped on top and slammed the man's hand to the concrete, causing the gun to slide across the floor. As he pulled out a taser gun and was ready to press the button, their eyes met. The man's fake mustache now dangled from his upper lip. He tore it away and pulled off his hat.

"What the hell, Toyer! What are you doing here?"

Toyer lunged his chest into the air, tossing Edgar to the side. Before he had the chance to continue, Edgar jabbed him in the throat with his fist. His windpipe bellowed like a draining bathtub.

Toyer covered his throat as the glasses slipped out of his hand and tumbled onto the concrete. Edgar slapped his ears on each side with his hands as hard as he could. The man's eardrums popped and hissed out air from underneath his eyeball sockets as church bells rang in his head. He tried to stand back up but Edgar was waiting. He quickly jabbed Toyer in the stomach with his fist, sending the man down for the last count.

Toyer accordioned into a fetal position and moaned for mercy. "Okay, you win. Stop!" he cried as he seesawed back and forth.

Edgar pulled out his pistol and pointed. "What the hell is going on? Who are you working for?"

Toyer rested on the ground for a few seconds until regaining his breath. The pain was still overwhelming but he did his best to block it out. He knew backup would arrive soon enough. All he had to do was stall. "Hey, Edgar, long time no see."

"Long time no see! We work in the same building. I saw you on the elevator yesterday, and now you're some kind of secret agent?"

"Why's that so hard to believe?"

"Because you're a damn accountant. You did my taxes last year."

"Best cover ever, wouldn't you say?"

Edgar did a double take. He now saw Toyer through different lenses. All his training and experience had prepared him for such a revelation but he'd never put two and two together.

"Now it's starting to make sense," he surmised, "my clearance level." He pulled Toyer up by the collar and asked, "Why are you tailing me?"

Toyer remained stoic. Edgar pushed even closer and sneered, "Who are you working for, the CIA, FBI?"

"Of course not."

"Then who?"

Toyer rubbed his jaw and said, "I can't tell you, and it's not important. What's important is that there's a Level 3 Alert out on you so you might as well cooperate and come in with someone you know, like me. Otherwise, no telling what might happen to you."

"What might happen? Not important?" Edgar twirled up to his feet and asked, "How the hell did this get so out of hand?"

"I don't know. My orders are to bring you in for questioning. That's all I know."

"Bring me in where? If you're not FBI or CIA, then who the hell are you?"

"I can't tell you. It's top secret."

"Top secret?" yelled Edgar. "You're a fucking accountant!"

A flashing red light reflected off the concrete next to the DDO glasses. Edgar picked them up off the ground. *So, he* is *wearing a Digital Data Organizer,* he pondered while studying them. *How's that even possible?*

"Hey, you shouldn't touch those. You aren't authorized."

"Nobody's authorized. How'd you get them?"

"I can't tell you that. Besides, they're just prototypes."

Toyer's eye twitched. Edgar was ready to ask another question when a message flashed across the lenses, "Almost there." The sound of tires screeching swirled down the stairway and echoed across the ramp.

"Shit!"

He tucked the glasses into his pocket and picked up Toyer's gun. Then he removed the clip and tossed it over the railing.

"*Greedness greaty*, Edgar. Why'd you do that?"

"Turn around."

"What?"

"You heard me, turn around and put your hands on your head. Now."

Toyer rose to his feet with a slow pirouette while lifting his arms in the air. Edgar pressed a Taser gun into his back and said,

"Sorry, I gotta go." 30,000 volts rattled Toyer's torso as he twisted and crumpled to the ground.

Another ding echoed throughout the parking garage. Edgar glanced at his CompWatch and shook his head. His Demeanor Score was now 350. *What is going on? This shouldn't be happening.*

He put on the glasses, activated the earpiece, and tapped on the temple. A full 3-D screen of the parking structure came into view. Two cars were about to make the turn down into the next level. He focused on an icon in the corner of the lenses and blinked. A map of the Metro Station tracks displayed departure and arrival times across the lens. A train was due to arrive at any minute.

Foam oozed out of Toyer's mouth as Edgar raced up the stairs and disappeared.

THE PHISH POND

THE TWO MEN ALL DRESSED IN WHITE stared into a set of monitors covering an entire wall in the white room. As a red light flashed, images of Edgar scampering across the street were shown on the screen. They focused in on his location and the tall man asked, "Do we call it in now?"

The short man yawned, rubbed the two-day-old bristle lining his jaw, and replied, "Not yet. I'm not sure what to make of this one. He's unpredictable, but I don't think it raises him to that level yet. Let's play it out first."

"He's got the glasses, though. That should be worth reporting."

"It is, but he hasn't done anything with them that's illegal yet. We need a fact pattern first; otherwise, it's all just conjecture and you know what that'll get us."

The tall man nodded and replied, "Yeah, in deep shit. Okay, I gotta piss. You keep an eye on him."

CHAPTER FIVE

ANOTHER WORLD

EDGAR HOPPED ON THE FIRST METRO train that arrived. It was the Express heading north away from his office but there was no time to wait for another. Through the DDO glasses he saw three men approaching the station from across the street. The next stop was in the San Fernando Valley. He removed the glasses and settled into a seat in the last row. The train car was half full of early-morning commuters scattered in clusters throughout.

Near the front, a group of maids exchanged morning greetings and gossiped about their employers. In the middle, college students studied and checked their social media feeds. Occupying the rear were a few older men sitting by themselves, each in his own separate world and still half asleep. They stared out the windows in an almost meditative state, allowing the natural sway of the train to overtake and dull their senses.

Edgar wondered what they were thinking. Were they contemplating a life full of bad choices that landed them a seat on the train or were they just happy to be anywhere except where they came from? Maybe they weren't thinking at all, but only daydreaming — feeling nothing but numbness.

He thought about his sister. The paths they'd both taken couldn't have been any more different, even though they came from the same womb and were raised by the same mother. His mind always drifted back to those early memories of sharing a room. The days of wrestling on the floor, eating candy they'd snuck out of the cupboard, and dancing with the curtains to the latest song on the pop charts. He missed the conversations they'd had in the dark, late at night between bunk beds. There were talks of spaceships, travel, and adventures into the unknown. What each one would do with their million dollars and how they'd save the world from itself. Then there were the revelations and shared secrets; the dark places created by their mother's boyfriends.

The day they remodeled the den and made it into another bedroom was bittersweet. On one hand, he now had the room to himself, but that lost camaraderie would never be the same. His nights were now filled with dreams of being lost at sea, searching for a passage back to the mainland. It was as if a part of his soul was missing and never to be found. That's how much he looked up to his older sister.

As the train rocked back and forth, dwindling away those precious souvenirs from his past, he found himself staring out the window in unison with the old men; how mesmerizing and peaceful it was.

An unexpected jolt sent him sliding across the seat and back to reality. He retrieved the DDO glasses from his jacket pocket to study. To the untrained eye, they seemed to be just like any other pair of cool hip frames. The thin contour around the lenses and stylish design was right out of a New York fashion show. Only around the temples did they differ, where it widened at the tip with bone induction earpieces. No doubt that's where the miniature quantum microprocessors and advanced chip technology resided that made them so dangerous.

He wondered how many people were actually able to use them. Rumors were that the body could only handle up to twenty-four hours of exposure before causing permanent brain damage. Even though that could never be substantiated officially, he felt nauseous and achy after only using them a few minutes. Congress passed a law to limit access and prevent any abuse until

Dill Electronics worked out the kinks. Only certain branches of law enforcement agencies could work on the development under stringent conditions, and even then they needed approval from the Senate Intelligence Committee. But as they liked to say around his office, if you keep someone in the dark, they'll never see the light.

The first limited edition of a dozen pairs of frames were never released to the public. Dill Electronics selected two law enforcement agencies to beta test them. Unfortunately, this mistake would haunt the company forever. The government seized control of the items soon afterwards and halted all manufacturing, using an obscure portion of the Patriot Act that was still on the books from the early 2000s. Within days, the Dill-DO 1000 had ceased to exist, at least on paper. All scientists working on the project were subsequently hired by the government, sworn to secrecy, and reassigned to different parts of the country.

He paired the glasses to his CompWatch, then placed them on his head. Slightly above a murmur, he commanded, "Engage."

The lenses lit up in split-screen-television fashion, flipping through channels at light speed. New data flashed by so fast that it left a taste of vomit in his mouth. Edgar clicked a button on the earpiece and held it down, slowing the movement until the images stopped. He rested his eyes for a moment and allowed them to readjust.

"Next stop, Ventura Boulevard in ten minutes," broadcast over the train's loudspeaker. "Transfers are available from there to Van Nuys or the Burbank Station." His sister lived nearby at their mom's house in Burbank. She'd been staying there ever since Leslie had moved into the Retirement Center. It wasn't ideal for the family, but better than renting to tenants.

The DDO glasses were still signed in under Toyer Wittler. Appearing in the corner of the lenses was his ID photo and the letters "BIG." underneath it. Edgar blinked rapidly while contemplating what BIG stood for. This caused the glasses to shift into gallery view, displaying an array of different screens. He recognized his face in one of them and dialed the thumbnail in closer.

His photo appeared with the words *"Level 3 Alert. Edgar Gorman was last seen at Cedars Sinai Plaza"* flashing on a banner. He scrolled down to read his profile:

"The suspect is wanted for questioning in relation to the disappearance of Diane Beatty in 2061. Subject is armed and has a history of psychopathic behavior possibly related to a brain aneurysm. Proceed with caution."

"What the hell," he whispered. He wondered just what Dr. Bevan had submitted in his report. Could his medical records have merged with his wife's? How could he be suspected of kidnapping or maybe even murdering a person he didn't even know?

As he directed the screen to zoom in on another file, it went black. "Engage," he commanded, but nothing came up. He blinked rapidly and only one screen with a blue box popped up. It read, "Sign In".

"You're not so dumb after all, Toyer," he hissed. With the glasses in hand, he mulled over his options. It was obvious that BIG had noticed activity in their database and deactivated the glasses. How to reactivate them without being noticed was the challenge. Signing in under his own name was a nonstarter. That would reveal his whereabouts and intentions, but was there another option.

"Go to Settings," he commanded while tapping the temple. A screen emerged on a lens allowing him to maneuver into GPS mode. He turned off the location function and powered down his CompWatch. Then an idea hit him. Since this was a prototype, it probably didn't have all the filters set correctly and maybe he could sign in under his wife's maiden name. Thirty seconds later, the DDO glasses flashed, "Welcome Evelyn."

Edgar pushed a button on the temple and commanded, "Take me to 1049 Sunnyvale Lane, Burbank." Images flickered across the lenses as wireless radio waves bounced off every open computer or phone nearby beaming signals to distant satellites and back. The lens adjusted focus on the house from overhead. The angle came in from a light pole on the corner of the street. "Zero in closer," he ordered. The camera view shifted to a lamppost in the front yard. Edgar saw the front of his mother's house clearly now. The garage door was wide open and a series of opened boxes lined the floor. Aluminum foil delicately stretched across the railing on the porch and up the columns on each side. There was also a strip of foil loitering in between each shrub leading up to the front door.

His sister, Lotty, marched down the driveway to a trashcan and tossed in a pile of papers. Then she went into the house for a moment, only to return with a pottery vase that she tossed into a box marked "Giveaway."

"What are you up to, big sister?" whispered Edgar.

Lotty wrapped newspaper around another item sitting on the garage floor and stood over a box marked "Attic." Even when alone, she talked to herself. Her short, spiked orangish-blonde hair stood rigid as her head wavered from side to side while she looked from one box to the other. Under her breath, she mumbled, "Giveaway, attic, giveaway, maybe attic." Without hesitation, she bent over and dropped the item into the "Attic" box.

After going back into the house, she returned a few seconds later, only to stop again. This time, she swayed in front of the boxes like a corn stalk blowing in the wind. While lifting the spectacles off her nose, she raised the glass-coated painting closer to her face. Her eyes ate up the designs and colors as she tried to understand their meaning. She flipped it over and examined her mother's signature and date. With a confident nod, she tossed it into the "Giveaway" box and reversed course back into the house.

Edgar ripped off the glasses and buried his nose into the palms of his hands. "Lotty, Lotty, Lotty," was all he could say.

With his eyes closed and lips puckered, he tried to slow down his breathing and think of what to do. Then he placed the glasses back on and zoomed in again. His sister was almost to the doorstep exiting the garage when he tapped the top of the frames and dialed her number.

"Hello."

"Lotty, it's Edgar."

"Oh, hey bro. What's up?"

Edgar continued watching Lotty through the DDO glasses as she stopped and stared at the ceiling. A sight he was very familiar with. "Oh, not much. What are you up to?"

"Cleaning house. It's long overdue."

"Yeah, like what?"

"Oh, you know, junk."

"Your junk or Mom's junk."

Lotty spun back around and studied the boxes. With her head slightly cocked, she replied. "Well, you know, I mean, of course, it's Mom's junk."

"How do you know what's junk and what's not?"

Her eyes ricocheted from one box to the next as her slim torso stood rigid. While mulling over a response, she pulled out a tissue from her pocket, blew her nose, and shook her head. "I need to go eat something."

Edgar exhaled with relief as he watched her stroll back into the house with the painting. "I see. Hey, I'm on my way over. I should be there in about a half hour or so. What's for lunch?"

Lotty grinned and stopped at the steps, "Your favorite, of course."

"Sounds wonderful. See ya soon."

Edgar smiled as Lotty hung up the call and entered the house. Then he touched the temple on the glasses again and asked, "Scan nearby." The images started moving from one house to the next as they passed by the train. He caught glimpses of people sitting in their living rooms, mowing lawns, cooking dinner, and making love in their bedrooms.

He paused the scanner and rewound it to the love-making spot. The visuals were grainy due to the low light but what he couldn't see soon came into focus as the glasses self-adjusted and advanced to "Jigsaw Mode." He marveled over how naïve people were to not think that they could be watched almost every moment of the day with the right technology. The farther away the train traveled, the grainier the images became.

He removed the glasses and spun them slowly in between his fingers. His vision went in and out of focus for a few seconds, followed by a short bout of light headedness. *Wow, these things are powerful*, he reflected. As everything gradually returned to normal, a thought occurred to him: *If I can zoom in on these people that easily, I'm sure BIG or whoever Toyer was working for could do the same.* While fumbling through the different modes using his earpiece, he cleared the present list of commands and cache history, disengaged the GPS locator, and powered the device off. Then he massaged the temple until the right shade of blue surfaced on the lenses and made them disappear into his jacket pocket.

CHAPTER SIX

COMING HOME

A HALF HOUR LATER, Edgar rang the doorbell to his mother's house. Several childhood memories reflected off the front porch window as he waited for someone to answer. There were scattered ruminations of long summer days filled with bike riding and hanging out with friends. Visions of his mother sitting on the porch swing with a different array of suitors passed by like boxes on a conveyor belt.

As the images faded through the glass panels, another episode entered his mind from more recent times. It was the last time Evelyn and he had visited the house. At first, he tried to ignore the flashback by focusing on the neighbor trimming her flower garden. Mrs. Darnell had been close to his mother. Even though they shared nothing in common as far as lifestyles, they bonded over the love of being outdoors. They'd take the neighbor dog for walks in the morning throughout the neighborhood. Twice a week they'd hike up into the canyons surrounding the Valley.

Mrs. Darnell was a Back-Ender who'd made it to retirement and was living comfortably. She also carried a Glock 19 under her blouse on her hip just in case. "Coyotes," she liked to say. "You can never be too careful."

"Not careful enough," Edgar's mother would rant as she recalled the story about the night Mrs. Darnell accidentally shot her son. "The old coot put a bullet into his leg thinking he was a burglar and then one into her big toe for good measure before she took her finger off the trigger." Leslie would wallow in the hypocrisy by adding, "I think she got 50 Demeanor Points for that one. Go figure."

Yet the flashbacks about his wife would not relent. Since her death, they happened frequently. The same way a random spam email pops up on a social feed, they seemed to never end no matter what he did. It was as if Evelyn was trying to console him from the grave and give him strength to carry on. Unfortunately, that wasn't how they left Edgar feeling. The memories filled jagged spaces in his heart while passing over the good times and leaving them in the shadows.

He recalled the last time Evelyn was at the house:

❧❧❧

It was a Sunday. Leslie, Edgar, and Evelyn were sitting at the kitchen table talking about her diagnosis. While Evelyn was crying with her head buried in her arms on the table, Edgar stroked her long hair and said, "Don't worry, there's got to be another way."

She shook her head and replied, "I don't see how."

Leslie rubbed her shoulder and said, "I can quitclaim the house over to Lotty and Edgar, then you can apply for a second mortgage. That would give you enough money to afford the surgery."

"Insurance isn't going to cover any of it since they don't consider it a medical necessity."

"I know," replied Edgar. "It'll eat up most of any loan amount we'd get. That means Lotty would have to go along with it too."

"She will," confirmed Leslie. "I'll make sure of that."

"You do know that you two aren't on best speaking terms, Mom. How does that work?"

"She'll want to make a deal with me. She's barely living from house to house and running out of friends who will tolerate her condition. I'll just guarantee that she can live here forever while I check into one of those retirement homes."

Edgar tilted his head and asked, "Why would you do that? You're still healthy."

"Maybe, but I can tell, my memory is fading fast. It won't be long before I burn the place to the ground or do something else stupid. I'm gonna need help soon. I can use up what's left of my SSI and live comfortably there for a few years."

Evelyn straightened up in the chair and cleared her nose. "I think it takes five years after quitclaiming before you can borrow on the house."

Leslie leaned back in the chair and winked, "Then I'll take the loan out myself."

Edgar looked to Evelyn and then to his mother. "It's worth a try."

༄·༄·༄

As the visions departed and the memory faded, Edgar was back standing on the porch. He wiped his dull eyes and sighed. Unfortunately, the bank denied the loan because of Leslie's health and Evelyn never had the surgery. In that moment, an aura of apprehension swarmed over him. The blood drained out of his head leaving him lightheaded, chasing contrasting black dots across the front yard. It was a sense of awareness, or, more exactly, full comprehension about his situation. His wife was never coming back and the chances of him ever being happy again were waning. He took a deep breath and ignored the inevitable.

Lotty did eventually move into the house and Leslie

willingly checked herself into the retirement home. When the front door of his mother's house opened, Lotty greeted him. "Hey Eddie, long time no see." She looked out onto the street and waved him in. Edgar had grown accustomed to his sister's dearth of human contact and even the random spurts of useless information. Usually, it was some sermon about the latest conspiracy theory or the true meaning of a classic rock song from the twentieth century. He'd learned to not let it distract from the conversation. With all of modern medicine's advancements, curing Asperger Syndrome was still as elusive as capturing a snowflake in your hand.

They hugged before entering the living room. Rusty nails and faded rectangles dotted the walls in the hallway where family photos once dwelled. The cold plaster had been stripped naked and seemed to be crying out for their mother's missing paintings.

The worn-out carpet greeted his every step with familiar odors of wet dog and whiskey from his childhood. Some smells brought back good memories, others not so good. He took in the scene with a cautious grin and asked, "Cleaning house, you say?"

Lotty nodded as she picked up a vase from the coffee table and shook it in front of him. "Yeah, this kind of junk." She added, "It's gotta go."

"Why? I mean, your mother made that, and she's still alive. Why's it so important to get rid of this stuff now?"

Lotty blinked hard as she searched for a reply. Her head wobbled when she tossed the vase on the couch and said, "My god, Edgar, she's not coming back to live here ever again. It's time I made it my house. How can I concentrate on my craft if I'm constantly reminded of her everywhere I turn? I mean, she hated my writing, she hated my singing, my playing, you name it."

"We all hated your singing."

"Hey now, that's not... well, really, was it that bad?"

"I've heard frogs that sounded better." Edgar smiled and

chuckled, "Just kidding, you have a wonderful voice. We just hated hearing it at four in the morning — on a school night."

Lotty's hands rose above her head, as if ready to conduct an orchestra, before replying, "I see, a joke. Always the funny guy."

"Hey, it kept me out of many fights over the years, especially with Mom's boyfriends."

"I'll hand you that. Of course, I had to step in and finish the job when you didn't."

Edgar smirked, "You didn't have to, you wanted to."

A concessional grin took shape as Lotty confessed, "That I did. That's what big sisters do."

Edgar wasn't sure how to respond. In a normal world, he should've been the one looking out for his sister but that just wasn't part of his DNA. Mother Nature had brewed a quirky set of traits and characteristics inside of him that seemed to bubble over when needed, with unpredictable results. It's what made him want to paint instead of watch football, it's what made him avoid violent situations, and it's what made him such a good FBI agent.

He pushed in closer and stood shoulder to shoulder next to Lotty. "Big sister?"

"Well, technically, not since you're taller and have a good two hundred pounds on me."

"Oh, now *you're* trying to be funny? It doesn't fit your...," Edgar waved his hand up and down her body before finishing, "your, what would you call this, outward disposition."

"It's a lifestyle. Besides, none of it really means anything in the scheme of things. I mean, relative to time, it's all just a blip on the radar screen."

"Speaking of radar, what's up with all the aluminum foil in the yard?"

"The more reflective objects you have around your house, the less the government can monitor your every move."

"Who told you that?" asked Edgar.

"I read it online." He watched her focus on the ceiling again. There was nothing but air surrounding her, but in his sister's mind, it was her comfort zone. Edgar decided to drop the subject altogether.

"Hey, where's lunch?"

"What?" Lotty froze for a second or two before registering what he'd said. "Oh yes, of course. Let's eat." Then she grabbed his hand and swung it back and forth like they were two kids on a schoolyard playground while escorting him into the kitchen. She opened the refrigerator door and pushed a button that rotated the shelf. Then she retrieved a plate and presented it with both hands as she humbly bowed, "Yours, my lord. A peanut butter and jelly sandwich, chilled to forty degrees and stripped of its crust."

Edgar clapped his hands and gestured, "Well done, my lady."

"Please sit. Milk or water?"

"Well, it has to be milk, of course."

"Of course." She opened the refrigerator and paused. "Uhh, yeah, we have no milk."

Edgar chuckled and replied, while peering over his sister's shoulder and noticing the empty shelves. "Water it is."

They both sat down and ate while trying not to let the peanut butter impede the conversation. In between gulps and bites, Edgar asked, "So, what in particular are you getting rid of?"

"Oh, you know, knick-knacks, old clothes, all the cheap artwork she used to buy at those garage sales, that kind of stuff. I need to make room for my stuff."

"Like what?"

"Water, canned goods, batteries, you know, stuff."

"What are you planning for, the apocalypse?"

"Shouldn't we all? The world is not a safe place. The government says we're safe, but I know better." Her eyes fluttered at a hummingbird's pace as she took another bite.

Edgar gave her a moment to recover. He'd seen this display

of erratic behavior before and knew it simply needed to run its course. "Well, I just visited Mom and she's not doing well. She couldn't remember a lot of things."

Lotty perked up. Her eyes widened as she said, "Oh no, that bad?"

"Yeah, I'm afraid so. You might want to go visit her sooner than later."

She nodded.

"Maybe we oughtta wait on tossing her stuff until she passes away."

Lotty lowered her head while evading direct eye contact. "Yeah, well, I don't know. I can't live around so much clutter."

"I remember your room. You're the queen of clutter."

"Yeah, but it's my clutter."

"But this is not your house."

"It will be soon. I mean, unless you want to move back here."

Edgar let this comment sink in. The thought of leaving his RV and moving back into his childhood home did have its merits: no rent, less hassles, more space. Yet, deep inside he knew reliving those memories was a pipe dream. People tend to remember only the good ones. Lotty had enough bad habits growing up. He couldn't imagine what it was like living with her now.

"No," said Edgar. "That's not gonna happen."

"I see." She felt the uneasiness in his voice but wasn't sure what to say next. Having long personal conversations and getting in touch with her inner feelings were not her forte. Those were her brother's qualities. After a moment, an idea came to her. "I know. Why don't you help me go through her stuff? That way, there'll be no hard feelings between us, and I won't have to worry about throwing out any of Mom's priceless treasures."

Edgar nodded and said, "Deal."

When lunch was finished, they both entered the living room and began divvying up their inheritance. After a few minutes of examining ashtrays, shot glasses, and porcelain cows, Edgar sighed and said, "You're right. She does have a lot of junk." He picked up a bag and said, "I mean, how many pairs of cheap sunglasses does a person need?" He pulled out a white set and added, "And in every color."

"Those were for my eighteenth birthday party, don't you remember? The 'No More Blues in My Pocket, Now Give Me My Money' theme we did."

"Oh yeah," he smiled, "that was fun. I still have the harmonica you gave out to everyone. Do the glasses still work?"

"I don't know. Turn it on and see if it'll play the radio."

Edgar fumbled with a switch on the oversized temple and frowned. "Nothing."

"What can I say. Just like everything else we buy these days."

Edgar noticed one of his mom's paintings lying on the couch and admired it. He held the 11 x 14-inch piece of unbreakable glass in his hand and angled it toward the overhead light. The colors burst out of the frame in all directions as the images mimicked layers of oil on a canvas. He tilted the frame upright with the edges straight, transforming shapes into figures and shades into vivid colors. "This, on the other hand, is not junk." While looking at Lotty, he said, "This *is* a part of our mother. Not some silly-ass trinket she'd collected over the years."

Lotty continued to avoid his gaze. "They don't even make those types of paintings anymore. It's all interactive holograms now."

"I know. That makes them even more valuable."

"Maybe," she mumbled.

"But you can't just throw them away."

"Well, what am I supposed to do with them?"

Edgar paused to study one of the paintings. "Boy, Mother does have an imagination."

"No kidding. I mean, look at this one. What are these things, aliens with six fingers? And the colors," she pointed and added,

"Look at the tits on this woman, and the lips, the hair. What is this?"

"It's your mother, that's what."

Lotty nodded, "You're right, but those are definitely not her tits."

"Well, I'm sure she wished they were."

His sister chuckled. "Boy, I miss you around here. Are you sure you don't want to move in?"

Edgar admired the subtle glow sweeping across her face and replied, "I want us to remain friends. That wouldn't happen if I moved back in."

She nodded, "You're right on that point."

"Tell you what, I'll take them off your hands. Box them up and I'll swing by and pick them up when I get a chance." He picked up another painting that was completely different from the others. It was a dinner scene where a group of children were sitting around a table laid out with a holiday feast. Colors with light shades of brown, yellow, and green totally contrasted his mother's vibrant portfolio. "What's this?"

"That one's definitely a giveaway," she said. "It's not even Mother's. I think it was one of her boyfriends'."

"Indeed, definitely not Mother's."

He turned the painting over and searched for a signature. There was nothing. "I kinda like this one. I think I'll take it back to my place now."

Lotty peered over his shoulder and said, "It does look like something you'd do."

"It does, doesn't it?"

She cleared her throat before saying, "You know, because you're a Back-Ender, the only career you could've taken as a painter would've been painting houses." She lowered her head and asked, "So why do you paint?"

Edgar fixed his eyes on the large picture window and replied,

"I don't know. On one hand it's torture, yet, on the other hand, it gives me solace. All my life I've just felt like I couldn't be a painter because it wasn't real. Do you know what I mean? Probably, not, since you are a musician and 'living the dream.' I don't know, something in the back of my mind, maybe it's inherited, you know, part of those old-fashioned blue-collar values in our DNA." He sighed and added, "Something just told me that it wasn't an option."

Lotty began to reach out her hand but then stopped abruptly before saying, "Well, you would've been a good one."

Her comment triggered a series of unchecked emotions inside him. The only person who'd ever made a similar comment before was his wife. In fact, she constantly encouraged him to pick up a brush. She was his biggest fan. He missed the unwavering idolization she exuded for no other reason than that it helped him carry on.

Before drifting further down that rabbit hole of reflection, he quickly changed the subject. "Hey, how you doing, money-wise, I mean? You still whole and everything?"

"Never better. I've been doing jingles for Dylan MacMillan. Not his main commercials or anything like that, but some of the online help videos, the hold music you hear when you call in, and he's been getting me some referrals too."

"I thought all the music was computer generated, like the voices answering your questions."

"Nope, it's all real. That is the music part. The answering service, I'm not so sure about."

"Well, I've seen those self-help videos and they're all bullshit. How he gets away with lying and deceiving people like that, I'll never know."

"Hey, if you can make money at it, then it's legal."

"How's that legal?"

"I don't know. It's just the rules. I didn't write them. I mean, go read it for yourself. It's all in there."

"Where?"

"In the Front-Loaders Bylaws."

"It doesn't say that in there."

"Well, something along those lines. I know I read it somewhere."

"Probably on Dylan MacMillan's website." Edgar paused long enough to gather his thoughts and asked, "What does it actually say in the bylaws? I'd like to know."

"You know, stuff about taxes, reproductive rights, energy rebates, healthcare options, all that stuff."

"Wow, I guess I should read yours just to see how different it is from mine. All mine talks about are different dental plans, maintaining a forty-hour work week, and how to budget your paycheck."

With a slanted smirk, Lotty replied, "It says more than that. I've read your bylaws and the healthcare benefits alone *almost* make it worth becoming a Rear-Ender."

"Back-Ender, dammit. What is it with you and Mom?"

"Please don't lump us in the same category. I still haven't forgiven her for letting Wild Bill throw me out of the house."

"Yeah, but she does regret it. She told me herself the last time I saw her."

"Really? Well, good. I wish she'd say it to my face."

"Maybe if you went to visit her, she would." Sensing the conversation was going downhill, he pivoted. "So, you actually get paid for creating music?"

"Very well, thank you. You'd be surprised"

"Well, ain't that the shits."

"And Dylan MacMillan is going to run for President soon, now that he's finally a billionaire and all, so I'll be working on his campaigns and creating music for that too."

Edgar didn't know whether to smile or frown. Adding Dylan MacMillan to the roles of Presidential candidates was troubling in itself, but on the other hand, his sister was thriving in that environment. He allowed a subtle grin to emerge and said, "I'm so proud of you. Mom would be too. You should go see her before it's too late."

"I will." Lotty chose her next words carefully. "So, Eddie, tell me. Do you ever regret not taking the million dollars up front?"

He studied his sister as he postured uncontrollably while considering how to reply. The similarities between their physiques were far apart. She was fair complected and skinny with the body of a palm tree. His body more resembled an elevator: tall and stout. Lotty had her mother's nose, but he had his father's eyes, from what he'd been told.

Edgar sat down on the couch and contemplated the question. After exhaling deeply, he admitted, "Of course, I do. If I'd known how tough it was going to be enduring this bullshit, I would've taken the million upfront and run."

"Don't beat yourself up. Thirty years of solid work in exchange for two million dollars and a lifetime guarantee of benefits is kick-ass. That's hard to turn down."

"You didn't hesitate."

"Well, look at me." She flexed her arm muscles before adding, "How far do you think I would've gotten in the FBI."

"You might have taken another job in government. Maybe at the DMV or the courthouse."

This time, they both laughed.

"Yeah, you're right," he added. "You made the right decision."

"So did you. You'll have your thirty years under your belt in no time and be living on easy street the rest of your life. And you're damn good at what you do."

Edgar unconsciously agreed. It was then that he realized the full significance of the choices they'd both made in life. His had been slowly splitting at the seams for years while his sister had stitched together a fairly prosperous career. "I'm glad it turned out well for you. Making a living as a musician is quite an accomplishment."

"A mediocre musician. I mean, half the stuff I create comes from pieces of melodies lifted from old public domain tunes. You can't keep reinventing the wheel when it comes to new music, but, hey, most people don't know the difference." She gently gasped and confessed, "But I am living the dream. My dream, and I get to sleep in whenever I want, stay up as late as I want, and do what I want. How many people do you know can say that?"

The words stung but didn't swell. Edgar knew she wasn't bragging or preaching, just telling it like it was. Nevertheless, he didn't want her to get too full of herself and replied, "Yeah, I guess so, definitely mediocre."

His sister chuckled and sniffed while covering her nose. She nodded before replying, "God, I miss talking with you."

Edgar placed a hand on his sister's cheek and enjoyed the tender moment before slapping her playfully while saying, "Me too. All right, I think we're done here. Just promise me that you'll never throw away anything that your mother made, okay?"

Lotty ran her finger over her chest and said, "Cross my heart."

"Good."

He turned on his CompWatch and reactivated the settings. A smile developed as a text popped up reading, "All clear."

"Well, I gotta go." Edgar began to order a driverless car, then hesitated. "Hey, is Mom's car still out back?"

"Yeah, but that thing hasn't been driven in ages. I doubt it'll even run."

"It's a Tesla. One of the last ones they made. It'll run."

They both agreed with a grin. He hugged her tightly while saying, "Love you. See ya soon."

"Me too."

Edgar grabbed the keys, walked over to the shed, and waved

goodbye. After opening the double doors and removing the tarp covering the car, he clicked the remote. It started on the first try. The car backed itself out of the shed into the alley and stopped. The driver's door opened and a bell dinged. As he sat into the bucket seat, a deep low digital voice asked, "Where to, Leslie?"

CHAPTER SEVEN

FBI HEADQUARTERS, WEST COAST

ISABEL MORENO STARED at the phone on her desk, tapped a button next to the receiver, and watched it retreat into the tabletop. Outside her office, a teenage boy in handcuffs was being escorted into the Interrogation Room. Two agents accompanied the teen in and soon came back out. One of them walked across the aisle to Izzy's door, opened it, and asked, "What next, boss?"

"Get him something to eat and let him watch TV. I have to take care of a few things first."

The man nodded and closed the door. Izzy ran her fingers over a picture frame on her desk and reflected, *Real wood. You don't see these around much anymore.* Smiling back at her was her husband and a younger version of herself from another place and time. There were no shades of gray in this photo, no wrinkled smiles, and not a care in the world on anyone's face. She rubbed the top of the frame and whispered, "Two more weeks."

She rose from the chair and headed down the hall to the Command Center. The room was dark except for a set of large screens on the far wall. A half dozen agents sat at separate desks staring into monitors. Izzy ambled over to the man sitting at the last desk and whispered, "Come take a walk with me."

The agent nodded and followed her out the door over to the elevators. "Let me buy you a coffee."

"Make it a mocha and you got a deal."

"Deal."

After visiting a kiosk outside the building in the courtyard, they sat down with their cups next to a fountain. The noise coming from the cascading water provided just enough cover to drown out any conversation that might be picked up by a nearby listening device. While looking over the area to make sure no one was watching, Izzy said, "I need you to do me a favor. It's about Edgar."

"Anything you want," the agent replied.

"Reinstate his clearance status to what it was yesterday and deactivate any alerts."

"Clearance status?" The agent hesitated before saying anything more and realized the less he knew, the better. "Will do." He nodded and walked away.

Izzy watched him enter the building and go through security. A few minutes later, the agent sent her a message reading, "Thanks for the coffee. You're welcome."

Izzy hit a button on her CompWatch and checked the roster of agents. A green bar lit up under Edgar's name reading "Active". He was back to normal. She sent him a text message and finished her coffee before returning to the office. An hour and a half later, a message alerted her on her watch. "About to enter the building."

She texted him back, "All good. I'll be in the Goldfish Bowl."

Downstairs, Edgar flashed his badge as he passed through the doors at FBI Headquarters. With the DDO glasses tucked away in his jacket pocket, he paused in front of the retina eye scanner. Then he rubbed his eyelids, brushed the lint off his shoulders, and looked straight ahead. The light remained red.

"Sorry, Agent Gorman, try the thumbprint."

Edgar wiggled his fingers and joked, "I hope there's a warranty on that contraption." He wondered about his boss's real intentions and whether he was walking into a trap. With one foot leaning toward the exit, he casually glanced over the guard's shoulder to see if anyone else was watching. The receptionist waved and smiled. *Kind of suspicious,* he surmised. Another guard winked at him as he passed by and headed out the front door. *Even more suspicious.* Smudges of faces hovered in the corridors down the hall. *Too far away to tell if they're watching, but too close for comfort.*

The guard laughed, "Yeah, it's been acting up lately."

Different options murmured like frightened children into his ears. If he ran, a guard would be waiting for him outside. That could be deadly. If he proceeded as if nothing was out of the ordinary, that could be even worse. He shrugged his shoulders and placed his thumb in the biometric fingerprint reader. A green light flashed overhead.

"You can go in now," ordered the guard.

As he walked away, he let out a silent sigh and thought to himself, *Thank God this place is still living in the dark ages.*

When the doors opened onto the twenty-first floor, he veered over to the kitchen and searched for a cup in the cupboard. After grabbing the largest one, he turned toward the coffee machine and noticed a Post-it glued to the front reading, "Out of Order."

"The fucking dark ages, I tell ya." Edgar growled and filled his cup with water.

As he made his way to the Goldfish Bowl, he removed the glasses from his pocket, cleared the dark tint, and placed them into position. In front of a mirror in the hallway, he stopped and reflected, *Wow, the nerds who designed these knew what they were doing.*

In the corner of the mirror, the words flashed, "Demeanor Score: 325. Down 100 points in the last 24 hours. Don't let depression affect your demeanor. Smile!"

Edgar shook his head and whispered, "How do they know that? Why do they care?" He removed the glasses and examined them. "Can they?"

Agent Moreno was daydreaming in the Goldfish Bowl as the suspect lay with his head down on the table. Her husband was in the process of remodeling their retirement home in Puerto Rico.

It had taken them years to move their money around and upgrade the home on the island. It was one of the many loopholes the government had left open after the Constitutional Convention following the Second Civil War.

Soon after Puerto Rico officially became a state, a series of hurricanes leveled the island. A liability protection clause inserted into the New Constitution allowed industries like insurance companies to deny claims based on the two-thirds principle. If claims amounted to more than two-thirds of the total value of properties in a disaster area, then the insurance companies were immune from paying damages.

As with all laws passed by Congress, the taxpayers eventually became responsible for those claims. Instead of rebuilding homes, the government decided it was cheaper to buy residents out. Thousands of dilapidated houses sat abandoned for years until Congress inserted a last minute clause in an amendment allowing government employees to purchase plots of land at the fair market value, but only if they built new structures up to today's standards.

When the Wupe Phenomenon, named after Professor Johann Wupe of the University of Illinois, entered their lives in the late 2040s, databases across the world were compromised. Massive solar flares disrupted most communications satellites orbiting the earth over a twelve-day period. Many cloud-based data systems were corrupted, causing personal digital information to be rearranged, deranged, inverted, and sometimes convoluted into total gibberish.

Consequently, the legal names of many citizens ended up scrambled like eggs within the databases of credit card companies, banks, the IRS, and even the Census Bureau. Names like John Smith turned into Tosh Jimson, Jane Doe became Dona Jeon — the list went on. Correcting them became such a costly and time-consuming endeavor that many victims just succumbed and kept the new names. It soon became a cultural badge of courage in many ways.

The scrambling effect didn't only happen with names, though. Legal documents, scripts, books, song titles, and anything else that could be uploaded to a cloud computing infrastructure all found themselves victims to this event. It took years to discover the errors and when side effects to the phenomenon started happening on a weekly basis, software virus programs had to be created to combat further changes.

As expected, not all the flaws in documents and laws were considered bad. Some benefited certain groups so they left them in place. One of those changes was contained in the Puerto Rico Land Purchase Agreement found in the New Constitution. The words "fair market value" had been changed to "airfare travel rate." In other words, each plot of land could be bought for the price of a plane ticket. Government employees snatched up real estate faster than you could click a button. By the time the rest of the world found out about the oversight, it was too late. Property deeds had already been processed, payments were made, and construction was well under way on most sites.

Every good government knows that the best way to dig out from one crisis is to create another. Within days, the embarrassing error was quietly swept under the rug and replaced in the news cycle with talk of a pending border closure with Canada. The mistake soon became forgotten by everyone, except, of course, government employees. As Izzy's retirement grew closer, conversations about windproof shutters, raising foundations, and basking in the sun filled the day like a clogged toilet.

The door opened and Edgar paused to take a drink. He knew the longer he took, the less intimidating he'd seem. Izzy had her feet propped up on the table. She opened the file on the notepad and slid it across. The boy was on the other side with his head still down, pretending to be asleep. They both knew better.

"Hi, I'm Agent Gorman. Sorry I'm late but I ran into an old friend and one thing led to another and, well, you know."

Izzy raised an eyebrow after hearing this last comment. "Old friend?"

"Yeah, Toyer Wittler from Accounting. You remember him, don't you?"

"Don't get me started."

"I thought so," he concurred.

As Edgar sat down, Izzy noticed him adjusting the glasses. A look of concern flashed across her face. Then she motioned to the boy and said, "This is Ketchum Tutaloo from Summerfield. He just turned eighteen a month ago."

Edgar lowered his head and shook it as he read the file. There wasn't much in it. The words "Financial Negligence" popped out. This made him clear his throat. He saw that the boy had a family and a sibling. That was a good sign.

An eerie silence filled the room with needles and pins as he finished reading. The Goldfish Bowl had been designed to be soundproof but, as an unwanted side effect, it made the interrogator's job even more difficult. A complete void of sound stirred up uneasiness and suspicion in most people. Edgar knew this so he stood up, walked over to the door, and propped it open.

"It's stuffy in here."

Ketchum's eyes opened as he lifted his head off the table. The sound of freedom coming from outside raised his interest. He rubbed both eyelids and took his first look at these aging FBI Agents. He wasn't impressed. He glanced from Izzy to Edgar and realized that they were either seasoned pros or desk-job flunkies. He wondered which would be better.

"You're Ketchum Tutaloo of 508 Vonnegut Lane in Summerfield, California?"

"Why'd they take my watch away? I wasn't doing anything bad."

"It's standard procedure, Mr. Tutaloo. Can you please answer my question?"

"Yes, I'm Ketchum," he replied as he rubbed his wrist.

"You live at home with your parents and sibling?"

"Yes."

"It says here that you recently graduated from Summerfield High and turned eighteen. One month later, you lost all your money and entered into Zero Sum Conclusion. Is that correct?"

Ketchum hung his head down for a moment, huffed, and nodded. Edgar asked as politely as he could, "Is that a yes?"

"Yes," he grumbled.

He glanced at his partner and sighed. Protocol required that he read him his rights and explain what was going to happen next, but this wasn't a protocol situation. That would happen soon enough when the Forest Dunes agents arrived. He only had a few precious minutes to understand what really happened to this boy, and then, barely hours to do anything about it.

Edgar paced along the table thinking of what to say. These types of cases weren't rare, but undoubtedly troubling. They were hardly ever resolved with a favorable outcome too. Izzy knew where his head was and added, "Ketchum, in a couple of hours, the Dunes agents will arrive, read you your rights, and ship you off to Ontario for processing. Then they'll send you off somewhere far away for a long time. Until then, you need to tell us everything that happened to you and how you got into this mess. You also need to be brutally honest. Can you do that, my friend?"

He gestured up and down.

"Good," interjected Edgar as he cleaned off the lenses. "Don't leave out any pertinent details but don't ramble on either. Our hands are kind of tied here once they show up."

Ketchum lifted his head and stared into Edgar's eyes. They were warm and inviting, giving him a glimmer of hope. His corneas reflected signs of sympathy, wetter than normal, almost tearing, and almost empathetic. He could tell that this case had hit a nerve with him. Maybe he'd seen it before, or maybe it was a little too close to home.

He began to speak. Edgar sat down, placed the Dill-DO glasses back on his head, activated the bone induction earpiece, closed his eyes, and said, "Engage." He wanted this to play out in his mind so he wouldn't forget any of the details. He wanted clarity and answers.

As Ketchum spoke, subtle details transformed into colorful visions across Edgar's eyelids. At first, it played like an old Kinetoscope. Disjointed choppy images flashed by one by one, trying to connect but not quite linking into coherent pictures. In the corner of the lens, a screen surfaced read, "Rub your finger over the edge to adjust." He made the adjustments, blinked a few times, and concentrated. He not only needed to see this, but also needed to be there too.

Gradually, the images leveled off onto one linear plane as the DDO device downloaded video feeds from hundreds of satellite sources and security cameras from around the world. He drifted into a semi-hypnotic state of consciousness, letting the ebb and flow of information move him from the present to the past, and then places somewhere in between.

Ketchum's voice narrated the dialogue but the device separated images, categorized them, and created a storyline from which to work with in real time. As he told his story, Edgar saw everything.

Ketchum's world became his own.

PART II

KETCHUM

CHAPTER EIGHT

SUMMERFIELD HIGH SCHOOL

IMAGES FILLED EDGAR'S HEAD as he listened to Ketchum tell his story. He found himself seeing most visuals from the young man's point of view, as if a camera had been imbedded into his brain. Had Dill Electronics figured out a way to access our deepest and darkest secrets? Some images blurred and shifted sporadically, but he soon learned to keep his focus on Ketchum's voice in order to see things clearly. The view shifted, depending on the narration, from the boy's viewpoint to camera angles in the corner of a room, to directly overhead, and then back, continually evolving.

Then he saw...

(TWO MONTHS EARLIER)

A gigantic Victorian wall clock stood mounted above the backboard in the basketball gymnasium. It read, "11:59." The last few students climbed the bleacher steps and scooted past annoying kneecaps and tennis shoes while finding seats. As the principal walked to a small table and chair sitting in the center of the freshly varnished floor, a wave of silence flowed through the crowd.

The last few whispers scattered when he picked up the microphone and raised his hand in the air. "All right, everyone take a seat and be quiet. This will be a short assembly, but a very important one. In fact, probably the most important one of your lives, so listen carefully. Those of you who have questions afterwards, and I'm sure there'll be many, can make an appointment with your guidance counselor to discuss any matters that concern you."

The principal sat down and signaled to a teacher standing next to an exit. As she dimmed the lights, a large screen on the far wall illuminated. On the display, the President of the United States stood on a podium draped with an American flag behind him. Patriotic music played in the background as he spoke:

"Thank you for gathering here today and I want to personally welcome our next generation of young Americans to what will, undoubtedly, be a pinnacle moment in each and every one of your lives. Three and a half decades ago, our country was in great peril. Foreign hackers were draining bank accounts at a record pace, poverty was at an all-time high, Medicare had deteriorated to the point of being nonexistent, government debt was over 500% of our Gross National Product, and our social security program, the safety net for most Americans as they entered their golden years, was insolvent. But America rose to the occasion, just as we have throughout our great history, and persevered. And as the chaos turned into hope, which then turned into solutions, a new anthem was born; one that resonates with this country's vision of what the American Dream means to every one of us."

The President turned around and pointed to a gigantic billboard behind him that read, "IT'S NOT ABOUT GREED, IT'S ABOUT GREATNESS." A low rumble of whispers resonated through the crowd.

"This slogan unleashed a dynamic force in this country that allowed the great American Dream, a concept envied around the world, based on the fundamental principle that all men are created equal, to finally be within reach of all Americans, and not just a few." Several students stood up and clapped as the audio sensors on the bottom of the flat screen digitally danced with each vibration. This caused the monitor to pause briefly. After a few seconds, the principal waved his arms for everyone to be quiet.

"A few short years after leaving NATO and the United Nations, our country was able to recalibrate the dollar to twentieth century levels and convert the economy to a virtual currency. This enabled us to properly eradicate poverty, eliminate welfare programs, and ensure that every American gets a head start. So today, we have come to this moment, with great excitement and anticipation, to talk about your future as young adults. Upon your eighteenth birthday, you will all become millionaires."

This time, the crowd stood up and went wild. Loud cheers echoed off the concrete walls and rattled the grill-covered windows. Students hugged each other and chanted "USA, USA, USA…" Again, the screen paused as the audio sensors turned different shades of green, yellow and finally red. The principal quieted the room once more. After he sat back down, the screen resumed.

"Each one of you will be given one million dollars from the Solid Start Initiative, or SSI as it's more commonly known, tax free. You can do whatever you want with that money: vacation around the world, buy a house, go to college, put it in the bank, the options are unlimited. It's yours.

"For centuries, most Americans have been forced to work their whole lives from the time they were sixteen to well into their golden years. If they were lucky, they made enough money to retire. Many who did were too frail and old to enjoy it. Many others never made it at all, but not anymore. The Solid Start Initiative allows every American to enjoy life while they are youthful and healthy, and maybe, just maybe, if you're ingenious enough and make the right decisions, you will never have to work your whole life."

This time, the whole gymnasium erupted into a roar. Students stood up, clapped, threw their hats in the air, and hugged each other, all except for one girl and Ketchum. They both leaned back on the bench and tried to disappear behind rows of blue jeans and skirts surrounding them. As the seconds passed, they both searched through the crowd looking for anyone else who was still sitting down.

As she turned from right to left, and he turned left to right, their eyes met for the first time. It was brief, but remarkable all the same. Both felt a connection on some level stretching the distance of that innocent stare. It was a glimmer of familiarity, maybe from a previous passing in the hallway, somewhere out on the street or maybe from a lucid dream. Either way, it was as if they both knew something that no one else knew, even though neither one had a clue as to what that nugget of knowledge might be.

Ketchum noticed her V-neck black sleeveless t-shirt and short blonde hair. Draped on her chest was a silver necklace, which was barely visible in the dim lighting. He couldn't make out the design but sensed it had special meaning to her. April gazed over and was immediately drawn to Ketchum's hazel eyes. The color was hard to make out from that distance but even in the low light they glowed around the edges in a fiery halo.

The surprise encounter made them both feel uneasy. April squirmed from side to side as Ketchum leaned forward and straightened up. They both became acutely aware of the awkwardness surrounding them. No one else was sitting. The dark lensed video cameras in each corner of the gym scanned the crowd one increment at a time. They were terribly aware of those. Without drawing attention, they both rose to their feet and stood up next to their peers. Again, the principal quieted the crowd and sat them back down while the President resumed his speech.

"But choose wisely, my fellow Americans, because, as you know by now, once that money runs out, you will have to go to work for the rest of your lives." As the President delivered this line, the crowd fell silent. Then he chuckled and continued, "I'm sorry, that sounds a lot worse than it really is. This is not a bad thing or a death sentence. It plainly means that you'll have to choose a career in one of our pre-approved specialties, enter a social service field of study, or become an Indentured Apprentice.

"For many of you, that would've been your only option anyway before Solid Start came along. Depending on your age, you'll be given an opportunity to choose from a variety of careers in order to support yourself just like Americans have been doing for centuries. And as you get older, you'll be able to move into less strenuous occupations that will allow you to work well into your golden years.

"There's also an alternative plan for those of you who wish to enter law enforcement, social services or the military. Our 'Thirty Years and Out' program allows individuals to serve their country in the most patriotic way, then retire with two million dollars instead of one, and enjoy a lifetime of full benefits. All of this will be explained in more detail later."

The President brushed his hand through his thin gray sideburns and added, "This is the trade-off we all must endure in order to prosper as a nation. Without it, we fail. Therefore, you must treat this as the opportunity of a lifetime, a chance to obtain the American dream like millions of others before you. A chance for greatness."

The teachers who'd been standing off to the side moved over to the aisles and began climbing up the steps of the bleachers. They paused at each step, counting heads and handing out stacks of pamphlets while asking the students to pass them down the row. The President paused for a few seconds before resuming, "Read your Millionaires Guidebook inside and out until you understand everything in it. There will be a test. You will be asked questions and must sign documents that will be binding by the laws of this country. Make sure you understand your options."

The President folded his hands together as if contemplating the last few words, "You've all learned the history of this great nation. You've all read about the consequences we faced because of the inactions by our forefathers. You all now understand the remedy that saved this nation from collapse and must do your civic duty, for God, and Country, and for the well-being of generations to come. I wish you luck. Thank you."

As the giant flat screen darkened, people rose to their feet and filed down the aisles and across the gym floor. The lights came back on and teachers continued handing out guidebooks to anyone missing a copy. Unlike the flyers distributed on the streets at night that randomly made their way into people's hands, no one dared throw these away.

Ketchum veered left from the moving herd shuffling out of the room. Standing on his tiptoes, he searched through the crowd for the girl but found nothing. She was nowhere to be found. As the last few students sauntered out of the gymnasium, he sighed and thought, *Another day.*

Next, he moved down the hallway and headed toward the counselor's office. When he arrived, a long line of students had already gathered, zigzagging around desks and across the floor. On the wall was an electronic whiteboard with a single word written in bold: "Appointments." He thumbed through the time slots for the next day, picked one, and wrote in his name.

"Got any ideas on what you're going to do with the money?" Behind him, Tusnig Dolan scratched the back of his neck as he reached with his other hand for the whiteboard.

"Not really. If I did, I guess I wouldn't be here."

"I guess not."

"Either way, it's a lot to comprehend. I mean, all at once, you know."

Tusnig agreed. "I think I may take the college deferment so I can get a discount on tuition, you know, wait until I'm twenty-one to take the money."

"That's an option," replied Ketchum. "Just make sure you finish or else you'll have to pay it all back."

"Well, that's the whole point, isn't it?"

Ketchum looked into his eyes and added, "I guess so. My luck, I'd flunk out or get a degree in something that's not on their list. Not to mention, having SSI track my every movement afterwards."

Tusnig shrugged and replied, "Hey, they track your moves anyway. What's the difference?"

Ketchum couldn't argue with those words. He studied his best friend's face hard for a moment. Beneath the thick angled eyebrows, dark skin, and brown eyes stood a kid who was worried to death. Tusnig was the starless night in a room filled with sunshine. His conspiracy theories drove others crazy, and the way he unconsciously rubbed the back of his neck could only be explained by the fact that he was always looking over his shoulder. Ketchum replied, "That's true."

Tusnig pivoted and asked, "Hey, did you get your SAT scores?"

Ketchum hung his head and swiped his shoe across the floor. "Yeah, what was yours?"

"1590."

His shoe stopped in mid-stroke as Ketchum almost fell over. Tusnig turned away and held his breath while waiting for a reply.

"Dude, that's like 99.9%. You can't get much higher."

"Ahhh, don't rub it in."

Ketchum put both his hands on his friend's shoulders and said, "Don't you ever be embarrassed about being smart. With those scores, you could do anything you want."

"I know, but I don't have a clue about what I want."

"What about being a doctor?"

"That's my dad's dream. In fact, it's almost every Pakistani's dream, but not mine."

Ketchum grinned and replied, "Still, it's a pretty good dream."

"You're right." Tusnig added, "But my Polygenic Scores were horrible. Said I was destined to be chubby and insecure."

"It's just a probability, T.D. They always get things like grit and desire wrong. Look at Dylan MacMillan."

"Still, it says a lot. It also said that I have a 50/50 chance of dying before I turn sixty."

Ketchum smiled and winked. "Those are pretty good odds in Vegas, my friend."

"Yeah, I guess. Hey, what was your score?"

Ketchum glanced down at his Millionaire's Guidebook and replied, "Let's just say, it's not as bad as you think, but not good enough — but my sperm count was higher than normal."

"I thought zero was normal these days."

"I guess so," contemplated Ketchum. "Still, that's one thing I got going for me."

"If you say so. I hear you can masturbate in public with any kind of numbers these days and get away with it."

"Ha, ha, ha. You're so funny."

Both boys walked back to the lockers and grabbed their books. After leaving the building, they veered down the hill and headed toward Highway 1. When they came to the row of trees separating the school grounds from the old highway, Tusnig said, "Hell, Front-Loaders have to wait three more years to get their driver's license as it is. Why not wait on the money? What a suck-ass law, you know, not being able to drive. I'm tired of fucking walking."

Ketchum poked at his friend's stomach with his hand and replied, "Yeah, but it's the only thing keeping that belly from falling out of your t-shirt."

Somewhere from above, a loudspeaker crackled and declared, "Watch your language, Mr. Dolan. That will be 10 points off your Demeanor Score." Mounted about twelve feet up in a wilting beech tree hung a security camera lens and speaker.

He recognized the principal's voice. "Really, Mr. Belmont, 10 points?"

"Yes, 10 points. Consider yourself lucky," replied the box.

As they hurried away, Ketchum groaned, "That camera's not even on school property. How can they do that?"

His friend shrugged and replied, "They're all connected to the same grid."

"What a suck-ass law indeed. Everyone used to be able to get your driver's license at sixteen. Now you get a stupid Demeanor Score instead. Let's get over to the old highway. At least they don't have cameras there."

By the time they'd made it down the hill to the coastline, the winds had picked up and the temperature dropped a good ten degrees. As they followed the path along old Highway 1, the waves crashed onto the pavement.

"High tide," complained Tusnig as he dodged a steady stream of saltwater meandering through the cracks in the chewed up blacktop. "These waves are getting more dangerous each day."

"I don't know," said Ketchum. "I think they're doing just what any living soul would do. You know, breathe in and out all night and day, grow larger, expand their horizons. Just like us."

"I think they're more like the Grim Reaper, constantly tugging and pulling at you, trying to pull you under."

Ketchum smiled at his friend and stared out into the sea. The crumbling highway that once handled hundreds of thousands of cars per day now sat helplessly, cowering to a relentless ocean as it pursued new real estate. At the last remaining jetty in the cove sat what was left of the abandoned Galley Museum. Now surrounded by water, it leaned in and rocked like a shipwrecked vessel. The rest of the bay had been taken back by the sea years ago. Tops of street signs and light poles reminded viewers where sidewalks once roamed and people gathered. Only the museum parking lot, which sat on higher ground in the next cove, provided a glimpse into the history of what used to be.

This had become an everyday ritual with them: measuring the water level and checking if any chunks of concrete had tumbled into the ocean. Nested on the second-floor balcony a mere three to four feet above sea level, a single seagull sat guard.

"We need to swim out there and check on your drone," said Tusnig as he tested another slab of concrete for sturdiness.

"Dude, I'm sure it's toast by now. If the salt hasn't eaten it away, then one of those birds has probably ripped it apart."

Tusnig squinted and covered his eyes as he gazed into the horizon. "Maybe, but we still need to see the place one more time, before, you know."

"I know. Let's wait until the water warms up a little."

"Warms up?" Tusnig tapped on his CompWatch and added, "It's almost ninety degrees right now."

"I like ninety-five."

"How about a boat? We just need to get out there." Tusnig refocused on the tiny flashing Demeanor Score snuggled in the corner of his watch face and added, "Just like I need to get those 10 points back from Mr. Belmont."

"What are you talking about?" asked Ketchum.

His friend punched a few buttons on his CompWatch and brought up a hologram as Ketchum stared in disbelief. A few seconds later he exclaimed, "There, done."

"What's been done?"

"Instead of deducting 10 points, I had them add 10 points onto my score." He angled his watch so Ketchum could see the screen.

"No shit, you can do that?"

"All day long."

"Amazing. Why bother with college, T.D., when you can do that kind of stuff. What else can you do?"

Tusnig blushed and lowered his head. "I don't know. Don't say anything. I could get into big trouble, you know."

"Damn straight, people go to prison for less," replied Ketchum. "Still, you need to convince your parents that you can make more money doing that instead of going to med school. How hard-nosed are they?"

"Very. My dad's already written to his alma mater about me."

"That sucks. Maybe you could do something to convince them otherwise, you know, make them a lot of money somehow online."

Tusnig kept his head down and replied, "It's not about money to them. It's about tradition and prestige."

Ketchum grinned and said, "I hear ya, but it's still cool as hell."

"Hey, let's cut through the old park."

Ketchum nodded and they followed a path another half mile before coming to a wooden sign mounted on two poles sitting on top of a circular parkway in the middle of the road. The sign was covered in ivy. Ketchum peeled back a layer of vines and read, "Summerfield National Park. Established in 2037."

"And decommissioned in 2057," added Tusnig.

"I can't believe it only lasted twenty years."

"Yep, this one and a hundred others across the country." They continued walking up the road as Tusnig elaborated, "These parks used to be run by MAGMA."

"No way. How come I never knew that?"

"They don't teach it in school. You won't find anything about it except in real books, and just the old ones."

"But why'd it close?"

"Well, from what I've read and what my dad tells me, the government turned over management to MAGMA in an effort to reduce the deficit and promote social awareness or something like that. One of the key points of the deal was that they would open a hundred new mini parks across the country and maintain the old ones."

"You mean like Yosemite Ski Resort?"

"Exactly. That used to be a national park with no ski lodge or indoor mall."

"That's hard to imagine."

"Well, there were a lot of them back in the twentieth century. Anyway, the agreement had a loophole in it where MAGMA could quit maintaining any park it saw fit after twenty years. That's when they shut this one down."

"How sad. It'd be cool to have a park so close by."

"It was all part of the agreement between the government and them, you know. That's how they were able to shut down the Internet. They said it was to prevent foreign hackers from infiltrating bank accounts, but I know better."

Ketchum rolled his eyes and replied, "You and your damn conspiracy theories."

"No lie. My dad has an old book at home that tells everything. It's an actual hardback cover, that's how old it is."

Ketchum started climbing the hillside. "I've heard enough for one day."

"Come over this weekend and I'll show you."

"Who was it written by, Chicken Little?"

His friend shook his head as they climbed over the hill and down into the canyon. It was strenuous but it saved them a good fifteen minutes. As they exited an orange grove, the small town of Summerfield came into view. Rows of colorful rocks filled front yards down the street as a variety of succulents lay scattered about the landscape. Shade coming from a string of King Palm trees threaded the space between sidewalks as jacarandas and other trees dotted the lawns. The long walk from the dead-end road to Vonnegut Lane was downhill and easy.

When they arrived at the intersection, Ketchum patted Tusnig on the back and said, "See ya tomorrow."

HOME SWEET HOME

THE TELEVISION IN THE LIVING ROOM blasted out a familiar commercial. *"My name is Dylan MacMillan. Some of you know me as "Dylan the Billionaire." I took a million dollars at the age of eighteen and turned it into a financial empire by the time I was twenty-one. How? Well, it wasn't easy. If you order my audiobook today, I'll teach you the skills needed in order to turn your million into billions."*

Ketchum's mother turned down the volume and shouted throughout the house, "Dinner's ready." Then she peeked into the study and smiled. On the wall, an interactive map of the United States stretched from one end to the other. Her husband was plotting destinations to visit across the country with digital push pins from California to New York. "Jonathan, dinner."

He spun around on his heels and replied, "Of course."

From the kitchen entranceway, Margaret hollered up the stairs, "Come on, kids, dinner's getting cold."

At the dinner table, Ketchum's mother read his Millionaires Guidebook in between bites. When she'd finished the back page, she laid it down on the table and said, "Things have changed a bit since I was in school. They didn't call it a Guidebook back then. It was just a brochure. I wish I still had mine to compare it with."

"Where is it?" asked Ketchum.

"They made us turn them in," replied his father. "We were the lucky ones, though."

"What do you mean?" asked his daughter, Shursta.

"Well, when they first issued million dollar checks, and they were actual checks back then, there were very few rules as to what you could do with them. You could deposit them wherever you wanted to, give them to anybody, even stash them under your mattress. It was easy to make money because all you had to do was invest it in the stock market and watch it grow."

His head swayed back and forth a few times before continuing, "Then, after a few years, everybody was in the stock market so, of course, it tanked. Suddenly, people had to find other investment strategies and some put their money in places that weren't so lucrative. That opened the floodgate to all kinds of problems, as con men and shysters offered up every type of get-rich-quick scheme you could imagine."

Ketchum winced and glanced at Shursta before asking his father, "So, what happened?"

"It took them a few years, but finally they got it back under control and things quieted down. Once they started monitoring web platforms and social media feeds, it became harder to get ripped off. It also became harder to get richer." He nodded to his wife while arching his back. Then with a swaggering smile, he added, "For us, though, we got in at the right time."

"Amen," replied Margaret. "Son, since your dad left his job at Dill Electronics, we've traveled the country dozens of times. We've even joined the Traveler's Century Club. This millionaire idea was the best thing that ever happened to us, and this nation."

"Yes, all you have to do is turn on the TV or look online to see how well people are doing. It's a great time to be alive," added Jonathan.

Ketchum wasn't sure what to make of these last few comments. He'd never asked his father or mother about money in the past. They'd just always had it when he needed it. Now that he was close to turning eighteen and about to inherit his own million dollars, his eyes were opening to the realities and possibilities surrounding him.

"So, what's that mean for me?"

His father inhaled before replying, "Well, I'm not quite sure what the process is now. According to this manual, you'll still get the money on or around your birthday and it will be deposited safely into an account. I don't know exactly how it goes from there. We'll see."

"We'll see?"

"We'll see."

Margaret realized that all this new information was a bit too much to comprehend at once, but knew her son needed to hear it. "The program has gone through many versions over the years. In the beginning, they did some housecleaning, you know, to get rid of any riffraff. Parole violators were sent back to jail, anyone with tickets was forced to pay them off, all kinds of crackdowns. They did a similar sweep about ten years ago and checked everyone's credentials to make sure people weren't cheating the system. It's just how it operates, son, they're still tweaking it to make it better."

"Is that what happened to our neighbors across the street?" asked Ketchum.

"Yeah, I think so." Margaret scratched the top of her head and wondered aloud, "What were their names? Martinez, I think... Jose and Anna."

"Carlos and Carmen were the kids." Shursta reached for her glass and asked, "Do you know where they went, Mom?"

"I don't know, but I have my suspicions. I think the parents were undocumented or something like that. Who knows where they ended up? I do remember an aunt from Arizona coming in and staying with the kids for a few days. Before you knew it, there was a foreclosure sign in the front yard and the kids were gone."

The silence that followed was only interrupted by the occasional scrape of a plate with silverware as they digested this revelation. There wasn't much else to say about the subject as none of the details were ever known to the public. Finally, Ketchum broke the ice and asked, "Do we have any avocado?"

"No, the store was out of them. Maybe next year."

Ketchum shrugged his shoulders and took another bite. Then he said, "I remember Carlos. Even though he was a couple of years older, he always let me hang out with him and his friends."

"You mean gang," chided Margaret.

"They weren't a gang."

"Well, they wanted to be."

Outside, sirens wailed in the distance and rapidly grew louder. By the sound of the squealing tires, they knew they were barely a few blocks away. Jonathan glanced up at his wife as she lifted his plate off the table. Their eyes met for a second before turning away.

The sirens made Shursta nervous so she asked, "May I be excused?"

"Of course. Finish your homework."

She rose from her seat and groaned. Before leaving, Jonathan waved her over, gave her a gentle hug, and whispered, "Love you, darling."

This brought a smile to her face as she ran upstairs. Ketchum had moved to the kitchen and was loading the dishwasher when Jonathan entered and asked, "Wanna take a walk?"

"Yeah, sure. Let me grab my coat."

They both stopped at the end of the driveway and zipped up their jackets. The winds had picked up that evening, sending an array of dead palm tree fronds swirling down onto the street. The giant leaves brushed against each other and crumpled like discarded newspapers. Across the street, a wooden swing surrendered control to a relentless breeze as it creaked and moaned.

"Which way?" asked Ketchum.

Jonathan lit an electronic cigarette and replied, "Let's head north toward the sirens."

In the distance, red lights blinked and faintly reflected off several picture windows. The sirens had ceased but they knew the incident wasn't over yet. It didn't take them but a little more than five minutes to arrive at the scene. A Summerfield police car was positioned on each side of the street, about four houses apart. In the middle was a red and white van with no markings except for large black letters on the side reading "Forest Dunes." Every light was on in the house.

"There's Max," said Jonathan. "Let's cross." Standing next to a police car was Max Calloway, an old co-worker of his from Dill Electronics. As they crossed the street and headed toward the car, the policeman motioned Max to move onto the sidewalk. Then the cop did the same to the other neighbors who'd come out of their houses to find out what all the commotion was about.

Max waddled in the direction of Ketchum and his father and reached out his hand. "Jonathan Mattock, it's been a long time."

"Yes, I'd say. How's everything?"

"Pretty much nullity naught, you know." He paused long enough to brush back his thick head of hair before saying, "I finally got that promotion."

"Oh, wow. That's nice."

"Yeah, I'm no longer on the floor. Heading up security now and stuck in an office behind a desk."

"Well, that's probably better than being on your feet, I'd suspect."

"Sure, but it doesn't do much for the rest of my body." He rubbed his stomach and laughed. Then he turned to Ketchum and added, "My, how you've grown, son. The baby shower we threw at work seems like just yesterday." Ketchum blushed as his bangs blew across his face. He brushed them to the side and turned his back against the wind.

"Yes, time flies," replied Jonathan.

Max massaged his chin and asked, "How's Margaret?"

"Still the same."

He nodded ever so slightly and added, "You still enjoying the money?"

"Oh yeah, we got into the program just at the right time. In fact, we're going on a trip to Yosemite here soon. I can't wait. How much longer for you?"

"I still have a long way to go. Five years, I guess."

"It'll be here before you know it."

Max nodded and mused, "Let's just hope that I'll be here too."

As an uneasy awkwardness teetered between them, the front door of the house opened wide and a female Dunes officer exited. Her department-issued blue and silver jacket was barely visible in the shadows of the porch — a phenomenon the two men were well aware of from their time on the floor at Dill Electronics. As the agent strolled into the light near the steps, her body vanished from sight. All they could make out were her face and hands. Max turned to Jonathan with raised eyebrows and said, "Still amazes me every time I see one."

"Me too."

The officer paced the porch with one hand holding a small black device and the other straddling her holster. "So, what's going on?" asked Jonathan.

Max searched the area to see if anyone was nearby and then moved in between Ketchum and his father before speaking. "The police got a call that the family who used to live there was back in the area. A neighbor saw a light on that shouldn't have been."

"Lived there? There are cars in the driveway and the yard is mowed. It looks like someone *is* living there."

"There is, but they're on vacation. This is the family that was there before them and had been sent off to Dunes."

Max and Jonathan locked eyes. He almost hated to ask. "A young couple?"

"No, they were in their late forties. Spies or something, I

heard. They were convicted of espionage, probably for NATO or the European Union, something like that. I never did get the whole story."

"Wow, how'd they escape?"

He lit a half-smoked cigar and puffed a few times before answering. "The cop wouldn't give me any details." Then he tossed the cigar to the ground and smashed it with his shoe. "Does anybody know these days?"

"And could you believe them even if they told you," replied Jonathan.

Max leaned back as a wrinkle surfaced on his forehead. "Exactly."

Just then, the side gate of the house swung open and a man took off running down the driveway. Close behind him was a woman. When they reached the sidewalk, she headed north and he went south. The Summerfield cop standing next to the crowd swung around in pursuit. Up the street, the other policeman tackled the woman as she tried to escape. Electric bolts of light shot into her body from his Taser gun.

The other cop didn't have the same luck. The man attacked him before he had a chance to reach for his gun and planted a knee into his stomach. Then he removed the pistol from the cop's holster and peered down the street. He jumped off the body and backed away a few steps. "Don't move," he shouted. The officer on the ground raised his hands in the air as the fugitive meticulously scurried away while scanning the perimeter for any movement from the spectators.

Max, Ketchum and Jonathan ducked behind a car but it wasn't fast enough. The man swung the gun around in their direction and yelled, "Don't move."

Max raised his hands and shouted, "Don't shoot."

The man motioned to Jonathan with the gun and demanded, "Give me the keys to your car."

"I don't have one," Jonathan yelled. A gunshot rocketed into the air. A woman congregating with the neighbors a few houses down screamed. Ketchum noticed a tattoo of symbols on the man's right forearm.

So did Max. He stepped up and tossed his keys into the street. "Okay, okay, here's mine. The black four-door."

The man retrieved them and clicked the fob. The side marker lights on Max's Cadillac blinked. He ran over to the driver's side and clicked the fob again. Right as he opened the door, a shot rang out. It landed slightly below his shoulder. The man jumped into the car, leaned into the steering wheel, and paused. With his bloody hand shaking, he reached for the button and started it. A subtle constant ding echoed down the block as he tried to pull the door shut. Before the interior light dimmed, a half dozen bullets riddled the windshield, shattering the glass. They pushed and pulled the man's torso deeper into the seat like a sewing machine needle dancing on a piece of cloth.

Across the street, two of the neighbors stood firm with their pistols drawn and holsters dangling from their chests. The agent yelled, "Stand down."

The Dunes agent closed in on the car with her gun drawn as the Summerfield cop maneuvered over to the passenger side. Splotches of blood covered the back window and reflected off the streetlight. The man's head now lay motionless on the headrest. When the agent shined her flashlight into the driver's seat, Max lowered his head and whispered, "Shit."

Jonathan patted his shoulder and said, "Don't you have insurance?"

"Yeah, but it's not my car. Belongs to the company." He stared at the two neighbors who were now holstering their firearms and patting each other on the back. Then he sighed and shook his head. "Damn vigilantes. They'll probably gain 100 points for that while I'll spend all day explaining what the hell happened to Corporate."

Jonathan gazed over at the crowd gathering in the street and added, "In the old days, that would've been streamed live on Facebook."

"What's Facebook?" asked Ketchum.

Jonathan and Max shared a moment and then shook their heads. "It's part of MAGMA now." His dad rubbed his eyelids and declared, "And the worst thing mankind ever invented."

Two other Dunes agents ran out from inside the house toward the car. One was talking into a radio on his helmet while the other shined a light down the street.

"What's the situation?"

"Everything's contained," replied the female agent as she pried the gun out of the dead man's hand. She pointed a black device at the corpse and clicked a button. A tiny red light illuminated. She turned to the other agents and nodded, "He's dead." As she backed away from the car, her short bright blue haircut almost glowed under the streetlight.

"I think it's time to leave," whispered Jonathan as he rubbed his boy's back.

Max understood and said, "Sorry you had to see this, son. Take care, my friend."

Jonathan and Ketchum inconspicuously slipped into the shadows between the streetlamps and walked away. As the Dunes officer ended her radio call, she glanced up the street and took notice of the silhouettes.

CHAPTER TEN

LATER THAT EVENING

WHEN KETCHUM AND HIS FATHER crossed the street and were within sight of their house, he asked, "Dad, what was that all about?"

"I'm not sure, son. So much has changed over the last few years. Forest Dunes is everywhere now, and I think they've taken over the whole prison system." He paused and gazed back toward the red lights in the distance. The wind had died down to a random gust here and there, but only after rearranging the landscapes of several neighboring yards with broken limbs and overturned planters.

"Could that happen to us?"

"What do you mean?"

"I mean, with the guns and all."

He hesitated to answer, but his son was almost eighteen now. At this point, there was no reason to protect him from the truth. Not telling him would do more harm than good. "Anything can happen these days."

"They actually shot him, though. How's that possible?"

"He had a gun and fired it. That's reason enough according to the law."

"Yeah, but..."

Jonathan firmly grasped his son's shoulders and said, "There are some 'rules of the road' you need to learn about how things are done these days: First, once you've become a resident of Dunes, they own you and can do whatever they want. Second, you have certain inalienable rights according to our Constitution, but only up to a certain point. It depends on whether you're a Back-Ender or Front-Loader. You need to know what they are. And finally, don't ever piss off someone carrying a gun. They'll figure out a way to justify killing you and getting away with it in the end."

Ketchum nodded and asked, "What was that tattoo on the man's arm?"

Jonathan scratched his head and replied, "I think they're Zero Sum markings. From what I've heard, they tattoo some of the people who go to Dunes for rehabilitation these days."

"Really? How's that work?"

"I don't know, and I don't want to know. Let's go inside."

They both entered the house to find Margaret fast asleep in the recliner. Jonathan grabbed the remote and muted the volume, then searched for any information about the shooting on the news. After flipping through the channels, he moaned, "Nothing. It figures." As he sat down on the couch, his gaze turned to his son. "Do you have homework?"

Ketchum nodded and sprinted upstairs to study. Jonathan spent the next half hour watching an old rerun from the Thirties. At ten o'clock, the doorbell rang. He studied his CompWatch which automatically connected to the camera at the front door. The noise woke Margaret and she gave her husband a concerned look. He patted her legs and headed for the door. "It's probably nothing."

At the door stood the three Dunes agents from earlier that evening. He recognized them immediately. Instead of inviting them in, he moved onto the threshold and let the door swing back against his shoulders. "What can I do for you, officers?"

The agent with the blue crew cut moved her eyes up and down Jonathan's body and confirmed to the other two. She stepped forward and asked, "Sorry to bother you, sir. I'm Agent Miranda

Conway and we're from Forest Dunes Agency. We wanted to know if you were present at the altercation on Julian Street earlier this evening."

Jonathan gazed at the agent and answered, "Yes. Why do you ask?"

The woman replied, "Just a routine inquiry. We questioned all the people who witnessed the scene and noticed you'd left right after the shooting."

"Well, it is a school night and I didn't want my son out too late."

"Is your son here?"

"Of course, but any questions you have, I can answer."

"Of course." The woman glanced at her partners and continued, "Were you friends with the deceased?"

Jonathan cocked his head back, a bit astonished by the question and a bit nervous about his answer. "I don't know. What was his name?"

The agent pressed a button on her CompWatch and presented the hologram of a mug shot. She reached out with her fingers and spun the photo in Jonathan's direction. "His name was Dormy Macruran. Maybe you knew him before the Wupe Phenomenon. His birth name was Ronald McMurray."

"No, he doesn't look familiar."

"How about his wife?" the agent swiped her finger and an image of a woman with dirty blonde hair and gaunt hollowed-out cheeks materialized.

"Alby?" muttered Jonathan as he stared at the hologram. For a moment, he tensed up, then quickly gathered his composure and added, "Yeah, I knew her years ago. She worked with me at Dill Electronics."

The three agents all made eye contact. "So when was the last time you saw Mrs. McMurray?"

"McMurray, I thought her last name was Rimbaru."

"That was her A.W. name. Her original name was Libby McMurray. Now we believe she goes by the name of Alby Rimbaru or a combination of both."

"I see. All this A.W., B.W., before Wupe and after stuff is so confusing. The last time I saw her was the day I left the company." Margaret and Ketchum had now positioned themselves at the doorstep behind him. They sensed that the conversation could go sideways with one wrong comment.

Agent Conway noted their appearance but kept her focus on Jonathan. "Do you know of any reason why Mr. McMurray and his wife would've come back to this area?"

"Quite frankly, I never knew they'd left," he replied. "What happened to them?"

"We aren't at liberty to say at this time. We're here gathering facts for the inquiry. Well, thank you for your time." As they walked away, Agent Conway stopped and asked, "Oh, by the way, do you have your credentials with you? It's routine."

Jonathan patted his pockets and said, "Not on me. I can E-Verify."

"I'm sorry, sir, but in situations like this we have to see a certified copy or 3D code."

"Really, I've been traveling the whole country for years now without needing a certified copy."

"It's a standard requirement now since Article 4.2 has been invoked."

"I see. The papers must be in the house." He turned to the half-opened door and asked, "Margaret, can you please get them?"

She was back at the door within seconds. Jonathan handed his ID card to the agent and smiled. The agent read the card and asked, "Sir, where were you born?"

"Cuba," replied Jonathan. As the three agents absorbed this comment, he added, "Guantanamo Bay. My father was stationed there in the late Twenties — you know, before they kicked us out."

Agent Conway ran her hand through her blue crew cut and handed the ID to the taller agent before saying, "Unfortunately, this card is not certified."

Jonathan chuckled, "Well, I mean who carries around the original certificate? I'm sure it's in the house somewhere."

"New regulations were implemented last year stating that all U.S. citizens are supposed to acquire an updated certificate from the DMV verifying their status. You are supposed to have a 3D security code that is kept on your CompWatch or card at all times. Were you not aware of that?"

"Well, like who has time to spend all day at the DMV?"

"It's the law, sir."

"Can I see yours while we're asking?"

The agent glanced over at her partners. The question caught her off guard. No one had ever asked her that and she wasn't sure if she had to answer. After a short pause, she responded, "Regulations do not permit it, but I do still need to see yours."

Margaret returned moments later and said, "I didn't see them in the file drawer, honey."

The agent rested her hand on an itchy holster and said, "I'm sorry, sir, but we're going to have to take you with us to the holding center until we can fully verify your status."

"Excuse me?" growled Margaret. She had come onto the porch and was now inches away from Agent Conway. The other two guards squared their shoulders with Tasers ready. Even though the agent had a good three inches on her in height, Margaret seemed to be standing on a ladder of intimidation, leveling the playing field. Ketchum's mom had a way of doing that with others when need be. It wasn't a natural instinct instilled in her at birth, but more of an acquired skill learned over the years when dealing with men.

Finally, the agent spoke up. "Ma'am, I'm just following protocol."

"I know what protocol is," barked Margaret. "I spent nine years in the State's Attorney's office before retiring and know exactly what you're capable of in the field. If you can't bring up my husband's official file on your watch, then go back to your van and search through one of the dozens of overpriced highly sophisticated surveillance databases you have rigged up in there."

The female agent signaled to her partner. One of them stepped toward Jonathan and took a photo of his face. Then he marched toward the van. While they waited for an answer, Ketchum made his way onto the porch and stood off to the side. The agent noticed and focused her attention on him. "I'm sorry, I didn't catch your name."

"Ketchum. Ketchum Tutaloo."

"What was your B.W. name?"

"Cole Mattock."

"If I recall, you were at the scene tonight too. Is that correct?"

"Yeah, but I don't know them at all."

Margaret, still in attack mode, glared at the woman and said, "He was just a child when my husband worked there. Of course, he wouldn't know Alby."

The van door swung back open and the agent stood up. He gave the thumbs up and yelled from the street, "All clear."

The two officers on the porch looked to each other and nodded. "We're sorry for the inconvenience tonight and we'll be on our way. Thank you for your time and cooperation." Then they backed up a step and turned to leave.

As they drove away, Ketchum finally exhaled. "Wow, what was that all about?"

"Commission," replied his mother. "They work off a commission. Every suspect they bring in, no matter what their status, whether they're dead or alive, makes them money."

"How bizarre. How did that happen?"

Jonathan brushed his son's silky head of brown hair and sighed, "The same way everything else happened: one cut at a time."

"Death by a thousand cuts," the boy replied as his mother gently nudged him back into the house. "That's what our history teacher called it. I wasn't sure what it meant at the time, but I get it now."

Margaret smiled, rubbed his arm and said, "It's late. Let's go to bed."

CLOSE ENCOUNTERS

The next day at school, Ketchum could concentrate on only one thing: the clock. Minutes ticked by at a glacial pace as he waited for his meeting with the counselor. When he finally did meet with her, all the questions he'd written down to ask answered themselves after reading them out loud. Her response each time was, "On page so and so of your manual…"

On the walk home, Tusnig was the first to notice movement on the second floor of the Galley Museum. Shadows filtered in and out of the sunlight shining through the windows. "Someone's out there."

Ketchum stared into the distance trying to get a glimpse of who it was. It was way too far away to get a good view. He spotted something on the far side. "Look, a rowboat. Where'd that come from?"

Then she revealed herself: a silhouette of a girl with short hair and a sleeveless shirt. She ambled out onto the second floor balcony, sat down, and splashed her feet in the ocean water. It was high tide again and the waves were billowing up over the levee and onto the abandoned highway. The sun was laying heavily in the west and casting long shadows over the sinking jetty. Ketchum knew it was the same girl from the assembly. It just had to be.

"I'm going out there."

"What, are you crazy?"

"I think I know who it is."

Tusnig thought about this for a moment and then understood. "The girl from the other day?"

"Yeah."

The ocean was on hiatus from its usual breezy self this afternoon as the wind was barely a stutter. A sky void of clouds except for a few ribbons drifting in from the east reflected shades of blue everywhere. The sun radiated down hard on the splashing waves. Tusnig watched Ketchum remove his jacket and shoes. "I have a lot of homework," he said.

"Suit yourself," replied Ketchum as he removed his shirt.

"What if it's not her?"

Ketchum laid his watch on top of the pile of clothes, turned to Tusnig and whispered, "It's a girl."

Tusnig simply grinned and agreed. "So be it. Three's a crowd anyway." He rocked back and forth on his heels until the silence became unbearable. Then he ambled away toward the hillside. "Later," he yelled into the wind.

Ketchum didn't understand what he'd said but waved anyway. Every few steps, Tusnig peered back over his shoulder to make sure his friend was still going through with it. When he reached the tree line, he turned and shouted, "Don't drown — and don't fall in love either."

Ketchum dove into the ocean. The tide was working against him, making every stroke harder than the next. After swallowing the first mouthful of seawater, his lifeguard training kicked in and he began using a sidestroke.

She was waiting for him when he arrived at the steps. He stomped onto the marble and wiped off his arms. Then he shook off any remaining water as the warm sun dried off the rest of his body.

She pointed and said, "Do you want to go inside?" Her body still lingered in the shadows under a curtain of darkness, obscuring her identity. When she stepped into the light, there was no doubt.

She was the girl from the assembly and even prettier than he'd expected. Her face was oval shaped and flush with color. The eyebrows, thin and dark, laced over a set of long eyelashes. When she moved from side to side, the necklace dangling between her breasts moved just enough to expose the outline of a respectful amount of cleavage. It wasn't deep but was definitely distinct.

He inspected the building to get his bearings and replied, "No, can we go around to the other side in the sun?"

She tapped her ear with her finger and said, "Sorry, I didn't hear what you said."

Ketchum wasn't sure what to make of this but repeated, "Can we go to the other side?"

"Of course," she replied.

He glanced back to the shoreline wondering if Tusnig was still watching. His friend was no longer visible but Ketchum knew he still lurked somewhere in the foliage. It was in his nature.

They walked in between fallen chunks of plaster and glass that covered the floor of the mezzanine. The wrought iron railing corkscrewed around the perimeter in double helix fashion, leaning inward and outward wherever it pleased. The rusted bars creaked with every passing breeze, as if to be complaining about its aches and pains to an empty horizon. Not a word was spoken.

They settled in on another balcony that faced westerly where the sun was in front of them. Any breeze that made its way across the water wasn't a factor in this spot. Ketchum brushed back his wet hair as he sat down next to her and tried to play it cool. Neither one was ready to say the first words. They were content with a few stolen glances here and there when the other wasn't looking.

April was the first to break the ice. "What was this place?"

"A museum. A famous one, in fact, you know, before all of this." He swirled his hand around a few times and she nodded.

She studied contours of the building, which resembled an ancient Roman country house. Red tile trim still separated most of the second floor from the third. Slabs of marble and travertine tiles held up the walls but were crumbling under their own weight. The sea floor below was slowly swallowing what was left of any foundation.

"I bet it was beautiful once."

Ketchum spun around on his rump and admired the architecture. "It still is, to me."

They both smiled. "I'm April."

"Ketchum. Glad to meet you."

"Likewise."

"You're new to the area?"

"Yeah, from up the coast, Old Oregon. My mother and I moved here to be closer to our relatives."

"No father?"

"Not that I know of."

"I'm sorry."

Ketchum wanted to say more but didn't know where to begin. Single parents were frowned upon and held up to a different standard than married couples. He wasn't sure how to continue without being offensive.

"She's my adoptive mother."

"Oh!" exclaimed Ketchum. Adoptive parents, on the other hand, were a completely different story and accepted with open arms. They were hailed by society as saviors and patron saints. "That must've been rough."

"Yeah, it was."

His comments had bounced the conversation from one ditch into another in a matter of seconds. The tumblers in his mind churned as he searched for any other topic to pivot to. "When do you turn eighteen?"

"In a couple of months. How about you?"

"Next week."

April searched Ketchum's face for any signs of fear. If it was there, she couldn't see it. Internally, though, a vicious tug of war battled back and forth between the options before him. What to do with the million dollars? Where to put it? Who to trust? Questions like these rattled around inside his brain filling spaces inside of spaces, consuming all his bandwidth.

"Have you decided what you're going to do with the money?"

"Of course not. Finish school, I suppose, and then go from there. Maybe college." He grabbed a chunk of plaster off the floor and skipped it across the ocean surface. "Even that's risky these days. You never know what career might be obsolete by the time you graduate."

"I hear ya. Even plumbers aren't a guarantee anymore."

"Exactly. My neighbor down the street says he's barely working because everyone has some kind of robotic plumbing module built into their system. He says there are more AI plumbers than there are toilets these days."

April laughed wholeheartedly. "That's funny."

Ketchum fidgeted from one hand to the other. No one ever laughed at his comments. He allowed the ocean waves to overtake the moment and soothe the apprehension he felt before adding, "I hear it's not so bad in Canada."

"Yeah, if you can get there. It's not that easy anymore. They've closed most of the borders."

"I guess you're right. It's all just fairytales these days."

Ketchum explored the contours of her copper-colored eyes as they glowed and glistened in the sunlight. They, no doubt, held the key that unlocked a pathway into her heart. Her facial expressions were another story, though. A slight lift of the cheek or a wrinkle across her forehead might have exposed volumes in other girls, but with her, they scarcely chipped away at the mystery behind them.

"The drone."

He jumped up onto his feet and scurried inside the building.

There was a deep crack running through the middle of the room in a serpentine fashion resembling an overgrown vine. It continued up the wall and through the ceiling. It was much larger than he remembered the last time he was there. Rays of sunshine filtered through small gaps in the plaster as water swished around underneath the floor. The twenty-foot-high ceiling slowly rocked back and forth, cradling the wooden beams as if holding on for dear life.

He scanned the empty room for any signs of the drone. Echoes of faint voices from a distant past seemed to dance off the walls in a low murmur as they moved around. In the corner, he found a broken plastic propeller that once carried the drone from the shore into the building.

He never understood why Tusnig guided it inside in the first place on that windy day. Maybe a breeze carried it so close to the building that he had no choice. Maybe he actually thought he could navigate it blindly inside using some kind of super X-ray vision. It didn't matter. There were laws against owning one anyway and the police would've eventually confiscated it.

April jumped over the gap in the floor toward Ketchum. "What are you looking for?"

"A drone. My friend flew it inside here a while back from the shoreline."

"I thought they were illegal, you know, like, unless you have government clearance or something."

Ketchum turned around and faced her. A combination of shadows and sunlight crossed her face like Indian war paint. Her short blonde hair spiking up from her head glistened in the sun. "They are, for the most part. I mean you can get an action figure drone that flies a few feet but that's it. Anyway, he didn't own it. We found it in a cave up in the hills. It must have been thirty years old. I was surprised it even worked."

She surveyed the room in a full three-hundred-and-sixty-degree motion and replied, "Too bad. That would've been cool to see."

The sky gradually changed colors as a few lingering clouds gathered on the horizon. They didn't have to squint any longer when gazing westward out the window. "We should head back," said Ketchum.

"What?" April pointed to her ear. "This hearing aid doesn't work too well in rooms like this."

Ketchum nodded. He wanted to ask, but knew he'd find out eventually. "It's getting late."

"You wanna lift?" She swayed her head in the direction of her rowboat as a cool breeze swirled around them.

"Definitely."

"Do you live near here?"

"Yeah."

"So this is your boat?"

"No, I borrowed it."

CHAPTER TWELVE

THE NASTY DEED

SILENCE FILLED the Interrogation Room at FBI headquarters as Ketchum paused and sighed. Edgar opened his eyes and said, "Disengage."

Ketchum stood up, arched his back and asked, "Can I use the restroom?"

"I'll take him," said Izzy.

As they left the room, Edgar rubbed his eyes and stretched. He removed the glasses, set them on the table, and with a whisper said, "Amazing, no wonder they're restricted." Recollections from an article he'd read years ago while it was still available on the Intranet came to mind. Most literature about them nearly vanished overnight after reports of people suffering permanent brain damage from extended periods of use surfaced.

The world had finally stitched together a quilted collage of fiber optics, radio waves, and microchips with the capabilities of almost reading a person's thoughts while reducing it down to the size of a needle head. Yes, no virtual stone had been left unturned when designing this baby. He examined the markings on the side of the titanium-plated headband. It read, "Model: DILL-DO 1000. Dill Electronics, Summerfield, California."

What a small world, he thought.

As he rewound the last few minutes of Ketchum's narrative in his mind, a feeling of emptiness quivered through the membranes lining his stomach. The boy's words had unlocked a sensation he'd never explored before because of the way things turned out between him and his wife: a paternal bond. He and Evelyn never had children. It was one of the hard choices they'd made early on in their marriage in order to enjoy the lifestyles they'd chosen. He didn't regret the decision, yet here he was wondering what could've been through the eyes of this young boy.

The thought of having children implanted itself in Edgar's brain. No matter how he tried to push it aside and think of something else, it kept creeping back in. It reminded him of a conversation he and Evelyn had had about starting a family. A conversation that changed their lives forever.

᷈᷈᷈

His mind recalled the day she received her ACP results and learned about possible health problems in her future. High blood pressure, cholesterol, and aneurysm were found everywhere in her family history. Edgar tried his best to keep her in good spirits but the facts weighed heavily against any kind of a positive outlook. "Don't worry, it's just a probability."

"It's more than that," snapped Evelyn. "I already have high cholesterol. High blood pressure is just around the corner, and who knows," she sniffed back a sob and added, "about an aneurysm."

"We can't let it affect the way we live, though. I mean, we can't keep waiting for something tragic to happen."

"I agree, but there are things we can do to mitigate the pain."

Edgar's focus narrowed in on his wife's last remark. "Like what?"

"Like having children."

Neither one said anything. They just let the comment linger in the air and breathe. The longer they were silent,

the louder it rustled around the room gathering momentum. What would life be like without children? Many couples didn't even bother with families these days, considering the costs and way children tied you down to a certain lifestyle.
Finally, Edgar replied, "It is a thought. I'm fine with it."
"I am too," she acquiesced."

சைசைசை

He fought the urge to reminisce further and tried to remember why he was there in the first place. Only a few minutes remained until the Dunes agents arrived. When that happened, there would be no time for reflection. After placing the glasses back on and thumbing through the temple settings, he commanded, "Call."

"Front desk."

"Jay, this is Edgar."

"Oh, hi, Edgar. I see you're still in the Goldfish Bowl. Everything okay?"

"Yeah, but we need more time. A few Dunes agents are arriving soon. Can you stall them?"

"You got it."

Ketchum and Izzy returned with snacks and drinks. The boy took a swig off a can of soda and sat back down. He seemed to be in better spirits now that he'd had the chance to tell his side of the story. Whether it made any difference or not, he didn't know.

"Shall we continue?" asked Edgar.

Ketchum eagerly agreed and resumed speaking. "It was the day of my birthday. Mom insisted we go out to dinner."

Edgar closed his eyes again and commanded, "Engage." This time, the images instantly flowed like wine.

சைசைசை

Margaret stood up at the restaurant table with her glass in hand

and said, "A toast. Our baby boy has finally turned eighteen and become a man."

His father raised his glass and added, "May the wind of prosperity forever be at your back."

Ketchum lifted his glass off the table and gently clinked it against everyone else's. Then they all saluted him and took a sip.

The waiter came out of nowhere and asked, "Would you like to see dessert menus?"

"I don't think that'll be necessary. Just the check, please." Margaret smiled and said, "There's a surprise dessert waiting for us at home."

As they all got up to leave, Ketchum noticed two people staring at him from a table in the corner of the room. One of them was April. He excused himself and walked over.

April smiled and said, "Happy Birthday."

"Thank you," he replied. Then he turned to the other woman and said, "You must be April's mother. Nice to meet you. I'm Ketchum."

"Adoptive mother," reminded April. She waved her arm and said, "This is the boy from school I was telling you about."

Ketchum grinned as the lady studied him from head to toe. "Well, *greedness greaty*, it's a pleasure to finally meet you, Ketchum." Her smile was gentle and sincere, but almost too sincere.

"Same here, ma'am."

"Oh, please call me Delores."

"I prefer ma'am, or Missus…"

"…Jones."

"Mrs. Jones."

"So, do you feel any different, I mean, turning eighteen and all?"

Ketchum rubbed his jaw and pondered the question for a moment. "Not really, just a little richer."

"Ha, you mean a lot richer." Delores reached out and placed

her hand on top of April's as she spoke, "It's a life-changing experience, you know. It's like having the world at your fingertips. You can do anything you want."

"Yeah, well, not quite everything," replied April.

"Oh, but you can if you invest it the right way." Delores grabbed a menu sitting at the end of the table. She pointed to an advertisement on the back. "Dylan MacMillan. You must read this book. It will change your life. My next-door neighbor took his advice and invested in real estate a few years ago. Not here, but in Michigan on a lake. He was able to buy lots with the money and, within five years, the price had doubled. Then he took that money and bought a few lots in Alaska. They've already gone up in value forty percent."

"Sounds interesting, but why Michigan?"

"It's the new Florida, my dear."

"Ahh, I see. Maybe I'll check it out."

Jonathan finished paying the bill and cleared his throat. Ketchum recognized the signal and said, "Well, I must be going. It was nice seeing you again, April, and meeting you, Mrs. Jones."

"Oh, here, not yet. I made you a card." April slid a makeshift envelope across the table marked "Ketchum." As she handed it to him, she glanced up and winked. Ketchum didn't know how to respond and merely smiled before turning away.

"Good night," was all he could think of to say while leaving the restaurant. As soon as the family SUV pulled away from the curb, he opened the envelope. The card was part of a restaurant flyer torn in half and folded over. Inside and scribbled in pencil, were the words, "Meet me tonight at midnight. Same place as before."

The rest of the night, one thought occupied every corner of Ketchum's mind. A salty sea breeze whistled through the kitchen while the family sang "Happy Birthday." The letters on his cake rearranged themselves in his mind to spell "April." Even the blackness of the night reminded him of her outfit.

Sneaking out of the house had become an art form for him over the years. He'd calculated the precise amount of time it took his parents to fall asleep, how to disarm the security cameras, and he knew exactly which doors caused the least amount of resistance once opened. The night air was unseasonably warm this evening.

When he arrived at the levee, a rowboat was docked and waiting on shore. April appeared out of nowhere as he jumped off the abandoned highway and trotted toward her across the sand. She was wearing a hoodie and holding an opened bottle of wine. Two plastic cups dangled between her fingers in the other hand.

"I'm glad you came. I don't know if I could've drunk this whole bottle by myself."

"It'd be fun trying."

"What?" yelled April. "The waves are too loud."

"What do you mean?"

She pointed to her hearing aid. "Lost most of my hearing when I was little. Spinal meningitis."

"Really," he hollered. "I'd heard that it'd made a comeback in some areas but never knew anyone who'd actually contracted it."

"Well, now you do. It's pretty common up in Old Oregon."

Ketchum smiled and helped her into the boat. He pushed it out to sea, then jumped in and grabbed the oars. "You act like an old pro at this," she said.

"There's not much to it."

On the ride over to the museum, they didn't say another word. The spattering waves on the distant rocks and a tugboat horn tooting somewhere far away from another bay were enough to entertain them. The water was calm at this time of night and the moon waned brightly in the southern sky. When they arrived, April tossed a sleeping bag onto the balcony and pulled herself up using the railing. Ketchum handed her the bottle and cups, then lifted himself out of the boat.

She unzipped the sleeping bag and spread it on the marble

floor. Then she pulled out an old digital radio and tuned it to a soft jazz channel. Ketchum started to pour her a drink but she reached up and stopped him. "I got it."

"You've thought of everything. I didn't realize I was so special."

April filled each cup half full and handed one to Ketchum. "Turning eighteen is very special. Happy Birthday."

They tapped the cups together and drank. The wine was a little bitter but it didn't matter. Neither of them were quite sure what it was supposed to taste like anyway. April laid her head down and Ketchum followed. He turned on his side and asked, "So what would you blow a million dollars on?"

"A new ear, for one. Even though it'd probably cost me a quarter of a million, if not more, it'd be worth it."

He brushed back her bangs and said, "Must be rough."

She didn't know how to respond. Rough was an understatement. If he only knew how this life-changing event had shaped her reality. "I get by," was all she said.

Her words were few and he liked that. Most girls he'd known needed to talk every second. Out of nervousness, he assumed, but still annoying. He rolled onto his back and sighed. Barely a handful of stars were visible above the skyglow of city lights and struggled for attention with every blinking light. "You can hardly see Orion tonight," he said.

"Have you ever thought about blowing your million on a space flight?"

"Sure, but it's not worth it. I mean, the short trips. How far does a million dollars get you these days if you do the return flight — a few months, a year or two? What do you do after that, work the rest of your life?"

"I'm talking about the long flights. The ones where you never come back."

"I've heard stories about them. My best friend says they're not even real. When you're a hundred light years away and have lost contact with earth, who knows what happens to you? They can't guarantee any kind of communication at that point. As far as we know, they may simply pull the plug and send you off on your merry way into oblivion."

"I guess so, but what a way to go. It still sounds romantic, though." April turned toward Ketchum and let her breath brush across his neck as she asked, "Is this romantic?"

"Indeed."

He tried to pivot with grace but it was clumsy in every sense of the word. She grinned and gently kissed his cheek. Then she lifted herself up and kissed his lips. Her hand had already unbuttoned his shirt as she rolled on top of him. Ketchum reached under her blouse and tried to undo the bra strap. The hook eluded every twist and turn of his fingers. April was now saddled on top with her spurs in his sides. She crossed her arms, then pulled the hoodie and blouse off her torso. Slowly, she reached around and removed that last hinge holding her bra in place.

"Are you a virgin?" she jested.

"Does it matter?"

As the strap dangled on her shoulders, Ketchum tried not to stare but couldn't help himself. He'd touched a few breasts in his life but never had he been so dominated by a girl in this manner. Never had he been this close to doing the nasty deed before, either. That didn't mean he hadn't seen it done online once or twice. There was always a restricted website popping up here and there that bypassed detection for a few hours before being shut down. Still, those videos constantly skipped over the good parts, meaning anything involving arousal of the senses, subtle kisses, or passionate moans. All those features were on full display tonight.

April was right where she wanted to be: on top and in control. To her, this was the sweet spot of any romantic interaction. She waited until his breathing became irregular before dropping the bra strap. She wanted him totally off balance and begging for more. No words were needed, only eye contact and a gentle touch. The slower she moved, the more he was aroused. It didn't take but another three minutes before they were both naked and lying on their backs gasping for air.

"Wow, that was awesome."

April was panting and didn't hear what he'd said. It didn't matter. Neither one of them had calmed down enough to talk so they just stared up into the night sky. After a few minutes, she rolled over and stroked his hairless chest, "This is nice."

A sensation of unbridled relief overcame him. He'd masturbated hundreds of times before but this feeling was different. It made him want to nestle her in his arms into a tiny ball of compassion. The fog had dissipated in the southern sky, revealing a multitude of stars. He even recognized Jupiter glowing near a large cluster in the southern horizon.

They sat for the longest time without saying a word. Finally, a cool breeze brushed off the ocean surface garnering their attention. It was enough to make April reach for the end of the sleeping bag and pull it over them.

She straddled Ketchum's torso and said, "I don't ever want this to end."

"Me too. I don't think I've ever experienced this level of peace and quiet."

"I wish we could stay here all night."

Ketchum jumped up and looked at his watch, "What time is it?"

"It's only one o'clock."

"My dad wakes up religiously around four o'clock, sometimes earlier, and can't get back to bed for hours. He paces the floor in the kitchen drinking warm milk or whatever else he thinks might help him sleep. That wakes my mother up too. It'll be hard for me to sneak back in if they're up. I'll have to leave around two."

"Sounds good. So what do we do for an hour?"

April grinned as Ketchum rolled on top of her and replied, "I say we keep doing what we're doing."

An hour later, April lifted herself onto her feet and began putting on clothes. "We should go." She brushed off Ketchum's attempt to help her with her bra and latched it around her waist. Then she slid it to the back and lifted it up in place.

"It's always amazed me how limber girls are."

"Someday, I'll show you a few of my signature moves." April winked as she pulled up her pants and lifted the blouse over her head. She laid the radio in the middle of the sleeping bag and rolled it up inside. Then she tied it off.

When they arrived back to shore, Ketchum jumped out and pulled the vessel on top of the sand. While lifting her out, he asked, "What are you going to do with the boat?"

"Don't worry, I just need to dock it over in the next bay. Piece of cake."

"How far away do you live from there?"

"Not far, just a few minutes from shore."

He brushed her bangs over to one side and out of her eyes, then gently kissed her on the lips. "I had a great time tonight. Will I see you tomorrow?"

"Of course."

"Sounds good. Thanks for a wonderful birthday present."

"The pleasure was all mine." She kissed him on the forehead, hopped into the boat, and rowed away.

Ketchum watched the darkness roll in as she faded away. He then examined his watch and trotted across the sand toward home.

April rowed hard against the current until she'd finally made it around the cape and into the next cove. The waves guided her into the dock with ease, where she tied the boat off and walked away.

In the corner of the parking lot, a white minivan sat under a tree and out of the light glowing from surrounding lampposts. The back door was unlocked. When inside, she untied the sleeping bag and spread it out over the lowered seat.

Rustling next to her was another sleeping bag. A head of hair popped up at the opening as her mother spun around from one shoulder to the other and yawned, "How'd it go?"

April lay on her back and replied, "I don't have a good feeling about this place. I think we need to find another town."

Delores rolled over and cleared her throat. "We'll do nothing of the sort. This one is perfect."

"This all just feels so wrong."

Her mother leaned on her elbow and scolded, "Young lady, I don't want to hear another word about this. Do you understand?"

"I feel like a goddamn hooker. Doesn't that bother you?"

Delores slapped April hard and replied, "It's not about you, you selfish little foundling. It's about surviving and keeping all our friends whole. Don't you ever forget that."

"It's not fair." April spun on her side and covered her head with the sleeping bag.

"You'll do what I say or else you can hit the road right now, without your hearing aid. In fact, give it to me."

April yanked the device off her ear and tossed it over. She closed her eyes and turned back on her side.

"Good night."

CHAPTER THIRTEEN

GRADUATION DAY

OVER THE NEXT FEW WEEKS, they made love. They made love on the marble floor at the museum in broad daylight, they made love on the crumbling stairs, and they made love in the rowboat drifting with the current. Nothing else entered their minds but total bliss. The obsession with each other turned into a full-time occupation between eating lunch, studying at the coffee shop, and walking home together after school.

"What's the very first thing you're going to do with your million?" asked April as they strolled along the abandoned Highway 1.

"Oh, I don't know, maybe a nice dinner. There are a couple of things I've been eying over the years, you know. Hopefully, I won't go on a stupid buying spree like some people do and end up broke the next morning."

"Yeah, for sure, but you should think about it now, you know, get that one thing you've always wanted right off the bat."

Ketchum thought about this comment and realized that everything he'd once wanted didn't seem so important any longer. Now that he was within reach of buying them, material things had somehow become immaterial. He shook his head and said, "I don't know." Then he stopped and gently placed his hand in hers. "Maybe I'll get you something. What's on top of your list?"

April brushed back his bangs and planted a soft kiss on his cheek. "You're on top of my list, silly boy."

He smiled and stared deep into her eyes. They'd both become comfortable with this level of romantic interaction lately. At first, it was awkward and uneasy, but now what he saw reflecting back seemed entirely sincere. He wondered if this was how love was supposed to feel. Since he had nothing to compare it to in his past, he surely hoped so. Whatever it was, this burning desire and raw passion had brought out a vibrant side of him he'd never known.

April let the moment sink in. It felt good, but even more significantly, it felt right. This wasn't supposed to happen. This was not the plan. Her life up until then had been filled with so much pain and hardship that her emotional spigot was drained completely. In its place, sheer numbness won out when it came to intimate relationships. She'd taught herself to deflect those sensations and shield her soul from the heartbreaks that were sure to come. Still, here she was falling in love and failing to care about the consequences. There were always consequences, though, especially when her adoptive mother was involved. But those were issues to be dealt with at another time. Right now, she just wanted to enjoy the moment.

"I've never been happier than I am right now," said Ketchum, "I hope the whole money thing doesn't change that. I've heard it happens a lot." He squeezed her hand tightly and added, "Promise me it won't."

"I promise." April focused her gaze on the crumbling museum in the distance. Every wave reminded her about how fragile relationships could be, how a sudden surge of emotion could wash away the foundation without warning. "Promise me something." She returned her attention to his eyes and warmed herself in their subtle hazel glow.

"Anything."

"If things don't work out between us in the end, I mean, like you said, money tends to change people, promise me that you'll only remember the good times we had, not the bad ones."

Ketchum didn't know what to make of this comment. It was as if she was trying to read the tea leaves before they'd even been served. Yet he knew that money did have a tendency to ruin matters just as easily as strengthening them.

"That'll be easy. They were all good." He kissed her on the lips for the longest time. Then they parted ways.

Tusnig watched from a distance. There was nothing he could say or do to change what was happening. Ketchum had found a new friend, with benefits. At first, his initial reaction was one of dismay and jealousy, but it quickly turned into admiration. He was happy for his best friend because his best friend was happy.

He'd read enough to know that these kinds of things usually run their course and end badly. Then he'd be there when the bottom fell out, just like he hoped Ketchum would be there for him. That thought, of having a relationship one day this passionate and this intimate, made him hopeful. Any notions to the contrary were brushed off like loose dander.

The day Ketchum's ID arrived with instructions on how to collect his million was a Saturday. He ran out of the house so excited that he'd forgotten to comb his hair or brush his teeth. April was waiting in front of the bank. When he squeezed her hand, the exhilaration passed through her like lightning.

Ketchum slid his ID to the bank teller under the glass.

"Do you have your Millionaire's Manual?"

He reached into his back pocket and pulled out the pamphlet.

"Please sign it and write your name and address on the back cover."

She handed Ketchum a pen and he complied. Then he pushed everything under the glass. She inspected the photo on the ID and looked him over. "Please look straight into the scanner." A flash of white light blinded him. "Place your thumb here and verify that you've read the document and agree to all the terms." Ketchum perused the screen and pressed his thumb on the device. A bell dinged while a green light glowed. "Thank you."

The teller left the counter and entered her supervisor's office. When she returned, the teller said, "A belated Happy Birthday." She pulled out her ID, swiped it alongside her monitor and pressed a few keys. A ding chimed on Ketchum's CompWatch as she said, "There you go, Mr. Tutaloo, verification that one million dollars has been deposited into your checking account. If you have a security chip implanted later, please return and we'll update it. Do you want any of that transferred into a secure savings account?"

"Not right now. Maybe later."

"Okay, your first transaction must be done in person at the ATM machine over there against the wall. It will take you through a series of security questions that you must set up and then, after that, you can do everything online. Please either memorize your pin number or change it to something else as soon as possible."

"Got it." Ketchum smiled and walked over to the machine. "I need to get cash."

"Cash," questioned April. "Why?"

"So I can frame my first dollar bill. It's tradition, you know."

He approached the ATM and typed in his account number. As he entered the password, April ran her hand up his back and gently rubbed his neck. Her fingertips tickled their way into his train of thought, causing him to press the wrong buttons.

"Shoot, I screwed up."

A message on the screen flashed, "You have two more attempts before being locked out."

April peered over his shoulder and said, "Just take your time. Take a deep breath and enter them slowly."

Ketchum nodded while unconsciously biting his nails. He pressed the keys cautiously, each time referring back to his password, and was in. Crisis adverted. After withdrawing the money, he returned to the counter and asked the teller for change and a crisp new one-dollar bill.

Outside of the bank, they turned left and headed straight for the guitar shop on the corner. In the window, a Starburst 1969 Stratocaster sat on a throne of stainless steel and rubber with an array of white lights beaming down from above. He stopped to admire it just like he had a hundred times before, then strode up to the counter and said, "I'll take that one."

The salesman brushed aside the request and with the indifference of a sixty-year-old roadie asked, "Birthday?"

Ketchum replied with a nod and added, "Plus that amp over there." He pointed to a vintage Marshall Combo behind the counter on a shelf. "And that strap, and a wireless cable, and these." He reached into a glass jar and pulled out a handful of picks. "Have it delivered to my house too."

When they left the store and rounded the next corner, a deluge of water met them head on. A city worker busy flushing out the fire hydrants motioned them to go around. April swiftly darted from one dry place to another before ending up on the curb. Unfortunately, Ketchum didn't react fast enough and was flooded with a steady stream surrounding his feet. His socks were soaked within seconds. He lifted the sole of his tennis shoe and ran his finger through a hole.

"Dammit!" he exclaimed.

He maneuvered around the rapid flowing river of city water and up on the curb, then they turned right at the next corner. At the end of the block stood a shoe store tucked away in a small mini mall. From the displays in the window, they could tell that the place was a bit too hip for the neighborhood. The Art Deco arrangements featuring shoe colors only found in children's drawings stood out next to the Hallmark card shop window a few feet away. Digital posters of skinny models posing in nothing more than a pair of sneakers and underwear while avoiding eye contact passed above him as they entered the store. Even the workers wearing black jeans cut off at the knees and sleeveless shirts seemed to be too cool to actually work for a living.

Ketchum strode up to the counter and said, "I want the most expensive pair of tennis shoes you have."

The salesclerk listlessly replied, "Birthday?" He nodded and they both followed the lady to the back of the store. "We can custom make whatever type of shoe you want. Please step into the 3D simulator."

Ketchum removed his shoes and stepped into a rectangular box where he pranced back and forth, on his heels and tip toes, then stood completely still. The clerk fiddled with the computer while explaining, "We use the digital light synthesis process here, or DLS as it's known to the rest of the world. Right now, the machine is printing your midsoles in a polymer bath. What kind of features would you like?"

A hologram screen swooshed in front of Ketchum with an array of options displayed. He scrolled through them with his feet still firmly planted and clicked on several features. A few minutes later, a bell chimed and a pair of red, white, and blue sneakers with sparkling stripes rolled out of a conveyor belt in the wall.

"There, they've finished growing." The clerk retrieved the shoes, placed them on Ketchum's feet, and said, "Give them a whirl." He walked across the floor and spun around in a half circle. "Tap the tips together twice."

Ketchum nodded and obliged. Lights flashed the colors of the American flag from one stripe to the next like a musically synced disco floor.

"Tap them again."

He nodded and once again clicked the toes. Fireworks lit up the room with all the colors of the rainbow spurting out from the soles. After an approving nod from everyone, he said, "I'll take them."

Outside the store, he put his arm around April and asked, "Dinner tonight? I'm buying. You pick the place. Anywhere."

April blushed and replied, "Of course. Let me think about it."

"Okay, I gotta run and do some errands. Text me later."

He kissed her goodbye and headed home. A digital ten-foot-tall billboard with Dylan MacMillan standing on a beach plastered across it caught his attention. "CALL NOW" was all it said, with an 800 number running across the bottom. He tapped on his CompWatch, dialed the number, and then hung up suddenly. A part of him knew better, but the other half was hearing April's mother from the other day in the restaurant. He dialed it again.

The number took his phone directly to a website filled with testimonials from every lifestyle. Sports stars, reality TV celebrities, and average Joes paraded across the screen in succession, all smiling and holding a wad of cash in their hands. He clicked on the "Buy Now" button and a menu surfaced. Each audio chapter cost five thousand dollars. There were ten.

"What the hell." He selected Chapter One, clicked the disclaimer box, and started listening to the book through his earbuds. By the time he'd made it home, he was on Chapter Three.

CHAPTER FOURTEEN

A SHORT GOODBYE

THE LAST FEW WEEKS of high school were just a blur. It was hard to concentrate on studies when you had a million dollars sitting in the bank ready to be spent. The teachers called it "Millionitis."

During English class, his teacher asked, "How many of you are planning on going to college?" She counted hands around the room. "Only five?" Tusnig inconspicuously raised his hand, without looking at Ketchum or making eye contact with anyone else. "Six."

She sighed and pointed to a boy in the front row. "Why not?"

"What's the point? So many jobs are lost to AI and automation these days that I might as well roll the dice on a couple of smart investments in real estate or the stock market. If I hit it big, I'm on easy street the rest of my life."

"But what if you make some bad investments? What then?"

The boy merely shrugged. "Then I'm back to square one, and I could always move back in with my parents."

The class laughed while the teacher revealed a subtle grin before replying, "Yes, but there's always the chance of entering into Zero Sum."

With the awkwardness of a newborn calf, he squirmed around in his seat and replied, "That won't happen."

The teacher decided not to pursue the exchange any further and deflected her next question toward Tusnig.

"Mr. Dolan, you had your hand up. Why are you going to college?"

An uneasy quiet filled the room, followed by a long pause. Tusnig looked around and realized that everyone was watching. Sure, many of the boys liked to tease him because he never fought back, but everyone knew he was as clever as they came and well on his way to being valedictorian of their class. Nobody was going to disrespect him today.

He sat up in his chair and cleared his throat. "I don't know. I'm thinking of becoming a doctor or something like that. I mean there's a big demand these days, you know, especially since they don't come in from overseas any longer."

"That's true," the teacher replied. "An extremely noble cause indeed. Some private practices are very lucrative."

"But what about flunking out? I heard you lose everything if you don't graduate," chimed in the boy in the front row. Tusnig sharply turned toward him and scowled. The last thing he wanted to be reminded of was failure.

"I don't think you lose everything but you would lose the money you paid for school, which is a lot," interjected the teacher. She studied her classroom and glanced at a camera up in the corner of her room. A darkened sphere recording and streaming every sentence she said reminded her that she had to pick and choose her words carefully. "Every one of you needs to realize that there are risks in anything you do in life. If that's too overwhelming, then there are several safer paths to take in civil service, law enforcement, or the military, where you defer the money until you put in your thirty years. In fact, you double your money that way and keep the benefits." She curtly smiled at the boy in the front row and added, "Or you can roll the dice on get-rich-quick schemes like the stock market."

A low rumble rolled across the room as she continued, "Throughout history, life has always been a challenge. It's what makes us human. In the old days, you had to be born into money in order to start out rich. A normal person struggled to make ends meet and spent most of their waking hours just trying to survive. That all changed with the SSI Initiative."

She walked over to the electronic whiteboard, picked up a digital marker, and began writing while continuing to lecture. "You've all been given a special gift that has only been bestowed upon very few in the history of this country or any country, for that matter. You are all destined to become millionaires. Just think about that. You'll all start out life without the burden of figuring out how to put food on your plate, how to pay rent, how to make ends meet. Yes, you must choose wisely on how to spend that money, but this is a golden opportunity for you to explore life, take chances, do what you are passionate about, and follow your dreams."

She pointed to the board and recited, "It's not about greed, it's about greatness." She continued, "You've all been born at a wonderful time in history, into a country that has made life for every citizen better than ever. Now you have every opportunity at your fingertips. Enjoy it." Then she turned to Tusnig and added, "You'll be a great doctor."

After school, Tusnig closed his locker and said to Ketchum, "I don't want to be a doctor. Why couldn't it be like it was in the forties? My dad said you could live off thirty thousand a year and make it last your whole life. It was so much easier back then."

"I know. I have an uncle living in Europe. He moved there before they restricted access." Ketchum shut his locker and added, "He's in his nineties and still hasn't run out of money."

Tusnig nodded. The bags under his eyes said volumes. Trying to live up to his dad's expectations had taken its toll. Ketchum tried to wash away the thick layer of guilt his friend had been born into and said, "You'll be fine. All you have to do is follow your heart. Your dad will come around eventually."

Tusnig halfheartedly agreed and then realized, "Hey, where's April?"

"She's sick."

"Wasn't she out yesterday too?"

Ketchum nervously grinned and replied, "Yes."

Later that night while jamming to music in his room with his new guitar, Ketchum's watch rang. It was April and she was sobbing.

"What's wrong?" he asked.

"Something's come up and we had to leave town for a few weeks. In fact, we're on the road now."

"On the road. To where?"

"Old Oregon."

So many thoughts stumbled around in his brain before he finally asked, "April, what's going on?"

There was silence on the other end for a minute and he could tell that she was moving around in the van. Then she whispered, "I'm pregnant."

Dozens of scenarios crossed his mind about what this meant: marriage, baby cribs, settling down, buying a house, then maybe even divorce later. There were no good options.

April cleared her throat and said, "Don't worry, it's all taken care of, or will be soon."

He knew what that meant and replied, "You're okay with that? I mean, if you get caught, they'll put you in jail and…"

"… I know," she interrupted. "I won't. Delores has a doctor friend up there who won't say anything."

"I see."

He ran his fingers through his hair and replied, "It's not how I'd like this to play out, but I understand."

"I gotta go. I'll call you when it's over."

He struggled with whether to say what he was thinking, but realized it was now or never. "I love you." It was too late. The other end of the phone had already gone dead.

CHAPTER FIFTEEN

JUDGMENT DAY

BACK IN THE INTERROGATION ROOM, Ketchum lowered his head and said, "Well, you can figure out what happened next. This morning, I got a call from the bank saying my account was empty — completely. In fact, it was overdrawn. April took it all. Before I knew it, SSI was at my door asking me to come with them. Then I ended up here."

Both Izzy's and Edgar's phones chimed with a message from Jay at the front desk. "I can't stall them any longer."

Edgar disengaged the glasses and put them in his pocket. Izzy stood up and whispered, "I'll take those. You're in enough trouble as it is."

As she removed them from Edgar's pocket, he asked, "And you won't be?"

"Believe it or not, I'm authorized."

"Well, I'll be. Why didn't you tell me?"

"The situation never came up. Besides, they'll drive you crazy if you wear 'em long enough." She turned to Ketchum and said, "Mr. Tutaloo, it looks like we've run out of time. I'm so sorry, son. We'll do what we can to track down this girl but the odds are that she's gone off the grid."

There was a knock at the door. Two Dunes agents opened it and entered. The one with the blue crew cut spoke first. "Agent Gorman and Moreno, I'm Agent Conway and this is Agent Terabush."

Edgar recognized them both. They were the same ones observed minutes earlier in Ketchum's memory feed. He studied her haircut and whispered to Izzy, "Same hair as Toyer."

"Glad to meet you," said Izzy.

"Is this the Zero Sum suspect?" Agent Conway motioned toward Ketchum.

"Why yes, it is."

"As directed by the Revised Constitution of 2033, Article 13, we are here to apprehend the subject, ascertain his status, and process accordingly."

Everyone turned to Ketchum, who was still sitting down. He recognized the agents from the other night at his house. So did Agent Terabush. "You look familiar." He read the name on the notepad and added, "Didn't we question you a while back regarding an altercation in Summerfield recently that involved the death of an escaped prisoner?"

"Yes."

The two Dunes agents greeted this news with a suspicious look of surprise. Coincidences usually meant connections in their line of duty. Izzy could sense the confusion and said, "Let's continue this conversation outside." As they exited the interrogation room and closed the door, she asked, "So, you two know the boy?"

A sense of command perked up within her spine as Agent Conway replied, "He was interviewed in an investigation a while back but nothing became of it. Two suspects had escaped a Dunes facility and the boy was at the scene with a group of neighbors when the incident occurred. The husband was fatally injured in a gunfire fight at the premises and the wife was apprehended. She's awaiting return to the Utah Flats Facility after we're done interrogating her. There're still some unanswered questions on how the couple managed to escape in the first place and make it all the way to the West Coast."

"What's your theory?"

"Our agency doesn't come up with theories, nor do we condone them. That is left to people like you."

"I see."

This new revelation sparked Izzy's interest. "Could we please have a copy of the file on the two escapees?"

The Dunes agents looked to each other but did not show any reaction. "As soon as you request it from headquarters, we'll have it sent over."

This comment didn't sit well with Edgar's boss. Her level of contempt for bureaucracy was only matched by her lack of patience. She crossed her arms and said, "Agent Conway, let me be frank. If you want to interview the suspect, then you'll send me the report now."

The female agent backed up a step and asked, "Is that a threat?"

The words burned Izzy's ears and triggered her to move in nose to nose. "It's whatever you think it is."

The repugnant smell of resentment briskly filled the air between them as neither one moved for what felt like an eternity. Both agents were sewn from the same cloth when it came to confrontation. Finally, Agent Terabush stepped up, tapped on his CompWatch, and said, "There, you have everything. Thank you for your time."

Tensions eased and piercing glares soon turned into pretentious smiles. As the two agents turned toward the Interrogation Room, Izzy put her hand on the doorknob and asked, "So what will become of him?"

"Most likely, he'll be sent to the Arizona facility for re-habilitation and training. We get way more teenagers than you'd think."

"Does anybody look into these cases? Any studies on the causes or correlations?" asked Edgar.

"I'm sure they do, Agent Gorman, but that's not my area

of expertise. Thank you for your time. We'll conduct the exit interview now."

An alert dinged as the lights above each exit of the office flashed. They all looked at their watches in stunned silence. The message read: *Level 3 alert for an Edgar Gorman. Height 6' 3", 210 pounds. Suspect is to be apprehended immediately and taken into custody for questioning.*

"Taken where," asked Agent Terabush.

A few seconds later, the message changed to: *taken into custody to the Dunes headquarters in Ontario for questioning.*

"How weird is that?" said Izzy as she peered up at a camera hidden in a circular dark sphere in the corner of the room.

"The revised message or the first one?" asked Agent Conway.

"Both."

"Indeed."

The three focused their gaze on Edgar, who looked to Izzy. There was nothing to say or do. In a tone that bordered on gratification, the Dunes agent said, "Agent Gorman, I must ask for your weapon and ask you to please come with us."

"This is all a big mistake," pleaded Edgar.

"BIG doesn't make mistakes," retorted Agent Conway.

"BIG? What's that? I thought you were part of Dunes."

"We are, but MAGMA recently created BIG as an alternative law enforcement agency and is moving certain responsibilities and security matters over to the new department going forward."

"Like what?" asked Izzy.

A callous sneer formed as Agent Conway tried to control her sentiments. "Like, your job."

Izzy locked eyes with Edgar as they both realized the rumors which had been floating around office for weeks were indeed true. Everyone at the Bureau had brushed off the gossip and attributed it to recent salary cuts and layoffs. The government had a way of creating background noise when needing to justify the means to an end, and this time, it had seamlessly succeeded in ending it all for the FBI and its staff.

"I don't believe you," retorted Izzy.

Agent Conway pulled up a hologram on her CompWatch and spun it around in Edgar's boss's direction. It was a secret directive issued by Congress outlining plans to transfer all control of the FBI over to BIG by the end of the year.

Izzy read every word, slowly allowing her legal expertise to carefully decipher its significance. As her lips moved in conjunction with the words on the screen, a look of concern crystalized on her forehead. Even though these wrinkles were jagged and broken, they clearly conveyed a message: Her world was changing while the rest of the world remained oblivious to the consequences.

She sighed and asked, "Where are you taking him?"

"To the van, for now. After interviewing Mr. Tutaloo, we'll take them both to Ontario."

As the agent moved in to escort Edgar, Izzy intervened. "No handcuffs. He'll go willingly."

"Agent Gorman?" questioned Agent Terabush.

He nodded.

The elevator door opened and Toyer Wittler, still wearing his shorts and Hawaiian shirt, marched over toward them with two other agents dressed in black from head to toe. Toyer had an ice pack wrapped over one of his ears.

"There he is," he yelled.

Edgar glanced up and whispered to Izzy, "Shit."

Toyer noticed the other two agents as he and his entourage moved in. "Miranda, what are you doing here?"

"I could say the same to you, little brother."

"I knew it," exclaimed Edgar under his breath.

Toyer placed both hands on his hips and asked, "Where are they?"

"Where's what?"

Toyer turned to the two other men and said, "Search him."

Izzy jumped in front and growled, "There will be no searches done on these premises without a warrant." With a smug smile, Toyer switched apps on his CompWatch and swiped. A chime dinged on both Edgar's and Izzy's watches. As Izzy brought up the file and read the warrant, she sighed, "Looks legit." Then she stood aside. Edgar removed a pair of white sunglasses from his coat pocket and handed them over.

Izzy looked on in disbelief as she discreetly felt the outside of her jacket. The pair she'd taken from Edgar a few minutes earlier was still there. One of the men in black handed the glasses to Toyer. He placed them in a bag and lifted the ice pack back up to his ear. "You do know it's illegal to possess this device. Only authorized personnel are allowed to operate them."

"Then how'd you get them?"

"Very funny." Toyer glanced at Miranda before remarking, "This must be your lucky day, Agent Gorman. Two offenses within hours of each other." His fingers dribbled across his CompWatch as he said, "This one will hurt."

Edgar's watch dinged, "Your Demeanor Score has been reduced by 100 points."

"What the hell, Toyer?"

"All within MAGMA guidelines." He aimed his next comment at Izzy and said, "He must make the Bureau very proud."

"Careful now, little man. I'd advise you to keep your words soft and sweet. You never know when you might end up eating them."

"I doubt that," snorted Toyer. "Why are you even still here? Didn't my sister tell you the good news?"

"That's enough, little brother." Agent Conway motioned to Agent Terabush and ordered, "Take him to the van and meet me back here to conduct the interview." He nodded, grabbed Edgar's arm, and walked away. Then she grimaced and asked her brother, "What are you wearing?"

"I was undercover," replied Toyer.

"Are you still undercover?"

"Well, uh, no, of course not."

"Well, then you need to get back into uniform. BIG needs to lead by example, not with shoddy appearances." With a curt nod she added, "Right, Agent Moreno?"

Izzy watched her colleague and good friend heading to the elevator and resisted the temptation to wave as the door shut behind him. Without answering the question, she asked, "Are we done here?"

Agent Miranda acquiesced.

A few minutes later, Agent Terabush joined his partner in the Interrogation Room. Agent Conway sat down in front of Ketchum while her partner stood to the side. She placed a recording device with a camera on the table, turned it on, and then firmly folded her fingers together. "I'm Agent Conway from the Forest Dunes Corporation. Are you Ketchum Tutaloo?"

In a voice slightly above a whisper, Ketchum said, "Yes."

"For the record, let it be stated that the suspect is indeed Ketchum Tutaloo of Summerfield, California." She pulled up a screen from the device and continued, "It says here that this morning at 4:00 AM, you entered into Zero Sum Conclusion. Is that correct?"

"That's what I'm told."

"It also states in the Millionaire Agreement you signed at the bank that, at any time, if you are overdrawn in your account, for any reason, you are to be given a prompt digital hearing to determine your status. If found delinquent, you are to be sent to the Forest Dunes facilities immediately. Are you aware of this?"

"I did read something about it in a brochure," replied Ketchum.

Agent Conway signaled to her colleague who pulled out another notepad and set it on the table. He scrolled a few times on the screen and a hologram of an android human robot sitting behind a bench materialized in the notepad. "This is presiding SSI federal judge, Mark Lanyard, of the Central Court District of California. Please state your business."

Agent Terabush replied, "Your honor, I have before you federal case number 382563 between the Dunes Corporation and Ketchum Tutaloo, also known as Cole Mattock, in B.W. times. At 4:00 AM on June 19th, 2068, the defendant entered into a state of Zero Sum Conclusion."

The judge seemed to be studying a screen in front of him and reading the brief. A few seconds later, he said, "I see that the defendant is eighteen years of age and has been in possession of this money for over twenty-four hours. Is that correct, Mr. Tutaloo?"

Ketchum cleared his throat and replied, "Yes, it is, your honor, but I have no idea how…"

"… Please just answer the questions," interrupted the digital judge. "I also see a document you signed at the bank stating that you agreed to all of the terms in the Millionaire Fund Disbursement Agreement. Is that true?"

This time, Ketchum hesitated. He wasn't sure what to do. From the looks of things, this hearing was just a formality to an already predetermined conclusion. He wasn't going to be given a chance to speak and definitely wouldn't receive any kind of empathetic embrace from this polished assortment of computer chips. An idea came to him, "Your honor, I request that I be provided with a defense attorney, sir, as soon as possible, if you please."

Judge Lanyard looked up from the paper in his hands, set it down, and replied with a mechanical timbre, "Son, it states clearly in the Millionaire Fund Disbursement Agreement that you've waived all rights to any legal representation, including an attorney. Did you not read your agreement?"

Ketchum bowed his head and replied, "Not really."

"Therefore, I must…"

"... Wait," he shouted. "The girl who stole my money. She tricked me. Can't we get her in here for a statement or something, you know, as evidence?"

"What girl would that be and how did she trick you?" asked the judge.

Ketchum found himself out of breath. His nerves were shot so he tried to relax and respond. "April, April Jones. There's got to be footage of her at the bank with me."

Agent Conway thumbed through the notepad and said, "We do have footage from the bank as evidence." She rewound the video back to the incident and stopped it on a frame taken by a security camera of April's face. She lifted the image off the notepad and asked, "Is this the person you're referring to?"

"Yes, that's her. April Jones."

The Dunes agent turned to the judge and asked, "Your honor, may we do a background check on the potential witness in question?"

"Approval granted."

Agent Conway dragged the snapshot of April's face over to another folder marked "Federal Database." The screen came to life with a set of photos revolving and looping in a circle. Everyone waited. A flicker of optimism emerged on Ketchum's face, as this was the best news he'd received all day. Within seconds, a window popped open with April's photograph and the following data:

Name: April Suzanna Jones
Born: April 13, 2049
City: Port Orford, Oregon
Died: October 11, 2067

Ketchum could not believe his eyes. He stared at the screen, then to both agents, and finally to the black-robed humanoid waiting stoically on the screen. "Wait, that can't be right. You just saw her on the video. How could she have died? Run it again, please."

Judge Lanyard flinched, as if to have been woken from sleep mode. "I see the data is in. Your witness is deceased, therefore cannot testify on your behalf. The evidence is inadmissible." His image shifted in tiny digital increments toward Ketchum's voice. "Ketchum Tutaloo, this court finds you guilty of Zero Sum Conclusion. As stated in the Revised Constitution of 2033, Article 13, Section 4, you are to be escorted to the Ontario docking station. There you will be processed and transported to the Dunes Gila Bend Facility in Phoenix, Arizona, for rehabilitation." He slammed the gavel and concluded with, "Case is closed."

The screen went black.

Agent Conway stood up and nodded to her partner. "I'm sorry, Mr. Tutaloo, but there's nothing that can be done. Please come with us."

Ketchum didn't move. He couldn't move. Every bone in his body rejected his new reality and made him unsure on what to do next. "This doesn't make sense. It's got to be a mistake," he pleaded.

"The Forest Dunes Corporation doesn't make mistakes, Mr. Tutaloo."

CHAPTER SIXTEEN

MIXED-UP GOOFY OLD WORLD

ON THE RIDE TO ONTARIO, hardly a word was spoken between Edgar and Ketchum. They were two random people, who'd never met before, that'd been plucked out of obscurity and tossed together like a salad of mixed greens. Edgar had relived Ketchum's last few months as if it were his own, but Ketchum felt a connection too. Their circuits were communicating in parallel, not series. Instead of just being on the outside looking in, Edgar felt like his ultimate outcome was somehow linked to this boy.

He studied his newly acquired partner through a different lens now. Ketchum's dark hair and slender build reminded him of Lotty. In another dimension or set of circumstances, Ketchum could've been his brother. Even more bizarre was the realization that this boy could've been the son he'd never had. This admission made him uneasy at first, considering the path he and Evelyn had chosen, but as he watched the boy run his hands through his hair with his head between his legs, a warm sensation of unfounded fondness came over him.

His emotional connection to both Ketchum and April made no sense and he fought the urge to accept it. Nevertheless, it was already under his skin, it was already part of his memory in some subconscious state that couldn't be erased. He felt the boy's pain, he felt the love between them both, he even felt April's struggles.

These newly discovered sensations were invigorating, but also dangerous. He wondered what else these DDO glasses did to the brain. It'd only taken minutes for another person's life and experiences to permanently embed themselves in with his own history. They were now inseparable sparks of consciousness melded into solid lucid memories. He wondered if he would now dream Ketchum's dreams, anticipate his next move, or even feel his future aches.

The dark plastic sphere mounted in the top corner of the cab reminded him that every movement was being watched. Everything he said could be used against him so he had to choose his words wisely. If he was to explore this phenomenon further, it would have to be discreetly. His only worry was that Ketchum had already capitulated and felt there was nothing to lose. Still, he needed answers.

"Did you get to say goodbye to your family?"

Ketchum stared straight ahead, rocking with the sway of the road, alive but numb, breathing but not living. His thoughts traveled in a circle of confusion taking him back to that assembly all the way through this morning. Each stop along the way, he searched for signs that he'd missed, clues that would right this completely unfounded wrong. There were none.

Edgar repeated the question.

He heard him this time. The man's voice had become a soothing beacon of hope earlier that day. Now, it was just another voice. He debated whether to respond or not. What was the point? Still, he'd been raised to be polite, especially to his elders.

"They're out of town. My mom tried calling the State's Attorney directly for help, but there was no answer."

Edgar digested this morsel of news and said, "I'm sure she's still trying. We all are."

"I don't know. She said something about MAGMA knows best. That it'll all work out in the end."

The words rang hollow. He knew all too well what MAGMA was capable of and "knowing best" was not on that list. "Tell me about your family," he asked.

Ketchum debated whether he should engage or just ignore this aging agent. What good would it do him now? Yet, what was the harm? His mind wandered back to better times as he pondered this question.

"My mother's smile, I can still see it now. She has the greatest smile, soft and sweet. She's always been there for me. I mean, when I was younger, that is — not so much lately." He cleared his throat and continued, "I have a sister. She's a year younger, and pretty annoying, but growing up she had the funniest whistle when she talked." He grinned and shook his head before adding, "I don't know, it had something to do with her teeth or tongue or something. The doctors finally fixed it but I sure do miss it." His head swayed with the rhythm of the van as he wondered. "I think she did too."

His voice dropped in pitch with the next few words. "Then there's my dad." After a long pause, all he could muster to say was, "He taught me how to play guitar." Memories of his father flowed by like airplane lights blinking in the clouds: a bit foggy and silent. What he remembered of those early days were just blurred visions now, replaced with snapshots of his dad reading travel brochures and planning trips. His parents were on a mission to see everything and enjoy everyone they'd known for as long as possible, or until their money ran out. Yet, how could he blame them? "My dad, is, how should I say, a busy man."

"Hold onto those memories, kid. No matter how mundane or meaningless they might seem. At least you have them."

"What do you mean?

"I never got to meet my father. He died before I was born. No memories at all, just a few photographs."

"April never met her father either. She was adopted. At least, that's what she told me."

Edgar could feel the pain in Ketchum's voice with those last few words. Even more, he felt the pain in his own heart. These newfound emotions were troubling and somewhat overwhelming.

It was as if he had no control over them or the consequences they presented. There was no way to separate their worlds any longer. An unexpected side effect, or curse, depending on how you looked at it. He tried his best to suppress the anguish it conjured up.

Ketchum did like this man's spirit. He'd been nothing but kind to him. At that moment, he realized that he wasn't even sure why Edgar was there in the first place. "So, why are you here? Are you escorting me to the station, and making sure I don't do anything stupid, again?"

A fragile grin emerged as Edgar contemplated an answer. Somewhere in a room deep inside a mountain or underground secure bunker was a pair of eyes watching and ears listening. "I'm not sure why I'm here. Unfortunately, I don't think my situation is much different from yours. We'll see."

The van slowed down and turned into a parking lot located in an industrial complex. The wheels squealed as it inched up to the gate and addressed the monitor. "Agents Conway and Terabush here to deliver the two detainees."

The gate opened and the van continued around to the back and entered a large building as a set of doors lowered behind it. Then the two jumped out and walked to the rear of the vehicle. Agent Conway opened it and pointed to Ketchum. "You, go with him to the train station."

Ketchum jumped down as Agent Terabush led him away from the light and into another van. Then she turned to Edgar and said, "I don't know what you did to land in this godforsaken place, but you've made my job so much easier."

"What job is that?" asked Edgar.

"Why, your job, of course. Although I'm still in consideration for Agent Moreno's position too. We'll see what happens over the next few weeks."

"So it's really official."

"It's official. The Federal Bureau of Investigation is no longer, and will now be known as Bureau of Intelligence Gathering, or BIG." Then with a flagrant flair of superiority she added, "You can count on that."

Edgar did everything he could not to react. This woman was jabbing him with verbal punches and pokes so much that he could feel the mental bruises all over his body. "You know, Miranda, or big sis, or whatever Toyer calls you, you can occupy my physical space and title, but that doesn't mean you'll ever replace me. BIG can't just step in and garner the respect the FBI has held for centuries."

"Sure we can. In a few months, the initials "FBI" will be forever "MIA" in the minds of most Americans."

Edgar shuffled off the hardened bench and stepped down from the bumper of the truck. He was almost afraid to pry any deeper into this subject but it was in his DNA to ask more questions. "How's that?"

"How's that? If you don't know by now, especially in your line of work, then we've already succeeded." Agent Conway placed a set of handcuffs on Edgar's wrists and leaned in. "In a few months, the bureau you once knew will be just a faint memory, wiped clean from the Intranet, you know, something to be forgotten and never again cherished — kind of like your wife."

In a flash, Edgar reached for Agent Conway's throat. With both hands clutched firmly around her neck, he growled, "Don't ever say anything about my wife again."

A circus tent full of red lights flashed above as Dunes guards rushed in from all directions with their guns drawn. Edgar released his grip as Agent Conway rubbed her neck. With a satisfying sneer, she said, "Thank you for that. You've again made my job even easier." She glanced at the guard and ordered, "Put him in a straitjacket and take him away. He's obviously showing more psychopathic traits and needs to be medicated immediately."

THE PHISH POND

THE TALL MAN IN WHITE paused the large screen in front of him on Edgar's image. Then he zoomed in on his face and said to the short man, "Rick, the heat sensors are rising. We should've predicted another uncontrollable social disintegration. Just look at his metrics: the engagement rates, impressions, monetary value readings are all negative. His Zero Sum acceleration rate is off the charts too."

"Recalibrate the algorithm to Level 5. Let's start a medication regime of Carbamazepine and Lithium to see if we can mitigate his behavior."

The tall man shifted focus to another monitor, pushed a button, and said, "Good work, Agent Conway, or should I say, Director Conway. I guess it's still a little premature. The detainee can now be admitted as a patient and we'll take it from here."

Agent Conway looked up at a camera in the corner of the hangar and winked. "Thank you, Roger."

CHAPTER SEVENTEEN

IN THE MIDDLE OF TURMOIL COMES...

IZZY WOKE UP AROUND 6:30 the next morning. She slid off the bed and lumbered into the bathroom. Then her CompWatch rang. With a yawn, she answered, "Agent Moreno here."

"Boss, there's been a development in the Dunes case connected to that boy and the two agents from yesterday. I thought you might be interested. The woman they captured a while back escaped last night. Apparently, she slipped out of the sensory handcuffs and shut down the defense perimeter in her cell. None of the alarms were tripped so she walked right out of the building undetected."

"Really. Who was guarding her?"

"The Dunes agents, at one of their facilities."

"Well, that won't look good in their new branding campaign."

"No, indeed. The report says they only had one guard on duty after midnight and then one at the gate. New protocol, I'm told. They're reviewing security camera footage right now."

"The high costs of cutting corners. These companies will never learn. Has the report been circulated to other agencies yet?"

"No, we're still in charge, at the moment."

There was a long pause as Izzy contemplated her next move. She was weeks away from retirement so there wasn't much they could do to her jobwise. Yet she knew the government had other ways of making one's life miserable.

"Sit tight and do nothing. I'll get back to you."

"Ma'am?"

"You heard me."

"Understood."

Izzy found herself standing in the living room after hanging up the phone. She'd unknowingly wandered through the whole house while talking. As she returned to the bedroom, she stopped and admired a painting on the wall in the hallway that Edgar had given her years ago. There was something about its connection to the past that she loved.

Most paintings these days were digital pigments captured in holograms, either sold to the highest bidder or rented on the open market. This painting was different. For one, it was oil on canvas, a time-consuming process rarely used in the art world today. She noticed that the colors didn't vary much: lots of shades of orange, green and blue.

It was Edgar's interpretation of Seurat's masterpiece, *Sunday Afternoon On The Island of La Grande Jatte*, with one uncanny difference: the setting was a nudist colony. Each naked body was proudly displayed in full detail, with no more than an umbrella or hat in their possession. Her gaze turned into a smile as she imagined Edgar in a makeshift studio at home applying vivid brushstrokes and singing off key. He'd never been able to carry a tune. It was something that drove him crazy when they were in the car together with the radio on, but in a good way.

She moved into the kitchen and flipped on the TV. While waiting for breakfast to print in the 3D microwave, she turned up the volume. "*Unemployment remains at an all-time low as the number of millionaires continues to climb. The Treasury Department reported a thirteen percent increase in revenue over last quarter...*"

Izzy grabbed breakfast and a briefcase out of the closet. "Moreno Castle, transition into Daytime Mode, please," she instructed as she closed the door behind her.

A half block away from the destination, she parked her car. No matter how hard they tried to disguise them, federally issued automobiles stood out wherever they went. If she had any hope of making contact with someone on the side street, she had to proceed with the element of surprise.

As she shut the door and walked down the main boulevard, a white limousine slowly cruised by with two people hanging out of the sunroof. Hip-hop music blared from the grill as the passengers shouted at the top of their lungs, "*Greedness greaty, millionaire baby, greedness greaty, gonna make more...*" The magnetic logo on the side of the door read: "How to Make a Million Dollars Last" by Dylan MacMillan." She shook her head and continued to the next block.

At the corner, she pulled out the pair of DDO glasses from her pocket that she'd taken from Edgar the day before. Yesterday, when he'd handed Toyer another white pair, she nearly choked on her own disbelief. *Clever boy*, she thought, *I taught you well.*

She placed them on her face and commanded, "Engage." Within seconds, the layout of the building came into view on the lens. It was an abandoned apartment complex on a dead-end street that the escapee had lived in before getting married. In fact, it was the only other residence she'd known her whole life besides the Summerfield address. The chances of her going back there were pretty good.

"Scan for images," she said as she took a few more steps forward. The building glowed with infrared shapes on her screen. "That's odd," she whispered. "Apparently, it's not as abandoned as we thought."

A skinny older man sat on the steps in front vaping on a cigarette. The building stretched from the alley to the end of the street. Izzy sauntered up and cleared her throat. The man glanced at a broken out window on the second floor of the building, then said, "May I help you?"

Izzy sensed the eyes upon her but kept her head down. From

the data pouring in through the DDO glasses, she could tell that most of the suspects were women and children with no firearms drawn. A thick layer of dust and smog smothered the stucco exterior of the building. Only a few blotches of the original paint under the gutters were left unscathed. The smell of burning wood drifted by from a third-story window.

She flashed her badge, double-tapped on her forearm, and a hologram opened. After a couple of swipes, an image developed. She turned it toward the man and asked, "Have you seen this woman? She goes by the name of Alby McMurray or maybe Libby Rimbaru."

The man took a good look at Izzy and studied her face. Then, in a Southern drawl, lifted right out of the first Civil War, he said, "I remember you. It must've been a good twenty-five years ago when you busted me."

Izzy took a quick step back, a knee-jerk reaction when sensing danger. "I don't remember."

"Of course you don't. Maybe you remember the date, Fourth of July, back in 2042. I was part of a roundup down at the pier. Vagrancy, I believe was the charge, back when it was still a misdemeanor."

Izzy nodded as her glasses digested this information and loaded images from that day. A video of man being handcuffed by a much younger-looking agent played in the corner of her lens. "I was just a field officer back then, working with the local police. Green as a dollar bill, my friend. I'm surprised you remember me."

"Oh, I remember all those kinds of moments." He spit something silky into the bushes and smiled wide, showing a mouthful of missing teeth. "That one sent me off to Dunes for the first time. What a fun trip that was. How could I forget? I even got this lovely tattoo as a souvenir to remember it by." He stretched out his arm, revealing three black Zero Sum symbols inked into the skin. The sum sign, a two-way pointing arrow and numeric zero, were all too familiar to Izzy. She'd seen them a hundred times on suspects apprehended off the streets over the years. The bitterness dripping off the man's lips didn't go unnoticed.

Izzy stared straight into the man's eyes with as much sincerity as she could muster and said, "Sorry, that wasn't my intention. What's your name?"

"Clem. Clem Chotter."

"That's not a name, that's a side dish."

"Isn't that what I've been all my life? Gals like you are the main course, kiddo. I'm just a throwaway side dish that loses its luster after cooling."

"A tasty side dish, though," responded Izzy in an indulgent tone. "What was your real name, you know, B.W.?"

Clem chuckled and responded, "Matt Collier, ma'am. And yours?"

"Agent Moreno."

The old man appreciated the agent's candor. The sooner he was rid of her, the better off for everyone. "Let me see that photo again."

Izzy swiped on her watch and asked, "So, have you seen this woman?"

"Doesn't look familiar."

"Is that a yes, or no?"

"No."

She knew he was lying but, at this point, there wasn't much she could do without taking this interview up a notch and calling in backup. Suddenly, shadows moved on the second floor as heat sensors blinked in the corner of her lens. She did her best not to tip the man off but it wasn't good enough. Clem stood up and stretched his biceps, no doubt, signaling those out of sight of a possible situation. A squeaky door opened and echoed in the distance. It caught Izzy's attention. She watched for a reaction from Clem, but none came. Then the form of bodies came into focus on her glasses, running from the rear of the building toward the end of the road.

Izzy darted for the side wall and raced around the corner. When she entered the back yard, the shape of a man and women dashed by on the other end of the building. Following as fast as her feet would take her, she made it to the edge of the wall, stopped, and pulled out her revolver. "Give me the camera angle to the end of the street," she ordered the DDO glasses. While carefully peeking around the corner, she observed a woman's image entering a large sewer drain. From an aerial view streaming to her lenses, images of a drain running under old Highway 1 to the ocean materialized.

The man had fallen into a ditch and twisted his ankle. He was hobbling toward the drainpipe while dragging his left leg. Izzy tucked her pistol into the holster and sprinted around the corner. Right as the man was about to enter the sewer pipe, she tackled him to the ground. They both rolled down the hillside a few feet before coming to a stop at the bottom of a ravine. She turned him on his back and sat on the man's chest while holding his shoulders down with her hands.

The man was a frail-looking creature with thinning hair and dark black skin. A shadow of fear covered his face, with eyes reflecting back a lifetime of hollowed-out promises and shortcomings. She loosened her grip after feeling his collarbone beneath a layer of weathered skin. This man was no threat to anyone, as far as she could tell. Footsteps echoed down the tunnel so she reached for her handcuffs and spun the man onto his stomach.

Then the man began reciting a haunting phrase that made Izzy cringe. "*Greedness greaty, going crazy. Greedness greaty, one, two, three, four...*" She tried turning him over on his back but he resisted with all his might. As he delivered those fatal last words, drippings of death rushed through his veins, "... *five, six, switch.*"

Izzy watched in horror as the man's eye sockets rolled back into a kill position, leaving behind the whiteness of his soul in their place. The man gurgled up a few gasps in between short spurts of air before his body stiffened. The retinas of his eyes returned, staring at Izzy and silently screaming. She jumped up to her feet and backed away. A few seconds later, he was completely still.

She placed her fingers on his neck to check for a pulse, but there was none. It was a sight she'd witnessed before but had never gotten used to. The tumblers in her head churned as she recalled the chant when she heard a splash echoing down the tunnel.

The old drain wasn't quite tall enough for her to run through it upright, so she leaned over with her gun in position and skirted ahead. When she came out on the other side, her eyes swiftly assessed the surroundings while adjusting to the light. There was no movement anywhere. Carefully, she walked over to the edge of a concrete slab jutting out over the ocean. She waited for a head to rise to the surface but it never came. She continued waiting, counting the seconds: one minute, two minutes. No one could stay under water that long. After a few more minutes, she paced up and down the shoreline searching for any signs of a head or body. There were none.

How could this woman just vanish like that, she wondered?

"Play back any facial recognition or movement from this spot over the past five minutes," she commanded. The DDO glasses accumulated several different feeds from above and one from a cargo ship miles off the coast. The images were grainy due to a light fog floating across the harbor. On the lenses, she saw a woman exiting the tunnel and running toward the ocean. Then she was gone.

Once again, she ordered, "Run that sequence back." The glasses replayed the video and she watched the woman exit the tunnel. Then, as soon as the woman made it to the edge of the concrete, the screen turned white. "What the hell? Switch to satellite mode."

The video replayed the same sequence from an aerial view. Izzy adjusted the feed and zoomed when a message flashed in front of her eyes, "No confirmed identities."

Izzy cursed and demanded, "Recalibrate."

The lenses blinked back the message, "Error loading."

She ripped the glasses off her head and growled, "Prototype piece of shit." Then she surveyed the horizon. The morning fog was burning away in spots as the sun now beamed down in slivers onto the shoreline. Her gaze moved along the coast but all she could see were a dozen or so offshore oil rig platforms in the distance. Beyond that, a few smokestack flames burning away excess methane from deep in the ground.

Lurking near the tip of the jetty was a yellow-colored buoy. A large tag bobbed on top of the water reading "Gooble." No doubt, it marked a series of supercomputers being cooled at the bottom of the ocean floor below. She wondered for a second if the woman could've swum down and possibly found an air chamber hidden around the steel housing. Then she realized it was way too far away and too deep.

She returned to the edge of the concrete at the tunnel exit and examined the wall below. As the waves crashed against the platform, rising and lowering ever so slightly, she caught a glimpse of an opening. There'd been rumors floating around about rogue settlements living under washed-out bridges and coverts throughout the coastline but didn't think they were real. Now she knew better.

With a shrug and a sigh, she walked back through the tunnel to the other end. The corpse of the man was where she left it so she walked down the hill to identify the body in hopes that it would provide some clues as to what was going on. She positioned the glasses back on her head and pressed a button on top of the frame. "Photo recognition software, analyze and report."

A snapshot of the deceased man appeared on her lens and a set of photos slid across a screen. One by one, the software categorized facial features and searched the database with lightning speed. A few seconds later, it stopped on a picture that barely resembled the man. The subject looked years younger with a full head of hair. A smile stretched across his face showing a set of pearly whites fully intact.

Below his chin, the words "Possible Match. Fingerprint Verification Warranted" flashed in red letters. Izzy knelt down and lifted the man's hand off the ground. She brushed away the dirt and used his palm and fingers for processing. The DDO glasses clicked a photo and chimed. The words "Identity Confirmed" popped up underneath the picture from their database.

The file read:

Name:	Michael Trahan
Born:	December 20, 2033
City:	Los Angeles, California
Status:	Front-Loader
SSI:	Seventy-six hundred dollars

She pressed the button on top of the frames and asked, "Employment record." The screen rolled down and displayed:

Occupation:	Systems Analyst
Employer:	None
Last Employer:	Dill Electronics (terminated)
Year:	2057-2066
Reason:	Low Demeanor Score – Rehabilitation

completed at Dunes Nevada facility in 2067 and a score threshold of 500 points reinstated.

Izzy struggled to understand what she was viewing on the screen. It didn't even come close to resembling what she witnessed on the ground. The system said he was thirty-five years old, but the corpse told another story. Draped in gray hair and weathered skin, the ragged-looking man appeared to be closer to sixty in age. She also wondered what could've happened to this young man with such a promising career that caused his Demeanor Score to drop so quickly. That was never a good sign.

CHAPTER EIGHTEEN

THE THRESHOLD OF ENGAGEMENT

IZZY RUBBED THE BACK OF HER NECK as the stiffened muscles throbbed for attention. Leaning over in the tunnel had triggered a familiar reaction of pain and discomfort, courtesy of old age. Retirement couldn't come soon enough. As she peered over at the apartment building, a child peeked out of a second story window. A part of her knew it was dangerous going in alone, but another part knew it was her best shot at finding any clues to what was really happening there.

When she made her way to the front of the building, the old man was back sitting on the steps vaping. Izzy decided it was time to twist a few arms. She walked over to Clem and with a gentle but firm voice said, "I need some answers."

"I wish I had them."

She removed the glasses, sat down next to the man while staring straight ahead, and with an indifferent wave of her hand said, "We can either do this the easy way where you take me upstairs and I ask your friends a few questions , or I call in a SWAT team and let them go in guns a-blazing. You decide."

Clem turned off the vape pen and exhaled. "You make a persuasive argument. Come with me." Then he stood up and walked toward the front door. About a half dozen steps in, he glanced back and called out, "You coming?"

Izzy peered into the old man's eyes; they were narrow but deep green, the color of life. Then she put the glasses back on and followed. At the top of the stairs, the hallways going both ways were long and dark. Clem turned left and dragged his frayed tennis shoes down to the end.

Izzy rested her right hand on the handle of her pistol and carefully made her way behind him. While searching the area from left to right for any movement or noise, she tried to anticipate the next scenario. Many came to mind, but none of them looked promising.

At the end of the hallway, Clem opened a door. Izzy expected a shower of sunlight to spill out but instead there was nothing. Complete darkness inhabited the room. The old man ambled in and faded to black. Izzy drew out her gun and stopped near the edge of the door with her back against the wall. "FBI. No sudden movements and show me some daylight."

A window blind spun in circles as sunlight brightened the room and hallway. Clem called out from the window area, "It's cool. Come on in."

In the corner of the room were about a dozen people standing or sitting on pillows. Several boxes lined the walls with plastic bags jammed full of clothes and utensils tossed on top. The stench of stale air whirled around as Izzy moved to the center of the room. She did a full sweep of every corner before lowering her weapon.

"What is this?" she asked.

"This is my family," replied Clem.

She scrutinized each face: black, white, brown, male, female, old and young. "A pretty diverse family indeed. Are they all Zero Sums?"

"No," answered Clem. "Check 'em out."

Izzy tapped the top of her CompWatch until it displayed a scanner. She swished an animated dial a few times until a camera lens emerged on her glasses. Then she pointed it at the first person and said, "Eyes wide open." A small flash of light filled the person's face, making them blink incessantly. "Front-Loader at seven thousand, six hundred." She moved to the next person and flashed the camera again. "Front-Loader at seven thousand, six hundred." Then, onto the next, "Seven thousand, six hundred."

With a rigid brow, she turned to Clem and asked, "They're all just above the threshold. How'd you do it?"

"Threshold of what?"

"Don't be coy with me. You know what I'm talking about. The Threshold of Engagement — TOE. The point where MAGMA dips their toes into your business."

"You're implying we somehow manipulate the system, Agent Moreno. That's illegal." Clem firmly stood his ground as the sunlight gleamed across his face. They stared at each other long enough to acknowledge an understanding between them. She wasn't there to arrest anyone for being penniless. She was there to catch an escapee and ask questions.

Clem glanced over near the doorway where two women stood with their backs against the wall. They looked ready to bolt at any minute but his eyes reassured them that everything would be fine. Izzy noticed too and nonchalantly moved around the room, studying each person while making her way toward them. Yeah, they were all destitute and homeless, for sure, but they weren't broken.

She stopped in front of the two women next to the door and said, "You two look familiar."

"We get that a lot," replied Delores as she glanced at her daughter.

She couldn't quite place where she'd seen them and asked, "I see. Where are you from?"

"Old Oregon. We're down here visiting friends." Delores smiled at Clem and added, "We used to be neighbors."

Izzy turned to April. She resembled a photo in Ketchum's file but couldn't be certain. She said, "Please open your eyes."

Delores massaged April's shoulder and interjected, "She's a bit hard of hearing. Make sure she reads your lips or talk louder."

Izzy nodded and mouthed the words with the elegance of a fish breathing underwater. "Please open your eyes wide."

Delores shook her head and added, "You can talk normally, just not too fast."

"Sorry." She turned to April and repeated, "Please open your eyes wide." April acquiesced while Agent Moreno shined the reader into her face and watched the screen.

Name:	Alice Marie Johnson
Born:	June 13, 2050
City:	Port Orford, Oregon
Status:	Front-Loader
SSI:	Seventy-six hundred dollars

"Amazing," she exclaimed. "Clem, I'm impressed." She sensed an unflagging camaraderie amongst the group that caused her to reflect on her own life. Of course, there was a bond between her and other agents. Anytime the balance between living and dying lies in your partner's hands, you're going to form a special bond. Still, this felt different, more organic.

A ring chimed on her CompWatch, sending a message to the screen from headquarters. "They're coming," was all it said. Izzy knew what that meant.

She turned to Clem and said, "We have company. I suggest that anyone who shouldn't be here leave now." Everyone picked up their belongings and shuffled out the door. The swiftness with which they moved told her they'd been through this drill before. Within seconds, the room emptied except for Izzy and Clem.

The old man walked over to Izzy and shook her hand. "I hope you find what you're looking for, Agent Moreno. I appreciate you letting us go. It's not easy these days for people like us."

Izzy didn't need to ask why. She already knew the answer. In this situation, there wasn't time to carry on a philosophical conversation about why or how or even explore the options. Time had run out. Clem reached into his pocket to pull out his vape pen when a card fell on the floor. Before he could pick it up, Izzy had beat him to the punch. She stood back up and read it. On one side it said, "Mama Cravens' Café," with no address or phone number listed. She flipped the card over and found a series of words followed by numbers and symbols handwritten in ink.

This twentieth century form of communication mesmerized her as she studied it from back to front and back again. It was a relic in its own right. The only people who used business cards these days were either from an older generation or those who wanted to keep its information secret. She kept concentrating on the words and symbols as she asked, "Where'd you get this?"

"I don't know, just picked it up somewhere."

Clem started to gather his belongings off the floor when Izzy firmly grabbed his arm and stopped him. "No, I mean it. Who gave you this card?"

The exchange had suddenly taken on a very somber tone as Clem sensed that Izzy wasn't going to let him leave without answers. The faint sirens in the distance now felt just around the corner. Clem fought the urge to make direct eye contact but Izzy wouldn't let him escape her gaze. Finally, he relented. "The girl. The one you were looking for."

"Do you know her name?"

"She goes by Alby McMurray these days."

"Do you know where's she's going?"

"I don't know."

Izzy wasn't sure what to say. She knew of this café but only in a very clandestine context. Never had she met someone randomly off the streets who also knew about it. She nodded and said, "Your loyalty to your peers is very commendable but it's probably going to land you back at a Forest Dunes facility for the rest of your life." She glanced out the window and added, "You don't have time to get away. Let me take you in myself and see if we can prevent that from happening. Besides, I have a few more questions for you about this card."

Red and blue lights were now flickering off the walls while car doors slammed out on the street. Clem nodded and said, "It's a deal."

❧❧❧

Outside, Delores and April had already jumped into their van and taken off down the street. They ran the light on the corner and turned right. At the next light, a couple of patrol cars and an unmarked black sedan raced through the intersection with their sirens flashing. The two stared straight ahead until they'd passed by. Delores gazed into her side mirror and said, "Coast is clear." They both let out a sigh of relief.

"Can I have my hearing aid back now, Delores?" growled April.

Delores unlocked the glove box and retrieved it. "Don't take that tone with me, young lady. I've gotten us this far so how about a little gratitude."

Gratitude indeed, thought April. She studied Delores's face as she drove through the changing light and occasionally glanced at her side mirror. The years had been unkind to her complexion. She still remembered the day her stepmother picked her up at the private orphanage in Port Orford. With a cigarette in one hand and her belongings in the other, Delores ordered her into the van. She'd been barking orders ever since.

April was one of the lucky ones, they told her. Most children at her age had very little chance at adoption. Orphanages were running over with unwanted babies and getting limited assistance from the government. All the non-profit agencies had dissolved long ago and were converted into private housing units for discarded children. They received very generous stipends for housing kids up to the age of twelve. After that, the money phased out and most organizations either gave potential parents hefty financial incentives to adopt or just put the children to work. At first, April was grateful. She'd been saved from a life of servitude and hard labor, but when Delores realized that taking away her hearing aid was comparable to putting April in chains, the gratefulness turned into resentment.

As the van turned the corner, something in the back rattled around. April turned around to investigate. Everything she owned in the world was stacked up against the rear in a makeshift vagabond dresser composed of cardboard boxes and garbage bags. Her life had been reduced to a few square feet full of bad memories and misery.

She wondered where she'd be today if she'd stayed in Old Oregon. Probably living on the streets or shipped off to Dunes by now, maybe even dead. Very few orphaned children ever saw a dime of their million dollars when they turned eighteen. That's because very few of them lived past that age, and the benefactor was always the guardian. You either moved on quietly or were silenced completely. There was a saying she'd heard many times back in the chilly unlit corners of her dormitory late at night; "Orphans are born naked and hungry, then things get worse."

Delores saw something in that skinny twelve-year-old back on the playground at the Port Orford Mission of Hope. A grifter can spot another grifter in an instant and April had potential. She was a bloodhound when it came to weeding out the truth from bullshit. She could spot a false narrative before a person even finished their first sentence. The tone of voice, a person's body language, or a quirky facial expression was all she needed to figure out what she was dealing with. That's what made her so valuable to keep around.

They'd managed to stay one step ahead of the inevitable these last several months by turning a few tricks here and there scamming unsuspecting newbies out of their millions — and all the while keeping a small legion of co-dependents off the Zero Sum List and out of trouble. These weren't any normal bunch of co-dependents, though. No, they were all interconnected in some way through that abandoned apartment building.

In an earlier time, they'd been neighbors all living the California dream and ready to take on the world; transplants from around the country hoping for a shot at fame and fortune. But fate had another destiny for them. Whether it was an unexpected sickness in the family, a job that never panned out, or a deal gone wrong, any way you sliced it, they were all living barely below the radar and thankful for it. They knew if they stuck together as a team, they'd be stronger than on their own.

When Delores stopped at the next red light, an unmarked sedan coming from the opposite direction crossed the center dividing line and skidded into the middle of the intersection. Two agents jumped out of the car with their guns drawn and pointed at the van. A loudspeaker belched, "Please come out of the car slowly with your hands in the air."

Delores turned to her daughter and sighed, "This isn't good." April wiggled her finger around in her other ear as the words eluded her.

They both exited the van with their hands up and leaned against the vehicle. One policeman asked for their IDs while the other kept one hand on his holster. Delores glanced at April and mouthed the word "Smith."

April began to reach into her coat pocket but then hesitated. The tumblers in her brain quickly assessed the situation, stopped, and started going in the opposite direction. Would she ever have another opportunity like this to make a clean break? Could she actually go through with it?

Delores sensed that something was wrong. April's motions weren't smooth and orchestrated like they'd practiced. Her daughter had called an audible and was ignoring the playbook. She pulled her ID out of her jacket pocket and said, "Here you go, officer." Then she turned to April and asked, "April, honey, give him yours."

The officer inspected Delores's fake ID and then addressed her daughter. "Young lady, do you have any identification?"

A moral tug of war ensued as April's eyes darted from her adopted mother to the officer and back. She wiped the perspiration off her forehead and exhaled deeply. "Yeah, it's in the car."

Delores opened her mouth but caught herself mid-syllable. "Hon..." April had already started walking toward the van. There was nothing she could say at this point.

April opened the door, reached under the seat, and removed a thin wallet secretly secured against the frame. The second officer followed close behind and watched her every move. When she pulled out several driver's licenses from the wallet and fumbled through them, the officer said, "Ma'am, I'll take them, all of them."

"Here," said April as she handed him the wallet and pointed. "These are the real ones."

THE PHISH POND

BACK IN ONTARIO, Edgar had been carted into a small room a mile away from the train station for interrogation. The lights overhead were exceptionally bright and hateful. The walls reeked of a sterile whiteness so clean that sound waves hesitated to breathe. It made a person want to ask permission to exist.

He'd been strapped to a stool so tall that his shoes barely touched the ground. That was no small feat for a person of his height. His eyes opened for the first time in hours as he spun around on his tiptoes trying to regain a sense of balance. The drugs they'd given him earlier were wearing off.

His mind raced from one thought to another as images flashed by like a deck of cards being dealt by a faceless dealer. Memories pivoted and flipped through his conscious with little meaning or recourse until, finally, one vision of him and his wife planted itself firmly into view.

❧❧❧

It was a moment he'd suppressed whenever possible, as the mere thought of it made him uneasy. Evelyn was sitting on the couch in their living room, coughing hard and vomiting onto the floor. As the volume rose from her uncontrollable outburst, Edgar looked on like a helpless child, unable to stop the eruptions and unwilling to accept their implications.

"What do you want me to do?" he cried.

"My eyes," cried Evelyn, "they hurt. I can't breathe." She put out her arm so Edgar backed away and gave her space. Then she swallowed hard as her left eyelid drooped down over the cornea. Her voice quivered while she struggled to form her words. "I can't go on like this forever."

"I'm not asking for forever," he replied, "but now is way too soon."

"I know, I know," she whispered with a nod. Then she inhaled deeply and exhaled before lying down on the couch to rest, "but we need to make a plan."

Edgar watched in silence as the vision blurred and disappeared."

࿔࿔࿔

Back in the Phish Pond, a high-pitched squeal interrupted the moment as a man's voice, too indifferent to be threatening but firm in its delivery, cleared his throat and said, "Good morning, Mr. Gorman."

Edgar fought against the urge to close his eyes and drop his head while mumbling, "Many mutters for the mabsoot and greedness might macarize, but gawdelpus, a menticidal mistake has been made."

The voice in the wall replied, "I'm sorry, Mr. Gorman, I didn't quite understand that. Can you please repeat it?"

Again, Edgar grumbled, "I'd be mabsoot to mabble gut with more gyve and guff, but a menticidal mistake has been made."

Another man's thinly veiled voice reverberated in the background barely above a whisper. Then both men began talking loudly over each other until someone put their hand over the microphone, muffling it. Inside the observation room, the tall doctor said, "I don't care what the manual says, Rick. It could be an allergic reaction."

Rick threw his hands up in the air and replied, "What's it matter, Roger. We are going to note that seizure in our report and ask the questions we're supposed to."

In the other room, Edgar continued to ramble incoherently. They listened over the speaker until Roger said, "I'm going in."

He grabbed a briefcase off the table and entered the room. After opening it and removing a needle, he assertively squirted out fluid from the end. Then he inserted it into Edgar's shoulder and removed the straps holding him in place. Edgar immediately perked up and stopped talking. Just as swiftly as he entered, the doctor exited.

A few seconds later, a voice came out of the wall and said, "I'm afraid you've had an allergic reaction to the medicine we gave you. We'll have to monitor it closely to make sure it doesn't worsen. That would not be good."

Edgar arched his back and stretched. The shot had rejuvenated him beyond expectations. He glided off the stool, landing hard with his left foot, but repositioned himself without tumbling onto the floor.

"Are you comfortable, Mr. Gorman?"

Edgar peered over to a two-way mirror and chuckled, "Are you kidding me?"

"Good," came the reply.

"Did you not hear me?" asked Edgar.

"Yes, we did. Your response means that you are lucid and coherent. That's what's needed in order to continue. My name is Doctor Tamalitis and I'm joined by my colleague, Doctor Wheeler. We are here to ascertain your state of mind and suggest a medical treatment plan going forward. Our goal is to rid you of any psychopathic impulses you may be experiencing and guide you down a solid path of recovery to where you can eventually be reintroduced into society in a safe manner."

Edgar lifted his arm up over his head to block the bright light. After rubbing his eyes and squinting, he said, "Doctor, can you define, 'eventually' and can you please do something about the light?"

The lights dimmed. "That should be better." He cleared his throat and continued, "I'm sorry, but I can't explain it at this time, Mr. Gorman. Various factors go into making that determination. Now that you understand what's expected of you, let's get started. I'd like to proceed with the first phase by asking a few questions.

"When did you first start having psychopathic impulses?"

A long pause followed as Edgar realized exactly where he was and what was happening. Answering the question could be seen as confirmation of a problem, but not engaging could also be an admission of guilt. Then he noticed that the walls were padded from floor to ceiling. Even with the lights dimmed, the white color of madness screamed from every corner, telling him to beware.

He took a deep breath and said, "I don't have psychopathic behaviors."

"I see," said the speaker. "Do you know a Doctor Diane Beatty?"

"No."

"Do you have trouble sleeping at nights?"

Edgar knew there was no good answer to that question. He searched for a reply that would not be too incriminating. "Occasionally, but don't we all?"

"I'll ask the questions, Mr. Gorman. Thank you."

Roger picked up a notepad off the table and flipped back to the top page. Then he wiggled closer to the microphone and said, "Hello, Mr. Gorman. This is Doctor Wheeler. I'd like to ask you two important questions. First, do you believe everything you hear and see?"

Edgar stiffened his shoulders and sat erect. At first, his eyebrows signaled confusion but then a reply rose confidently. "Of course not."

Roger nodded to Rick and wrote down the answer on the notepad. "Question number two: Do you think it is always best to tell the truth?"

Edgar's torso hunkered down while contemplating an answer. Once again, there was no good one. "Occasionally?"

Roger flashed his eyebrows at Rick and noted the response. Then his fingers skipped around on the pad and he said, "Very good. Thank you. One more thing, can you please finish this rhyme: Greedness greaty, going crazy. Greedness greaty, one, two, three, four."

"Five, six, switch!" Edgar's face glowed with delight. Memories of a similar childhood rhyme uncontrollably guided his response.

Roger looked to his partner smugly and tugged on his collar. "I think he's ready to be activated." Then he smiled and returned his gaze to Edgar. "That will be all for the day."

CHAPTER NINETEEN

DUNES LOADING PLATFORM, ONTARIO, CA

"HAVE YOU EVER been convicted of a felony?"

The scruffy man standing on the platform next to the boarding dock hesitated. "Uh, no. I mean, yes."

The crossing agent's eyes peered through her reading glasses at the large screen in front of her. Then, without moving her head, she looked up and focused on the man himself. She didn't like what she saw: a week-old beard, dark tanned skin, uncombed hair, and a wrinkled shirt lined up one button off. His appearance told the agent more about this man's life than any database could ever reveal. It was a suitable metaphor for an otherwise dreary story that she didn't want to hear. They were all dreary stories in this line.

She waved to the security guards standing at the doorway near the entrance to the platform, then opened the optic scanner. "Step up to the yellow line, please."

The man turned his head and caught a glimpse of the two guards approaching from the doorway. Their inconspicuous white and red Dunes jackets slipped through the crowd like patches of fog in the morning sky. He half smiled and slowly stepped forward. His eyes scrambled from left to right to left while sizing up his options. There were none.

As his feet touched the wide yellow line painted on the

wooden plank, the crossing agent said, "Look straight into the camera."

The rest of the passengers standing behind him moved to the side as the two guards hustled up the aisle. The scruffy man smiled and glanced back again before leaning into the cotton-draped booth and stared into the camera. A bright white light illuminated all three walls of the curtain. Then there was a flash.

The worn-out letters on a wooden sign precariously dangling above the booth became visible in that brief moment. What was left of any paint chips on the sign reflected the words:

IT'S NOT ABOUT GREED,
IT'S ABOUT GREATNESS.

When the light dimmed, most of the words faded out of sight. Someone had taken the now ubiquitous national slogan and scribbled out "IT'S NOT ABOUT," "IT'S ABOUT" and "NESS" with a marker. Then they wrote the letters "NESS" next to the word "GREED" and added a "Y" to the word "GREAT." The two words "*GREEDNESS GREATY*" were all that remained visible.

The man rubbed his eyes and blinked several times while stepping back. "Please wait here until your Memorial comes up," said the crossing agent as she focused on the monitor in front of the podium. A blank screen stared back. After a minute, she banged on the plastic casing and cursed under tightened lips. Still nothing. Then she pushed a reset button under the table and said, "It'll just be a minute."

The old man nodded. Any delay was better than facing the consequences. As the aging machine rebooted, the agent brushed the dust off the display panel. Finally, the screen loaded. She logged in and read his Status Report. Then she clicked on the corner box and reviewed his Penalty Sheet. "Five citations for Anti-Government Propaganda, six warnings for Disorderly Conduct, and three convictions for Loss of Income.' Looks like you posted bail with what was left of your SSI savings." She stared into his vacant eyes and studied his sunburnt face trying to understand where he'd gone wrong, and then sighed, "Pity."

"Please check my Commendations and Demeanor Score. They can't be that bad."

The crossing agent agreed and clicked on the lower left hand of the screen. Her lips moved as she read each line outlined in blue, "'Impressive. Front-Loader with Six commendations for Active Volunteer Participation and four Sworn Statements of Improved Conduct.' It looks like your score was at 650 until two months ago. Now it's at 120. That's way below the Threshold of Engagement and what has activated Zero Sum." She wanted to ask what'd happened but caught herself before speaking. Getting involved never produced favorable results and usually led to an occasional ulcer. She immediately shifted her attention to the two guards now standing behind the man. "I'm sorry. Take him away to the Yucca Mountain Gate for processing. Sector Three."

"No! No! I beg of you. Check it again."

The two guards each grabbed an arm and escorted the man down the platform onto a lower deck. The passengers waiting in line watched them march away while all saying in unison, "May the Lord be with you." Below, on the wide dock leading to an old diesel locomotive, sat a series of mismatched train cars. Spray-painted graffiti covered each one, labeling them in such a way that you could easily tell which cars had been switched out or moved around recently.

When the guards made it down to the next level, the dock narrowed. Then the condemned man tried to wiggle out of their grasp and yelled, "No, not there!" The younger guard shoved a Taser into his side and pulled the trigger, sending fifty thousand volts into the man's chest.

"What are you doing?" cried the older guard. The prisoner's body fell limp. His head drooped forward and his eyes closed fast as his shoulders collapsed. Both guards scrambled to secure their grip. "For Christ's sake, now we have to carry him."

"He wasn't cooperating. Just following protocol."

"Fuck protocol. Get a better grip and carry him over your shoulder."

They both turned sideways and threw the man's arms over their necks. After a few grunts and moans, they continued moving.

"Jesus, he's heavy."

"What'd you expect? Don't ever do that again."

With the next step, the older guard tripped over a loose board in the floor that sent him stumbling to the ground. "Shit."

When the younger guard tried to secure his grip over the limp body, the prisoner opened his eyes and bolted up.

"What the…"

The scruffy man elbowed the younger guard in the stomach causing him to lean forward and release his grip. The older guard tried to react and jump to his feet but the man was too quick. He kicked him hard in the chest, sending him off the platform and down to the ground below. The guard moaned in disgust as a sandy mixture of oil and thick tar stuck to his body.

"He's getting away."

The prisoner ran back up to the main platform and darted toward the exit, all the while pushing people out of the way and jumping over barriers. When he opened the door leading into the next building, a single unrepentant shot rang out. The bullet landed squarely in his back causing him to arch up and glide helplessly to the floor.

A gray-haired woman in her late sixties lowered her revolver and smiled. She turned to the younger guard and shouted, "Invoking Article 2.2 of the Revised Constitution. I surrender my weapon but plead self-defense for the greater good of the country."

The guard ran over and asked, "How'd you get that weapon in here? It should've been confiscated at Interrogation."

The woman smiled and repeated, "Article 2.2 of the Revised Constitution."

"Okay, okay, but you're not getting off that easy."

By now, the older guard had crawled back onto the platform, wiped off the splotches of tar and marched over to the woman. Then he gazed at the doorway where the dead prisoner lay. "Lady, if you only knew the number of headaches you just created. Why couldn't you have done this on public property?"

"Article 2.2 of the Revised Constitution," was all she said.

"Well, if you think you're gonna collect an extra 100 Demeanor points for this little shenanigan, you'd better think again." The older guard's eyebrows straightened as he let out a sigh and barked, "Take her weapon. Damn vigilantes."

Another man in a red and white Dunes jacket with blue armbands stumbled past the crowd. He walked with a sideways swagger that made you wonder if he was coming or going. With his shaved head neatly concealed under his official Dunes cap, he flipped up his collar to cover the tattoos on his neck. Then he smiled cordially at the passengers in line as he passed them by and chuckle-whispered, "*Greedness greaty, going crazy. Greedness greaty, five, six, switch...*"

When he stopped in front of the dead body, the older guard said, "Here you go, Harold. You know what to do."

Harold mumbled under his breath as he dragged the corpse into the other building. As the two guards followed behind him, the crossing agent resumed the processing of passengers. Ketchum took a few steps forward in line. The man in front was a step slower and his foot caught the heel of the man's shoe. "Sorry."

They briefly made eye contact. His larger-than-life ears and nose seemed out of place on such a small head. The combination of oversized body parts seamlessly attached to undersized appendages created a physique so unfamiliar looking that only a loving mother could've appreciated it. Ketchum's eyes were drawn to the man's lips. They weren't moving. Even though the man said nothing, Ketchum knew what he was thinking: *Don't draw their attention.*

They both quietly moved on in line while the next person was processed. As the sun rose into the eastern sky, a cloud of mist swirled around the loading dock. All the moisture from the chilling nighttime breeze had surrendered to the warmer dryer air being baked by the heat. It rose up forming a cloud in the atmosphere. A purple gleam of light burst over the horizon causing the precipitation to dissipate into thin air. As this ecological firework display fizzled to the ground in fading shades of red and blue, passengers standing on the platform sang in unison to their version of an old hip-hop song from the twentieth century, "Wupe! There it is. Wupe! There it is."

They all chuckled and laughed for a moment and then returned to their normal business. Even though this naturally occurring phenomenon happened almost on a daily basis now, it still brought the same response each time. Much like a full moon on a clear night or the northern lights, people never grew tired of watching it. Only a few knew why it happened. Even fewer cared.

Methodically, the line hobbled along until the sun was now high enough in the sky to filter into the loose grid of wooden planks stretching above the platform. It was lunchtime. The carts rolled out with warm meals served by young volunteers from the local communities. Most of them had committed a small misdemeanor offense or some other social mishap that had been deemed "undesirable" by the local authorities. They knew that a low Demeanor Score automatically triggered a higher level of scrutiny so gaining a few extra points volunteering was a good way to stay above the Threshold of Engagement.

The stench of body odor and soiled feet lingering in between the rows was now replaced with the smell of French fries and hot dogs. They served food that one could eat while standing on their feet and nothing more. Many of the men and women had been in line waiting to be processed for days. At night, they were given a card with a number and told to come back in the morning. Of course, there wasn't anywhere for them to go except to an open spot on the platform where they might be able to catch a few winks.

None of the passengers knew exactly where they were going, but they all knew it wasn't somewhere nice. Nice things didn't happen to SSI exiles. For them, there were no other choices, as they'd exhausted all other options available. Fortunately, the camp options on where they'd be assigned were many, depending on the degree of the crimes and the skills they possessed. Some camps in the north were more like retirement resorts with outdoor sporting activities, weekly dances, and swimming pools. Those in the south didn't fare as well. Manual labor was mandatory and if a person didn't already possess adequate working skills, they'd be taught one soon enough.

As the temperature rose above 120 degrees, the line moved a little slower. Those suffering from asthma or respiratory ailments placed wet bandanas or masks over their noses to help with breathing. Any time the hazy wind blew in from the east, they knew it wasn't safe.

The man standing in front of Ketchum had just finished staring into the optic scanner and was rubbing his eyes. The crossing agent checked a box on her list and said, "Flagstaff to the Mountain Retreat Center."

The man nodded appreciatively and mumbled an almost inaudible thank you. He snatched the ticket from her hand and followed the wide green line painted on the dock that led down to a waiting shiny electric train. As he scurried away, he glanced over at Ketchum and smiled. Ketchum complimented him with a bow of the head and a slight grin.

"Next," shouted the agent.

As Ketchum stepped up, the sun was now directly overhead. A checkerboard pattern of black shadows and white sunlight radiated through the canopy blanketing the heads and shoulders of passengers below. The contrasting images created a hazy glow over the platform, almost celestial. It was enough to distort a person's vision unless you were wearing sunglasses. Of course, the only people wearing sunglasses were the guards.

"Name."

"Ketchum Tutaloo."

"Birth name?"

"Cole Mattock."

She continued, "Age."

"Eighteen."

The agent peered up from her screen, lifted her head back, and examined the young man from head to toe. They didn't come any younger than this and every time she processed one, she knew something horrible had gone wrong. There was either a story of lies and deceit behind his fate, or reckless abandon. One look at Ketchum and she knew which one was true.

"Have you ever been convicted of a felony?"

Ketchum paused and rubbed his ear. "Could you repeat that?"

The agent stared straight ahead and let all the air sink out of her chest as the wrinkles around her eyes frowned. She felt her blouse shedding its grip around her stomach in that brief moment, signaling she had to let go of any thoughts or feelings she might have over the matter. She inhaled and said, "Have you ever been convicted of a felony?"

"Is Zero Sum considered a felony?"

"Not if it's your first time."

"Then, no."

They locked eyes for a moment. A wonderful shade of bluish grey glowed in this young man's eyes under the high noon conditions. The kind of eyes she could've fallen in love with thirty years ago. She couldn't help feeling a bit melancholy in the moment. This abruptly led to a sensation of remorse for what she was about to do.

The agent returned her gaze to the monitor. Then she clicked on the box in the lower corner. One citation came up on the screen, but it was a serious one: "***Financial Negligence***." The words at the bottom of the screen read, "Suspected SSI Fraud. Case closed for lack of evidence."

Her instincts were confirmed. At this point, there was no use in asking any more questions. She knew the justice system had already run its course and nothing would change that outcome. She gazed into his eyes once more. They were still hopeful. She knew this wouldn't last long where she was sending him, but it was nice that the young man hadn't completely capitulated.

The agent handed Ketchum a ticket. "Here, you'll need this. Good luck. Please proceed to the Phoenix Gate: Arid Sector Three." She pointed to the large sign on the lower dock dangling above a wide orange line.

Passengers in line fixated on the young boy and watched him march down the long wooden dock. This time, the "May the Lord be with you" chant was disjointed and riddled in discord. Obviously, their hearts weren't into it.

The two guards escorted him down the dock but remained a few steps behind. It was a show of courtesy and respect that they'd been trained to do even though they each had a hand on a Taser just in case the boy hesitated. Speckle-colored steam hissed underneath the dusty diesel train waiting at the end of the plank. They didn't expect him to run like the scruffy old man before him. No, the boy was too young to risk everything that way and too naïve to know any better.

Still, the sight of such a young lad heading off to the Dunes contradicted everything the line of people understood about the world they lived in. They wondered where he'd gone wrong in such a short time. They wondered about their own pasts and tried to correlate some relevant event where they might have met a similar fate. One by one, they indiscriminately turned their gaze back to the line.

The acidic smell of diesel fuel sifted up from underneath the dock. It reminded Ketchum of the days spent in his dad's garage stripping an old wooden table and cleaning up with turpentine. It was an antique table made of actual hardwood, not the resin composites and plastic used today. As Ketchum and the guards grew nearer, bells chimed from the engine and caboose compartments signaling that the departure time was near. A snakelike hiss exhaled from the brakes and greeted them upon their arrival. The train was already full of passengers and the lights had dimmed inside each car.

The porter waited at the steps. "Well, look what we got here," snickered Harold in a high-pitched voice. Harold's protruding forehead squeezed tightly into his cap as his lower lip dripped out drops of what first appeared to be tobacco. He reached for a chocolate candy bar on a shelf behind him and took another bite. His mouth chomped bits of caramel, nuts, and chocolate through his crooked teeth as Ketchum followed him down the aisle. The porter staggered past each seat from side to side and waved Ketchum on.

About halfway down the train car, a tall man was trying to sleep with his knee sprawled out into the aisle. Harold pulled his Taser out from his holster, pointed it to the floor, and clicked it. A flash of electricity singed the aisle runner, filling the cabin with the distinctive stench of burnt rubber. The passenger frantically twisted out of the way, sat up in his seat, and whined, "What the hell?"

Harold snickered up a breath of contempt and continued down the aisle. As he made his way toward the rear of the cabin, other passengers grumbled and moaned with every nudge and flicker of his gun. Some of them had been waiting on the train for hours. Their patience had been tested and teased to the point of insubordination.

The only space left was a window spot in the last row. A large black man with his eyes closed occupied the aisle seat in a very unaccommodating recliner. His knees touched the back of the one in front of him while his forearms and hands caressed the armrests. Fresh scars extended across his biceps and neck resembling teeth marks or, more likely, Taser burns.

Harold stopped in the aisle and cleared his throat. Nothing. He reached down with his billy club and tapped on the metal seat frame. The man opened one eye and said, "This seat's occupied."

Harold nervously chuckled and stiffened his shoulders while replying, "I remember you. This ain't your first rodeo, now is it, cowboy? What was it, about seven years ago you were here?"

The man closed his eye and exhaled. Harold rattled the club between two metal bars and said, "We need the seat. It's the last one. Don't make me..."

Before Harold uttered another word, the man reached out, clamped onto the baton and yanked it out of his fingers. "Don't make me what?"

Harold placed a hand on his Taser but didn't lift it out of its holster. "I don't want no trouble. The boy just needs a seat."

The unmerciful midday sun sifted in through hollows of the canopy overhead, making it hard to breathe. For anyone exerting nervousness or a rise in blood pressure, panting was the only option. Harold nearly hyperventilated as he waited for an answer. He glanced down the aisle searching for backup but there was none. The other guards were nowhere in sight. An uneasy smile slithered across his face as he added, "Now there, let's don't do nothing you'll regret later. These things can get out of hand real quick, you know, and what d'ya think happens then?"

Ketchum stood there motionless. He wanted to take a few steps back but knew any sudden movement might trigger an unwanted outcome. This reaction was totally unexpected. He wondered if this was how every situation would be handled going forward. Was this the new norm? His instincts kicked in. "Never mind, I'll just stand."

The two men both turned their heads toward the boy, welcoming the comment. It didn't take long for Harold to speak. "Well, there ya go. Problem solved." He chuckled and returned his gaze to the passenger, adding, "How's that sound to you, mister."

The man stared at Ketchum for the longest time while contemplating his next move. Then he glared at Harold. His face poorly masked the obvious spite brewing inside. At any moment, he could rip the porter apart and serve him up as snacks to the rest of the passengers, but what would that get him? Harold grinned and whimpered onto his dripping chin. The man returned his gaze to the boy and said, "Have a seat."

"Thank you," peeped Ketchum.

The man stood up and towered over both Harold and Ketchum. He handed Harold back his baton and waved him away. "Shoo."

The porter backed away and swiftly retreated down the aisle while singing, "*Greedness greaty, going crazy. Greedness greaty, five, six, switch...*" Each time he finished a verse, he nodded to another passenger. Ketchum stared in disbelief wondering what it meant. The porter chuckled and retired into the next car while the black man moved to the aisle in order to allow Ketchum to pass. Ketchum scooted by and settled into the window seat.

CHAPTER TWENTY

ALL ABOARD

AS SOON AS HE SAT DOWN, the train jerked suddenly and started rocking. The bells had ceased ringing but were soon replaced with the metallic sound of steel upon steel. The wheels crept out of their cozy positions and began their journey forward. Ketchum lowered the upper half of his window to allow the breeze to flow through. It brought welcome relief but also signaled the beginning of what was to certainly be a hot and dry trip through the California desert.

Ketchum hesitated to speak first. Instead, he returned his gaze out the window. Within minutes of leaving, they passed through the Redlands Way Station. This was the last stop on the rail line until reaching the state of Arizona. The train cruised along at twenty miles per hour as required while within city limits. It was fast enough to prevent any drifters from running alongside trying to catch a ride while slow enough to handle the occasional suicide victim lying on the tracks.

Cheerful bliss coming from children playing along the track echoed through the train car. In the distance, partially opened windows and unhinged screen doors dangled from shelters and abandoned houses. Hand-written signs were plastered everywhere directing people on such matters as where to dump their waste, when to attend church, and who to seek for medical attention. Dusty canvas tents lined the empty lots in between structures. A few residents stood around rusted trashcans warming their food over fires and brewing coffee.

Once the train reached the outskirts, the landscape changed dramatically. The countryside transformed from a sparsely covered tree line into a wide, open abyss of wilted cactuses and golden sand. Rows of tar-covered mounds stretched across the landscape in linear fashion like mosaic tiles. Dormant oil pumps resided in between rows with their horse heads teetering up or down and sometimes in between. They seemed to salute the train when it zipped by, perhaps as a mechanical show of respect for its continued service and another job well done.

The train crooned along at full speed now on a downward slope through one of the many dips and rises across the rose-colored plateau. Ketchum leaned his head against the glass and gazed out into the void of endless horizon surrounding him. Nothing could survive in this heat during the day except for a few birds. An occasional vulture glided through the orange haze above, undoubtedly searching for scraps of the less fortunate that'd journeyed across its dominion.

As his head swayed back and forth to the rhythm of the rolling train track, his eyelids grew heavier. It had been a long day on top of a very long week. *How could so much have gone wrong so quickly*, he wondered? He hung his head low and groaned. This garnered the attention of the man next to him, who'd closed his eyes right after sitting back down. He peeked over at the boy just to make sure nothing was wrong, but then resumed his slumber. Obviously, he was in no mood for a friendly chat.

Ketchum dosed off within minutes. Although his body was resting, his mind continued to race from one lucid thought to another. Snapshots of events from the last few months trickled by like water drops splashing on the surface of some elusive lake. They spread in concentric circles taking with them pieces of different memories, mixing and blending them in ways that made no sense. Of course, nothing made sense right now.

He was supposed to be lying on a beach sipping on a cocktail while thinking of ways to spend his money: rubbing elbows with other millionaires in posh nightclubs, hopping on private jets with friends, and going to other cities just to watch basketball games. Dining in restaurants where there were no prices on the menu would all be second nature.

Those visions came and went until he found himself back on the broken patio lying on top of the sleeping bag recalling the nights with April. How could he have been so naïve, so stupid? Maybe it was just the lure of something so forbidden that did him in, pure teenage hormones. Or maybe he was madly in love, a love so overwhelming that it made him blind.

He wondered who she actually was. According to the state of California and the virtual judge, she'd died, but how could that be? Was it that easy to manipulate a database? One thought of Tusnig and he knew the answer to that question. Still, the series of events that followed afterwards was just as puzzling. The lightning speed at which SSI moved and labeled him insolvent went against everything he'd been taught in school.

Although his mother did try through her connections, she'd been told that protocols had changed. The country was entering a new phase of the Solid Start Initiative and implementing different procedures. The changes were mandatory and non-negotiable.

His family felt powerless those last few hours before extradition. Even Jonathan's old friend, Max, tried to help but to no avail. Dill Electronics was a major supplier of surveillance equipment to Forest Dunes so he figured maybe someone up higher in the chain of command could pull some strings. Hours later, he'd been unable to reach anyone on the phone. Voice mail and comment boxes were the only options. Finally, time had run out and everyone knew that the cavalry wasn't coming to save the day.

The only real alternative to rehabilitation at Dunes was prison. It was the first option always offered. Even though he'd be able to remain close to home by checking into an institution in Chino, that would be a near death sentence for a boy like him. Rehabilitation at the Dunes facility in Arizona was the only real option. After all, how bad could it be? There he'd be able to learn a skill or trade that would allow him to return to society someday and live an almost normal life.

"Almost" came with its own caveats, as he would now be under constant surveillance and have to report to the authorities on a monthly basis. There'd be blood tests, urine tests, polygraph tests, polygenic tests, cognitive intelligence tests, and anything else to insure he'd never again be a burden to society. If he failed, the first option became his only option.

CHAPTER TWENTY-ONE

EYES WIDE OPEN

THE SCORCHING WIND seeped in as the train built up speed. Some passengers raised their windows because the breeze coming in from the outside was hotter than the air around them. When the train turned around a tight bend, it sent most of the snoozers banging against the object next to them. Some moaned and stretched, then returned to sleep. Others opened their eyes and yawned.

The smell of burnt skin lingered painfully through the back of the car but hadn't yet registered in Ketchum's brain. His head wobbled against the glass window when the train rounded the turn sending a burst of heat to his singed cheek, waking him up.

"Holy shit!" he shouted.

He instinctively placed his hand on his face and leaned back into the seat. His fingertips glided over the freshly formed crusty patch of skin. Through his reflection in the window, the damage was clear. It felt worse than it looked. The big man sitting next to him awoke after hearing the outburst and opened his eyes.

"You should get that taken care of when we arrive. There should be a first aid kit in our dormitory." The man hadn't spoken a word the whole trip until now.

Ketchum gently caressed his face and said, "I will. I'm Ketchum Tutaloo."

He reached out his hand and they shook. "Double Down."

"That's your name?"

"That's what they call me, and for good reason." The man smiled, showing off a set of pearly whites that would've made any movie star envious.

"Have you been here before?"

"Yeah, but as a guard, years ago."

"I see."

Double Down peered into the aisle and focused on Harold, who'd just stirred from his own senseless siesta and was getting ready to report for duty.

Ketchum hesitated to ask about anything else. The chances of it being a pleasant story were slim. "What's that?" He pointed out the window. In the far distance, steel frames rose from the ground in tic-tac-toe formations casting a prism of colors across the desert land. Semitrailer trucks moved along a vein of gravel roads going to and from the site.

"We're crossing the Arizona border. They're building a desalination plant near Yuma."

"Yuma, the ocean's that high now?"

"Close enough."

Ketchum lightly pressed his fingertip on the glass and hastily removed it. "It's gotta be 140 degrees out there right now."

"At least," said Double Down. "They mainly work through the night and sleep during the day."

"They?"

The man nodded and replied, "They, maybe you. You'll see."

Ketchum wasn't sure how to absorb that comment so he just brushed it off. "You have an accent. Where're you from?"

"Baldwin Heights, but I grew up in the Midwest. A little shithole south of Chicago called Carbonville. It doesn't even show up on the maps these days."

"Why's that?"

"No one lives there anymore, my friend. Zero Sum Diffusion,

they call it. Once a town becomes insolvent, everyone has to move away"

"I didn't know they did that with towns and cities. I thought it was just people."

"Oh, they don't advertise it," lamented Double Down. "I mean, you won't find it in any corporate SSI report or on the nightly news, for sure." He focused his attention on Ketchum and added, "The government doesn't tell you all this because the government's not in charge anymore."

"Why, of course it is. How do you think we got here?"

"Really? Think about it, son. Who arrested you and put you on this train? Was it the government? No siree, it was Dunes and SSI."

The conversation made Ketchum uneasy so he straightened up in his seat and asked, "I thought SSI was a government program."

"Used to be, back in the beginning, but slowly and surely, one layer at a time, the government turned it over to a private firm like they've done with everything else."

"Death by a thousand cuts," recited Ketchum.

"Exactly. They bring in the EPA and deem an area uninhabitable. Do you know who controls the EPA?"

Ketchum shook his head.

"It's a privately owned corporation now whose biggest shareholder is, of all companies, Shale Oil. It doesn't matter what the reason is: radiation, a chemical spill, too much fucking garbage on the street. If they want to condemn a place, they can do it in a heartbeat. That's what they did to my hometown." The disdain in Double Down's voice splintered across the room.

"That's harsh. I had no idea."

"Of course you didn't. That's because Mega, Alpha, Gooble, Macrohard, and Appo control everything you see, hear, and do. MAGMA is flowing everywhere these days." He nodded and readjusted himself with his back firmly against the seat cushion before continuing, "You aren't old enough to remember and, quite frankly, most people didn't realize it at the time, but after the Media Reform Act of 2037 was voted in by Congress, everything changed for news outlets. Hell, they weren't even able to write about the changes without being shut down."

"I read about the Second Civil War in high school and how people were given a choice to become Front-Loaders or Back-Enders but don't remember anything about a Media Reform Act," responded Ketchum.

"That's because they don't want you to remember it. Even though the Second Civil War barely lasted a few days, it changed everything. I lost a few friends who'd been living in the South. Hell, they were just kids, wide-eyed freshmen in college and protesting everything that was wrong with the country." Double Down shook his head, inhaled the memories, and exhaled the grief.

"Anyway, the politicians knew that dividing the Union by states wasn't an option anymore. Pockets like Athens, Georgia, and Austin, Texas, would be sitting ducks for retribution if those states seceded from the Union. The same for Bakersfield and most of rural America. That's when they came up with the concept of Front-Loaders and Back-Enders. Instead of choosing *where* to live, all you had to do was choose *how* to live." He lay both palms out flat and demonstrated: "Did you want more health care or less taxes, fewer bible sessions or more guns? Quite an innovative concept at the time, and it worked."

Then he relaxed his shoulders and gazed around the train car to see if anyone was listening in. "One of the most important parts of the peace accord that you hardly ever hear about was a declaration, or I should say, a compromise on what constituted 'real news.' Newspapers and broadcasters were forbidden to circulate any kind of negative stories or anything politically toxic from then on. You wonder why these stories aren't in your news feed. That's because they control what you see and what you don't see."

"But how?" asked Ketchum. "I see stories and political posts all the time and from all around the world."

"Algorithms and censors. They sterilize every post and make it fall in line with what the government, or private government, deems as acceptable. Type in the word 'moral' and see what comes up. Instead of a definition about what's right and wrong, you'll find that the main description says, 'Anything written in the Bible.' Compare that to an old dictionary from the twentieth century, if you can find one."

Ketchum mused, "I bet my buddy, Tusnig, has one."

"I bet he's read it too," nodded Double Down. "After the war, everything changed for news organizations. They were already hurting as it was. I mean, as soon as a reporter broke a story, it was plastered everywhere on the Internet within minutes. They couldn't make any money. Soon, all the main news outlets went belly up, which meant that reporters were out of a job. Private companies stepped in, marvelously, I must say, and took them all over. Plus, they did it in a way that made it sound like they were the heroes by rebranding it all as part of MAGMA. I mean, hardly anyone knew what really happened and even less actually cared."

Ketchum nodded but was almost afraid to ask the next question. What he'd thought was going to be a quiet train ride had turned into a nonstop lecture. He thought about changing the subject, but curiosity got the best of him. "How were they able to do that?"

A thinly veiled grin surfaced as Double Down answered. "They nationalized everything under the banner of PBS. That pleased all the liberals to death. They all jumped for joy singing 'Hallelujah' and rode off into the sunset thinking they'd won." The big man shook his head and continued, "Dumbass liberals. They were always so gullible when it came to trusting people. Everything was peaches and cream for a few years, but gradually PBS and NPR and any other silly acronym you could think of began changing its programming. One by one, all the talk shows out there about the alt right or alt left vanished. Instead of loud yelling from some talking head, you had sweet little stories about herbal gardens being grown underground. Social media algorithms were altered to prevent any spread of misinformation, whether it was good or bad. Soon they became milder and more sterile, while the country became calmer. It was a really good thing, at first."

He snorted in the last of his childhood memories and sighed deeply. "People were nice to each other for once. Decades-old rivalries and feuds dissipated. TV shows stopped airing sex and violence all night long, and everyone became very patriotic. It was a wonderful time to grow up."

This new information was hard for Ketchum to grasp. Everything he thought he knew had been wrong, according to his new colleague. Everything he'd been taught in school was nothing more than the abbreviated sanitized Cliff Notes version. Could this be true? Then it occurred to him. "I thought everyone became patriotic because they were rich."

"Yeah, that all happened around the same time too. A perfect storm, if you think about it." Double Down shook his head and resumed, "Put a million dollars into somebody's pocket, and they'll forget about a lot of things, especially when you recalibrate the money into mid-twentieth century levels. All of a sudden, a million dollars felt like ten million and all your problems faded away." He lifted his arms in the air, letting them metaphorically float weightlessly. "All your troubles just faded away."

"How come my parents never said anything about this? I mean, they were around then too."

"It was a dark period in our history. I mean, the first Civil War was bad enough. I bet your history books told you that it was fought over state rights, didn't it?"

Ketchum nodded.

"Well, guess what. I'd be chained up on a plantation somewhere in the South if it hadn't been for that war. That's what it was really about." He rubbed his wrist and continued. "The Second Civil War tore families apart, brothers and sisters, many died. Nobody wanted to talk about it afterwards. They wanted all the negativity to go away, and it did, especially when people started receiving million dollar checks."

Ketchum nodded and let this revelation sink in. He gazed out the window where the sand and rock languished in the heat, soaking up ultraviolet rays like strokes of paint on a canvas. Colors blanketed the horizon in subtle shades of yellow, orange, and red, sprinkled with streaks of white. The fragile Joshua tree that'd once branched out across the terrain with its twisted tentacles had all but vanished.

As the heat refracted off the sand creating an ocean-waving mirage across the countryside, Ketchum found himself back in Summerfield, watching sprays of saltwater crash against the abandoned museum. The image juxtaposed against his current situation brought a tear to his eye. He quickly wiped it away. The last thing he needed was to show any emotion or signs of weakness where he was going.

CHAPTER TWENTY-TWO

A NEW BEGINNING

A HALF HOUR LATER, the train headed in a northeastern direction toward the Gila Bend Mountain facility west of the abandoned metropolis of Phoenix. The mountain range rose and dipped, one telephone pole at a time, across the desert for miles like a roller coaster. Over the years, it had transformed from a popular hiking destination into a natural inhospitable barrier on the southern border of the facility. Ketchum barely made out the guard towers along the ridge but he knew they were manned with infrared cameras. Thirty-foot-high poles lining the fence equipped with laser range finders were positioned strategically in blind spots and valleys as far as the eye could see.

As they approached the entrance, Ketchum sat up in his seat and stared out the window. They were about to enter a tunnel through the mountain. "Hold your breath," warned Double Down.

Ketchum caught a glimpse of the man inhaling deeply before complete darkness overwhelmed the train. The stench of sulfuric acid swiftly filled the cabin and singed his nose, causing him to raise his shirt up over his face. He closed his eyes and bent down. By the time his head came to rest on the back of the seat in front of him, they were through the tunnel.

"What was that?" he cried.

"Sulfur from the copper mine. This time of day, the wind quits blowing and it just sits there. They say it's harmless, but they say a lot of things."

As the train slowed down and wound its way into the station ahead, several armed guards approached the passenger cars. Dressed in tan fabric from head to toe, they disappeared and reappeared like birds floating in the ocean waves. Tiny portions of faces and hands emerged here and there as vapor hissed from the engine and the brakes squealed against steel.

Harold strode up and down the aisle yelling, "Gather your belongings and head out single file to the rear." He seemed to relish the excitement as the train ride came to a halt. While zigzagging down the aisle, a bead of runny snot rolled down his upper lip as he snickered, "Nap time is over."

Double Down stuck out his leg and caught Harold's foot just enough to send him stumbling against the back door. The guard turned with his Taser and glared. The big man had his hands firmly gripping the arms of the seat, just waiting to spring into action.

Harold grunted and said, "Your day will come, cowboy. You're not one of us anymore. Remember that."

Double Down didn't say a word. He merely stared straight ahead and ignored the temptations brewing inside.

The train stopped under a large canopy that jutted out from the platform. Passengers exited the hot, stale air inside the cabins just to find hotter air breezing along outside. It felt like leaving a sauna bath and jumping into a roaring fire. Tumbleweeds rolled across sandy pathways and huddled together in corners of buildings, seemingly knowing when to cross the roads and when to get out of the way.

A combination of cinder blocks, tile roofing, and battered stucco covered most structures, never reaching up beyond two stories high. One could only guess it had something to do with the heat and costs of trying to cool down the buildings. Every second story view had their shades pulled down at five o'clock in the afternoon and rightly so.

Each person waiting in line passed under a horseshoe-shaped

scanner after exiting the train, triggering a subtle beep followed by their name recited in digital English by a sincere-sounding female voice. When Double Down walked through, the announcer responded with:

David Downey
Afro-American
6' 4"
245 lbs.
Front-Loader
Zero Sum

Everyone boarded a driverless open-air tram which had a guard stationed on the front and back of each car. An automated voice, no doubt a close relative of the woman inside the horseshoe, repeated every few seconds, "Please step all the way inside and be seated."

"Where're they taking us?" asked Ketchum.

Double Down studied the station and surrounding buildings searching for any familiar faces before replying, "Home."

As soon as the tram moved, monitors positioned above every other row lowered down and turned on. Then the President of the United States materialized. "Good day, my fellow Americans." In the background, an array of flags waved in the breeze over the National Mall in Washington. The President's wavy hair and bangs lay firmly on his head as he proceeded to speak:

"You have all been willing participants in this great American experiment known as the Solid Start Initiative. Unfortunately, by your presence here today, we must assume that your efforts have come up short. That doesn't mean you should give up hope or be left out in the cold. We are a compassionate nation conceived on liberty and justice for all, where everyone is entitled to a second chance.

"As you know, our Solid Start Initiative has been key to eradicating poverty and welfare in this great country. People no longer wander the streets wondering where their next meal will come from, where they will sleep at night, or how they will make it through the day. With this program, we've been able to help those in need while saving our country from certain financial demise."

Ketchum's mind wandered back to earlier in the day when they passed through Redlands. The images of burning trashcans and broken windows made him question what he'd just heard. He decided not to give it a second thought, considering his circumstances.

The President continued: "Over the next few months, you'll receive training, be given opportunities to learn a new skill, develop a craft or trade, and receive the finest education possible in order make you a more productive citizen. If you do well, you'll eventually be reintroduced into society with the opportunity to once again become a valuable participant in the great American dream. And remember..."

The President pointed above his head as the camera swung over to the side of a stage where a banner read in bold letters, "IT'S NOT ABOUT GREED, IT'S ABOUT GREATNESS."

"Good luck, and may God be with you."

The monitors all darkened but didn't recede back into the ceiling. Instead, another video began:

"Welcome to the Gila Bend Mountain Facility. This wonderful natural beauty was commissioned twenty years ago as a refuge for Zero Sum associates and a training ground for citizens to be reinstated back into society. When you arrive at your dormitory, you will receive bunk assignments, a clean set of sheets, and all the necessary provisions needed to make your stay as comfortable as possible. Please follow the signs once exiting the tram and feel free to ask for help or directions from any of the welcoming staff while you are here. Good luck and God bless America."

Double Down leaned over and whispered, "Do not ask for help." His eyes said volumes.

When they arrived at the dormitory, passengers unloaded the tram and headed straight for the doorway. The building was made of the same concrete and stucco that formed most of the compound's structures. Robots scooted along the perimeter armed with built-in machine guns and night sensors. They patrolled each sector like bulldogs, questioning anything that moved.

Double Down looked to Ketchum and nodded. Inside the dorm, large fans swirled and spun throughout ten-foot ceilings. A row of bunk beds lined each side of the room with a six-foot walkway in the middle. There were no curtains on the windows and no door locks on either side. Privacy was not an option. Harold stood at the entrance holding a jar filled with folded pieces of paper. He ordered each person to reach in and grab a slip. As the new tenants opened their slips, he shouted the number and directed them toward their new bed.

Ketchum ended up with a spot in the corner of the room on the bottom bunk several rows away from Double Down. They both nodded to each other after finding their accommodations. Double Down was intimidating as hell when you met him head on. Yet, on the other hand, he had a motherly disposition once you got to know him. Either way, he was somebody you wanted on your side in a place like this.

Time passed at a lazy crawl. Most people were still in shock and adjusting to their new surroundings. Making friends and exchanging stories were the last things on their minds. Everyone tried to act busy inspecting their beds for bugs, checking out the bathrooms and showers, and peering out the windows without drawing attention.

Ketchum found the first aid kit in the bathroom and rubbed a little antibiotic ointment on his wound. When he returned to his bunk, a set of wrinkled faces followed his every move. No doubt, they were wondering how a person with such smooth skin could be suffering the same fate as themselves. He lay down on his bed and tried to ignore the thoughts and questions he saw in their expressions.

About an hour later, a ragged-looking old man entered pushing a metal cart. He scooted down the middle aisle slowly dragging his left foot while hunching over the handle as if it was the only thing keeping him upright. He stopped at every bunk and offered tenants bologna sandwiches, water, and napkins. Once a person accepted the food and thanked him, he would simply glance up for an instant with a welcoming gesture, then proceed to the next set of beds. Every once in a while, he'd chew on his gums or snort something inaudible under his breath.

Double Down apparently recognized the man and put his hand on his shoulder when he came by. "Is that you, Herbie?"

The old man stood erect and studied Double Down's facial features. The expression in his eyes remained distant. Instead of acknowledging him, the man simply smiled and recited fragments of the same old nursery rhyme from earlier in the day, "*Greedness greaty, going crazy. Greedness greaty, five, six, switch...*" Then he snickered and moved on.

As he approached each subsequent bunk, Herbie stopped and repeated the baffling refrain before handing out food and drinks. When he reached Ketchum's bunk, the boy didn't even look the old man in the eyes. Why, he wasn't sure, but all he could think of was the porter on the train chanting the same slogan before departing Ontario.

Everyone went to bed early that night. They were all instructed to be ready in the morning for a full day of orientation and training. What that meant was still a mystery as there were no ex-millionaire pamphlets to read or other welcoming speeches delivered. Just silence. In a way, it was only fitting, as hours on a wretched steamy train inhaling diesel fuel was enough to tire even the strongest of souls.

In the morning, a digital alarm blasted over speakers hanging on each side of the dormitory. Everyone sleeping promptly jumped to their feet, except for Ketchum. With a sluggish yawn, he slumped back down on his pillow and closed his eyes. It took more than an alarm clock to rouse most teenagers and Ketchum was no different.

CHAPTER TWENTY-THREE

THE REUNION

AS THEY WALKED ACROSS the compound to the cafeteria, an array of repetitive slogans blared out from all sides of a digital billboard stretching two stories high on the guardhouse:

"Residents of any Dunes property are not allowed to possess any communication devices whatsoever."

"Residents of any Dunes property are not allowed to leave the premises without written consent from a supervisor."

"All rights granted by Article Six of the Revised Constitution of the United States of America are hereby revoked until further notice."

The list went on.

The guardhouse was positioned in the center of the compound where all paths met. No matter which direction you walked, which direction you looked, signs greeted you like a nagging backache. To make matters worse, motion detectors automatically triggered vocal recitals of each and every rule any time a person came within a few feet of a building. And like that omnipresent radio jingle or television commercial playing from break to break, everyone knew the rules by heart after a few hours.

At the bottom of each sign, the same iconic slogan followed people everywhere: "IT'S NOT ABOUT GREED, IT'S ABOUT GREATNESS." Some of the staff wore the slogan on their sleeves or on hats like a medal of honor. Some had even tattooed it on their skin. It had become a symbol of patriotism ranking right up there with apple pie.

In small print below each slogan were anecdotes by famous celebrities and important politicians crooning praise about its value:

"Had it not been for this statement and the principles behind the philosophy, America might not exist today."

"These seven words have made our nation great once again."

Again, the list went on.

While eating breakfast, Ketchum noticed that one of the guards standing next to the kitchen door was staring at him. He dared not stare back but glanced over every so often when the man wasn't watching. He observed a medium-built male well under six feet in height, wearing the standard issue uniform and hat, with a dark complexion. Nothing out of the ordinary compared to other guards. It wasn't until their eyes met did he make the connection. Somewhere in his past, they'd known each other, but he didn't know where.

The guard stepped to the middle of the room and cleared his throat. "May I have your attention, please." He waited until the room went silent before saying, "Everyone needs to finish up their meals and head to building #7 immediately."

Two other guards joined him in the center. One of them the size of Double Down placed his hand on his pistol and reiterated, "Immediately." The whole group of new arrivals hurriedly rose from their tables, emptied their plates, and left the room.

They were all led into an air-conditioned building lined with rows of seats and desks. A white electronic board positioned between the American Flag and the official SSI flag covered two walls in a large room. A bell rang. Then a man wearing a plaid sport coat entered, stood behind a large desk, and commanded, "Please stand and recite our pledge of allegiance." Everyone rose to their feet and followed along. After finishing the salute, he pulled down a list of rules, using his fingertips on the whiteboard. Next, he pointed and said, "By tomorrow, you should be familiar with the rules and regulations that will be followed during your stay with us here at Forest Dunes. They are non-negotiable."

He scoured the room from one end to the other looking for any signs of dissent, then continued, "You will be given a series of tests over the next few days which will help us establish a baseline of your skills and experience so we can determine where you would be best suited to work. You'll find some of these tests to be very simple, and others extremely difficult. But don't worry, they're not designed to set you up for failure, they're there to help you succeed.

"After that, you'll be given a physical examination in order to assess your overall health, and then be sent off to different sectors of the facility for training purposes. There you'll establish residency and begin the process of learning a new skill or trade which will allow you to eventually integrate back into society. Good luck and do your best."

As the teacher turned to leave the room, an older man in the front row raised his hand. The teacher stopped and acknowledged him, "A question?"

"What if we don't pass the exam or are not capable of working?"

The teacher firmly replied, "There's a place for everyone here." Then he addressed the rest of the group, "Remember, church services start at 10:00 a.m. in this same room on Sunday. Class dismissed."

On the trip back to their dorm, Ketchum noticed the guard from the commissary standing in front of the building. Even through his reflective sunglasses, Ketchum sensed that he was watching him the whole way.

Double Down noticed too. "You have an admirer, I see."

"Right?" replied Ketchum.

"Could be a good thing, or it could be really bad."

"What do you mean?"

Double Down leaned over and in a low voice said, "They tell you that homosexuality doesn't exist."

"What's homosexuality?" asked Ketchum.

"See what I mean. The word might've been removed from the dictionary but the emotions still exist in many. We just don't talk about it."

"Emotions?"

Double Down simply shook his head and said, "Oh, you'll find out sooner or later."

The rest of the afternoon was spent playing cards, board games, and hanging out on the bunk beds. At certain hours of the day, it was too hot to do anything that involved going outside. Even the guards were nowhere to be found but you knew they were there all the same.

The next morning at breakfast, the same guard stared at Ketchum from across the room. This time, he stared back long enough to make the guard uncomfortable. The guard turned away and ducked into the kitchen. A few minutes later, he returned with a couple of empty boxes that he carried out the front door. This routine continued for another ten minutes until he vanished completely.

On the way back to the dorm, the guard showed up again walking behind Ketchum and Double Down on the pathway. When they both passed the central building, the man caught up and said, "I need you two to carry some boxes. Follow me." The guard turned around and marched them over to a supply shed tucked away in the corner of the compound. He ordered them to grab a few and carry them to the commissary.

When they returned to the shed, he pointed to Double Down and said, "Go back to the commissary and grab the empty water jugs. They're stacked next to the cooler." Double Down nodded and turned to Ketchum just long enough to let him know that he had his back. Then he went on his way.

As soon as he was out of sight, the guard motioned Ketchum

into the shed. He shut the door halfway, took off his sunglasses and said, "Ketchum, it's me, your old neighbor."

Ketchum studied his face as images from his childhood flashed by and fled while trying to remember. He saw a vague resemblance in the eyes and cheekbones.

"Carlos?"

"Yes, you remember."

"Barely. That was a long time ago. What happened? I mean, your family disappeared overnight."

"It's a long story. I'll fill you in later. I need to warn you now before it's too late."

"Too late. For what?"

Carlos grabbed both shoulders and stared in Ketchum's eyes. "Whatever you do, do not take that physical exam. Once they implant you with a chip and tattoo, there's no escape."

"But why would I want to escape? They're going to train me."

"There is no real training," replied Carlos, "at least, not like they used to. Most of that was abolished months ago. Dunes finally figured out the best way to deal with new arrivals."

"How's that?"

"By eliminating them."

Ketchum's jaw hung in shock as he absorbed the implications of this comment. His head shook with disbelief while studying Carlos's face. Yes, it was the same boy he knew as a child, but a decade had passed since knowing him. Could he be trusted?

"Why would they do that? I mean, how could they get away with it?"

Carlos rubbed his fingers together and whispered *"Mas dinero,* my friend. This company has been trying to reintroduce reformed prisoners for a long time now. It's just not working. It costs much less to make some of them disappear. They don't get rid of everyone, only those with few contacts on the outside or the ones that cause trouble — like your friend." He glanced outside before adding, "The problem is, you just don't know who stays and who goes away. I know I haven't figured it out yet."

"How... why... I don't get it."

Carlos gave him a minute to let it sink in while peeking out the door for any movement. Then he added, "I know it's a lot to absorb, but believe me, don't get the physical."

"Well, how can I stop them?"

"You don't. You have to escape."

"How? I don't know this area. Where am I going to go?"

Carlos saw Double Down walking back across the grounds toward the shed. "Can you trust your friend? He's been here before and knows the area."

"I think so. I'm not sure."

"I guess you don't have a choice. It'll be tough without him, but you decide. All I can tell you is to be back here behind this shed on Sunday night three hours after lights are out. There will be a backpack with supplies and instructions." He peeked out the door and exited. "Good luck."

That night, Ketchum couldn't sleep. He tried to recall those days with Carlos as a child. His mother called them a gang but he knew better. They were more like cousins than a gang. They were fun times, carefree, innocent, but a little dangerous. Carlos had no fear and didn't hesitate on a double dare. Ketchum wondered what happened to his sister, Carmen. She was a couple of years younger than him but as cute as they came. He knew she had a crush on him but didn't pay it any mind. When you're that young, girls were more of a nuisance than anything. He'd heard rumors that she'd returned to Summerfield but had never seen her around town.

He also didn't know whether he trusted Double Down. After all, he once was a staff member himself. As far as Ketchum knew, he could be a plant or spy. He observed the guards and staff with a new sense of awareness now, looking for any signs to confirm what Carlos had said. There were none.

Telling Double Down wasn't a choice by the time Sunday rolled around. He detected something was amiss by the uneasiness in Ketchum's voice and stiff body language. He didn't hesitate to agree to come along either. From the moment they'd set foot in the camp, he noticed that none of the guards smiled or joked around like they used to when he was one of them. They all seemed to be watching over their own backs and wary of each other. Something had changed indeed.

When Ketchum told him the plan, he hung his head down and said, "I bet he's sending us to the Indian reservation."

"Why there?"

"It's not under MAGMA's jurisdiction, at least as far as I know. Going southwest would lead us right into a military base and north of us is Interstate 10. They patrol that area pretty hard. West is the old, abandoned wildlife refuge where there's nothing but death. Northeast is what's left of Phoenix and we don't want to go there for sure."

There wasn't much the two could do but lie on their beds and wait until the lights went out. They had no belongings to pack, no friends to say goodbye to, and no idea of what was in store for them next. Time dragged like a tiger tugs on an elephant.

Double Down was the first to rise. Ketchum saw his silhouette signaling from across the room. He rose quietly and walked over to his friend's bed. He could call him a friend now, even though they'd only known each other for a few days. Anyone willing to risk his life and follow you into the unknown was a friend in his book. As he made his way across the floor, he wondered what his old pal Tusnig was up to these days. Back home, he'd been the only friend Ketchum had. No doubt, he was the only friend Tusnig had too. Now, they both were coping with their new reality.

Not a word was spoken as they exited the dorm and surveyed the compound. They avoided the guardhouse and any cameras by circling around back and following along the perimeter. That meant they'd have to deal with the robot patrol, or Rat Patrol, as referred to by the residents. They were everywhere and anywhere, never sleeping, appearing out of nowhere, and disappearing into thin air.

When they made it over to the next building, the two paused to listen. No matter how hard the designers of these AI machines tried, they couldn't quite master completely silencing them under desert conditions. Every time a relentless barrage of dust and sand kicked up around the compound, another rotating joint gummed up. The wind breezed along like dragon's breath, methodically injecting bursts of heat into the air throughout the compound.

"I hear one," whispered Double Down.

"Where?" He put a hand over Ketchum's mouth and a finger to his lips.

Approaching from the office building north of them came a six-foot-high robot covered in black non-reflective coating that rendered it nearly invisible. Nothing but the laser sensors positioned every few inches apart on the top, middle, and bottom glowed in the darkness. Even then, they could only be seen at certain angles. When it moved into the light coming from the guardhouse, its black covering turned gray and discreetly blended in with the background.

Double Down was exceptionally familiar with these devices. One of his jobs while on the Dunes staff was maintenance. He'd worked on hundreds of these machines over the years. Even though they were an efficient mechanism to have when it came to surveillance, they did lack one important feature: instinct. He picked up a handful of rocks off the ground and tossed them in several different directions. The Rat stopped and pinpointed a laser on each place where one had landed. Double Down waved his hand and the two darted over to the next building, then took cover.

When they were out of listening distance, Ketchum whispered, "What was that all about?"

"The Rats are programmed to do one thing: survey the compound and alert the guards whenever there's movement. When they notice something moving, their sensors fixate on the item for however long it takes to determine whether it's a false alarm or not. There're only twelve sensors on any given machine. If you throw twelve rocks, that renders it incapable of tracking a thirteenth item, or fourteenth."

With a triumphant snort, he added, "It'll take the guards a minute or two to show up and investigate. Then it will take them another five minutes to disarm the Rat and send it back on its merry way."

Ketchum scratched his head and replied, "That seems so archaic."

Double Down nodded again. "It is. Every time the Dunes Corporation tried out a new model with more humanistic characteristics, it ended in a complete disaster. When they introduced quantum physics into the equation, the results were even worse. The lawsuits alone almost bankrupted the agency. Finally, they realized it was safer to make their humanoids not so human." He smiled and added, "We need to keep going. They may spread out and search the neighboring buildings once they find nothing."

When they arrived at the next building over, they listened again, then jetted over to another. Soon, they were behind the shed and panting.

"There it is."

"Hold on," said Double Down, "it might be booby-trapped." He knelt and examined the package, then lifted it gently over on its side with a stick. "Okay."

Ketchum picked up the backpack, unzipped it, and pulled out a sheet of paper. "We need to head north as far away from the main gate as possible. There is a white building near the far north side next to a fence. It says to wait there for a signal and further instructions."

"Let's go."

A good twenty minutes had passed after retrieving the backpack and making their way to the northern part of the compound. When they arrived, they found themselves surrounded by manmade walls of fully loaded dumpsters and large plastic trashcans. The stench from yesterday's dinner in the overfilled containers filled the silent air. Lighting was sparse and unwittingly positioned at angles that hardly covered any of the exposed surfaces. Even the Rat Patrols didn't bother watching this area.

Double Down peeked at his watch. It was in stealth mode illuminating only numbers at a forty-five degree angle. "Should be soon." They both sat down in the dirt and enjoyed the peace and quiet. A warm breezed drifted by unfurling their emotions and soothing their souls. It was a welcomed change from the last few hectic days of uncertainty and surprises.

In the distance, a rustling sound sifted through the blackness. Then a flashlight swung over the sidewalk as a pair of legs approached in the light. "Ketchum," whispered the dark shadow, "where are you?"

"Over here." Ketchum stepped away from the wall and waved. The legs and flashlight raced over to where he was standing and came into view.

Carlos smiled and said, "Hello, again, my old friend." He hugged him tightly and said, "Follow me."

CHAPTER TWENTY-FOUR

THE ESCAPE

BEHIND ANOTHER STORAGE SHED wedged into the corner of the compound was a rectangular concrete platform surrounded by dirt with a metal hatch on top. Carlos pulled a set of keys out of his pocket and opened it. Nothing but complete darkness greeted them from the exposed earth walls lining the hole. He flipped on a flashlight illuminating a set of wooden stairs leading to the bottom.

"Down here. Take my flashlight and follow the tunnel as far as it will take you, which is about a mile. You'll see another door like this one at the end. Be careful when you open it. It's near a road and you might be spotted."

"What do we do after that?" asked Ketchum.

Carlos helped them down the stairs and said, "There's a backpack with supplies at the other end. Take it with you and head southeast. You'll find an Indian Reservation about fifty miles away. If you can make it there, you should be safe. It's probably best to travel at night when it's cooler, but that has its own set of problems."

He reached down and shook Ketchum's hand. "Good luck, my friend. If you make it to the reservation, ask for my sister, Carmen. I think she's still there."

"Thanks."

The guard looked to Double Down, handed him another flashlight, and just nodded. They both understood. As the door closed, a moment of pure surrealism overcame them both. The surroundings were foreign, yet familiar. They were safe, yet in more danger than ever. They knew where they were going but had no idea when or how they'd get there.

Ketchum was the first to ask. "I don't know. Are we doing the right thing?"

"We don't have a choice," replied Double Down. He flashed a beam of light over the room. There were pickaxes leaning against the wall next to wooden shelves lined with hard hats. A cool breeze brushed by their faces, no doubt from deep within the tunnel. A stack of empty paper wrappers huddled up against the wall, each one stuck together with a piece of used gum.

"The sugarless gum was used to help the workers salivate. That way, they didn't have to carry as much water around." Double Down reached down and picked the top piece off the pile and put it in his mouth. "Umm, hard as a rock," he jested as he spat it out.

He started moving down the path without saying another word as Ketchum followed. They soon found themselves walking on top of a set of railroad tracks. Bits and pieces of copper ore lay scattered along the ground, blending in with hundreds of fragments of blue and green hydrated copper, malachite, and azurite rocks. The path sloped heavily downward for a good half mile before coming to an intersection. Heading both left and right were other carved out rock tunnels dipping even deeper into the earth.

"Hear that?" said Double Down.

"No, but I smell something rotten. Kind of like spoiled milk," replied Ketchum. Double Down shined the light down into the side tunnel and a swarm of bats shot out past them, barely missing Ketchum's ears and shoulders. "Holy shit!" he cried as he ducked down.

Double Down just put his elbow up and continued shining the light. "Look, it's glowing down there. Let's check it out. Watch out for bat dung. It's slippery."

They both ventured deeper down and soon found themselves at the entrance of another cave. When Double Down shined the flashlight beam inside, a stunning array of colorful stalactites and stalagmites covered the walls. A golden cathedral of rock formations filled the room, reflecting back veins of copper that flowed like velvet curtains to and from the floor. They felt the heat generating from the glow immediately.

A trickle of water dropped into a puddle in the center. Ketchum bent down to touch it when Double Down barked, "Don't! Probably contaminated."

"What makes you think that?"

"Why else would this still be here? They would've mined these walls a long time ago." He turned in a full circle while gazing above his head and added, "No, I'd say there's a reason they haven't touched this place. And that's reason enough for us to leave."

Ketchum unconsciously started scratching his arm and replied, "You're probably right."

They left the cave and continued down the railroad track for another half a mile or so. The elevation began to climb up slowly. There were several offshoots of tunnels along the way which they chose to ignore. Most were smaller than the cave they'd seen earlier.

At the end of the tracks, the slope leveled off and a thick rubber bumper mounted to a post came into view. They hadn't seen a mining cart of any kind on the whole path. Something caught Ketchum's eye as Double Down scanned the walls and found a ladder. "What was that back there, next to that desk?" They both walked over to look. Next to an old wooden desk was a crate marked "Explosives." Ketchum lifted the lid and it was empty. "Of course."

Double Down tried to open the drawers on the desk but they wouldn't budge. He shook them vigorously but nothing. Then he pulled away the chair and reached underneath in the middle. "Bingo." They heard a click and the side door on the left popped open. He shined the light inside and smiled. "Looky there." At the bottom of the drawer was a pistol and a box of bullets. "This could come in handy," he said as he loaded the gun and stuffed the bullets in his pocket.

The backpack contained food, water, Mylar blankets, and more batteries for the flashlights. Double Down climbed up the ladder, opened the hatch, and peeked out. "Looks clear." It was still dark outside. They both slid out into the predawn air and ducked behind the platform. The moon and stars were fading in the east but the sun had not yet shown itself. In the distance, headlights of a truck heading toward them shimmered off the blacktop road. They stayed low and waited for it to pass. To the southeast, a silhouette of a large mountain range embraced the entire horizon. The truck's taillights slowly melted into the murkiness of the mountain as it passed through a tunnel.

Ketchum stared at the colossal peaks ahead of them and asked, "How do we get over that? Crossing it will take forever."

Double Down studied the area from left to right and said, "Let's go through it."

"How do we do that? We'll be spotted for sure."

"I got an idea. Follow me."

They both raced over to the mountain base near the tunnel and next to the blacktop road. "Help me with these boulders." After dragging several large rocks onto the road blocking it completely, they sprinkled sand and dust in between each one. "That should do it. Let's just hope the next vehicle is going east." Then they waited.

Dawn was nearly upon them when another pickup truck approached in the distance. "Wait for my signal before jumping in the back," ordered Double Down. The truck's headlights slowed as it approached from a vanishing point beyond their view. While kneeling on one knee and hiding behind a boulder, they watched the truck slow down and eventually stop. Two men exited cursing every step of the way as they slid rocks off the road. When they opened the doors and started to sit back in the cab, he ordered, "Now."

Double Down and Ketchum raced up and quietly timed their climb into the back bed with the shutting doors. Everything went seamlessly until they realized they hadn't jumped into an empty bed. Ketchum felt around trying to determine what it was underneath him. Right then, Double Down whispered, "They're bodies." Shapes of human bodies took form as the sun slowly rose over the mountaintops. Ketchum's first impulse was to jump back out but Double Down clamped his hand over his mouth and held him on the truck bed until he settled down.

The truck gradually picked up speed and continued its journey to the foot of the mountain. Mounted spotlights illuminated the tunnel and blinked flashes of bright white light every few feet. The glow of the headlights reflecting off the granite walls revealed a road so narrow that only one vehicle could pass through at a time.

Ketchum wrestled with the limited floor space around him until he was on solid ground and not on top of anything. Soon he noticed that the bodies were still warm. Then he realized they were still breathing. How could this be? He placed his hand on the chest of one man. The heartbeat was strong, in fact, too strong. The man's chest thumped wildly pounding out an uneven rhythm of pulsations rising and falling with no sense of direction. It was as if his heart wanted to jump out of his body.

Then the man's eyes suddenly opened wide as his torso tensed up, exuding sweat and fear through his pores. Ketchum sensed the man's urge to scream but he remained silent. Then, the body fell limp. His eyes closed and he exhaled loudly.

This garnered Double Down's attention. He carefully turned around to see what was happening. "Shhh...."

"It's not me, it's him."

Double Down looked to where Ketchum was pointing and then back at him. All he saw was what appeared to be a corpse.

Another light flooded the truck bed for an instant and slowly faded to black. He grabbed Double Down's hand and placed it on the man's chest. "He's alive."

Double Down quickly pulled it away and recoiled. It took him a few seconds to absorb the revelation before cautiously feeling around the man's nose to confirm his breathing. Then he rolled him over and checked the person on his other side. It was a woman in her forties. Again, warm air coming out of her nose.

"They're all alive," he exclaimed in a low whisper. "What's going on?" He shook the woman's shoulders, "Wake up, wake up." There was no movement, just a quick fluttering of the eyelids. Then nothing. "It's like they're drugged."

"My thoughts exactly," replied Ketchum. "It's gotta be. Why else would they be so comatose?"

The truck slowed down at an intersection with red flashing lights at each corner. It turned left without fully stopping and headed downward deeper into the mountain. There were no lights in this tunnel, only the glow of headlights hovering over and around the front cab.

"Shit! What do we do?" cried Ketchum. "We're supposed to just pass through this place."

"I don't think we have a choice now," whispered Double Down.

Ketchum agreed with a nod and began to shiver as the temperature dropped while the air thickened. The scent of sulfur lingered everywhere, making it harder to breathe. Double Down rubbed his nose with his sleeve and coughed.

"I think we're almost there. We should get out before the truck stops."

Ketchum nodded and added, "As soon as they start to slow down, let's go."

"Agreed."

It wasn't long until the truck downshifted and the brakes squeaked. "Now."

They both swiftly rolled over the tailgate and landed flatfooted behind the moving vehicle. As it traveled on, they darted for cover behind a pile of boulders off to the side. "Keep moving," ordered Double Down.

They shuffled from place to place trying to keep pace. The vehicle sputtered and downshifted again before coming to a complete stop. A large aluminum door buried into the rock was exposed in the headlights. The driver pushed a button in the visor and the door slowly rolled up. Projecting out from underneath the door was the subtle glow of red lights as the truck entered and continued on.

Double Down hesitated, "Hold on. Wait until the door starts to close. If someone spots us, split up immediately. Later on, meet back here at this door when you can. No one leaves without the other, got it?"

He looked to Ketchum for reassurance. "Got it."

They both waited until the truck cleared the opening. Then Double Down gestured, "Now."

As they slid under the door and ducked under cover, an undeclared bond began to form between them. They both understood that in order to survive, they'd have to work as a team. There were many ways out of this place but very few paths to freedom. The best way to see that path was to work together.

CHAPTER TWENTY-FIVE

DOCTORS, SCIENTISTS, AND BEARS, OH MY...

AS THE DOOR slowly lowered, they slid underneath and crawled over to the nearest cover. Stacks of boxes six feet high and wrapped in cellophane lined a pathway of tire tracks leading deeper into the room. As the truck puttered along another fifty feet or so before coming to a stop, Double Down whispered, "Move along the walls and stay low."

The driver and passenger walked to the back of the truck and lowered the tailgate. A tiny woman in a white lab coat approached and the driver handed her a bag. "Here's breakfast from the cafeteria."

"Thank you. I am getting hungry." She pointed and said, "Take the bodies to the first room."

"Will do."

Granite walls and spotlights hovered over the area as the two men unloaded the truck bed. There were three glass enclosures in front of them: One where they laid the bodies on the floor, the one next to it containing only a chair sitting in the middle, and the third lined with blinking machines and colorful lights. Another man in a white coat was typing on a laptop as the tiny woman entered the room. She waved her hands around like a chimpanzee while studying a white board. Each press of her finger against the board dug deeper under her colleague's skin as he reacted with his own flighty display of hand gestures and facial expressions.

Then the two technicians left the control room and walked toward the middle one with the bar stool. "I don't care what the manual says," said the man. "It changes from week to week anyway. We are going to ask just one question and decide from there. Deal?"

"Deal, but remember, this is supposed to be a reeducation camp, not..." she spun her pointer finger around in a circle and added, "This! Whatever happened to the Three R's: reeducate, revise, and redistribute?

"My word, no one has used those terms since Dunes took over."

"Exactly."

The female technician entered the first room, opened a box in the corner and removed a large canister. As she walked over to the middle room, the man held open the door and said, "If it makes you feel better, I'll do it today."

"Thank you." Then she inserted the cannister into a slot in the floor and twisted it into place. The man motioned to the driver and passenger and said, "You can take your break now. See you in a half hour." He smiled as the two disappeared behind a door built into the rocky walls off to the side. Then he turned and shouted to a guard situated in the corner and ordered, "Bring a male subject into the Observation Room."

Both technicians returned to the control room, punched a few buttons, and jotted down notes into a digital notepad. A ten-foot-wide glass enclosure rose from the floor encircling the stool with three thick walls that stretched ten feet up to the ceiling. The guard returned carrying a man who looked to be in his early sixties. He placed the subject onto the chair in the glass encasement.

"We need to get closer. I can't hear what they're saying," said Double Down. They both stealthily slid in behind the truck which was now directly in front of the three rooms.

The male technician entered the glass enclosure and injected the limp body with a syringe. It immediately perked up and became conscious. The woman in the control room turned on a monitor above her head and stated, "Front-Loader Subject Number 14, Trial number 9. It's June 25th, 2068."

The male technician nodded and turned to the old man, "How are you feeling, Number 14?"

The old man rubbed his eyes and scanned the surroundings. "Where am I?"

"We'll ask the questions here. You've been brought to this place as directed by Article 13, Section 7 of the Revised Constitution for violating the terms of your SSI handbook and entering into Zero Sum Conclusion."

The man nodded and said, "Understood."

"So, subject Number 14, how are you feeling?"

"The name's Jake, and I'm fine."

"Duly noted."

The monitor brought up images of the man's bone structure and internal organs. As the female technician dialed in a few settings, she touched the frame of her glasses activating a microphone and stated, "Blood pressure 130 over 82, pulse 75." She made a couple of entries on the digital notepad and said, "All organs appear to be healthy."

The male technician followed suit with a tap to his earpiece and replied, "Good" Then he waved off the guard, "That'll be all. Thank you." The guard exited behind the same door in the corner where the two workers had gone earlier. Then the technician clasped his arms behind his back and paced the floor in front of the man. "Subject Number 14, you are here today because your Futures Exchange Value has gone into negative territory. The chances of you recovering from this deficit while rehabilitating at the Gila Bend Facility are very slim. In fact, your scores could negatively affect the scores of other members of your family."

"But I don't have any family. They've all passed away."

The male technician stopped, turned toward his colleague, and raised an eyebrow before answering. "Duly noted. Subject Number 14, are you aware of the new Accelerated SSI Structural Timeframe program, or ASSIST for short, that began a few months ago?"

"Why, no." For the first time, the old man became acutely aware of his surroundings. He cautiously scanned the glass encasing and asked, "What is this room?"

"That is not your concern, Subject Number 14. Again, I'll ask the questions."

The old man blinked rapidly and ran his hands up and down his pants legs. Then he swiveled and swayed around on the chair as a film of silky sweat began to form on his forehead. The female technician updated her colleague, "Pulse rate is up to 91, blood pressure 160 over 95."

The male technician inconspicuously nodded and put his hands in his coat pockets. When the patient skirted off the chair and pressed against one of the glass walls, the technician calmly said, "Subject Number 14, please have a seat." The old man peered over at the doorway and reluctantly acquiesced. The technician continued, "As you know, you were inserted with a hydrogel microchip upon arrival to this facility. Do you know why?"

The old man squinted inward and tugged on his bottom lip. "No, not really."

"It was inserted as instructed by the new ASSIST program which has been developed by Dunes Corporation in order to assure that the original Solid Start Initiative remains strong and healthy. It will allow the company's new goals, and in turn, the goals of the whole nation, to align with our current needs in order to maximize efficiency."

The old man glanced at the doorway again and said, "I'm not sure what you mean."

"Come on now, Number 14. What is this country's motto?"

"Uh, you mean, 'It's not about greed, it's about greatness'?"

"Exactly. You've had a long and meaningful life, yet here you are today. That means you've come up short and become a burden to society. For the good of the country, for the good of your neighbors and friends and generations to come, it's time to stop being greedy and embrace greatness."

The female technician turned on a neon sign mounted on the control room wall displaying the American flag glowing in red, white, and blue. Patriotic music slowly ascended from hidden speakers as images of the first settlers, revolutionary soldiers, Ronald Reagan, families playing in a park, and more soared across the glass panels surrounding the subject.

The male technician firmly dropped his arms to his side, glared into the old man's eyes and commanded, "It's your patriotic duty."

The old man's head darted from the female technician, to the male, to the door and back before asking, "Are you saying you want... you want me to kill myself?"

"Well, we don't condone suicide, Subject Number 14. It's still illegal nationwide, but there are other ways to serve your country proudly," reminded the male technician. "Just say those magical words and you'll have done your country a great service. Do you remember them?"

"Why, yes."

"Then say them along with me: *Greedness greaty, going crazy. Greedness greaty, one, two, three, four...*" The technician rolled his arm in the shape of a donut and waited for a response from the subject but none came. After what seemed to be an eternity, he clutched his hands tightly and dropped his shoulders.

The female technician turned down the volume and faded the visuals from view. Ketchum and Double Down looked on in shock as streams of terror filtered down the old man's leg. Ketchum whispered, "He peed his pants!"

As the old man sat there, frozen in fear and drastically trying to comprehend his situation, scattered thoughts pulled and tugged between his temples while those fateful words dangled off his lips. Yet, they never came. After a minute or two, the male technician looked to his CompWatch and said, "What the hell, it's not going to happen." He snapped his fingers and the female technician pushed a button. Gas swiftly seeped into the encasing from above as a fourth wall rose from the floor sealing the man's fate. It soon engulfed the whole ten-by-ten enclosure while he frantically slapped at the panels and screamed. His eyes seemed to eat up the rest of his face while streaks of red dripped down his cheeks. His hands clawed at his throat as if digging for more pockets of air.

The male technician left the room and shut the door behind him, which immediately smothered and silenced the cries from inside. He entered the control room as the subject collapsed on the ground. The woman gazed at the monitor and announced, "There's no heartbeat." She tapped on the control panel and the glass encasing submerged back into the floor while hidden ceiling fans sucked out the poisonous gas.

The technician opened a bag on the counter, took a bite of a burrito, and said to his female colleague, "Call in the guards to cart him away and bring in another subject."

Ketchum and Double Down watched from behind the truck and quickly ducked when the two guards came in and entered the middle room. As they carried the body away, Ketchum whispered, "Holy shit. What was that all about?"

Double Down rubbed his eyes and chin. "Wow. That was bizarre. I've read a few things on the Dark Web about this kind of stuff but thought it was all conspiracy theory bullshit until now."

"That was no bullshit."

"Indeed. That was Soylent Green-type of shit in there. Now I know why your friend was so adamant that we didn't get the physical."

The two men who'd driven the truck into the mountain

returned from lunch and headed toward their vehicle. Double Down gripped the back bumper and said, "We need to get out of here."

"Soylent Green?" questioned Ketchum as he slowly rose to his feet waiting for a response.

Double Down peered over to the two men and then to his colleague before replying, "I'll fill you in later."

They jumped back into the truck when the men opened the doors just as they'd done earlier. One of the men waved and yelled to the guards, "See ya tomorrow." Then he fired up the truck and drove away. Double Down and Ketchum huddled close together at the front of the truck bed as the vehicle exited the mountain and headed toward Phoenix.

Fifteen minutes later, the truck came to a four-way stop and pulled over. "I gotta pee," said the driver as he exited and walked behind a large boulder off the road.

The passenger opened his door and moaned, "Me too."

Double Down gently rolled over on his side and whispered to Ketchum, "They must be done with their shift. When they come back, let's overtake them." He removed the revolver from his jacket and cocked the trigger. The driver was the first to return. Double Down leaped from the truck bed, pointing the pistol at the man's head and said, "Don't move!"

The man raised his hands in the air and replied, "I don't want no trouble, mister. This is just a job."

Ketchum peered over to the passenger who was zipping up his pants and coming back toward the truck. When he saw the gun, he tapped on his sunglasses and began to speak, "This one's on his phone," shouted Ketchum.

Double Down spun around and fired without hesitation striking the man's arm. "Put your hands up." The man raised one arm in the air while dangling the other at his side. When he realized blood was gushing out of his injured bicep, he covered the bullet wound with his other hand. "Get over here," Double Down commanded. The man took two steps forward but then sped off toward a large boulder. With a grimacing sigh, Double Down narrowed his eyes, aimed, and fired. The running target dropped like lightning into the soft sand.

While his back was turned, the driver crept in quietly and tackled Double Down to the ground. They rolled around exchanging grunts and fists until the gun hurled from his hand and landed next to the truck's tire. Both men wrestled in the dirt, pulling and tearing at each other's clothes.

Ketchum squeezed the guard rail and froze. He wasn't sure what to do or how to do it. The driver landed an elbow into Double Down's jaw, knocking him onto his stomach. His friend moaned and swayed while trying to shake off the blow and get back on his feet. The guard grabbed a large rock and raised it over Double Down's head. As he was ready to strike, Ketchum jumped off the truck, picked up the pistol, and fired without hesitation.

The blast reverberated across the desert into a desolate canyon and back. The smoke swiftly dissipated into the parched air. Double Down crawled over on the ground to examine the body for a heartbeat. There was none. He rose to his feet and removed the gun from Ketchum's hands. "Thanks for saving my life." Without saying another word, he dragged the dead bodies over to the large boulder and hid them both out of sight.

Ketchum stood shellshocked and stoic as he watched the corpses slither away. Any innocence that was left of his youth was forever lost in the moment, seeming to follow in the shadows of the two dead bodies and bury itself in the sand. His eyes trailed Double Down as he returned and got in the vehicle. All the while, he said nothing and ignored the tears that lingered but would not drop. What was there to say?

"Let's get out of here before somebody comes," Double Down said as he started the engine. His voice brought Ketchum out of his trance, triggering him to instinctively move around to the other side, open the door and hop in.

They plugged in the GPS coordinates for the Indian Reservation and drove away. Traveling on the main roads was too risky so they veered off onto dirt paths or abandoned fields whenever possible. A few dilapidated buildings scarred the landscape, clinging to what was left of wrought iron frames and crumbling piles of mortar. A helicopter crossed overhead at one point and hovered above. Double Down picked up a ball cap with the Dunes logo from the seat and waved it out the window until the chopper flew away.

A few minutes into the drive, Ketchum peered out over the endless array of eroding mesas and quietly said, "I suppose our lives will never be the same again."

Double Down glanced at his compadre before returning his gaze back to the road ahead. He'd already had his chance to make something of himself in this world, but Ketchum's life had been cut short before it'd even started. There weren't going to be any pool parties, extravagant gifts, or excursions on a yacht in his future. Nor was he likely to ever find a true love or see his family again. The prospects made him weep inside but he did his best not to show it. "I'd say we're marked men for sure. I don't know how you recover from that." He reached over, rubbed Ketchum's full head of hair, and added, "But there's a new self-defense clause in the Constitution that makes it legal to shoot someone in pretty much any situation. It's our word against theirs, and since there were no video feeds streaming up to the Intranet, and since they're dead…," he glanced over and winked before finishing his thought, "…I guess we can say whatever we want. Sooo, anything's possible."

Ketchum gingerly nodded and gazed out over the horizon. After a few minutes, he asked, "So, what's Soylent Green?"

Double Down snickered up a smile with a small grunt thrown in while recalling the memories. "It was an old movie from the twentieth century, probably a hundred years ago, I guess, where food was scarce and the world was overpopulated and dying — you know, real dystopian shit. Anyway, at the end of the film, the detective figures out that the food they've been eating *is* people. He yells at the top of his lungs, "Soylent Green is people, Soylent Green is people!"

Ketchum rocked his head back and forth while declaring, "Boy, that gives new meaning to the phrase 'going green.'"

"Where do you think those shamrock shakes come from?" A rosy grin emerged on Double Down's face as they both laughed.

"I need to see this film," said Ketchum.

"I don't think it's out there anymore. Maybe if you dig deep enough on the Intranet you might find it."

This comment sent Ketchum's mind wandering as his gaze turned to the vast landscape of rocks and sand outside his window. "So, what was it like when the Internet was unregulated?"

"Total chaos at times, at others, pretty amazing," replied Double Down. "You could find the answer to any question at your fingertips at any time and uncensored. Still, at other times, there was so much misinformation out there that it was hard to know what was real and what wasn't."

"Like what?"

"Like conspiracy theories about the government and a secret deep state. Who do you think works in government? I'll tell you who: people, ordinary citizens just like you and me. It may be slow to change and have stupid policies once in a while, but it's definitely not organized enough to create any kind of deep state. They're just not that smart." His eyes tightened as he turned to Ketchum and growled, "Private corporations, on the other hand, meticulously think these things out in board rooms filled with Harvard grads. All behind closed doors, too. That's the real enemy."

An uneasy silence filled the cab, accompanied only by the steady hum of rubber moving along the pavement. Double Down's grip tightened on the steering wheel as his breathing became louder with each passing field. Ketchum stole a few glimpses of his friend in between fumbling through his backpack and checking the side mirror but dared not stare too long.

Up ahead, a sign read, "Tohono O'odham Nation — 1 mile." They turned on a blacktop road and drove up to a lowered gate stationed next to a guardhouse before stopping. Two armed Indian guards came outside and approached their vehicle.

"State your business," said one of the guards as he warily inspected the visitors.

Double Down glanced over at Ketchum and then at the guard, "Uh, Carlos from the Gila Bend Facility sent us. Said you could help, you know." He paused for a moment as he wasn't sure what to say next. "Is Carmen here?"

The Indian guard looked up at his partner who'd just returned from surveying the perimeter of the truck. When their eyes met, he nodded. "Come on in."

PART III

ONE YEAR LATER

CHAPTER TWENTY-SIX

DILL ELECTRONICS, SUMMERFIELD, CA, 2069

ONE YEAR LATER

EDGAR DRAGGED his baton across the chain link fence as he walked the perimeter. An alarm chimed from his CompWatch at midnight signaling it was time for a coffee break. He headed to a side door of the warehouse, stood in front of the eye scanner, and entered when it buzzed. Automated forklifts zipped by carrying stacks of boxes down the aisles and depositing them in their final resting places.

A plump man wearing a hard hat and bursting out of his company-issued long white jacket stood on a platform above the fray directing traffic. "Evening, Agent Gorman."

"Fucking asshole," replied Edgar as he passed by. He stopped in front of a grease-covered sink basin to wash his hands. When he reached over to the automatic soap dispenser, nothing happened. "Fucking dark ages," he whispered.

He ran his hands under the water and caressed his wedding band. It was more than a year after his wife's death, yet he still didn't have the heart to take it off. While gazing into the worn-out mirror, one question kept circling the back of his mind: *How could I have fallen so far so fast?* In between the jagged dark spots hovering over the corner of the glass, his Demeanor Score read 395. *What do you know, better than yesterday*, he surmised. As he stared at his reflection, visions from the last few weeks of his wife's life came into focus. She was lying in bed with a cold wet rag on her forehead moaning.

❧❧❧

"Make it stop," she cried. "Make it stop."

Edgar stood next to the bed with heavy arms and the weight of the world on his shoulders. "Put your hands on my temples," she commanded. "Press hard."

He sat next to her and squeezed. "I am," he replied. "What else can I do?"

Evelyn turned on her back and looked him in the eyes. "You know what you have to do. Just do it. I don't want to know how but just do it."

Edgar hung his head and sighed."

❧❧❧

Slowly the images faded as Edgar closed his eyes, trying to savor them a few moments longer. It did no good. He brushed the dust off his shoulders and wiped his badge clean. Even though it only said, "Dill Electronics Security," it was still something to be proud of. When placed over his heart every evening before his shift, he felt almost human again. A sense of dignity emerged and gave him purpose. Of course, it wasn't anywhere near the amount of pride he felt when it read "Federal Bureau of Investigation," but it still garnered a nominal level of respect. The fact was, there were no badges with the "FBI" logo any longer. They'd all been reassigned to pawn shops and wooden knick-knack boxes resting on closet shelves.

A television monitor in the break room broadcast the day's news from earlier in the evening. A blonde-haired woman with perfect teeth recited from a teleprompter: *"It's been a year since*

Congress approved placing the 37th Amendment to the Constitution on the ballot, delegating several branches of our government's security to private firms. Voting for the nationwide referendum will begin in a few days. All registered voters will receive notification as to when and where it takes place. Please remember to reboot your phones whenever requested.

"The private firm Forest Dunes just reported a savings of fifteen percent over last year's budget after transitioning the FBI into the newly formed Bureau of Intelligence Gathering, or BIG for short. The company attributed most of the cost reductions to moving operations out of the Washington D.C. area and decentralizing offices throughout the country. Physical buildings have been reduced to a handful, which house technicians and research personnel, thus saving millions of dollars. Agents now travel the country in cars, RVs, and planes in order to avoid detection. This has reduced the threat of attacks that devastated the FBI and Homeland Security in the Fifties. It's unknown whether cyberattacks have increased during this time but authorities have stated, for the record, that damage has been minimal.

"In other news, a polar bear was spotted off the coast of Greenland this morning in what is being hailed as a triumphant rebuttal to environmentalists who had written the species off as extinct. The Speaker of the House tweeted, 'Where there's one, there are many.'"

"Gorman, in here, now," yelled a burly, gray-haired man standing in the doorway of an interior office. His demeanor was nothing short of intimidating, but deep inside, his heart was in the right place. He'd taken Edgar in when no one else would. Word spreads quickly about agents who've been blacklisted. Nevertheless, Max Calloway didn't like being told what to do and subtle threats made him even more rebellious.

"Shut the door," he barked as Edgar entered and sat down.

"What's up, boss?"

Max looked into a mirror and adjusted his tie before speaking. Knowing that Edgar was one strike away from being sent to Dunes meant he had to do everything by the book with him. "Alert levels have been increased to yellow in this sector, as we have reason to believe there is a possibility of some kind of attack or breach."

"Based on what intel?"

"It's classified."

"Then how'd you get it?"

"Here, smart-aleck." Max slid a folder across the table. "Dill Electronics isn't as low level as you might think."

Edgar opened it and found pages of documents with handwritten notes from another meeting. Sharing computer files or even printing them was dangerous in his line of work, as you never knew who was monitoring them. He could barely read Max's writing but did manage to decipher a few scribbles. Truncated sentences lined the page with cryptic passages like "Cyber Threat," "Lots of chatter," "Cross check," and "Dunes."

He pieced together the story as Max rattled off textbook phrases of normal protocol just in case anyone else was listening. His boss had already swept the room for concealed cameras this morning but there was always the chance he'd missed a spot.

Edgar nodded and said, "I see."

"Good. I'll keep you apprised of any new developments, but be on the alert for anything unusual." Max stretched his arms and asked, "What time does your shift end?"

"Six a.m."

"So does mine. Thank God it's Friday." He subtly winked and added, "Now get back to work."

Edgar knew what that meant. Max would be stopping by his favorite watering hole after his shift for a drink or two before heading home. If he wanted more information, all he had to do was stop by.

The bartender was turning off neon lights and propping the front door open when Edgar entered. Max was sitting at the bar with an unlit half-smoked cigar cushioned between two fingers.

With his seat strategically placed against the wall and in the middle of the room, he had a bead on everything coming and going. He was already halfway done with his first beer when he yelled to the bartender to bring two more, while spinning the cigar in the air.

Edgar sat next to him as the beers arrived on the counter. He raised his drink and said, "To your mother."

Max lifted his glass, clanked it against Edgar's, and downed the rest of it. "To your mother." Then he slid the empty glass to the edge of the bar and grabbed the full one. "You have kids?"

Edgar looked down, then gulped before replying, "No. we wanted to at first, but you know how it is. We just never could afford them and then — well anyway, it wasn't going to happen with my wife's condition and all."

"I'm real sorry about that. Although they can be a pain in the ass, losing one is about as bad as it gets."

"Are we talking about kids or spouses?"

This brought a smile to Max's face. Edgar's sarcastic humor was his best quality. Even though he could be incorrigible and downright annoying when it came to following orders, he always managed to break the ice with a good one-liner or colorful anecdote. Max had learned to adjust to his style and tolerate the bad stuff because he was so good at his job. Not to mention, highly overqualified.

"Both, I guess. I haven't spoken to my daughter in six months and I'm not even sure where my son is. Ever since Veronica left, they've just kind of gone their own way."

"Why's that? I thought you were pretty close to them."

"Money. It's all about money. They were hoping to inherit our millions when we both died. See, my parents were killed in a plane crash so we collected on their life insurance. Then when Veronica filed for divorce and married another man, she raised that guy's rug rats and ended up cutting my kids out of her will."

"That's pretty cold. Why would they blame you?"

"It's not just that. They also found out about the bad investments I made with my share of the money and that put them over the edge."

"Investments — like what?"

"Oh, you know, stocks, ETFs…" He lowered his head and mumbled, "…time shares."

"Time shares. You didn't!"

He sighed and said, "Unfortunately, but the place is so damn beautiful, and who wouldn't want a condo on an island somewhere? Fiji had it all — the beach, snorkeling, a hut surrounded by water, peace, tranquility."

"And more water."

"Indeed. We bought it twenty years ago. I mean, it wasn't so bad then and the place was a steal. Sure, during high tide it was a little scary, but now, oy."

"*Greedness greaty*, Max, what happened?"

"Well, the company we bought it from said they were moving all the huts further inland and that we'd be able to simply transfer ownership. What they didn't tell us was that they were selling everything to another firm. Come to find out, that firm wanted us to pay a transfer fee that was almost as much as what we'd paid for the home in the first place."

"Is this a US firm?"

"Of course. If it'd been a foreign company, we could've filed a complaint, but now, we're stuck."

"Right, corporations can't be sued."

"You got it." Max lit his cigar, took a toke, and added, "That made it nearly impossible to do anything, unless you spent a ton of money on lawyers, and, if I'm going to do that, well, I might as well just pay the damn fees."

"Kind of a Catch-22."

"Catch-22? Wasn't that a movie or a book?"

"Was. You can't watch it or read it anymore."

Max shook his head and continued, "Anyway, they don't understand or just don't care. They only want their money."

Edgar patted him on the back and said, "That's just sad."

He sighed again and replied, "Yeah, but it's not all bad news. When the kids left the house and went their own way, it made me realize that I didn't need to keep grieving for Veronica or take care of the thankless snots. It made me realize that I needed to start living my own life again."

The bartender rolled an empty keg by their stools and disappeared into the back room. Max gazed up over the long counter that stretched a good thirty feet. It butted against a long rectangular window looking onto the street outside. Every once in a while, a head walked by or a truck would flash along the glass momentarily. The day was still very young, but his heart wasn't quite ready to greet it.

He emptied his drink and set it on the end of the counter. When the bartender returned, he declared, "Two more."

"Well, good for you," said Edgar. "Life's too short, right?"

As the beers arrived, Max turned his head and said, "Right. Anyway, that's not why I wanted to talk to you." He rubbed his five-day-old beard and added, "I thought you might be interested in this other development at work, since it involved a few players from your past." He opened a hologram reading "Class of 2069," zoomed in on one of the young cadets standing in line, and slid it over to Edgar. "Does this person look familiar?"

Edgar scrutinized the image intently. "Yeah, how could I forget. April was her name. Connected with this boy, Ketchum Tutaloo."

"I thought you'd remember."

"Remember? I think about the two of them every day. I wondered where she'd gone to. I searched high and low and here she was, right under my nose."

"Don't get yourself all wrapped up in a bun. When BIG wants to make somebody disappear, they do."

"I guess so. She looks convincing."

The young woman was dressed in a dark blue uniform with a BIG badge on her chest. Max counted backwards, "Three, two, one," under his breath and then dissolved the hologram. "An 'Alert' notice popped up when I received the memo. When I read it, I thought it was worth bringing up, considering it was the last case you were working on before, you know, all this goofy stuff went down."

"Goofy is putting it mildly."

Max rolled the cigar between his fingers and said, "I know. What you've gone through this last year must've been a complete nightmare. I can't believe it took this long to straighten things out."

"But the Dunes Corporation doesn't make mistakes, Max."

He chortled up a grin and took another swig before saying, "Don't we all know that? Anyway, I can't change the past, but just thought you'd find it interesting that the girl who'd swindled that poor boy out of his million somehow became a BIG agent."

"Very, and now the boy is missing."

"Yeah, I saw that in the file too." He flashed another hologram and said, "And then there's this. When headquarters sent the photo of the graduating class around, of course our security team cross-checked it with the employee roster. Your name came up over a dozen times in connection with this April lady and Ketchum Tutaloo."

"Why's that? I only met him once and I've never even met her."

Max leaned back on his bar stool and replied, "How strange. Apparently, the cross-check connected you to the boy and girl at their school, his home, in a bank, a store, and a few other places."

Edgar's eyes widened as he realized what had happened.

"Oh... my... God." He downed half of his new beer and fumbled with the label on the bottle.

Max sat motionless and observed. That was what he was good at. He could tell more about a completely silent person than one who wouldn't shut up. He cleared his throat and asked, "Is there something you want to tell me?"

Edgar looked him straight in the eyes and added, "I was never at any of those places with April and Ketchum. I was only there in his head."

"I don't understand. How's that possible?"

Edgar glanced around the bar to see if anyone was nearby before whispering, "DDO glasses. Do you know what they are?"

"Of course I do," replied Max, "but how'd you get your hands on them?" He then squirmed in his seat and added, "Don't answer that."

Edgar merely smiled.

"Well, that's a relief. I thought I was going to have to take away your clearance credentials and ... you know."

"Fire me? Why? Just because I knew him?"

"Hey, they're paranoid as hell in Corporate. You do realize that we are a security systems company."

With a slight nod, Edgar pondered this last comment. "I guess so." As Max closed the visual file on his watch, Edgar noticed another photo popping up and pointed, "Hey, is that the suspect who escaped from Dunes?"

"Why, uh, I believe so. Let me look." Max clicked on the photo and an image emerged. "Alby McMurray, aka Libby Rimbaru. It says she's still at large."

"That's her. Gotta admire someone who can evade the authorities that long these days."

"Indeed. She's kind of cute in this photo." He swiped the screen and added, "Not in this one."

"That's what years at Dunes will do to you. Do you mind

sending me the file? I'd like to read up on her, you know, see what makes her tick."

Max glanced sideways and smirked. "I know that look. Don't say another word because I don't want to know." He tapped on the lens and said, "There you go. It's on the shared drive." Then he stood up, and said, "I'd better get out of here before I break any more laws. Now that I don't have to fire you, I can leave with a clean conscience and attend my Pilates class."

"Pilates?"

"Hey, you gotta start somewhere. Have a good weekend."

As he rose from his stool, Edgar asked, "Oh, by the way, did you ever hear anything back about Izzy?"

"No, I haven't. Isn't that strange? It's been a month now and no word from her." Max sighed and added, "It looks like she's just kind of slid off the grid."

"She married your cousin, right? What about him?"

"He's not returning my texts or calls either. We were pretty close too. Anyway, Izzy disconnected her phone and now the emails keep bouncing back. I can't figure it out."

"I wouldn't have this job if it weren't for her. Yet she wouldn't just drop off the map unless it was for a very good reason, would she?"

"I'm not sure. Lots of people go missing these days. Anyway BIG has officially closed the inquiry and declared her an Emancipated Agent."

"Meaning?"

"Meaning that she's been retired long enough and no longer a liability to the company. They've deemed themselves free and clear of any responsibility. As far as they're concerned, it's none of their business."

Edgar snickered and took another drink of his beer. "Quite convenient."

"Hey, when your liabilities outweigh your assets, you're liable to end up on your ass. That's our new company motto."

"That's every company's motto these days."

He winked and said, "Have a good weekend. I gotta go."

"You too."

The bartender continued cleaning up and carting bottles from the back to the front. He looked innocent enough but maybe that was intentional. Edgar had learned to trust nobody, not even Max these last few months. His memory wandered back to the early days with his wife. Yes, they were a bit of a struggle, but what fun they had. The years of traveling around the country in their RV with no road map and not a care in the world were the best. Then he imagined what it would've been like having Ketchum as a real son. He seemed to be such a good boy from what he'd observed.

That line between what he'd observed and what he'd experienced had all but been erased now. The memories intertwined forever because of the DDO glasses. The feelings were too real for both kids. He wondered what Izzy did with the glasses after their last meeting. Did she fall into that trap too? They were known to drive people crazy if you wore them too long. Was that why she'd disappeared?

Edgar took the last swig from his beer and contemplated everything that'd happened in his life. There was a good chance that these emotions would keep him up all morning. Thoughts were kryptonite when it came to sleep. Sunbeams from the glass window pane at the front of the bar stretched across the floor exposing dust floating in the air. He couldn't feel the heat, but sensed it. How closely that described his present situation made him chuckle. Instead of sitting on the sidelines licking his wounds, he should've been back in the game making things right. Then he finished his drink and whispered, "Maybe it's time to turn up the heat."

CHAPTER TWENTY-SEVEN

REDEMPTION WITH A "WHY"

EDGAR LEFT THE BAR and headed home. When he pulled into the Leisure Life Trailer Park and stopped to get his mail, the manager ran up to the car. "Hi Edgar," he puffed. "It's the end of the month. I need your rent money by tomorrow."

"I know, I know. You'll get it. Don't be such a turd."

"Well, I also have to fill out that damn questionnaire again, but this time it's with BIG."

"Only a year and a half more to go, then you won't have to bother with it ever again."

As he drove away, the manager yelled, "That does me no good right now. I'm tired of covering your ass and making you look good." When Edgar was out of earshot, he added, "Especially one as sorry looking as yours."

Edgar parked the car next to his RV, got out, and brushed off the cobwebs stretching from the wheel well to the tire. He entered and switched on the lights. The sun was now peeking through the tree line on the east side of the park. Jagged rays of sunshine blanketed the fiberglass on the outside of the trailer so he flipped on the air conditioner and pulled the curtains shut. Originally, he'd moved up to Summerfield to enjoy the cooler ocean breeze weather, but lately it had been hotter there than inland. Why, was anybody's guess. At least, he still had the solitude to enjoy.

The RV wasn't much to take note of: twenty-eight feet of fiberboard, foam, aluminum, and plastic molded into the shapes of household items, kitchen comforts, and appliances. What it lacked in luxury, it made up for with pointless accessories. On the walls mounted with stick-on hooks were everything from his first book report to a family portrait dangling over the toilet. Several of his mother's pottery masterpieces were poignantly placed in corners and underneath shadows.

He lifted one and studied it. The base of the vase curved nicely while the other half spiraled up like a wrung-out washcloth. The hole at the top was barely big enough for a flower or two, making it not worth the time and effort. An ashtray sat on the table with colors more vibrant than his mother's paintings. The bottom was off center just enough to where it teetered off balance with each cigarette.

Why he kept his mother's useless creations was beyond explanation. There were many times he'd come close to tossing them in a dumpster but something in the back of his mind wasn't ready to let them go. In a way, they brought a certain level of peace and solitude into his life. The wobbly ashtray was a nice reminder on why he'd quit smoking in the first place. The nicotine highs regularly threw his whole body out of whack. The paintings that he'd lined up above the front cab were a daily reminder that he needed to pick up a brush and apply a few strokes himself. Yet, there were other demons he needed to conquer before letting those types of pleasures back into his life.

The items were also a constant reminder of another place and time, another era, another period of his life when everything was carefree and simple. The scattered memories of his mother shaping a piece of clay on a potter's wheel or quietly humming while adding touches to her latest colorful composition now meant more than ever.

A set of white LED lights blinked around the refrigerator as he opened the door and pulled out a bottle of beer. This was the only home he knew now and it was paid for. He sat on the couch and turned on the TV. A newscaster with glossy silver hair and sharp cheekbones announced, *"Another oil reserve was discovered in Alaska today, making that twenty-three in the last thirty years. Experts estimate the added production will fuel the energy demands of America well into the next century. In other news, a new ski lift at Yosemite National Park has opened to the public this week and skiers are saying that it's one of the most beautiful runs in the country..."*

There was a hard knock at the door. Edgar turned down the volume, reached for his gun and clicked off the safety. He sandwiched it between a pillow and the mattress above the two front seats next to the door just in case. He didn't get many visitors these days and the only one he was expecting had already caught up with him at the mailbox.

Carefully, he walked over to a window and peeked out. It was a man and woman dressed in black slacks, blazers, and dark sunglasses. He immediately recognized Toyer Wittler, who was still trying to grow into that first mustache but failing miserably. The agent sneered through a thin set of lips while running his hand over a short blue crew cut. He was a frequent visitor to Edgar's place but today wasn't a scheduled visit. At least, not one he remembered.

Then there was the woman standing next to him. The image was eerily familiar: a slim but firm torso, neatly dressed in a uniform, with polished patent leather shoes and an attitude that exuded confidence yet inexperience. The woman stood back away from the door so she could be easily seen and acknowledged. Edgar recognized that M.O. too.

He cracked the door open and removed his hand from the pistol. "May I help you?"

"Hello Edgar, can we come in?"

"Today's not a scheduled visit."

"I know, but we're authorized to make unannounced visits when warranted. It's all in the agreement you signed."

Toyer nodded to the younger agent. She removed her sunglasses and said, "I'm Agent Jones from BIG. We only need a minute of your time."

The blood drained from Edgar's head as he recognized April's face. He wondered why the girl would show up at his place now. How could this be a coincidence? Something was terribly out of alignment here.

"Certainly."

Edgar took a few deep breaths to calm himself down and stood rigid. Then he brushed off his shoulders, buttoned up his uniform, and tucked his shirt under the belt. April scanned the area around the RV searching for any movement from neighboring trailers before following Toyer up the stairs. Once inside, Edgar opened the refrigerator door and asked, "Beer?"

A grimacing scowl brushed underneath Toyer's peach fuzz as he answered, "No, thank you, we're on duty."

Edgar couldn't help but snarl up a smile while grabbing the bottle opener. He opened the bottle and plopped himself onto the front passenger seat while waving the other two toward the couch.

"Please, have a seat."

The two agents jockeyed for a level spot on the worn-out foam cushions. Toyer opened a notepad and typed away in the BIG database while Agent Jones took in the trailer décor. Edgar inconspicuously stole a few glimpses of her while taking sips of his beer. Visions from his early days after graduating the academy kept flashing back. She had the same outward bravado, the false deep tone in her voice, almost as if she'd just hit puberty, and the inability to make direct eye contact without giving away clues. Those were all characteristics that would evolve over time and recede as she learned her craft.

He chuckled internally at the word "craft." Was it truly a craft, or more or less a way of simply coping? It wasn't in his nature to lie or be aggressive like most agents. In fact, his best qualities were subduing a suspect with charm and politeness. That was the main reason he was such a good agent. His boss recognized these skills early on and used Edgar to diffuse the tension whenever a situation called for it.

"Quite an interesting collection of... stuff you have around here," said April.

"The paintings and pottery aren't mine. They were my mother's."

"Were? I'm sorry for your loss."

"Oh, don't be. She lived a long time and enjoyed every minute of it." Edgar glared at Toyer and added, "I wish I could say the same."

Toyer stopped typing into his notepad and straightened up. "There now," he announced as he raised his head. "Well, as you know, it's been a full six months since your release from the Dunes Psychiatric Ward. As required in the agreement between you and the state, BIG is to monitor your situation and make routine checkups, then report your progress back to MAGMA. After two years, a review will be made of your condition and any continued observation will be determined at that time."

He then grinned and addressed Edgar directly. "It's been my utmost pleasure being your caseworker these last few months. We've had some wonderful memories together."

Edgar spun from side to side in the captain's chair and took another sip. He knew he had to choose his next few words very carefully. Most of his past sarcastic remarks had done very little to help his cause. In fact, they had only succeeded in knocking his Demeanor Score down to dangerous levels. Toyer knew this all so well and relished any chance to throw in a jab here or there.

"That we have," was all he said.

Toyer nodded and glanced down at his notepad before saying, "I'll now ask you a series of questions to determine this week's status." He cleared his throat and recited:

"What are the colors on the American flag?"

"Red, white, and blue," replied Edgar.

"Have you had any desire to commit a crime or bring harm to any individual?"

"Of course not."

"Have you consumed any alcoholic beverages or used any illicit drug substances this week?"

"Just beer."

"How many?"

There was a long pause. Edgar contemplated what to say knowing that they'd already accessed his digital files and knew exactly what he'd purchased. "Twelve, no, maybe a whole case, twenty-four."

"Have you engaged in sex with anyone of the opposite sex?"

This question always got under Edgar's skin. He'd long suspected that Toyer threw it in himself, off the record, just to get a rise out of him. "Kiss my ass."

He swiped a few more times and Edgar's CompWatch dinged. His Score had dipped to 345. "What the hell, Toyer!"

Another ping and the score dropped to 320. "Profanity directed at a BIG agent by a parolee is considered reckless insubordination. Would you like to try for more?"

"When did 'hell' become profanity?"

Another ding and his score dropped to 295. Edgar went silent.

"Better. Please answer the question. Have you engaged in sex with anyone of the opposite sex?"

"No," defiantly replied Edgar.

"Have you engaged in sex with anyone of the same sex or in between?"

"Not yet." He glanced at April and winked. Even though he had no interest in having a relationship with a person of the same sex, he knew this would get under Toyer's skin terribly. Plus, he'd learned over the years that certain words were not detectable in Demeanor Score algorithms and wouldn't be interpreted as derogatory or self-incriminating. Words like "maybe," "I don't know," and "not yet" were too ambiguous to be converted into a calculable figure.

Toyer arched his back and shivered as he imagined the horrible act between them. "Well, I... we must... it is forbidden."

"It's a joke," replied Edgar. "*Greedness greaty*, you are so gullible."

They all three laughed half-heartedly and released a cohesive sigh of relief into the room. Then, to add insult to injury, Edgar added, "Besides, you're not my type."

This time, April and Edgar let out a laugh so loud that it echoed off a metal sheet of artwork hanging over the window. April lowered her head and tried to contain herself with a subtle snort.

The smear rubbed Toyer all the wrong ways and he replied, "I'll definitely have to include that remark in my report. Insulting an agent." Another ding on Edgar's watch and his score fell 25 points.

Edgar let out a long sigh and struggled to catch his breath as he replied, "Oh, that one was worth it." He allowed the moment to linger while absorbing the ramifications of his actions.

Toyer stood up and turned to April. "Agent Jones is officially taking over as your caseworker going forward. I'm needed back in the office, so I'll be on my way." He handed April the notepad and nodded to them both. "Good day."

With that, he quickly exited the RV. April gazed over to Edgar, as the sound of popping gravel spurting out from Toyer's tires filled the parking lot. Edgar's mind wandered off to some elusive place between redemption and regret. He wondered what would become of him after stumbling over so many bad decisions in life. It was all there on his chart and reflecting off his Demeanor Score. He remembered what his mother had said during that last visit. Did he have a cause worth dying for? A resounding 'No' echoed inside.

April interrupted his train of thought. "Well, now that that's over, let's see what we can do here."

She opened the notepad and loaded Edgar's case file. In his rush to leave, Toyer had forgotten to submit the last portion of the report. A green rectangle glowed in the middle of the page reading "Submit." She hit "Escape" and backtracked a few steps on the form until she came to the summary. Then she highlighted his last few comments and hit "Delete."

As Edgar finished the last swig of the beer, he analyzed his new caseworker with renewed interest. Was this still the unsuspecting grifter that'd destroyed several boys' lives, or a girl looking for her own kind of redemption?

"There, no need to get off on the wrong foot here. Toyer's comments have been permanently stricken from the record." April slightly lifted a cheerful cheek while adding, "It's a pleasure to be working with you, Mr. Gorman. I look forward to our next meeting."

She hit a key on her notepad one last time and Edgar's CompWatch dinged. His Demeanor Score increased 25 points. April rose from the couch and Edgar followed suit. They shook hands as she said, "I'll see you next week at the scheduled time and day, Mr. Gorman."

Edgar locked the door behind her and wondered if his first impression could be so wrong. He'd made reading people's faces an art form over the years but this person did not fit the mold. Nothing in her mannerisms connected her to the person he'd seen a year ago in Ketchum's mind. His body deflated onto the couch like a hot air balloon. Did he finally get a break when he least expected it? Good news was just life's little way of keeping him off balance and today was no exception.

As he opened another bottle and took a swig, the cabin bed above the driver's seat caught his eye. Leaning against the window on one side was a lifetime's work of canvases and frames. Instead of being proudly displayed in an art gallery or even on the wall of his home, they sat hidden and forgotten, relegated to existing only in the crevices of a dingy corner of his RV.

He pulled the paintings out into the light and laid them on the mattress. While admiring his crude interpretations of Munch and Seurat, he smiled. Most people would say they were creative, if nothing else. Yet anyone who'd ever observed them never used the word beautiful or exquisite. Piled in the corner sat his unfinished works: a few sketched charcoal drawings smeared into canvas, some half-completed watercolors dripping with several shades of the rainbow. These sketches weren't even allowed the privilege of being praised by friends or fellow artists. No, they weren't ready to show. Still, each time he viewed them he whispered that someday, someday soon they would.

Then there were the other paintings of his mother's lined neatly across the wall above his bed. When juxtaposed against his, you'd never imagine that the two people who'd created them were related. The colors flew off the fractal images like paintballs splattering against a wall. Yet, when you viewed them from the right angle, oversized heads of birds and dogs popped out of the frames, turning the experience into a more hallucinatory enlightenment instead of a geometric enigma.

He pushed the artwork back into place and covered it with long pillows before stepping down from the cabin bed. Then he turned up the news on the TV and plopped back down on his couch to unwind. The anchorman smiled and delivered the morning news. *"It's been another banner year for the stock market and profits are projected to continue at this same pace well into next year. On another note, a survey done by Gallup Polls states that the overall approval rating for Congress and the job being done in Washington has risen to 74%. This is the highest rating ever recorded in the survey's history.*

"In other news, out-of-wedlock births have reached an all-time low in several parts of the country. This is being attributed to the abstinence-only educational programs being taught in schools today, along with the rise in the number of marriage licenses issued..."

The chatter soon became background noise as Edgar yawned. He downed another gulp and sprawled out on the couch with a blanket. Before setting his beer down, he drained the last few drops into a cactus sitting on the counter that'd bloomed overnight. The vibrant yellow petals had already enjoyed their moments in the sun earlier that morning. "Every flower must grow through dirt," he purred, while wondering what it would be like to exist so easily. A little sunlight, very little attention, and even less water were all it needed to blossom into something lovelier than before. It gave him hope.

CHAPTER TWENTY-EIGHT

CONFESSIONAL

A WEEK LATER, April showed up at Edgar's door at the prearranged time. She pulled into the trailer park driving a banged-up late model electric car. As she exited the vehicle, Edgar noticed her hair wasn't rolled up in a bun like before. Instead of the company-issued uniform, she sported worn-out bluejeans, a black V-neck t-shirt, and that ever-present silver necklace.

Edgar opened the door before she had the chance to knock. "Sweet ride there."

April blushed and replied, "Yeah, BIG is big on stealth surveillance and not attracting any attention. If you ask me, I think they're just cheap."

Edgar couldn't help but smile. In the back of his mind, a voice kept saying, *Don't make me like you, bitch. I know what you did.*

April stopped at the bottom of the steps and said, "Why don't we take a drive? It's too nice a day to sit inside."

Edgar glanced over the interior of his RV, ran his finger over a dusty lampshade, and asked, "Where're you thinking about going?"

"How about the pier?"

"Sounds good."

On the drive over, April swerved through traffic as if driving a bumper car, churning up enough of last night's dinner to make Edgar nauseous. Finally, while holding onto the handle mounted in the headliner, he asked, "Do you always drive like this?"

April blinked rapidly and leaned back in her seat. "Oh, sorry. I wasn't even aware. Bad habit."

"Thank you." Edgar released the handle and lowered the back of his seat. "I thought I might lose it there for a second." He let out a sigh and asked, "So, why the beach?"

April glanced over while entering a parking lot and said, "Your place is bugged. Has been since you were released."

Edgar's head slowly wobbled as the car bounced over a speed bump and replied, "I suspected as much but couldn't find anything."

"You won't these days, unless you get rid of your CompWatch, TV, refrigerator and anything else with an electric cord."

"A little bit like Big Brother, don't you think?"

"A lot like Big Brother, you mean."

They exited the car and moved toward the end of the pier. An unrelenting breeze and overcast sky engulfed the wooden platform. Perfect weather for fuzzy video feeds and static microphones. Every few feet, they stopped to gaze into a shop window or browsed through a few knick-knacks displayed out in front. Although April's hands fumbled through layers of cotton shirts, her eyes were scanning the perimeter through her sunglasses. There was nothing out of the ordinary as far as she could tell, but, as any good agent knew, that's how it was supposed to look.

Halfway down the pier, a fisherman reeled in a large mackerel and tossed it onto the deck as tourists gathered around. It flopped defiantly, evading the hands of a small boy who was trying to place it in a bucket. At the end of the platform, the sun broke through the cloud cover and now blanketed the sea with a warmer breeze. To the north, yellow-colored buoys dotted the middle of the bay with the word "Gooble" written on them.

April gripped the wooden rail and peered out to where a crumbling pile of stucco and red tiles lay stacked on the end of a jetty. The old museum had finally lost its battle with the sea.

With each crashing wave, another memory inched closer to the ocean floor.

She discreetly frowned and wiped back a tear. Often, she'd wondered what had happen to the boy she was with on that cold marble slab. He was different from the others. That one hurt and she never forgave her adoptive mother for forcing her to go through with the whole scam.

Edgar felt the pain too, knowing Ketchum as he did. The memories were still vivid, almost as if he'd been the one lying on that sleeping bag with the girl, dreaming about their future together and revealing their deepest secrets. When he'd heard that Ketchum had gone missing, he did everything in his power to find out the details, but these days his powers were waning and the inquiries went nowhere.

"What is that out there?" asked Edgar, while already knowing the answer.

"It's an old museum. Sad what's happened to it."

"You have a special connection to the building?"

"If you only knew." April squeezed the railing and stared straight ahead. Her sunglasses hid the pain well but the strain of the past was visible everywhere else, from her slumping shoulders down to the buckling knees.

Edgar offered a comforting smile and said, "Demons from your past or pleasant memories?"

"A little of both." April leaned into her next reply with a sigh and said, "I've had my regrets, but I'm a changed person now."

"For the better?"

"That's an odd question, Mr. Gorman. What are you implying?"

Several thoughts entered Edgar's mind. He wasn't quite sure why he said what he did. His response was Pavlovian in nature, a verbal knee jerk reaction. Did he want to poke the bellicostic bear here or lull it back to sleep? *Ah, what the hell*, he thought, *it's now or never.*

"The last case I worked on before being, how do we say, reassigned."

"You mean, committed," retorted April.

Edgar nodded, acknowledged the jagged comment, and continued, "Call it whatever you want, but it was all a big mistake and the Bureau knows it."

"The Bureau doesn't exist any longer, Mr. Gorman, and as you know, BIG doesn't make mistakes."

"They've programmed you well, Agent Jones, or should I call you, Agent Johnson, or some other alias? I was there for Ketchum Tutaloo's interrogation after he entered Zero Sum. I know it all."

This verbal hand grenade exploded like a shaken soda can in April's face. Part of the agreement with the agency in return for testifying against her stepmother, Delores, was that her criminal history would be sealed from public view. Yet, here was a man who somehow knew her deepest and darkest secrets. She was impressed and anxious at the same time.

April's eyes watered slightly before she turned away, brushing them off with her sleeve. Edgar couldn't decide whether this was all part of an act or actually legit. He'd seen this girl in action and knew how good she was, but his instincts told him otherwise.

"I'm sorry."

"No need to be sorry," said April. "I should've known it would come to this one day. You can run from your past, but you can't hide from it completely."

"Don't I know that," replied Edgar.

They both laughed nervously and enjoyed the moment. Then April lowered her head and said, "I really loved him. I know you might find that hard to believe but, after everything went down, he changed me, and I got out."

A breeze, reeking of salty air and dead fish, whisked by, ruining their moment. Edgar studied April's whole body, trying to weed out any hints of deception. Did it pass the smell test?

Seagulls squawked with vigor at the scene, seeming to unwittingly debate the question themselves. Yet he felt a change happening to him inside with every step he took away from his own past. Why couldn't the same be for April?

"I believe you, for some reason. I don't know why, but I do."

"Thank you. That means a lot." April gently sniffled and asked, "Do you know where he is?"

"Not a clue. He disappeared days after arriving at Dunes with another guy. No one's heard from them since — at least, none of the people I know."

"None in my world either. It's the reason why I became a BIG agent in the first place. I figured that if anybody knew, they did. Turns out I was wrong."

Edgar leaned on the railing and said, "Maybe we should pool our resources together and see what we can find out."

"Sounds good."

They both nodded and shook hands. Then Edgar stood rigid and stared directly into April's eyes before asking, "What would you do if you found him?"

April smiled and gleefully replied, "I'd squeeze him as tight as I could and never let go."

Her confession felt sincere. She didn't blink, she didn't tear up — it was nothing but barefaced honesty. It was crystal clear now that this girl had truly changed. Edgar swiftly turned away as the revelation made his own eyes tear up.

"Are you okay?" asked April.

"Yeah, just the sea air." He wiped away any remaining doubt and added, "Then we need to find him."

"Agreed." April cracked her knuckles and wrung her hands. "Wow, I'm so glad I got that off my chest. You don't know how hard it's been this last year carrying all this guilt. I mean, ever since he went away, a part of me has seemed to be… missing. I don't quite know how to describe it."

Edgar grinned and replied, "You were in love. It's a hellacious thing and it shows no mercy."

"I guess so."

As they walked back to the car, Edgar inquired, "So, something's been bugging me all day and I just have to ask. Didn't you used to wear a hearing aid?"

"I did indeed. Very observant."

"Hey, it's second nature, you know."

"Of course." April unconsciously rubbed her ear and said, "Part of the agreement with the agency was that they'd expunge my record and make the old April disappear. I convinced them that having a hearing aid would always blow my cover and they agreed. Instead of a signing bonus, I got a new ear."

"That's wonderful, and a game changer, I bet."

"Definitely." April glanced at her CompWatch and said, "Well, I need to head off. You're not my only case, you know."

"No problem. I've enjoyed our little heart-to-heart talk here. This all doesn't feel like normal agency protocol, though, unless BIG has changed strategies."

"I've never been normal, Mr. Gorman, and the agency knows it." She smiled and added, "I just wanted things to get off on the right foot between us."

"That they have," agreed Edgar.

April scooted in closer and spoke the next few words a little over a whisper: "I know you weren't crazy."

"Thank you." Edgar nodded and grinned. Then, with a flair of sarcasm, he replied, "Well, maybe a little bit, but aren't we all?"

CHAPTER TWENTY-NINE

THE DECISIONS WE LIVE WITH

APRIL DROPPED EDGAR off at his trailer and sped away. While watching her merge into traffic, he noticed two children playing tag and racing from one tree to another on the other side of the trailer park. Instinctively, he dialed a number.

"Hey, bro," answered Lotty.

"I was thinking about stopping by today. Are you busy?"

"Always, but never too busy for you. Come on by."

"Great, I'll be there in a couple of hours."

With that, he loaded in her GPS coordinates and summoned a driverless car to carry him away. During the trip, he logged into his work database to see what information, if any, it had on April. The typical early school data and training in the academy were there but nothing about a criminal record. Nothing about a father came up either. She searched the database for Delores and found that she was doing ten to fifteen years at the California Institute for Women in Chino. The list of charges and convictions for robbery and identity theft were long. He entered the section containing the court transcriptions but they were heavily redacted.

When he typed in "Ketchum Tutaloo" and searched, the database forwarded him to the Dunes public website. The boy's photo turned up with the words "Missing" written underneath. He tried to access more information, but a message glaring back read, "No further information is available."

Traffic was light so he made good time on the freeway. After his mother's death, he and his sister had drifted apart, seeing less and less of each other. A big part of him didn't want to be reminded how well she was doing. It only made him regret not taking the million dollars when he had the chance. The first thing he noticed when the car pulled up was that the lamppost had been removed, along with all the aluminum foil. The house had recently been painted and new plants lined the perimeter. Lotty answered on the first knock.

"Little brother, what a pleasant surprise. It's been a while."

"I know, I know. I've been busy."

Lotty looked at his outfit and said, "Who dresses you in the morning?"

Edgar grinned and lightly pushed her out of the way as he entered the living room. "Look who's talking? There are other colors besides black, you know."

"Black is not a color. It's an attitude." She stiffened her shoulders and tried to look bigger than she really was as she shut the door and followed him into the house.

He stopped, turned around, and hugged his sister tightly. "Um, I miss you. Sorry for not coming by more often. Of course, you could always come by my place too, you know."

"And what, squeeze into your tiny trailer and sit around drinking cheap beer? Come see what I've done with the back yard."

She guided him to a set of huge glass sliding doors and clapped her hands. They parted like the Red Sea, opening to a patio deck covered with limestone, flowers, and rattan furniture. A kidney-shaped pool occupied the back half of the yard, with a small waterfall spilling out from an above-ground spa. Mediterranean palm trees lined the corners as different shades of green, yellow, and orange filled in the landscape between them.

"Holy shit, this is beautiful," exclaimed Edgar. "When did you do this?"

"Shortly after mother died." She walked over to a table under an umbrella, sat down, and poured a glass of water from a pitcher. "Dylan MacMillan had a good year, which means that I had a good year."

"Obviously," he replied.

"Yes, it's very exciting. The music industry is slowly moving back toward using real musicians instead of all that computerized keyboard algorithm crap. And now that some of the classic rock songs are entering the public domain, I have a treasure trove of material to work with."

"Good to hear. I'm proud of you, sister, and mother would be even prouder." Edgar sat down next to her and noticed the gleam in her eyes as the words sank in. She'd actually managed to look at him directly without turning away. That made him even more pleased.

Lotty placed her hand on his knee and said, "You're always welcome to move in with me, you know. This is still your home as much as mine." She leaned back and added, "Especially since you won't let me buy out your half."

"That's my retirement plan, you know," said Edgar. "In due time."

"Well, even if I did buy you out, you're still always welcome."

"Thanks."

Lotty took a sip and asked, "So what brings you here today? Are you meeting someone in L.A.? Maybe a new woman in your life, a new job, searching for the meaning of life?"

Edgar laughed. "No, nothing like that. Just wanted to see you."

She shook her head and replied, "I really missed you when you were gone. I didn't think you'd ever come back. I mean, if anyone's crazy in this family, it's me."

He snorted. "So true."

"What a shitty deal you got."

"It's all in the past now."

"Still, I have a friend who's an attorney and he could look into having your record expunged."

Edgar perked up and quipped, "You have a friend? When did you get a friend?"

"Eat shit and die, brother." Lotty wiggled in her chair and placed both hands on her glass. "I have lots of friends now. That's what happens when you don't have to work for a living."

"I wouldn't know," replied Edgar. He leaned back and rocked in his chair while absorbing this last comment. It hit home hard. He realized that he was the one without any friends and the one friend he did have was missing.

A familiar chime rang on both their phones. The message "Please reboot your devices" showed up, but this time, another communication followed: "The Nationwide Referendum adding the 37th Amendment to the Constitution is on the ballot in every state and voting will start in one week."

"These damn reboots are irritating as hell," said Edgar as he covered his CompWatch completely with his hand, shutting it down.

"I know, but it's for the good of the country."

This last statement puzzled him. "When did you become so patriotic?"

Lotty sat stoically in her chair and replied, "Everyone should have a sense of duty, especially when it comes to such an important vote. I know I'm voting."

"Lotty, you've never voted for anything in your whole life. In fact, I don't recall you ever even registering. What happened to all the conspiracy theories about the election being rigged and our vote never counting?"

Lotty watched her CompWatch reboot and replied, "I never said that."

There was a long pause between them. As the waterfall flowed gently from the spa softening the dialogue, Edgar studied his sister's face closely. She'd always had a small twitch on the side of her eye that acted up whenever her brain moved too fast. Today, it remained motionless.

"So, sister, how are you voting? Do you want Dunes to take over Homeland Security and the FBI permanently or not?"

"Why, yes, of course. Don't you? They'll be able to run them way better than the government has."

"What about the national parks?"

"I think they've done a wonderful job with them. I mean, what's wrong with a few upgrades to increase foot traffic."

"I think they were pretty crowded as it was."

"Maybe, but by widening all the roads, and adding a few more hotels and ski lifts, that kind of stuff, now everyone can enjoy them."

"Everyone but the animals that live there."

Lotty merely shrugged her shoulders and directed her gaze from the pool to the waterfall and then back to the table. She took a drink and said, "The government's done a pretty piss-poor job of running things. I think it's time for a change."

Edgar just peered over at the waves rippling across the water and replied, "I used to be part of that government, remember."

"Yes, and look what they did to you."

"That wasn't the government. It was MAGMA."

"Still, it was wrong."

Edgar pondered this comment while watching a spider web glistening in the sun between the two lawn chairs. In a way, his life had been reduced to a single strand of silk stretching across two barriers. On one hand, it was precariously thin, exposed to the elements of scorn and ridicule. On the other, it had withstood the test of time and adapted to his ever-changing world.

"What's that saying, 'What doesn't kill us makes us stronger'?" said Edgar as he continued observing the spider web.

"My god, you sound like Mother now."

He laughed, "So true."

Lotty leaned into the table and folded her hands together before saying, "I'll tell you my theory about life, and it's not pretty, but all the same, it's how I view these things. I think some people are just born lucky. You know, they grow up on the right side of the tracks and always catch a lucky break. And then there are others who I think have some kind of secret compass that guides them along. You know, like they'd made these decisions before in another life and know exactly what to do all the time, sort of like being reincarnated. Does that make sense? Probably not, but can you imagine what it'd be like if every time you had to make a decision, a memory from another life popped up in your brain and said, 'Do this,' or 'No, don't do that.' Wouldn't that be cool?" Then she slapped her hands on the table and added, "Then there's the rest of us unlucky stiffs."

Edgar mulled this over and nodded, "You know, you kind of make sense. I'm not saying that I agree with you, but I can't say it's impossible." His eyes narrowed as he asked, "When did you become so smart?"

"Must be in the genes."

"No doubt."

"Speaking of jungles and the outdoors, can you imagine how much fun it would've been being able to go to a water slide at Zion National Park when we were little?" She lightly shook her head and added, "Much better than that godawful camping excursion mom's boyfriend made us go on."

"Oh, I don't know. I thought that was fun."

"Edgar, there is nothing fun about drinking water out of a canteen and sleeping on the hard cold ground."

"To each his own, I guess."

Lotty rocked back on her chair for a moment, then said, "Hey, I found a box of Mom's things that I need you to check out before I toss them."

"Toss them? You've already cleaned house and whitewashed away almost all her memories as it is. Don't you want something to remember her by?"

"Edgar, your relationship with her was completely different from mine. She threw me out of the house, remember?"

"She didn't throw you out. She let her boyfriend throw you out."

"The same thing."

Lotty's voice wavered. She was right. Even though the two had come from the same womb, you'd think that they'd been raised by two different mothers. Yet, when you cut through the thick onion-skin on the outside and peeled away the layers of tears, it was less about their mom and more about her boyfriends. It was all about timing with Lotty. She had to deal with the wrath of Wild Bill growing up, while Edgar enjoyed play dates with Chip.

He wondered how different things would've been if his real father had been there. Edgar knew so little about him, as he died soon after their mother found out she was pregnant with him. His father had no living brothers or sisters and any distant relatives were living incognito in the Chicago area.

"I guess so," he said. "Let's go look at the stuff."

"I'll bring it out," replied Lotty. She stepped into the house and returned seconds later with a shoebox. Then she slid it across the table to her brother and said, "It's not much, but you never know what might mean something to you, so I kept it."

"Thank you," replied Edgar. He removed the lid and fumbled through odds and ends like fingernail clippers, political pins, business cards, and earrings. Nothing jumped out as worth keeping until he came across a colorful card with red, black, and gold swirls on each corner and a Mardi Grás mask in the middle. He'd seen the design somewhere before. He lifted the card out of the box and read, "Mama Cravens' Café – dial BEST-RECIPE." On the back was a recipe for fried chicken with the handwritten words, "Don't get me started." Those words had special meaning to him. They reminded him of Izzy every time he heard them. While tucking the card in his pocket, he said, "I'll keep this. You can toss everything else."

Lotty nodded and replied, "Perfect. Consider it done."

Edgar watched her march the box over to a trash can and dump it inside. He stood up and stretched. "I have to get back home. Your back yard is beautiful. See you soon."

They both hugged and headed into the house. At the doorway, Edgar whispered in her ear, "I love you. I know you love me too, although you'd never admit it."

Lotty gripped him tightly and replied, "You bet."

"See you soon."

While driving home, he analyzed the card and wondered why his mother had it in the first place. Where had he seen that name before? He turned it over and read the recipe: flour, salt, pepper, egg... something was missing but he couldn't quite place it. He read the ingredients again. Then it hit him: cooking oil. There was no mention of oil anywhere, yet he knew that cooking fried chicken without it was like breathing without air. *How strange*, he thought.

When he turned the card back over and read the words "Don't get me started," a warm smile emerged. It was Izzy's favorite catchphrase. He'd heard her say it a million times over the years and couldn't imagine it appearing there without a reason. This couldn't be a coincidence.

With a confident nod, he dialed the number. The line on the other end picked up after one ring. "Press 1 for English, 2 for *Greedness*." Edgar froze. *Did I hear that correctly,* he questioned? After a few seconds, the recorded voice repeated, "Press 1 for English, 2 for *Greedness*."

Edgar couldn't resist and pressed "2." The line rang and the same voice answered, "Press 3 for *Greaty*."

He complied.

The recording immediately transferred to another line. Dead space ticked across the airwaves as the silence wavered in between static and heavy breathing. Someone was on the other end of the call but not ready to respond. Edgar waited. Every bone in his body wanted him to speak but his mind knew better. His training had taught him better. So he waited.

Finally, in a low subtle voice, a woman said, "Hello."

"Hello," Edgar replied.

"Are you looking for the missing ingredient?"

His hunch was right. Vindicated but still unclear where this conversation was heading, he decided to play along. "Yes."

"Meet me at noon tomorrow in front of Mama Cravens' Café."

"But I don't know where it is."

"You do now." Then the line went dead.

Edgar's stared at his watch after the caller hung up. He noticed that it ended barely a few seconds before a tracer could be put on it.

He turned the card over and reviewed the ingredients again. Sure enough, no oil was mentioned on the list. Then he flipped it back over. Right before his eyes, an address slowly surfaced underneath the words, "Mama Cravens' Café." It read, "512 Olive Street. 12:00 noon tomorrow."

How did I miss that? he mused.

He swiped his CompWatch and held his finger down on the lens until the Maps program came up. Then he commanded, "Show me 512 Olive Street in Summerfield, California." The address was an empty lot. This didn't make sense so he reviewed the card again but the address had vanished.

"What the hell is going on?" he whispered while examining both sides.

Next, he maneuvered the hologram around a full 360 degrees to see what else was in the neighborhood. All he found was a liquor store and a café residing on the other side of the street. He zoomed in on the marquee in front of the café. Corners of a few faded letters dangled in between paint chips but none of it was decipherable. *That must be it*, he thought.

The driverless car pulled into the RV park and stopped in front of his trailer. He ended the trip and exited the vehicle. Once inside, he sat down, opened his laptop, and searched the address in other towns and cities nearby, but nothing fit as well as the one in Summerfield. The thought of calling Max entered his mind, but he realized that could do more harm than good. How far would he stick his neck out for an employee when the chances were very real that it could bite him on the ass as well?

An uncontrollable urge to scratch every part of his body overwhelmed him. It'd been two days since he'd bathed. It'd been two days since he'd had a decent meal. After a shower and dinner, he watched a little TV and fell asleep on the couch.

MEMORY LANE

THE NEXT MORNING, a little recon mission felt in order so Edgar left his trailer early and headed over to Olive Street. Knowing your terrain before the start of a battle was always a plus and the same logic applied to walking into an unknown situation. Just as the Maps progam had shown, a liquor store stood on one side of the street with an abandoned restaurant next to it. Nothing but vacant lots occupied the other side. Several tire tracks trailed through the dirt, randomly crisscrossing each other. What that meant was anyone's guess.

With time to kill before his meeting, he decided to go to a nearby diner and grab breakfast. As he was driving on the main road, he passed a street sign with the name "Vonnegut Lane." He knew it well. Images from being in Ketchum's head kept flashing by with each telephone pole he passed. The temptation was too much so he turned at the next corner and circled back around the block. Slowly, he cruised down the road looking for anything that might be familiar. Well-manicured lawns and splotches of shade underneath palm trees triggered even more memories. His car seemed to know right where to pull over and park.

Edgar closed his eyes and tried to envision Ketchum's house from memory. Then he opened them and surveyed the block. One by one, he clocked and categorized each structure until it clicked. There it was. He unzipped his jacket and checked his revolver to make sure the safety was off. Then he stepped up to the house, knocked on the door, and backed away a few steps.

A young girl in her teens opened it and said, "May I help you?"

Edgar stood silent for a few long, uncomfortable seconds. His initial instinct was to introduce himself as Agent Gorman, but he quickly realized what kind of trouble that would get him into. As he searched for an alibi, a row of ants marched across the porch floor. To most, they were as ubiquitous as fallen leaves, but today, they were special indeed.

"Good morning, I'm from Dolby Pest Control. I was told that you ordered an inspection of your home and wanted a quote on fumigating the house."

"I didn't call an inspector."

Edgar peered over the woman's shoulder and said, "Maybe someone else placed the order?"

"No one else here would've called that in."

"Hmm, how peculiar. We got a call yesterday and…" Edgar pulled an old receipt out of his pocket and pretended to be reading it. "Yes, this is the address."

The woman stiffened up and replied, "I'm sorry, but you have the wrong house."

"Oh, please forgive me. So this isn't the Johnson residence?"

"No, this is the Mattock residence."

"Ah, sorry for the mixup, ma'am."

Edgar walked back to his car as a young man, a bit overweight, with glasses and a dark complexion, passed by. He dawdled with his key fob as the man greeted him with a "Good morning," then skirted up the driveway, swung his backpack off his shoulder, and knocked on the front door of the house.

༒ ༒ ༒

Ketchum's sister opened it and scurried him inside while closing it behind her.

"What's going on?" asked Tusnig.

Shursta peeked out through the curtain and replied, "This guy just showed up at the house with some cockamamie story about working for a pest control company. I'm not buying it."

Tusnig peered over her shoulder and said, "Interesting. He looks familiar. Did you catch his name?"

"No, he didn't say."

He then focused his attention on Shursta and asked, "Where's your mom and dad?"

"Still on vacation somewhere. They should be calling in any minute now."

"I see."

She brushed back his bangs and pulled him in closer. "I'm so glad you're here. These kinds of things freak me out. I don't know what I would've done without you this last year and all."

"It's been tough on both of us. He was my best friend, you know."

She hugged him tightly and replied, "I know." Her CompWatch rang. "There's Mom now." She turned on the TV and selected a setting on her watch. An image of Margaret and Jonathan came onto the large life-size screen in vivid color. They were laughing and holding ski poles, wearing only shorts, t-shirts, boots, and goggles.

"Hi Mom, hi Dad."

"Hey, honey. How's everything at the house?"

"Everything's fine. The plumber fixed the garbage disposal and your package arrived. Where are you at?"

"We're in Yosemite skiing. The snow-turf is perfect."

"Snow-turf?"

"Yes, it's a combination of artificial turf and dry snow. You must come the next time and try it out."

Shursta glanced at Tusnig and rolled her eyes. "Will do."

"Is that Little T.D. there with you?"

"He's not so little anymore, Mother."

"Hello, Mr. and Mrs. Mattock," droned Tusnig.

"Please keep an eye on our little girl, T.D.," replied Jonathan. "Now that she's a bonafide millionaire and all, you can't be too careful."

"I will."

"We just have to get her to shake loose of some of that cash and enjoy it. I don't think she's spent a dime since it landed in her bank account."

"For good reasons, Dad."

Jonathan lowered his head and placed his hand on Margaret's shoulder. "Understood." Margaret wiped a tear from her eye and laid her hand on top of his. Everyone knew what she meant. Ketchum's tragedy was still fresh in their minds and Shursta was determined not to follow suit. Another skier slid behind the couple so close that it made them both hop aside. Then another group passed by, shouting something inaudible.

Margaret lowered the goggles back over her eyes and said, "Well, we have to go. We're in a bad spot. Talk to you soon."

"Okay, love you both. Bye."

And with that, the screen went black. Shursta squared off in front of Tusnig and put her arm around his waist. "Shouldn't we tell them?"

"No," he replied. "They're not ready and who knows what they'd do."

She lightly shook her head and said, "It just doesn't seem right."

A female voice from the top of the stairs chimed in, "He's right, Shursta. They'd post something online or tell a friend. You know they've drunk the Kool-Aid and bought into this whole subversive ploy that everything in the world is wonderful and as long as they still have money, they'll stay drunk."

"But what if both Ketchum and I sit down and talk with them. Maybe we can convince them."

Alby glanced at Tusnig and replied, "I think the only way they'll change is to see it with their own eyes. Seeing is believing and that's what we intend to do."

"Aunt Alby's right," inserted Tusnig. "Most people don't care what's happening in the real world. They like fuzzy stories about caterpillars and how great this country is doing."

"Yes, but that's about to change." Alby had moved down to the bottom of the staircase next to the couple. She'd gained back a good twenty pounds since her escape from Dunes. Her rosy cheeks and short haircut made her look ten years younger. While living in safe houses throughout the area over the past year, she'd developed a regimen of lifting weights, exercising in place, and devouring everything she could read.

"According to GRID, there's been a major breakthrough and the sooner we get everyone together to talk about it, the sooner we'll change the world."

⋙⋙⋙

Edgar took one final glance at the house and the shifting curtain before hopping in and driving away. When he turned the corner onto Olive Street, his foot instinctively slammed on the brakes. The previously empty parking lot had transformed into a carnival. He swiftly pulled over and parked on a side street, then walked to the scene. Festive music filled the air as a dozen food trucks circled the center of the dirt lot. Rhythmic samba drumbeats echoed from one truck while dancehall reggae vocals filtered through in the middle. A buzzing sitar reverberated in the distance.

A crowd of people wandered from truck to truck chomping on

tortillas wrapped in foil, miniature buns dripping with cheese, and cotton candy. Aromas from all over the world blended together, creating a potpourri of flavors and smells. At one end, the sharp smell of chili peppers nearly singed the nostrils while a savory hint of curry hovered in the air fifteen feet overhead. Smoky scents of barbeque swirled by, each one exuding different layers of brown sugar, vinegar, and campfire odors. Everyone laughed and smiled as if they didn't have a care in the world, and why would they? They had the dress, the haircuts, and the swagger of a newly minted generation of millionaires.

MAMA CRAVENS' CAFE

THE POLICE PRESENCE was sparse, with an inconspicuous officer posted on each end of the street, but Edgar knew better. Any pair of sunglasses blending in with diners could be an undercover agent. The cameras mounted on each street light no doubt covered all the pertinent angles. A mental cash register rang up every detail and lodged them in the back of his mind for safekeeping. Such were the ways of an ex-FBI agent.

He casually strolled around the circle studying menus and nodding at bystanders when necessary. Everything appeared to be a normal, typical weekend gathering in a hip part of the city. That is, until he spotted a truck on the far end of the caravan with a small marquee running across the front reading, "Mama Cravens' Café."

Bingo!

Edgar approached the truck and perused the menu while a highly spirited New Orleans-sounding jazz trumpet and trombone rhythm section blared from a tiny speaker suspended by two wires under the overhang. It became obvious after reading a few entries that this truck only specialized in one thing: chicken. There was grilled chicken on a stick, Cajun chicken, chicken étouffée and, of course, fried chicken, just for starters.

A young Hispanic girl peered out from one of the two windows and asked, "What can I get you?" She was pleasant looking with dark eyes, thin dark hair, and a light brown complexion. Behind her, a woman with her back to them was flipping meat on a grill and preparing meals. Barely visible in the corner sat an older lady smoking a cigarette.

Edgar smiled and hesitated a little too long before replying so the girl moved to the next window and bellowed, "Order's up, number 107." A couple approached and she asked if they needed any napkins or condiments. After they'd left, she returned to the other window and repeated, "Did you want to order something?"

Edgar wasn't sure what to say. He'd been given no instructions and there were very few clues. The only reply that came to mind was, "Do you have fried chicken that hasn't been cooked in oil?"

The girl backed away a step and glanced at the woman sitting next to her. The old woman lowered her head to light another cigarette, then lifted her chin high enough to see over the counter. She scrutinized Edgar with the precision of a tailor sizing up alterations on a new customer's dress. The cook stood rigid and still. Then she set down a spatula and slowly turned around.

"Izzy!" whispered Edgar. The gleam in his eyes was instantly met with the motion of Izzy's hand as she swiped it across her neck. The message was loud and clear.

"Yes, we have that," replied the old woman. There were four other people now in line behind Edgar impatiently waiting for their turn. The woman asked, "Anything to drink?"

Edgar nodded. "A beer."

He paid and the woman gave him a number. As the cook returned to work and others ordered, Edgar stepped to the side and sipped on his drink. There was so much to think about and analyze but the last thing he needed to do was draw attention. His body leaned against another truck as he scanned the surroundings with nothing but his eyes. One by one, each person's movement was categorized into different threat levels as they minded their own business.

"Number 512, where you at?" shouted the old woman. Edgar

examined his ticket and handed it to her. The old lady held out a set of colorful Mardi Grás beads. She leaned through the window and lifted them in the air. With an accent as if paddling down the Mississippi Delta to a Cajun bayou, she said, "Here, Beb, you can't eat at Mama's without dis *dreegailles* around your neck." Edgar tilted his head and the lady draped the beads onto his shoulders. Then she handed him the chicken plate and went back to the other window.

As soon as Edgar took his first bite, a familiar voice whispered into his ear. "*Hola.* Don't say a word or look around. They can't hear me if you keep that necklace around your head."

The chicken in his mouth floated on a bed of saliva, as he'd forgotten to swallow. With a mouthful of food, he asked, "Can they hear me?"

"No one can if you keep talking like that," jested Izzy. "They can't zone in from afar but if they're standing next to you, they'll hear your normal voice."

"Got it," garbled Edgar.

"Please swallow before you suffocate," commanded Izzy.

Edgar smiled and obeyed. Then he sighed, "God, I miss talking to you. I thought you were dead."

"Hopefully, everyone else thinks that too."

"But why?" he asked. He tried not to stop and stare but his head kept circling back toward the food truck.

Each time Izzy scolded him. "Keep your eyes turned away. You never know who's watching."

"What happened to the DDO glasses?"

"Don't get me started. They're a pain to use but I still have them."

"Good. They were pretty handy."

She nodded and casually glanced around to see if anyone was approaching before saying, "Edgar, do you remember a memo circulating the office a few years ago about a manifesto? The one posted a few years after the Wupe Phenomenon?"

"Of course. You told me to look out for it and let you know if anything else came up, but then, well, you know what happened next."

"I do indeed. After you were taken away, my associates and I had to take evasive actions and come up with another plan. As I predicted, the new bureau swept the report under the rug and buried it." She placed another order of food on the counter and smirked. "That turned out to be a stroke of luck for us."

"I bet," replied Edgar. "But who is us?"

Izzy grinned and turned away. "You'll meet the rest, soon enough. In the meantime, say hi to Carmen taking orders, and that's her Aunt Claudia smoking a cigarette in the corner." Both women discreetly nodded.

With her back still to him, at the grill flipping pieces of chicken and chopping them up, Izzy continued, "Anyway, the manifesto was posted without much fanfare at first. After all, it had all the usual silly stuff in it that you always see, like end of the world predictions and the coming Rapture, that kind of crap, but also in it was an attachment with a manual on how to shut down the Intranet."

"For real?"

"Real enough to garner our attention."

"I thought that was impossible."

"Implausible, but not impossible, at least, here in the United States. See, when the government nationalized Internet providers back in the Forties, they had to create a network system capable of handling the egress and ingress between different platforms in order to limit access to certain websites. That meant it all had to be linked together. Even though that system is highly encrypted and guarded very well, it still has its vulnerabilities."

"I see. So what happened?"

"The FBI was alerted immediately and sent their agents into this organization's database to erase all the information before it could be viewed any longer. Unfortunately for the Bureau, five copies had already been downloaded."

"Did they locate them?"

"All but one."

Edgar swallowed his last bite and tossed the container into a trashcan. Then he asked, "So, what does this all have to do with me?"

"*You* are in possession of the missing copy."

The words stopped Edgar in his tracks. He slowly turned and gazed into the food truck booth.

"You're doing it again — turn away," barked Izzy.

His eyes zeroed in on his old colleague as he placed the sunglasses on top of his head. The words had left him speechless. They now tumbled through memories like unpolished rocks searching for any glint of clarity. Nothing came to mind.

Izzy turned and faced him with another basket of food in her hand. For the first time in a long time, he was able to see her eyes. The years had been kind to her brown complexion. Inside her pupils, a soul reflected back vibrant and strong. It made him realize just how much he missed his old companion.

"Please explain before my head explodes."

"Turn away and I will."

Edgar sipped his drink and casually meandered over to the shaded area of another truck.

Izzy continued: "One of your mother's boyfriends was ex-military and part of a clandestine cyber unit." She set the basket down and returned to the grill. "You don't leave those types of units willingly. You either work there for life or simply disappear one day."

"I remember one guy who died in a car accident. Is that who you're talking about?" asked Edgar.

"Exactly. He'd downloaded the manual but didn't know what to do with it. He knew it was important and could certainly do some damage if in the wrong hands but had his doubts about turning it over. The only option was to change his identity and reemerge elsewhere. Your mother was a perfect cover."

"Did she know?"

"Yes," she replied. "She was too smart not to figure it out. In fact, we think she helped him hide it in a way that would keep it safe and out of sight. Some way that would identify the code when needed without revealing its identity. We believe it's still around but don't know where. Maybe in the house or maybe even with you. That's what we were hoping you'd be able to help us with."

Edgar winced and thought hard. "I can't think of anything."

Izzy nodded. "Let me know if something comes to mind."

A black sedan pulled up on the corner of the street and two heads with blue crew cuts surfaced over the hood of the car. He knew this was trouble. Out of nowhere, three other men in black suits approached from the other direction. Edgar moved a few feet away from the food truck and put on his best poker face.

When Director Conway and her brother were within a few feet, he said, "Miranda, long time no see. Did you miss me?" Then he turned to her brother and added, "Why, Toyer, so you left me to be closer to your sister. How heartwarming."

Director Conway held Toyer back and she responded, "Hello, Edgar. How's that security guard gig going? Saving a lot of boxes from falling?" Toyer offered up his best sarcastic laugh but it fell way short of its mark. After a few seconds, Miranda waved her hand to shut him up.

Edgar ignored the comment and replied, "So, what do you want?"

"There's a lot of Intranet chatter going around about a group planning some kind of a... how should I say... I believe they call it a Virtual Algorithmic Manipulative Insurrectional Takedown."

"Those are pretty big words. Don't you think you should dumb it down a little for Toyer here so he understands?"

"*VAMIT* for short, Mr. Gorman," retorted Toyer. "Kind of like what comes out of people's mouths when they see your picture."

Edgar's eyebrows twisted in confusion. "Why, Toyer, did you just try to be funny, or was that a downright insult? Because if it was, you suck at both."

Toyer swiped at his CompWatch, then patted it firmly. Edgar's watch pinged. "There, I believe that puts your Demeanor Score under 250. I'm afraid you'll have to come with us for a refresher course at the Rehabilitation Facility."

Edgar arched his back and leaned in. "A what? You can't do that."

Director Conway inserted her rigid frame in between the two and placed her nose directly in front of Edgar's. "Yes, we can, Mr. Gorman. As a precautionary measure, anyone known to have a history of psychopathic tendencies can be taken into custody for evaluation at any time." She waved the other three agents over and said, "Search him."

The stingy smell of cheap cologne overwhelmed Edgar as the agents fondled his pockets and searched from top to bottom. One of them removed the beads from around his neck and studied them. He peered over to Director Conway who motioned him to toss them into a trashcan. The other agent pulled the card out of his pocket and handed it to his boss.

She read it carefully as her eyes narrowed and forehead tightened. "Mama Cravens' Café. Now why in the world would you have this in your pocket?" The director raised her head, took a few steps back, and surveyed the food trucks nearby. She checked off each one with a nod until she came to Izzy's.

The marquee on the front now read, "Bubba Blue's Barbeque." She rubbed the side of her face hard as she tried to recall if that sign had been there when she arrived. A blues guitar wailed out from the speakers as the old woman leaned out the window and asked with a strong Southern accent, "Ya'll gonna order or just scare all da customers away?" With her good eye glaring down at Toyer and then over to Director Conway, the old woman cocked her head and spat a wad of chew into the dirt. Then she leaned back and wiped her mouth clean with her arm.

Toyer unconsciously took a few steps behind his sister and asked, "Are you hungry?"

Director Conway didn't know what to make of the woman but understood her body language. "No," is all she said.

Her eyes crossed over the food truck from left to right and then up and down. Izzy was nowhere to be seen. Instead, Carmen now manned the grill and yelled, "Order's up." Then she handed a plate to a couple of teenagers and returned to cooking.

Director Conway took one last look at the card and then tucked it in her jacket. "Take him away."

THE PHISH POND

THE LIGHTS in the padded white room were dim. Images of Edgar's childhood played on three of the four walls. A party reflected onto one of them complete with the singing of Happy Birthday and an immediate wail from a fearful, crying toddler. On the rear wall were scenes from the first day of the Second Civil War. A teenage Edgar blushed and gestured from his window to the neighbor girl across the street as she waved back. It was nighttime in his backyard on the third wall with that same girl, who'd now mushroomed into a woman. He was asking for her hand in marriage.

Edgar spiraled around on the stool before regaining his balance. The shot he'd been given earlier was wearing off. A loud squeal reverberated through the room as a man cleared his throat and spoke: "Hello Mr. Gorman. We meet again. How are you feeling?"

Edgar lifted his arm and flashed the middle finger toward the large two-way mirror. Then he mumbled, "Many mutters for the many in good greedness, but gawdelpus, a menticidal mistake has been made."

The man covered up the microphone as muffled sounds of voices arguing reverberated. The door opened and Roger entered with a syringe, squirted fluid out the top, and injected it into Edgar's arm. He instantly sat up on the stool rigid and alert.

Roger left the room and Rick began to speak. "Mr. Gorman, I'm sorry that you've returned under Zero Sum conditions again. It's with great displeasure that we have to initiate the second round of therapy treatment. I'm afraid that it won't be as pleasant as the first."

Edgar lifted his head and gazed into the mirror, searching for anything but his reflection to appear. He didn't know how much more of this he could handle. The sleep deprivation, constant injections, and mindless questioning that had taken place over the last few days were wearing him down.

There was a long pause as Rick waited for a response but none came. "Mr. Gorman, we know you're somehow involved with this GRID organization and the virtual takedown they are planning. It will only make things better for everyone if you just come clean and tell us what you know."

Edgar asked, "Why am I here, and what's GRID?"

"The Group Restoring Internet Democracy, of course." Rick crossed his arms and added, "You know why you're here. You know you could end it all right now, or anytime you want by just saying it. Clearly say those patriotic words, Mr. Gorman, and everyone can go home for the night. Just repeat after me, 'Greedness greaty, going crazy.'"

At that moment, the lights went out everywhere and all three screens died. Then, a loud boom shook the building. Scattering across the floor were shards of concrete followed by flumes of smoke rising in the air, obscuring everyone's view. Voices shouted as chaotic chatter bounced between the walls.

A large black man shot out of the newly formed hole in the wall, raced across the floor, and leaned against the hidden door going to the control room. A second man, more or less a boy, followed behind him and ran over to Edgar. He grabbed him by the arm and said, "Follow me."

Edgar looked up and smiled. "Ketchum?"

"No time to chit-chat, come with me."

Ketchum helped Edgar off the stool and led him over to the smoky crater. Outside next to the building was an uncovered manhole. They both scrambled over to the hole and Ketchum carefully guided Edgar down a ladder. When he was down to the lower level, the boy yelled to Double Down, "All clear." Double Down backed away and slapped an explosive device on the outside of the building while keeping an eye out for any movement. Red lights flashed from each corner of the room as a deep metallic voice warned, "Alert, Alert, Code Red, Alert, Alert..." Underneath a cloud of smoke, the three faded away.

Roger and Rick opened the door and ran into the room without hesitation. While leaning out the recently formed hole, Rick gasped and exclaimed, "They do exist. It's actually for real."

"Call Director Conway," barked Roger. Before Rick dialed the number, another explosion shattered what was left of the building smothering the two under a pile of rubble.

CHAPTER THIRTY-TWO

IF YOU LIKE PIÑA COLADAS

THE SMELL OF SULFUR and pepper cut through Edgar's sinuses like a dull razor, making him cough and rub his eyes. Ketchum reached for a handkerchief from his pocket and placed it over Edgar's mouth.

Double Down nodded, pointed into the tunnel, and said, "Go on. I'll be right behind you."

Ketchum clicked the toes of his tennis shoes twice and red, white, and blue colors sparkled down the smoky corridor. "Follow me."

The ground rumbled above immediately after Double Down spun the wheel on a large metal door, tightening the seal. The vibration caused the walls to crack, but they held firm. As calm filled the void left by the muted mayhem, Double Down turned to Ketchum and said, "Mission accomplished." A fraternal nod between them signaled that it was time for the next phase of the rescue.

Ketchum was still holding Edgar's arm when he turned to him and asked, "Can you travel? It's a long walk where we're going."

"You bet," replied Edgar.

"Here, keep these beads around your neck the whole time, do you understand?" Double Down pulled out three sets from a backpack and handed one to Ketchum.

"I've seen these before," replied Edgar as he draped them over his head.

"Good. They'll scramble any signal that might be tracking us."

Once they were all at the end of the next doorway, Ketchum pressed a button on the wall. Gears churned as a roller chain strapped on the side plate began to move. Soon, a set of lights flickered down a corridor underground illuminating a tunnel stretching as far as the eye could see.

"Where are we?"

"An abandoned Metro Line. It was supposed to be the last connector to downtown but then Forest Dunes took over operations and shut it down."

"I wonder why."

"Just like everything else, money," replied Ketchum.

Double Down brushed the dust off his pants and interjected, "And because nobody in their right minds would live out here except Dunes workers. Too fucking hot."

The three climbed the steps to another tunnel that existed between the metro line below and the paved freeway above. The tunnel stood eight feet high but only six feet wide. In the middle, running along both the top and bottom, were large pipes securely clamped to the walls.

"Where are we now?" questioned Edgar.

"A DWP underground power line. After the great fire of 2039, DWP was forced to put all power lines underground. Whatever you do, do not touch those pipes. Even though they're insulated, you'll still feel a little jolt."

Edgar's eyebrows curled while studying the pipe above with intense scrutiny. He zoomed in to read the writing and then followed its shape down the corridor. His hand uncontrollably rose into the air, wavering between a state of cautiousness and curiosity before tapping the pipe with his fingertip. A spark flickered so strong that it made him jump back a step.

Ketchum shook his head and turned to his partner. "It happens every time."

There was a light exchange of laughter between the three before Edgar squinted and asked, "Why are you two doing this?"

Double Down glanced at Ketchum and said, "Izzy. She called it in. Said it was urgent and imperative that you be rescued today before it was too late."

"Too late? Too late for what?"

Ketchum stood at the entrance and asked, "What was the last thought going through your mind before we showed up?

"Killing myself," he exclaimed. "I actually considered it."

"Of course, you did. That's what they do. That's their end game when everything else fails. When caught on camera, it's all perfectly legal, too." Double Down's lips tightened as he tried not to get worked up. "They've figured out a way to reduce the population and make people believe they're doing it for the good of the country. How ripe is that?"

"Pretty amazing. I'm Edgar, by the way."

"They call me Double Down."

"Thanks for saving me, Double Down." He turned to Ketchum and added, "You too."

The journey from Ontario to Los Angeles took most of a day to complete. There was only one open passageway that serviced the massive web of pipes and wires underneath the metro area, but it stretched from Ontario to Downtown Los Angeles and then on to Santa Barbara. All other pipes ran perpendicular to the main corridor.

At certain junctures, they had to move into other abandoned tunnels because the passageways were too small for people to travel through.

"Where are we now?" asked Edgar.

"These tunnels were supposed to connect certain freeways together but were never finished. In fact, they're not even on any city maps so we can avoid anyone who might be following us."

"How's that possible?"

"From what I understand, the city tried to connect all the freeways through underground tunnels decades ago but the project went kaput after funding dried up. Years later, they purged all the old records when they upgraded systems. No one had the foresight to think someone might need to know what was where, and actually, no one really cared."

Double Down stopped walking and brushed away the dirt covering one of the plaques on the drilling equipment. "That turned out to be a godsend for us. Fortunately, one of our associates was able to find an old copy of the map in an abandoned library."

"A nice stroke of luck," replied Edgar.

"You bet." Ketchum opened a door to another tunnel before adding, "And here we are, our own little underground railroad. Let's go. This place gives me the creeps."

When they arrived at L.A.'s Union Station, Double Down opened a side door that led onto a Metro track line. He cautiously peered each way, studying every corner, and said, "There's a camera on the left. We'll have to wait for a train to pass by before crossing."

They sat at the doorway for a good five minutes until the floor started shaking. Ketchum peeked out and said, "It's going north. We need a southbound train if we don't want to be seen."

He shut the door and sat back down next to Edgar. The six-foot-wide corridor didn't leave them much room for privacy or stretching out. The close proximity to each other made everyone nervous. Edgar couldn't help but steal a glance at Ketchum every chance he could. It didn't go unnoticed.

"Why do you keep staring at me?" he asked.

Edgar turned away and replied, "Sorry, it's just that... back in the Interrogation Room a year ago, I got to know you pretty well."

"How's that? I mean, we, like, hardly talked for more than an hour or so, and I think I did most of the talking."

"You did, but I had the upper hand when it came to understanding what'd happened to you."

Ketchum scratched his head in confusion while Double Down listened intently. This discussion piqued his curiosity, as he'd become very protective of his young friend during this last year of living underground. "Are you talking that gibberish again, mister? I don't think the drugs have fully worn off."

Edgar chuckled and let his head sway to the train noises in the distance. "No, it's nothing like that. Sorry, I need to explain. I was wearing a pair of DDO glasses."

"Whoa, you can see everything going on and everybody around you with those things. Very advanced technology and dangerous."

"Exactly," replied Edgar. "That's what I had on the day we interviewed you, Ketchum. They allowed me to see what you were seeing, every aspect from every camera view in the places you'd gone to, all the way to reading your thoughts and being inside your mind."

Ketchum's eyes bounced from Edgar to Double Down a few times before lowering his head. Flushed with this new information and realizing what it meant, he cleared his throat and croaked, "Everything?"

"Everything." Edgar reached over with his hand and raised the boy's head. "There's nothing to be embarrassed about. It was beautiful. I feel like I know you better than myself." He smiled and added, "I know I definitely *like* you better than myself."

Ketchum evaded eye contact at first, but eventually gave in to the temptation. When their eyes did meet, he felt the connection too. Somehow, their virtual bond had become physical. "Even at the museum?" he asked.

Edgar nodded subtly and smiled. "I know it's a lot to comprehend, but don't worry, it's all locked up in here and not going anywhere." He tapped on his forehead and winked.

Double Down wasn't sure what to say, if anything. He'd only known Ketchum for a short year now and the details around his

Zero Sum Conclusion were sketchy. Talking about being swindled and duped by a girl were not something the boy wanted to share readily, as it made him irritable. He understood. After all, he had his own demons to deal with.

"That's a heavy load to lay on him, mister. It's like finding someone's diary and reading it in front of them. No wonder they're outlawed."

"Outlawed to everyone but law enforcement. I don't have them anymore. If I did, I sure wouldn't be here — and please, call me Edgar."

"So what happened after I was sent away?" asked Ketchum. "Did you ever catch her?"

"No, but I did see her again — in fact, recently. Believe it or not, but April's a BIG agent now, and she's my case worker."

"How bizarre," said Double Down. "That's so absurd."

"No doubt." Edgar focused his gaze on Ketchum again and revealed, "I think she's changed, though, and for the better. In fact, she's still in love with you and regrets everything she did. That's why she turned her mother in to the authorities and got out."

"She did what?"

"Yeah, her adoptive mother's the one who forced her to do what she did in the first place. April couldn't handle it after what happened to you so she turned her in and now she's doing 10-15 years at Chino."

This new information cracked open that shell of a soul Ketchum had been hiding in this last year, as images from his time with April rose back up. So many questions came to mind: How much should he believe? Was it all just a mistake? Did she really love him? Did he still love her?

Edgar sensed that the conversation was too much for the boy and shifted gears. "I'm still confused about why I'm so important to everyone."

Double Down heard the conviction in Edgar's voice and

empathy in his tone. Everything told him that beneath it all, he could be trusted. He straightened up against the wall and tried to stretch his legs. "It'll all make sense once you meet the rest of the group, but somehow, somewhere, your mother hid this formula or computer code, or whatever, after her boyfriend turned up dead. She knew what he was up to and realized the importance of this information."

"Where'd she meet him. Do you know?"

"Well, from what I'm told, your mother met him at a rally protesting some cause. I can't remember what, probably the SSI Initiative or the new Constitution. He was a former systems analyst and smart as a whip when it came to hacking into databases. When he stumbled upon this code and realized what it was, he kind of freaked out. Apparently, he'd talked to one too many friends, and then came the car accident."

"But why shut down the Intranet?"

"We're not shutting down the Intranet, we're opening the Internet like it used to be, where everyone can see everything all over the world. Think about it — MAGMA controls everything, what you think, say, and do. They've done a pretty good job over the last couple of decades reprogramming everyone into acting a certain way. I mean, give a person a million dollars and they'll believe anything, and forget everything. As long as people have money, they don't care about social injustice, world affairs, or political discourse. They believe that poverty's been wiped out, religion is the answer, and being a good citizen is the best way to show patriotism. This Demeanor Score bullshit has made everyone into a snitch."

Ketchum was back to his old self again and wanted in on this conversation. "On top of that, now they're going for the final kill by gradually placing control of the whole federal government into private hands. No more oversight, no more accountability, and no one will know the difference."

Double Down slowly rose to his feet and stretched. Then he said, "When society grows complacent and doesn't question authority, authority grows more powerful. It's just human nature. I'll guarantee you that the people in charge are eating avocados behind closed doors. When's the last time you had a ripe avocado, or any avocados for that matter? They're methodically erasing words from our vocabulary in the hope that someday we'll forget them altogether. Try looking up the word and see what you get. I'll tell you what you'll get. Nothing more than a few entries saying it's a color."

"I'd almost forgotten what they tasted like," said Edgar. "What else?"

"How many people do you know who have returned from Forest Dunes in the past few years?"

"A few."

"And how long have they lasted?"

"What do you mean?"

"I mean, they're doing and thinking the same thing that you were thinking in that bunker before we showed up. All you have to do is say a few words and your pain is over. It's the ultimate form of survival of the fittest, but we're not going to let that happen."

Edgar asked, "Who's we again?"

"GRID." Ketchum stood up to brush off his pants before adding, "You'll meet the rest soon enough."

Lights shined on a wall down the track and the silhouette of an engine came into view. They all huddled by the door. Ketchum removed a handkerchief from his pocket and tied it around his face. He handed another one to Edgar and motioned him to do the same. Double Down followed suit.

"Okay, on the count of three."

Ketchum was the first to jump down on the track as the train passed by, followed by the other two. They scurried across and climbed onto the other platform. Before the train made it around the bend, they were at the door leading to the open drainpipe and out of sight. Edgar pressed the handkerchief closer to his face as the sewage smell overwhelmed him. His eyes burned while tears dripped down his cheeks.

"Blink," ordered Double Down. Edgar complied as they disappeared into the darkness. They climbed a ladder leading up to a manhole cover and Double Down lifted it with his shoulders while surveying the area. It was nighttime and pitch black. "Good, no signs of traffic. Let's move." Then he braced his back against the cover and pushed hard. It popped off with ease. Quietly, he slid it to the side, exited, and helped the other two out. Then he replaced the cover and followed everyone down the street.

CHAPTER THIRTY-THREE

GRID

THE WAVES CRASHING against the rocks woke Edgar when the car pulled into the parking lot. He opened one eye and stared at the waning moon now receding into the horizon. An elusive glow scattered across the water as he peered into the distance. Worn out from the long trip and days of interrogation, he'd fallen asleep in the back seat during the drive from Union Station. He yawned and stretched. Ketchum exited and opened his door while helping him out. Double Down walked over to the edge of the parking lot and said, "The sun will be up soon."

They left the lot and trekked down to a single-lane blacktop road. The path weaved from one walkway to the next along the ocean cliffs until winding onto a dirt lane. "They're not answering," grumbled Double Down as he pushed aside the overgrown weeds. "We'll have to go in through the ocean."

"Again," cried Ketchum. "What's up with that?"

"Security reasons, I guess." He looked to Edgar and said, "You'll need to lose the jacket and shoes. We're going for a swim."

After they undressed, Double Down motioned the two of them to follow him into the darkness. A path emerged through the last rays of moonbeams leading them down to a ledge overlooking the water below.

"It's about a twenty-foot drop so be careful when you dive in."

Edgar yawned and gazed over the ledge. "What's down there?"

"You'll see. Just hold your breath and stay with me." Double

Down pulled a tiny rope out of his pocket and tied it around Edgar's waist. "On the count of three…"

All three dove into the ocean. The current initially pulled them out to sea but quickly reversed course with the next wave. Soon Edgar was rolling around in sand and water ten feet under the surface. The seconds ticked by swiftly while he struggled with the current. Just as he was about to run out of air, something tugged his body deeper into the water. It was as if Poseidon had reached down with his trident and whisked him away on a chariot of seahorses. The next thing he knew, he'd burst through an opening in a concrete wall and found himself in a hollowed-out cavern. The three of them were now wading in a rapidly moving pool of water two feet deep. Ketchum lifted Edgar to his feet. With his legs firmly planted, they all moved toward a set of steps.

Once on dry land, Double Down grabbed towels off a rock, tossed two to the others, and used one on himself. "Change into these clothes. They might not fit perfectly but they should suffice."

"These aren't shoes, they're slippers," moaned Edgar as he snuggled into a tight t-shirt and sweats.

"It's all we got, sorry."

A light glowed off in the distance down the tunnel. They all carefully crept toward it while keeping their eyes peeled for any movement. Edgar heard the murmur of strange voices drifting in and out of earshot. Lights flickered and grew brighter as they approached. When they were within a few dozen yards of the entrance, the sound of music and laughter gently bounced off the rocky walls. By the time they were within a few feet of the opening, the volume was so overwhelming that he expected to find a raging party going on. Instead, the instant they entered the main room, several rifles and pistols were pointed at their heads. Behind this wall of armed resistance was an antique boom box sitting on a table blaring out music and sound effects.

A woman walked over and pushed the button. The music

stopped. She turned around and said, "Welcome, Edgar. We've been waiting for you."

Edgar's eyes adjusted to the lighting. A lantern on a table in the background lit the hollowed-out cavern, revealing dozens of prints and other artwork plastered on the wall. Black light posters of U2, Nelson Mandela, and the Grateful Dead glowed next to newer reproductions of Greenpeace, Crack Whore Babies, and Smokey the Bear. Banners reading "IT'S ABOUT GREED, NOT GREATNESS," "IT'S TIME FOR REAL CHANGE," "POWER TO THE PEOPLE," and the like lined the perimeter of the ceiling.

As people moved back and lowered their weapons, their faces came into view. Edgar asked, "What the hell's going on here?"

Double Down scuttled around him and hugged a woman that Edgar recognized from an FBI photo. Her face was much fuller now and her physique was in top shape. "Good to see you again."

"Same here," replied the woman.

He turned to Edgar and said, "This is Alby. She's the one coordinating everything for us."

"I remember you from the escape last year," Edgar said. "I'm sorry for the loss of your husband."

Alby replied, "Thank you. We knew it would be risky returning. We just didn't count on a couple of vigilantes getting in the way." Then with a solemn nod, she added, "I'm sorry about your wife and the loss of your mother. She was a very special person."

"You knew her?"

"Of course. Many of us did, at one point or another. My father was one of those boyfriends she kept around. They dated from time to time, but she and I hit it off splendidly and remained in contact."

"Was he killed in a car accident?" asked Edgar.

"That's the one. Chip was his name. He taught me everything he knew about cyber security." Alby's light brown eyes darted back and forth across Edgar's face, as if trying to unlock a secret code inside his head. "He liked you a lot, I remember. Not so much your sister, though, but you."

"Why me?"

"He said something about, your heart was in the right place." She rubbed Edgar's arm and added, "That's what your mother used to say too. She said you kids were night and day when it came to personalities. She couldn't believe that you both came out of the same womb."

Subtle laughter filled the cavern. Ketchum and Shursta pushed their way through the crowd and hugged. "It's been a while, brother."

"That it has, sis."

"How're Mom and Dad?"

Shursta grinned slightly as hints of sarcasm dribbled off her reply, "Still living the dream. You know."

"On vacation again?"

She nodded and turned to Edgar. "Sorry for being rude to you at the house. I didn't know who you were at the time."

"No problem. I wasn't sure why I was there in the first place. Something just told me to stop by. I'd have been suspicious too."

A voice from the dark said, "That's the sign of a good agent."

Edgar's eyes opened wide, "Izzy! I'm so glad to see you again."

"Me too." They hugged for a long while. Izzy closed her eyes and tightened her grip around him. "I thought we might lose you there for a minute in Ontario."

"You're not the only one." Edgar uncurled his eyebrows and said, "Thank you, but I'm still not sure why this is all happening now."

"Sit down. Let me try to explain."

Edgar lowered his arms and plopped into a chair. "I'm really thirsty. Do you have anything to drink?"

A tall skinny old man pulled a bottle of whiskey out of a

cabinet, unscrewed the cap, and poured some into a cup. "Here you go."

"Who's this?" asked a suspicious Double Down as he leaned across the table with his own cup.

"This is Clem Chotter," said Izzy. "He's been involved with another organization similar to ours for years. It appears that we weren't the only group working on this Mama Cravens project. Anyway, I checked him out and he's good."

Double Down nodded to Clem after he poured him a drink and replied, "If you say so."

Clem asked Edgar, "Another shot?"

Edgar nodded and Clem poured one into his cup as Izzy continued, "We are GRID, or the Group Restoring Internet Democracy." She pointed to the graffiti on the walls. "Years ago, this organization was founded by a group of concerned citizens who were afraid that the government and private corporations had gone too far with controlling what we see and what we don't see."

"Censorship."

"Correct. Anyway, your mother and my father helped form this organization after all the news organizations and Internet feeds were taken over. Not many people even noticed the changes. They happened so slowly and sometimes over decades. Just think, every time you updated your CompWatch, it tightened the stranglehold they had over what information went in and what came out."

Edgar downed his drink and asked, "Do you have any water?"

Izzy nodded and Ketchum brought over a can. Then she continued, "You see, when the government realized that Social Security was going bankrupt and came up with the million dollar scheme, they also realized that there was a golden opportunity to save even more money by privatizing all of their agencies. It was a win/win situation."

"Capitalism at its finest," interjected Alby. "Less government means less hassle."

"Whoa, whoa, whoa. When you say government, who are we talking about? You know I used to be part of that government."

Izzy took another sip before explaining, "It's not really a government any longer. I mean, sure, we still have elections but private corporations determine who will win before anyone casts a ballot. Think about it, who took over the Presidency this year?"

"The Vice President."

"Correct, and where did the President go?"

"To head BIG," replied Edgar.

"And where was the Vice President four years ago?"

"Head of Homeland Security, I think."

"Do you see a pattern? How could two men have all that power without help from other sources? asked Izzy.

"Oh, it wasn't just them," said Alby. "There was plenty of money to be made all around so everyone in the private sector who could jumped on board to make it work."

Izzy spun Edgar's seat around and asked, "Do you remember what the nightly news was like when you were a kid?"

"Sort of, but not really."

"That was by design. The changes were subtle and slow. Gradually after the Second Civil War, the news went from ranting political commentary from talking heads to stories about the benefits of butterflies and bees. The world seemed calmer, tensions were brought down a notch, and then, everyone became rich. At least, for a while."

"Wasn't that a good thing?" questioned Edgar.

"In a way, but not everybody became rich, did they? It was all a ruse. You never saw stories about the homeless or less fortunate in your news feed, did you? But do you think poverty has been wiped out?"

Edgar replied, "Absolutely not. I saw it every day on the streets."

Izzy nodded, "Yes, but not many did. After a while, people

just assumed that it'd been eradicated because that's what they were told. Out of sight, out of mind."

Tusnig entered from the other room and said, "We intend to restore things to the way it was before all this happened. Open and free. That's where you come in, Mr. Gorman."

"Please, call me Edgar. You make me feel really old."

"We are, Edgar," replied Clem, "and running out of time."

"So, how do I fit into this?"

Tusnig sat down in a chair next to him and opened a laptop. "We were able to piece together parts of the code from the original manual that was on a flash drive Alby's father had hidden in the attic of their home."

"I stumbled upon it while cleaning out the house before putting it up for sale a few years ago." Alby glanced at Izzy and continued, "That's when I realized what was at stake here. Wrapped around the flash drive written on a piece of paper were the words 'Mama Cravens' Café.'"

"Mama Cravens' Café? What does that have to do with everything?" asked Edgar.

"It was a dream of your mother's. My dad was a great cook and your mom always said they should open a restaurant together. In fact, they were working on it the night he was killed. That's how I knew you needed to be involved."

"Who's Mama Cravens?"

"I don't know, an inside joke between members, I presumed. It's not important. What did happen was, when I plugged the flash drive into a computer, it sent a message to Izzy."

Alby slid the bottle of whiskey across the table and poured herself a drink. She sipped it and said, "After hooking up with Izzy and finding out about this algorithm and what it was capable of, I went to work on figuring out how to make it work."

"Yes," interjected Tusnig, "we've been able to piece together parts of the code based on similar formulas, but something is missing here and we were hoping you could fill in the blanks."

"When you say missing, missing how?" asked Edgar.

"A device of some kind or maybe a string of code embedded in an item that could be extracted later," said Alby. "Hell, even a poem or lyric might contain the information. My father was too paranoid to leave the whole formula in one place. He would've separated parts out and kept them somewhere else in case it fell into the wrong hands. It would be something that would contain the code without revealing its identity. We know he hid it with your mother and went through your sister's house but didn't find anything."

"Does Lotty know you were there?"

"Of course not. She doesn't have a clue as to what we're up to."

"Good, because that would send her over the edge." Edgar smacked his lips and thought hard. "Nothing comes to mind."

Tusnig scratched the back of his neck as his mind churned away. "Did your mother keep anything special around the house — a diary, notebooks, weird photos, unusual keepsakes?"

Edgar tapped his finger on his lips while repeating, "Diaries, notes, weird photos." His eyes closed as he dug deep into his memory. "Weird photos! I mean, no, she didn't have weird photos but did she ever paint the weirdest and wildest looking paintings. Plus, the pottery she made. If that's not unusual, I don't know what is."

"Where's this stuff now?"

"At my place."

Double Down grabbed the Mardi Grás beads from his backpack and said, "I think it's time for a road trip."

"You bet!" exclaimed Edgar.

CHAPTER THIRTY-FOUR

PAINTED INTO A CORNER

DOUBLE DOWN TURNED the corner and announced, "We're here."

They entered the trailer park and Edgar whispered, "Turn off your headlights. The manager's a complete asshole." The old man was watching TV in his living room as usual. Through the window they saw him sitting on a recliner, sipping on a drink with his dog at his side.

"He seems harmless," said Double Down.

Edgar leaned forward and said, "He's worthless."

"I take it that you owe him money?"

"Maybe."

They both smiled at each other. All the lights were off in Edgar's trailer when they pulled up. Alby squinted into the darkness and asked, "This is it?"

Edgar blushed and replied, "Hey, it's paid for. Besides, after all the doctor bills with my wife, there wasn't much left over. In fact, there was nothing."

Alby nodded. "Sorry to hear that."

Her delivery was sincere but restrained. Edgar knew that somewhere in her past, this woman had gone through a similar hell. You don't end up at Dunes without being betrayed by someone, if not yourself. Her role in all of this seemed essential, which led him to wonder if she'd planned her escape from Dunes based on the events that were now happening or if she triggered them by showing up.

"Thanks," he replied.

The car door dinged on the other side as Izzy got out. She tapped on the hood and snorted, "Edgar, what are the chances that you have a painting of dogs playing cards on the wall in there?"

Edgar slowly walked around the car and replied, "You're about ten years too early to find that one. I'm working on it, though."

She surveyed the outside of the rundown motorhome from top to bottom and interjected, "You mean, working *toward* it."

When all the car doors to the sedan closed, a message popped up on their CompWatches: "Voting will start on passage of the 37th Amendment to the Constitution in twelve hours."

"Shit, we don't have much time," said Alby.

"What do you mean?" asked Edgar.

"When private corporations take over permanently, they'll be able to remove all the government safeguards, which means they will control the Intranet completely. That means they can change security protocol and rewrite all the algorithms and codes. That means our algorithm might not work any longer."

Ketchum, who was leaning on the car hood, said, "Then the game is over."

Edgar peered over at Ketchum. A patch of peach fuzz cuddled his chin, trying to hide what was left of his childhood. He'd grown up so fast this last year in terms of political views and his outlook on life, yet his body was still struggling to shed the innocence of puberty. He was now a seasoned pro when it came to love and heartbreak. It was hard to tell whether the experience had left him bitter and jaded. If it did, he hid it well.

Then he turned to Izzy. He loved the warmth in her eyes. They were a soft brown and rounder than most. He'd never noticed the gray streaks trickling through her bangs, maybe because she'd always colored her hair when she was his boss. After retirement, that all changed. It's not that she quit caring what she looked like. No, it was more of an epiphany, or to be more precise, a resolution to quit denying the inevitable and embrace old age. Trivial matters like looking younger didn't seem to be important when just getting out of bed was a challenge.

"How well did you know my mother?" he asked.

"Not that well. I met her at a party a long time ago soon after the Civil War." Izzy grinned and gleefully recalled, "Boy, was there excitement in the air back then. Everyone was talking about the changes and what was going to come — and what was going to go away." She rubbed her chin and stroked her thick head of hair, then added, "That's when she introduced me to her boyfriend and the rest is history."

The sounds of cars driving by on the main road and crickets chirping filled the air as Double Down checked his rifle while walking the perimeter. "Don't let the quiet fool you. There's probably an APB out on us by now. It only takes one street camera to trigger an alert."

Edgar fumbled with the spare key he kept under a gnome next to the steps. Once inside, Double Down clicked on a flashlight and said, "Keep the lights low to the ground."

"It smells like fish in here," said Alby.

Edgar peered under a plate in the sink and replied, "Salmon, to be exact. I didn't plan on being gone so long, you know."

When he dumped it into the trash and sealed the bag, Double Down bumped into the tea kettle on the stove with his rifle. Edgar caught it before it fell to the ground. As he placed the pot into the cabinet above, visions from one of his last conversations with Evelyn emerged from a hidden corner of his mind and replayed vividly.

❧ ❧ ❧

It was the week before she died. They both sat on the sofa reading the rejection letter from her insurance on the laptop. Once again, they'd denied her request for additional testing. The words "requested," "lack," "medical," and "necessity" glared back at them through the liquid crystal screen like headlights in the rain — each one warning of the pending danger ahead; each one dripping with cynicism about her condition; each one slowly washing away any hope for a recovery.

Edgar rose from the couch and walked into the kitchen. He lifted a vial of pills out of his pocket and studied the label. The reality of what he had to do was sinking in and smothering his sense of virtue. Yet, what did virtue ever have to do with empathy? With a wavering hand, he fondled the vial between his fingers before returning it to his pocket. He picked up the steaming kettle from the stove, poured a hot cup of tea, and added some honey.

Back in the living room, he handed it to Evelyn and said, "Here, this will help." She forced a smile while he stroked her hair and closed his eyes.

She laid her head in his arms and asked, "Do you think there's a heaven?"

Edgar opened one eye and replied, "No … well, maybe. I guess you might want to hedge your bets on that one."

She tapped on her watch and commanded, "Elixir, play happy tunes." Music filled the room while she caressed his arm and said just above a whisper, "If they find out, you could go to prison."

"They won't find out," Edgar assured.

"What if…"

Edgar put his finger to her lips to quiet her. "They won't find out. Just follow the script like we planned in case anyone is listening."

Evelyn squeezed his arm and blinked. "I'm gonna miss you."

"Not as much as I'm gonna miss you."

"I guess you're right." She half chuckled and added, "Just don't mope around after I'm gone, you know, or else this will eat you up inside." She sat up and emphasized, "And then you'll end up just like me."

He contemplated this thought as he stretched his legs, "Maybe I should go with you. That would simplify things."

She slammed her hands into his chest and scolded, "Don't talk like that. You need to go on for both of us. Dammit, use what time you have left on this planet and live, enjoy what you have, maybe save the world from itself."

Edgar nodded and replied, "I will, I promise." He closed his eyes again and let his thoughts run wild."

࿇ ࿇ ࿇

"Where's the stuff?"

Izzy's question brought Edgar back into the moment. He shut the cabinet door and motioned toward the bed above the driver's seat. "Up there are the paintings. The ceramics are everywhere." He pointed to an ashtray on the table and over at the vase.

Ketchum stepped onto the ladder and climbed on top of the bed. With a flashlight tightly secured between his lips, he fumbled through a pile of pillows before seeing the frames lined up against the wall. "Got 'em." One by one, he pulled the paintings out and handed them to Double Down who was standing next to him.

Double Down carefully laid them on the table and asked, "Is that all of them?"

"Yes," replied Edgar, "but not all of these are my mom's. Some are mine."

Ketchum peered over his shoulder and said, "Let me guess, this one and that one."

"Correct!"

"Not bad, Mr. Gorman. You missed your calling."

"I hear that a lot." Edgar studied the one closest to him and recalled the memories behind it. It was the last painting he'd ever finished. After his wife died, he just couldn't quite get over that hump because his heart wasn't into it. His painting career entered into a creative time warp of sorts, lost in the past and always emotionally beyond his reach.

Alby leaned over Edgar's shoulder for a quick look. "They're nice," she said with an appreciative nod, "very nice."

Double Down stacked the 11-by-14-inch fractal images on the table. Taking great care with each one, he opened his backpack and inserted them.

Izzy's CompWatch pinged. There was a message from Tusnig. "*BIG is there. Get the hell out.*"

"They've found us. We need to go now."

Outside, a set of spotlights shot out of nowhere and blinded the trailer. "This is Director Conway from BIG. We have the place surrounded. Come out with your hands up."

Toyer grabbed the mic out of his sister's hands and added, "Yeah, we got you now."

"Who was that?" asked Ketchum.

"Her idiot brother. What do we do?"

Double Down looked to the others and said, "We have two choices. Either we give up or go out with our guns a'blazing."

"Jesus," replied Edgar, "why so dramatic. Let's just drive out of here."

"What do you mean? This thing actually runs?"

Edgar smiled, "Sure it does. I think."

"When's the last time you started it?"

"Uh, when I moved in, but it's never been a problem. The battery is fully charged."

Izzy tugged on her Mardi Grás necklace and said, "I thought these mute pedals would keep them away longer." Then she pushed a button on the temple of her earpiece and said, "Tusnig, switch to level two."

"Mute pedals?"

"Yeah, what'd you think they were called?"

Edgar caressed his necklace and said, "Tusnig, no need to shout. I can hear you clearly."

"Okay folks, somehow we have to do this quickly and do it in a way where we don't get pelted with bullets." Izzy closed all the curtains and added, "I doubt the walls on this contraption are more than an inch or two thick. That won't even stop a pellet gun. Any suggestions?"

Edgar raised his hand. "I have a flare gun above the sink."

Double Down perked up and said, "That's a start." He grabbed the flares and gun out of the cabinet. "I'll shoot them at the agents. Maybe that will give us a little time to get away."

"Or better yet, shoot one into his landlord's trailer and cause a diversion," replied Alby.

"It's worth a try," said Izzy. "We must act fast, though. Double Down, you shoot them through the skylight and, Edgar, you be ready to get the hell out of here once all hell breaks loose. Everyone, stay low to the ground. Once the firing starts, try to hide behind something solid."

Izzy's eyes focused on Ketchum with the weight of the world resting on her next comment. "You take the backpack and whatever you do, protect those paintings at all costs."

"Will do."

She rummaged through Edgar's cabinet and pulled out a pack of cigarettes. With them raised above her head, she said, "I thought you quit."

"It's unopened. I pull them out every once in a while when I feel the urge, and then I take them to church with me."

"Church, you're kidding, right?"

"No, you wouldn't believe how many times that pack has saved my ass," he smirked. "Every time I show them off to a preacher and get a few 'Hallelujahs' or 'Hail Marys,' depending on where I'm at, my Demeanor Score goes up."

"Fascinating." She admired the firmly wrapped packet for a few seconds and concluded, "That won't do us any good now." Then she tossed them to the side and rifled through the other drawers. "What else do you have here that might help us get out of this mess? There's no way this RV is going to outrun anything bigger than a skateboard."

"You have sixty seconds," Deputy Conway blared over the megaphone outside.

"Shit! What about the DDO glasses? Do you have them turned on?"

"No, I turned them off because they really mess with your mind. I put them into 'stealth' mode but I'm sure BIG had some way of accessing that data, even with them off. I guess it doesn't matter now."

Izzy activated the glasses and said, "Tusnig, can you see them?"

"Yes, syncing them up now," he replied.

"I have a little trick up my sleeve that I've been wanting to try for a long time." Izzy played with the dial on top of the temple and added, "Let's hope that Toyer has a pair with him now."

"I can confirm that," said Tusnig. "He's trying to listen in on your conversation as we speak but I have him blocked. Alby, connect the quantum laptop and I'll send you the video feed."

Alby patted a few keys and said, "I'm in."

"Good." Izzy peered over her shoulder and said, "Your view is much better than mine." Then she smiled before saying, "Okay, let's get inside Toyer's head."

"Make him do something stupid," said Edgar.

Alby maneuvered the touch pad down and around, then pressed a button. Toyer swiftly pointed his gun into the air and started firing. The other agents took cover as tree limbs and leaves pummeled them from above.

"What are you doing?" yelled Director Conway.

Toyer stared into the sky and said, "I saw them. Two people in the trees, with guns. Didn't you see them?"

"No," replied his sister. She peered up and said, "There is nothing up there. Don't do that again."

Everyone in the RV burst into laughter. "That was amazing," said Ketchum. "What else can you do?"

"Hmm." She searched through camera footage from Toyer's past. "How about a video of Toyer jerking off or something like that?"

"How about a video of Director Conway getting off?" said Edgar.

Alby searched through the database and said, "How about a video of the director getting it on with her old boss?"

"Perfect."

She isolated the video footage, opened a hologram on Toyer's glasses outside, a few feet in front of the other agents, and pushed "Enter." The hologram glowed in the dark as images of Miranda lying on her bed naked with a man almost twice her age came into view. A deep moaning sound filled the air as the agents realized what was happening. At first, there were a few snickers, but then outright laughter as Miranda groaned loudly, "Oh, oh, oh..." Toyer stood there stunned with disbelief and in shock.

Director Conway paced in the grass back and forth while pushing back any agent who even as much smiled at the video. "Stop it. Stop it now. I order all of you," she growled. Everyone ignored her. Finally, she ripped the glasses off Toyer's head and violently snapped them into several pieces before throwing them on the ground. Then she took the butt of her pistol and shattered the lens until the hologram dissolved.

Complete silence suffocated the parking lot as the director squeezed the palms of her hands. A brief flash of images fizzled and vanished while one last grunt dissipated over the park grounds. The lights had come on in several trailers by now as residents peeked out their windows.

"Get ready to fire," she commanded.

"We can't," replied her brother. "We need to recover the missing download first."

"Unbelievable." Miranda stomped on the remaining fragments and asked, "Do we have to bring them all in alive or just one?"

CHAPTER THIRTY-FIVE

ROAD TRIP

WHILE LOOKING OUT the RV window at the turmoil going on around the agents, Izzy quipped, "Well, that should rattle a few cages. Double Down, shoot off the flares and let's get the hell out of here."

Edgar slid into the front seat and tried to stay low. Ketchum and Alby unhinged a table from the floor brace, wedged it next to the stove, and huddled behind it. Double Down climbed onto a chair and quietly lifted the hinge holding the skylight in place. He loaded the flare gun and pointed.

"Ready."

"Let's do it," replied Edgar, "on the count of three."

The first flare missed the trailer and hit the window of a parked car. The effect was even better than expected as it shattered immediately and flames instantly engulfed the interior. His second flare landed in the landlord's bedroom, catching the curtains on fire. Edgar tried to turn the engine over. It sputtered and whined but wouldn't start.

"I'm giving you five seconds to surrender or else," blared Director Conway. "Five, four..."

Double Down fired another flare in the direction of the megaphone. It landed under one of the agents' cars and burst into a fiery display of red smoke and sparkling fireworks.

"Try it again, Edgar. Make sure you're pushing on the brake."

Gunfire exploded across the windows and walls. Double

Down jumped off the chair and ducked behind the table. Ketchum laid flat on his stomach, covering the backpack with his body.

Finally, the RV started. Edgar threw it into drive and floored it while still hiding under the seat. Outside, the blocks wedged underneath the tires scattered while the RV rocked and swayed. A power cord connected to the motorhome ripped out of the socket causing sparks to fly everywhere. The sewer hose popped out of the drain and bounced from side to side as the RV rolled off the concrete slab and down the gravel road.

Edgar channeled the memories of leaving for work every day and let them guide him out of the trailer park. He quickly turned right and followed the sounds of the dirt road straight out onto the street as chunks of feces and urine sprinkled onto the ground. When he felt the gravel firm up and turn into blacktop, he turned right again onto the main road.

"What the hell's that smell?" asked Alby.

"The sewer hose, what else."

"Maybe we can weaponize it," interjected Izzy. "Tusnig, what do you have?"

Bullets riddled the back end of the motorhome as it made its getaway. When the RV was out of range, the agents quit firing and all jumped into their cars.

Edgar ripped away the curtain covering the windshield and sat up in the driver's seat. While adjusting his mirrors, he hollered, "Tusnig, now or never. What do we do?"

The RV puttered down the street, gradually gaining speed. Flashing lights and sirens soon followed. "They're gaining on us," cried Double Down as he smashed the skylight and maneuvered himself into position with the rifle. He aimed at a set of tires and fired. A car skidded off the road but a barrage of bullets simultaneously splattered against the rear of the RV. "Anybody hurt?"

"All good," replied Alby.

"There should be a strawberry field on your left," relayed Tusnig. "Turn into it and head for the tree line."

"Strawberry field? What good is that going to do?"

"There are water pipes everywhere. Run over as many of them as you can. That should slow them down."

"Got it."

Edgar turned left on the dirt road and headed straight for a small twenty-foot-tall water tower next to a set of wooden crates. He managed to nick the crates, sending them scattering everywhere, and then plowed right underneath the tower, knocking out the main feed pipe. The truss poles buckled and fell like dominoes. Then he zigzagged across the field, smashing every hose and pipe in sight. Water spewed up, down, and sideways across the field, creating gushing peacock tails of liquid jetting high into the air. He turned his windshield wipers on while small chunks of feces and thick brown liquid dripped down over the glass.

Alby peered out the window and asked, "Is that what I think it is?"

"Cow shit. Only seems fitting," replied Edgar.

"Just what the doctor ordered, eh?" said Tusnig. "There's a steep drop-off after the tree line. You know it's there, but I don't think they do. Be sure to turn onto the dirt road right after you exit and, hopefully, they'll keep going straight."

"It's worth a try." Edgar floored the RV and sped off, bouncing over row after row of dirt as plates, glasses, and anything else hidden in the cabinets catapulted onto the cabin floor. He searched for the cleanest entry point into the row of trees ahead, set a course, and yelled, "This is gonna be rough, folks. Everyone get on the left side of the trailer and brace yourselves."

The RV barreled over several bushes with ease and trampled down the smaller saplings. Larger limbs scraped across the side with ear-piercing screeches. The BIG agents swerved and slid across puddles of mud while trying to maintain their speed. All the while, red lights gyrated across the field while sirens hiccupped from ditch to ditch. From time to time, a desperate gunshot rang out from a window but never came close to hitting the target.

"I see the edge coming up. Everyone hold on."

"It doesn't look like they're slowing down at all," chimed in Izzy as she adjusted the DDO glasses. "I count three cars on our tail."

Edgar tightened his grip on the wheel and as soon as he saw daylight beyond the trees, swerved sharply to the left. The RV twisted and bowed like a tree branch into the turn while teetering on two wheels. The open plateau stretched out no more than ten feet before making a sharp descent down hundreds of feet into a deep ravine. Edgar let off the gas allowing all four wheels to land but the vehicle slid sideways toward the edge. He quickly floored the gas pedal and turned the renegade tire the other way until it skipped back onto the path.

"We made it. Cross your fingers."

Behind him, the first squad car blasted through the tree line and hurtled into the air. It landed fifteen feet away as it propelled downhill like an Olympic ski racer. The next car tried to make the turn but started too late, causing it to roll over and Rock-O-Plane down into the ravine, where it came to rest next to the first car.

The last driver slammed on the brakes and tried to stop its descent, but the slippery slope was too unforgiving. The vehicle continued its ominous slide downward and ended up butting against the other two at the bottom.

The newly minted fugitives laughed and cried with joy. They peered out the windows at the buried headlights and watched the BIG agents get out of their cars. Before any of them could aim and fire, sewage runoff from the field cascaded downward in a diarrhetic spiral, sending them ducking for cover.

"That should slow them down for a while. Tusnig, how close are we?" asked Edgar.

"You're about a mile from the entrance. I'm not sure if the RV can make it the whole way. It looks like the ridge narrows down to almost nothing. You may have to hoof it the rest of the way."

"That's fine. We'll enter in the same place we exited. Please make sure it's unlocked."

"Will do. See you soon."

Suddenly, a police drone showed up out of nowhere flying in front of the windshield. It flashed tiny red and blue lights at the motorhome, making several attempts to obscure Edgar's view by zipping across it in erratic spurts. Then a laser beam pierced through the windshield and into his eyes. "What the hell! Somebody do something about this."

The mini speaker in the drone chirped out Director Conway's warning: "You cannot escape. We have pinpointed your position and locked in your GPS coordinates. It's only a matter of minutes before we arrive."

"She's lying. The lights on the drone would be white if they'd locked in our coordinates," replied Ketchum. Edgar stopped the RV and threw it into park. The road had narrowed to the point where the wheels barely hugged the edge of the ridge.

"I'll take it out." Ketchum propped a chair up under the skylight, calmly lifted his rifle up through the hole, aimed, and fired. The drone spotted him and darted to the side, zigzagging back and forth until he'd expended the whole clip. Then two gun barrels opened up from under the wings and fired a dozen rounds into the windshield.

Edgar ducked down and held his breath. Then he yelled, "Holy shit, we have to do something now!"

"I got this," barked Double Down. He pulled a pistol out from inside his jacket, kicked open the side door, and jumped to the ground. In one swooping motion, he rolled over, cocked the gun, aimed, and fired. The drone was too quick and maneuvered sideways while zeroing in on the target.

"Double Down, get the hell out of the way," yelled Ketchum.

It was too late. A rainfall of bullets riddled the dirt and pushed toward him through the sludge. They danced off Double Down's torso like pistons, each one tearing away cloth and flesh, flesh and cloth. Izzy pointed a shotgun out the RV door and fired blindly. Three of the four propellers shattered as the drone sputtered out of control, crashing to the ground. Then she ran over and crushed it with her foot.

She knelt and rolled Double Down over on his back. Blood seeped out of several holes as his white shirt quickly turned red. The others were now all out of the RV and standing over him. His eyes struggled to stay open while he gasped for air. Ketchum placed a towel over the holes trying to stop the bleeding.

"It's no use," whispered Double Down.

"No," cried Ketchum. Tears rolled off his cheeks as he hugged his friend and stretched the towel tighter. Images from a year ago in the Arizona desert ran through his mind. In that scenario, he'd been able to save his partner by reacting swiftly, but that was not the case today. A thin layer of guilt seeped into Ketchum's consciousness as he repositioned the saturated towel.

As all feeling drained from his body, Double Down sensed the grief in Ketchum's motions and tried to conjure up a smile. "You've been a good friend." His breathing was more erratic now and every syllable a struggle, yet he pushed on. "My best friend, in fact, but I need you to stay strong and finish the job."

"You can't leave me now," exclaimed Ketchum as he searched for the right words to say. "You promised to take me to Disneyland."

Double Down chuckled and coughed up blood. "I'm sorry."

Seconds later, he was gone. No one said a word. What was there to say? The game had risen to a completely new level now. It wasn't about ideological differences or the fate of mankind any longer. It wasn't even about life itself. No, this had gotten personal and there was no turning back.

Ketchum knelt over his companion and continued crying. Double Down had become a big brother to him over the last year by keeping him safe and being there when he needed it most. Now, he was on his own again.

Edgar placed his hand on his shoulder and gently squeezed. "I'm sorry." Ketchum's lips quivered as he cleared his nose and wiped it clean. They all paused and reflected, each person silently saying goodbye and absorbing the consequences of their actions.

Finally, Izzy spun in a circle and said, "We should leave. They'll be here any minute. Looks like we're walking the rest of the way. Make sure we have everything."

CHAPTER THIRTY-SIX

LET THE SUNSHINE IN

THE FOUR KICKED the mud off their shoes in the parking lot and walked down the steps leading to the ocean. They entered the corridor through the large metal door at the bottom of a stairwell and slammed it shut. Izzy secured the padlock and said, "That should do it."

They paused long enough to acknowledge each other's presence and then marched down the tunnel leading to the main room. By now, they were exhausted and thirsty.

Alby followed behind Edgar and tugged on the back of his shirt. He turned around and stopped as the rest of the group continued down the tunnel. Then she whispered, "I read your file."

"Really."

"Yeah, I had to know who I was dealing with, you know."

"Understandable." Edgar sheepishly replied, "I read yours too."

"Oh!" She snickered and let go of his shirt.

Edgar noticed a change in her disposition and said, "I'm sorry, just old habits."

"No, no, no. I get it. Under these circumstances, it was the smart thing to do."

He scratched the back of his head as he lowered it and confessed, "It was before I knew you were part of this group."

She blushed and turned her gaze down the tunnel at the rest of the group. They were now a good thirty feet in front of them. "I see."

"I'm sorry." Edgar gently grabbed her arm and added, "We need to keep up."

Their pace was slow as each person digested this news, wondering what deep secrets about themselves were now known and not knowing what it meant. Finally, Alby shook off any thoughts of trepidation and said, "Anyway, I found a few very incriminating entries in a BIG database regarding your wife's death. They were investigating it pretty heavily as an assisted suicide after they sent you off for rehabilitation."

Edgar's eyes opened wide. He looked ahead at the others, waiting to see if anyone had heard her. They all appeared to be more concerned about aching feet and too tired to care. "What kind of entries?"

"The kind that can get you sent away for a long, long time, if you know what I mean."

Edgar ran his hand through his hair and confessed, "It never happened. The aneurism killed her before I had a chance to do anything."

"That explains a lot and why they didn't pursue it." Alby softly caressed his bicep and grinned. "Don't worry, I deleted them from your record, permanently."

"Why would you do that for me?"

With a tender smile, she replied, "I don't know. Why wouldn't I, since I could?"

For a moment, their eyes connected on a different level. He wasn't used to random acts of kindness and it felt good. It stirred emotions inside that he hadn't known for years and wasn't sure what to do with them. "Thank you," was all he could muster.

Up ahead, they heard Ketchum call out, "There it is. We made it."

When they entered the main room, the rest of the group rushed toward them. "How'd it go? Did you get them?"

"Well, we got them. I'm not sure exactly what you're looking for but here they are," said Ketchum as he handed Tusnig the backpack and tossed his rifle into a box in the corner.

Shursta searched the room and gazed down the tunnel while asking, "Where's Double Down?"

The four paused and exchanged glances. Ketchum nodded to Edgar. "He didn't make it."

Clem's eyes opened widely as he gasped before asking, "How'd it happen?"

"Drone. He was trying to knock it down but it was too fast."

He nodded and lowered his head. Silence blanketed the room like a shadow's shadow. Each dark thought was met by an even darker reality. This was not a drill. This was not a game any longer. Even if they wanted to, they couldn't turn back because they'd all been identified and categorically labeled as enemies of the state.

"Let's see what you brought." Tusnig and Shursta removed the paintings and dumped them onto the table. One by one, they held them up to the light, examined the tops and bottoms, and ran their fingers over the surfaces. Tusnig even dropped a wad of spit on one and rubbed it in.

"What were you thinking, Mrs. Gorman?" he said as he continued scrutinizing every detail. "Come on, give us a clue."

Alby fumbled through the assorted ceramics and said, "I can't see how these would work." She pushed them to the side and lifted one of the colorful images up to the light. From top to bottom she reviewed the glass canvases as it changed shapes before her eyes. "I haven't got a clue as to what these are, besides pretty bizarre paintings." She gazed over at Edgar and added, "Your mother had one crazy imagination."

"She also had one crazy and bizarre past that she didn't like to talk about. Maybe they're a collage of some kind and you have to put them together like a puzzle."

Alby started rearranging them on the table. "Look at the

colors and weird shapes. They're repeated in different paintings. Maybe they do fit together."

Tusnig continued to scrutinize the one in his hand and asked, "When were these painted?"

Edgar wiped a splotch of dirt from his pants leg with a towel and replied, "I don't know. I guess it must have been twenty, twenty-five years ago, at least."

"What was popular back then?"

Izzy lifted one of the canvasses and replied, "There was a renaissance period after the civil war. A lot of rethinking about what America had been and should be. Some things that were popular in the twentieth century returned, like bell bottoms, drugs, religion, sixties music, and the sort."

Ketchum leaned over and caught the reflection off one picture and added, "And black light posters." He scooped up a painting and walked over to the wall. While maneuvering it in the black light from left to right, he exclaimed, "Look!"

Tusnig ran over and peered over his friend's shoulder. "I don't believe it." He grabbed another glass canvas off the table and raised it in the direction of the light. "I can see numbers and letters, but what do they mean?"

Alby picked up another and moved over next to Tusnig. "Yeah, I can see letters and numbers glowing inside of this frame too." They lifted each one and studied the images.

Tusnig turned his painting over and said, "I'm not sure what to make of it."

"Maybe there's a pattern, you know, in the order they should be arranged."

"We're gonna be here all day trying to figure this out and we're running out of time," said Izzy as she glanced at her CompWatch.

"Do you have another idea?"

Alby rubbed her chin and asked, "How many of them are there? I'm counting seven. Is that it?"

Ketchum searched the room and said, "Yeah, seven."

"Edgar, do you have any idea when they were painted?"

"You mean in what order?"

"Yes."

He examined the images from front to back one by one and laid them on the table. Then he rearranged a few while whispering under his breath. After a few minutes, he announced, "I think this is it, from left to right."

"Good." Alby lifted the black light off the wall and reflected it off the letters and numbers. "Tusnig, what do you see?"

Tusnig gazed into the images, moving his head from side to side. "I don't see anything. It's not making sense."

Shursta peered over his shoulder and groaned. She wiggled her way in front of him and said, "Sometimes I wonder about you geniuses. Especially when the answer is staring you right in your face." She turned a couple of frames over on their backs while rearranging another one by spinning it top to bottom. "There, try that."

"That's it!" he exclaimed. Then he reached over and kissed her on the cheek. "You're the genius in this family."

"One genius in the family is enough. Let's just say I am brilliant."

Tusnig smiled and studied the 11 x 14-inch paintings before him. "Let's see what happens if we insert this into the formula we already have."

He turned to Alby who nodded in agreement and grabbed her quantum laptop. She feverishly pecked away while studying the glass panels. Her lips moved as she read the lines of code one by one, stopping barely long enough to type a few keys. A few minutes later, she sat up straight and said, "It's done." Then she grinned and gazed over to Edgar. "Your mother was one clever woman. Let's see what happens."

Tusnig pecked a few keys on his quantum laptop and said,

"I'm in too. We're synched." Then he pushed his chair away from the desk and announced, "Now, we wait."

The room went silent again. Everyone glanced around as each set of eyes traveled between them in short but cordial encounters. The minutes ticked in uneasy increments, scattering the sounds of people snacking on sandwiches and drinks. Tusnig continued to watch his laptop while lines of digits and symbols flashed across the monitor. In the corner of the screen, a caption in a box with a yellow bar slowly moving inside read, "Calculating estimated time."

"How much longer?" asked Izzy.

"I don't know. This could take minutes or maybe days. It's never been done before so I don't have anything to compare it to."

"We don't have days." Izzy glanced at her CompWatch and exclaimed, "We can't scramble these signals forever without someone getting suspicious. Let's just hope they didn't spot us coming in." She peered down the tunnel where they'd come from and said, "Everyone go into Stealth Mode and link into Alby's feed. Send a link to Carmen and her aunt too. We need to hedge our bets."

"Why aren't they here?" asked Edgar.

"You can't keep all your eggs in one basket," she said. "If everything goes sideways, we still have someone on the outside to carry on the fight."

Alby pounded a few keys on the keyboard and responded, "Everyone, do it now." They all synchronized their CompWatches and glasses to the upload and locked it in.

Izzy then lifted her head back and refocused on the group, "Let's try to get some rest, if possible." She ran her hand over her lips and asked Clem, "Got any more liquor?"

"Sure, let me get it."

"Pour me one too," said Edgar. "It's been an extremely long day."

"I bet." Clem pulled a bottle of brandy out of the drawer and poured some into several paper cups. He handed one to Edgar and Izzy and said, "Bottoms up."

Edgar looked to his old partner, downed his drink completely, and exhaled "I miss hanging with you. Why didn't you reach out sooner?"

"It was too risky. Not until I got the call about them sending you back to Ontario did I realize we were running out of time and staying underground wasn't an option any longer."

"There's only one option left and let's hope it works."

Alby smiled and spun her chair around. "I'll take a glass of that too."

CHAPTER THIRTY-SEVEN

GOOD MORNING

THE MINUTES PASSED with still no confirmation on the program working. Tusnig and Shursta snuggled in the corner on top of a sleeping bag and tried to catch a few winks. Others laid their heads on the table or leaned back on a chair to relax, but no one was really sleeping. The faint sound of trickling water echoed in the distance as the stale smell of body odor warmed the room.

Without warning, an explosive blast shook the floors and walls of the cavern. Dirt and rocks plummeted down as everyone scrambled for cover. A half dozen Dunes agents appeared through the smoke with their guns drawn.

"Don't anybody move!" commanded Director Conway as the agents took positions around the perimeter. Edgar recognized Toyer, Agent Terabush, and April standing by her side. Then the director strolled around the middle of the room taking in each face. "So this is the infamous underground group, GRID." She placed a hand on one of the posters hanging on the wall and ripped it into shreds. "More like GERD if you ask me."

"Ha, good one, sis," interjected Toyer.

"Shut up," she snapped back.

She sauntered over to where Alby sat and said, "Ah, the elusive Alby McMurray: computer hacker by day, fugitive by night. Living underground so long that she looks more like a chipmunk than a human." Director Conway smiled and pivoted. "Then we have the two young lovers, so sweet." Tusnig and Shursta had locked in each other's arms after the blast but her comment made them both recoil and sit up.

Toyer sneered as the Director removed her gloves and stopped in front of Izzy. "Then we have the legendary law enforcement agent with the deepest and darkest secret of all. All these years you've been working behind the scenes for a lost cause and now, here you sit with nothing to show. I hope it was worth losing your retirement."

April crept over to the side of the room next to where Ketchum sat. The director followed her movements. "Poor, poor, Ketchum Tutaloo. The boy who was swindled out of his million dollars by a pretty girl. But you did manage to get your rocks off before losing it all. That's one consolation." She leaned in and purred, "It must make you very, very angry seeing her standing right next to you like this. Probably so angry that you'd want to get even somehow, maybe put your hands around her neck and..." Her last word oozed off her lips like molasses, "...Squeeeeeze."

The director smirked and slowly stood back up. Then she pivoted away, rubbed her chin, and walked over to Clem who was sitting in the corner. He'd been uncharacteristically quiet the whole time, leaning inside his own shadow. She typed and swiped on her CompWatch a few times and said, "It's about time you came through for us. I was beginning to wonder if you'd changed your mind. There, a million dollars has been inserted into your account. You can leave now." Clem sprang up out of his seat and vanished through the smoke-filled tunnel without saying a word.

"How'd I miss that?" whispered Izzy.

Alby periodically glanced over at the quantum laptop when the director wasn't watching. The upload bar was almost complete. The estimated time said less than a minute. Director Conway had circled the room and was now back in her space. "Quite a commendable accomplishment, escaping the facility and evading capture the way you did. You could've been a valuable asset for us at one time. Such a shame." She waved over to Agent Terabush and said, "I'm going to let you get credit for this capture. Take her back to headquarters and stage a press conference."

"Should I do it virtually or in person?" asked Agent Terabush.

"Invite all the usual suspects into the office. We need to get as much news coverage as possible." The agent nodded and handcuffed Alby.

Then he lifted her out of her seat and said, "Let's go."

As they passed by Edgar, she stopped and said, "It was nice meeting you. I hope we see each other again, some day."

Edgar smiled and replied, "Yeah, me too." Once again, their eyes connected as she smiled and winked.

"Get her out of here," barked Director Conway. The director focused on Edgar and approached his chair, "And finally, we have Mr. Smart Ass." She bent down, strangled the arms on both sides, and asked, "How do you like me now, Ex-Agent Gorman? Got anything humorous to say?"

A faint smirk emerged as Edgar replied, "Loved your little performance on the hologram back at the trailer park. Didn't think you had it in you."

The director smacked Edgar across the face with the front of her hand and then slapped it again with a backhand. Edgar's lip started bleeding as his head swayed in defiance. He grinned and relished his newfound state of insubordination as long as possible.

The director stretched her arms and confessed, "Boy, that felt good. I've been waiting a long time to do that. Shall we try it again?"

The quantum laptop chimed and flashed in large bold red letters: "Complete."

"What is this?" she asked.

Edgar wiped away the blood and replied, "The beginning of the end, Miranda."

Izzy took a sip from her paper cup, leaned back on her chair, and explained. "The Intranet, as you know it, has been shut down. No longer can you filter out websites and replace them with fluffy feel-good stories. No more censorship, no more false data, no more bullshit. Just reality."

"Why would you want to do that?" replied Director Conway.

"So Americans see the truth for what it is. No more watered-down spoon-fed versions of this Utopian landscape MAGMA has been painting. People will now have to learn how to carry on real conversations, make decisions on their own, and maybe even learn how to be creative again."

"People don't want the truth, they want comfort food for the mind. They want things to be like it used to be when everything was good in the world." Conway waved her hand from Toyer to the laptop and demanded, "Shut that thing down."

Edgar's CompWatch pinged and he winced. The director grabbed his arm and glared at his watch. "Who's that?"

"My sister."

"Go ahead and play the message. Maybe we can take her in too as an accomplice. Put it on speakerphone."

"I don't think so."

She still had a grasp on his arm and hit "Play" on Edgar's watch.

"Hey bro, Lotty here. The world is going crazy. Have you been watching your news feed? There's somebody talking about a drought in Africa that's killed half the population. Did you know that we landed on the moon over a hundred years ago? And they're saying that the President and Vice President aren't even in charge of the country. Plus, avocados, my god, avocados! The rest of the world has been eating them like candy. Oh, oh, and there's this lady talking shit about Dylan MacMillan saying that he swindled her out of her million but no one will do anything about it. It's just unbelievable."

Director Conway silenced the recording before it could finish. "Where are we at with that computer, little brother?"

Toyer slammed his hands on the keyboard and cried, "It won't respond." He held down the "Off" button and added, "None of the keys are working and I've already unplugged it but it's still running."

"Whose laptop is this?"

"Alby's," responded Tusnig.

The director pointed and barked, "Shut it down, immediately."

Tusnig sat up in his chair and answered, "I don't know how. Only she knows."

She stomped over to where he sat, pulled out her revolver, placed it against his head and said, "I'll give you until the count of three."

"Okay, okay, let me see what I can do." He jumped up and scurried over to where Toyer was sitting.

Shursta gulped back the fear and stared at the director until she finally lowered the gun. Then her CompWatch rang.

Director Conway swung around and snarled, "Who's that?"

Shursta gazed over to Tusnig, seeking guidance on how to respond. He locked eyes for a moment and confidently nodded. She turned and replied, "It's my mother and father."

"By all means," teased the director. "Let's visit with the folks and see how they're doing. We have time to kill. Put them on the video screen so everyone can watch."

An image of Margaret and Jonathan in a restaurant enjoying a glass of wine came on the monitor. "Shursta, are you all right? We heard on the news feed that there was a mass shooting at your school today."

"I don't go to that school anymore, mother. I graduated, remember."

"Oh, that's right," she replied.

Jonathan leaned into the picture and added, "They said it was the seventh mass shooting this month. Can you believe it? I had no idea."

Margaret nudged in front of him and interjected, "Hey, did you know there used to be a museum in the bay? That pile of rubble out there. I thought it was a ..." Her mother's eyebrows curled up in mid-sentence as she noticed Shursta's surroundings and asked, "Where did all those people come from, and where are you?"

Her daughter motioned around the room and replied, "These are my friends, Mom, and we're in a cave."

"Wait a minute, is that... Look here, Jonathan." She pointed at a spot on the screen. "Is that your brother standing behind you? I don't understand." Both were now squinting and staring back intensely.

Ketchum placed his hands on his sister's shoulders and said, "Hello Mother, hello Father."

"Ketchum, we thought you were dead. Now you're with your sister in a cave? What's going on?"

Miranda pushed her way in front of the camera and said, "I am Director Conway and I'm with BIG. Your son and daughter are being taken into custody and will be charged later today with crimes against the government." Then she shrugged and confessed, "Or whatever else we can come up with. If you wish to have any further contact with them, I suggest you get on a plane and head back to L.A. as soon as possible."

Jonathan and Margaret leaned back in their chairs and exchanged disbelieving frowns. "Well, we can't do that. We have a masseuse coming in at five, then dinner with our stockbroker at seven. The earliest we can be there is tomorrow morning."

"I see," snorted the director. "Well, that'll have to do, now, won't it?" She turned to Shursta and Ketchum and smiled. Then she pecked on Shursta's phone, turning off the video screen.

Ketchum spun around and stomped over to the wall in the corner of the room. He opened his fists and pounded them as hard as he could until the palms of his hands matched the color of granite. Then he turned around and glared at Director Conway. As he marched in her direction, April hurried over in his path and stopped him. Shursta laid her head on the table and cried. Tusnig tried to get up from his chair to console her but Toyer reached over and grabbed his shoulder.

"Okay, the peep show is over," growled the director. "Where are we with shutting this computer down?"

Toyer examined the screen and said, "It's still running."

"Mr. Dolan, you have thirty seconds to stop this thing from happening, whatever it is. Do you understand?"

Tusnig glanced back at her and replied, "I can't figure out her password. If I do it too many times, it will lock me out completely."

The director pulled out her pistol again, marched over to Shursta, and positioned it on her temple. "I'm going to count to thirty, and if you aren't inside shutting this program down by then, you can say goodbye to your girlfriend here. One, two, three…"

In that moment, Tusnig struck a key on the laptop and the lights went out in the whole cave. Only the glow coming from the green lights of a few devices sitting on the table and the laptop screens illuminated the room. He closed the monitors without hesitation, sending the whole place into darkness.

Before anyone could react, April grabbed Ketchum's arm and pulled him toward the ocean exit. Director Conway shined a flashlight on the two and yelled, "Where do you think you're going?"

April was tongue-tied as a stunned Ketchum wondered what was going on himself. Edgar stealthily retrieved a pistol from the box in the corner and moved into the light. He nonchalantly whispered to them both, "Get ready to run. I got this." Then he smiled and let the moment sink in. "Good luck," he added.

"I don't understand," whispered April.

"That makes two of us," said Ketchum as they shared glances.

"There's no time to explain. Just go on my cue." Edgar turned around and faced Director Conway. The flashlight was now squarely on his face. He did his best to stay in front of the two teenagers while keeping the light focused on himself.

The director swayed from side to side and asked, "What's going on here?"

"Too late." Edgar lifted his revolver and said, "You shoot them and I'll shoot you." He inhaled a new sense of purpose as the flashlight beams cast a warm glow over his face. He could hear his mother's words echoing throughout the cavern. This *was* a cause worth fighting for. This *was* a cause worth dying for. It felt invigorating. It felt liberating.

"Shoot? You do know that there are five guns pointed at you right now."

"Doesn't matter. My gun is pointed at you."

From her seat, Izzy cried, "Edgar, what are you doing? This isn't part of the plan."

He glanced over and smiled. "Ah, Izzy, it would've been nice to grow old together but it just wasn't in the cards."

"Edgar, don't do this."

He watched a tear form on her cheek as he replied, "It's too late. Don't worry, I'm finally in a good place now."

April and Ketchum continued to quietly slip farther away from the light radiating around him. Director Conway refocused her aim on the two and yelled, "I said don't move!"

The flashlight beams of every agent were now upon April and Ketchum. They froze. Izzy swiftly slid over to the box of weapons and retrieved a revolver. In one swooping motion, she fired and hit the director in the chest, then placed another bullet in her forehead. The other agents returned fire with a melody of muzzle flashes. Bullets pierced her torso with a force so powerful that it knocked her hard to the ground.

As the director's flashlight rolled around on the floor landing near Edgar's feet, April stared with disbelief. She grabbed Ketchum's hand, and like a cat in the night, slunk into the shadows and was gone. The agents that remained standing swung around toward Edgar with their pistols ready. "Drop your weapon and hands in the air," one shouted, as Edgar dropped the gun and raised his arms.

Toyer rushed over to where his sister lay on the ground. "Miranda, are you okay?" One of the agents shined their flashlight on the body as another one applied pressure to her chest. A velvet curtain of death oozed out of the wound on her forehead. The blank stare said it all.

"What do we do now?" asked one of the agents.

Toyer stood back up and surveyed the damage around the room. He glanced at his CompWatch and frowned. "No signal. I guess I'm in charge."

The others rushed over to where Izzy was and turned her on her back. Edgar knelt on one knee, brushed back her hair, and asked, "Why?"

She opened her eyes for a moment and smiled. "Sorry, old pal. It's all about greatness, not greed, remember?" Then she exhaled for the last time. He closed her eyelids and cleared his nose, taking one last mental snapshot before saying goodbye.

Toyer shined a light onto Izzy's head and then back to his sister's before screaming, "Was it worth it? Shutting down the Intranet and all... and for what? More turmoil, more needless bloodshed. What's wrong with you people?"

Edgar pushed himself up to his feet but continued to focus on his ex-partner. "What's the use of living if you can't think for yourself, can't form your own opinions, can't die for a worthy cause? This gal just gave her own life so two others could have one of their own." He nodded at Toyer and added, "Would somebody do that for you? I doubt it."

"What makes you think I'd want that?" Toyer sneered. "You

purists obviously don't understand people at all. They don't want to be informed, they want to be entertained. An hour from now, they'll all be clamoring for things to be the way they were. Nobody cares about worthy causes. They care about fancy cars, a roof over their head, and money in the bank. You've just created total chaos in their worlds and they're going to hate you for it."

"Maybe so, but it's still worth trying. Maybe you're underestimating human kindness and understanding."

"Maybe you're underestimating human nature." Toyer motioned the agents to come forward and snarled, "Handcuff everyone and get these wackos in the van before something else happens."

"What about the boy and girl. They're gone?" asked the agent.

"Don't worry, we'll find them later."

As Toyer and the agents escorted each person down the tunnel, their cell reception returned. An alert showed up on everyone's CompWatches, but this time the chime was different than normal. A pulsating low-frequency hum echoed between watches as a message read: "Voting for the 37th Amendment to the Constitution has completed. The amendment failed on a margin of 61.6% to 39.4%."

CHAPTER THIRTY-EIGHT

DUNES LOADING PLATFORM, ONTARIO, CA (2069)

AS THE SUN ROSE into the eastern sky, a cloud of mist swirled around the loading dock. All the moisture from the chilling nighttime breeze had surrendered to the warmer dryer air being baked by the heat. It rose up forming a cloud in the atmosphere that was inhaled instantaneously. A purple gleam of light burst over the horizon causing the precipitation to dissipate into thin air. As this ecological fireworks display fizzled to the ground in fading shades of red and blue, passengers standing on the platform sang in unison, "Wupe there it is, Wupe there it is."

Alby and Shursta sang along and danced as they stood in line with other passengers. After weeks of being cooped up in a crowded jail cell, they were both glad to just be outside in the open air.

"Hey, look over there. Doesn't that look like Dylan McMillan standing in line?" asked Shursta, squinting sharply.

Alby covered her eyes from the morning sun and examined the crowd. "It sure does, and look behind him just coming out of the other building. It's Edgar and Tusnig." The two men acted confused while studying a piece of paper in their hands. Soon, they made their way to the back of the line and fell in with the rest. Both women waved, trying to get their attention. Finally, Edgar noticed and gestured back. Shursta kept waving for them to come over but they hesitated at first. Eventually, they sifted through the crowd, apologizing along the way, but no one resisted the intrusion. No one was in a hurry to find out where they were going. Any delay was a good thing.

"I'm so glad to see you two," said Shursta as she hugged Tusnig, then Edgar.

Alby gently caressed Edgar's hand and agreed. "Me too."

Edgar pulled her into his arms and squeezed. Then he rubbed Shursta's shoulder. "It's good to see friendly faces for once."

"Did you notice Dylan McMillan in line back there?"

"No." Both Tusnig and Edgar peered across the platform.

"I'll be damned, it is. I overheard two guards talking on the phone about it. From what I could gather, there was a scandal about some foreign corporation that was bankrolling Dylan's enterprises all along." Edgar focused again on his friends and added, "It was all a Ponzi scheme. Apparently, he was below the Threshold of Engagement a long time ago but they were able to manipulate the system somehow. That all changed when the Internet opened up."

"There is a God," replied Alby.

"Karma," interjected Tusnig. "Boy, it's so good to see you all. They kept us separate and in isolation for weeks. I didn't know where anyone was until a few days ago."

"Same thing with us. We crossed paths in the cafeteria once or twice but they wouldn't let us speak to each other." Alby studied Edgar and added, "You've lost weight."

He patted his belly and replied, "Haven't we all?"

"I guess so. What have you heard?" asked Shursta.

"Not much. I don't think they've caught April and Ketchum. I would've seen him by now."

"Yeah, we haven't seen April either. Good for them."

Tusnig glanced around at the line of people waiting to board the trains and said, "Looks like we're finally being shipped out."

"No doubt, I wish I knew where we were going."

"Nowhere pretty, I can guarantee you that."

They all reflected on the moment and nodded. Reality had set in long ago on the day they were processed. A guard hobbled up the stairs from the dock with a flipped-up collar and tattoo-covered arms. Harold stepped onto the platform and walked by them. The distinct smell of body odor and chocolate lingered in the air as he sneered and mumbled under his breath.

"Speaking of pretty," said Edgar.

They all laughed.

Another guard at the end of the dock yelled, "Lunch will be served soon. Shore up the line."

People moved in closer to the wall and straightened up. The sunlight beaming down was blinding at this time of day. The temperature now was well above 100 degrees and rising. The scent of tar and gasoline drifted throughout the platform.

Shursta blinked away the moment and asked, "So, was it all worth it — I mean, opening the Intranet and all?"

"I don't know," replied Tusnig. "From what I've heard, most people want it back the way it was. They don't like seeing the truth. They want the fluffy stories about babies and kittens."

"So it was all for nothing?"

Alby glanced at Edgar and then to Tusnig before blushing. "Oh, I wouldn't say that. I'm pretty sure allowing the whole country to see things for what they really were had something to do with the 37th Amendment failing. A little splash of reality can go a long way sometimes."

"Indeed," replied Edgar with a defiant nod.

"So what happens now?" asked Shursta.

"I'd assume that Congress will have to reverse the trend and start returning everything to the way it was under government control, at least in theory. Who knows? Let's just hope the rest of GRID is out there fighting to make sure it happens."

"Boy, I'd like to be in that fight," mused Tusnig.

"No doubt. I hope we see each other again on the other side. And to think, Izzy made the ultimate sacrifice." Edgar lowered his head and rubbed his eyelids with his fingertips.

Alby placed her hand on his shoulder and pondered, "I don't know if I'll ever understand that one. I guess she just figured that they had much more to live for than she did."

"Well, I hope they make her proud," replied Edgar. And with a nod, the eulogy was complete. The carts of lunchtime snacks started shuffling down the platform as he added, "If we don't end up at the same place, it's been great knowing you all."

"Absolutely, it's been my privilege." Alby hugged Shursta and Tusnig, then turned to Edgar. "It's been fun." They both chuckled.

Tusnig gently squeezed his girlfriend's hand and said, "So much for enjoying our millions. I'm sorry I got you into this. You'll never get to travel the world like your parents now."

"Who wants to be like my parents? I don't regret any of it."

They turned their attention to a cart inching along the line and two servers handing out sandwiches and drinks.

"Good, it looks like lunch has arrived."

The food cart was now barely a few feet away. The smell of stale hot dogs and French fries sifted in and out of the platform with every breeze. Then Shursta noticed the tennis shoes of the man serving food. She recognized the red, white and blue stripes immediately. She examined his torso and legs as he stood with his back to them, retrieving cans of water from his cart. Then she noticed the girl with a hoodie covering her head and a silver necklace dangling from her neck.

She squeezed Tusnig's hand and pointed with her eyes. He nodded and cleared his throat, causing Edgar and Alby to take notice. Ketchum turned around and clicked the tips of his shoes twice. The red, white and blue stripes flashed brightly. Then the lights and video screens went dark across the platform. The mutter of confusion filtered through the crowd as the crossing agent pounded on her keyboard and cursed. April lifted her jacket revealing an automatic rifle under the apron. She raised it high enough for people to see and yelled, "Everyone, on the ground, now!" Ketchum fired a couple of rounds in the air as the crowd and guards dove to the floor. In the distance, Carmen and Claudia pulled back their hoodies and stood firm with rifles in hand. They all nodded to Ketchum.

Then April spun around toward Edgar holding a bun in her hand. With a devilish grin, she asked, "What would you like with your hot dog, sir?"

☐☐☐

ABOUT THE AUTHOR

Thomas grew up in a quaint small town in Illinois called Georgetown and studied at the University of Illinois. Later, he moved to Southern California with his family to work in the music industry.

In Southern California, he's had a successful career in the Film & TV Music Licensing field with Warner Bros., Universal Records and the Walt Disney Company. After the birth of his triplet daughters, Lopinski focused on writing literature and joined a writer's group made up of his peers in the music industry.

In 2012, he self-published his first novel, "Document 512," which won recognition and awards from Reader Views, Foreword Review, National Indie Excellence Awards and Best Indie Books. His second novel "The Art of Raising Hell" was published through Dark Alley Press in 2015 and won Best Young Adult Novel through Best Indie Books and was a semi-finalist for Best Literary Novel through Kindle Book Awards.

In 2022, Thomas released an album of original songs called "Unfinished Business" under the pseudo name "Pinski Thomas". The album can be found and purchased on Spotify, iTunes and BandCamp.

Thomas is also a member of the Independent Writers of Southern California (IWOSC) and has been a cancer survivor since 2006.

Visit: https://www.thomaslopinski.com/

www.ingramcontent.com/pod-product-compliance
Lightning Source LLC
Chambersburg PA
CBHW021341310726
48971CB00001B/238